Nanagin

Front cover design by Aleska Kirsten.
Map design by : "aja".
Date 5/02/2020

Published By

RockHill Publishing LLC
PO Box 62241
Virginia Beach, VA 23466-2241
www.rockhillpublishing.com

Nanagin

H. C. Kilgour

For Gina
for always knowing when I could do better,
and pushing me to do so.

Mountains

Islands

Grech

Xieng River

Upper River Fort

Grevasi

Javin Lake

Whendell

Tratolek

Agrielha Castle

Suilenroc

Tatat River

Lake Romann

Agrielha Cit

Drath

Grenadone

Bouyne

Middle River Fort

Suttan

Revod

Ohvenail

Greyault

Aylentowne

Bowtilmer

Westerlies

Móverth

Borders

N

Aldiera River
Averit Volcanoes
Wynsh River
Icchota Lake
Glensung Plains
Port Ligola
Edreba
Parav Forest
Mountains
Port Clire
Haggard Land
ueweba River
gress
Illeria
Eastern Ocean

Nanagin

CHAPTER 1

Soldiers filled the hallway, forcing Aron to push his way past as he followed silently behind his father and older brothers. Outside, lightning illuminated the stormy night sky to be quickly followed by a deafening clap of thunder. Rain steadily drummed against the corridor's windows, and at the end of the hall, the throne room loomed like a cavern, its doors hanging askew on their hinges, the wood blackened and warped. The stench of burning flesh and cloth permeated the air.

Aron peered through the doorway, speechless. Everything in the room was charred and covered in a thick coat of ash. Guardsmen lay scattered around, dead or dying, the agonizing cries of the living echoing off the walls. A thin layer of hazy smoke filled the air, causing his eyes and lungs to smart.

His father, Caius, strode across the room, deliberately stepping over men who cried for help. As Aron followed, he could just make out the shape of something that did not belong. He stared in disbelief; it was a young woman, dressed in a black shirt with sleeves that stopped above the elbow, dark blue pants of a coarse-looking fabric that fit like a skin on her body, and black shoes with white stars on the side. He had never seen such clothing. This person should not be here, yet, there she was, alive, and untouched by the blast.

As Aron drew nearer, he studied her features. Curly brown hair, riddled with hints of red, was splayed across the floor and over her shoulders. Freckles dotted her pale skin like haphazard constellations, and her lips were parted slightly, the sound of her breaths slow and steady. From the padding on her body, she was used to a life of luxury.

He knelt beside her and as his hand swept a strand of hair from her face, a sensation that sent chills and pins across his body caused him to pull away quickly.

His older brother, Braxton, prodded the girl's shoulder with the tip of his boot.

She did not stir.

Caius stood behind them, finding the girl of little importance, then walked over to a nearby solider, who barely clung to life.

Kolt, the second of the three Alagard boys, followed their father.

Aron was surprised Caius was not more interested in the girl, then realized it was not out of his father's character to ignore the subject of concern. Then again, the dying deserved priority.

The soldier's skin was cracked, the red of his flesh showing, and his breathing was labored, as if each gasp caused excruciating pain. "Sir," he croaked, "water, please."

Caius knelt beside him. "What happened?"

"Water," the man begged.

Caius' expression was as blank as slate. "Answer me and you will have your water."

The man reached toward him weakly. "Please."

Anger flashed across Caius' face. "Answer the question before I end your wretched life."

Fear sparked in the man's eyes and he began to speak, coughing every few words, "We were standing guard, when– a bright light filled the room. There was... an explosion..." He gasped and the words died in his throat as his chest ceased to rise and fall.

"Useless." Caius straightened up and turned to the girl. Stooping, he grabbed her wrist and satisfied with what he saw—or did not see—let her arm drop limply to the floor. Leaving, he ordered two guards, "Put her in a cell. If her condition changes, alert me at once."

Braxton and Kolt followed silently after their father while Aron lingered.

He looked at the girl again; she appeared so innocent. He felt a pang in his chest as he realized it was going to be stripped away. Two guards removed the girl and he strode after them, wishing there was something he could do to save her.

‡‡‡

Braxton followed his father and Kolt through the castle. No words were spoken, which was fine with him as it gave him time to ponder. The girl... young woman—she was no child, but certainly not older than his twenty-four years of age either—was mysterious and questions raced through his mind. Where did she come from? How had she survived the blast? Who the nastor was she?

Finding himself standing outside his bedchambers, he shook his head, pushed open the door, and glanced at his bed, which was in a state of disarray from his hasty departure. Deciding to forego a candle, he quickly slipped from his clothes and crawled back beneath the covers.

Tired as he was, it was difficult to sleep and get the girl out of his mind. There was something about her, though every time he thought he understood, the idea was swept away.

His dreams were strange that night. He started in a void, where he could hear nothing, see nothing, and feel nothing but the weight of existence. Pigments slowly began to add themselves to the dark backdrop, seeping in like a sunrise; they were dusky colors, mostly blues,

2

browns, and grays. Slowly the bolts of stain began to pull into rough shapes.

When those became clear, he could see two people, holding hands as they ran and instantly recognized one of them as the girl who had caused tonight's commotion. Fear was plastered across her face, etched into every pore of her skin. She pulled against the person leading her and began speaking. Whatever words were exchanged were muffled and sounded as if they were in a foreign tongue.

He tried to focus on the person she was talking to, but the face was blurry. The only thing he could see was an intense pair of blue eyes that felt familiar. He concentrated on them, but slowly they began to cloud. The world around him faded to shapes again, then to color, then to nothing.

When he stirred, sunlight was pushing through his window, and there was a knock at the door.

"Give me a moment," he called, throwing the covers back and quickly dressing.

Standing outside was a soldier.

"What?"

"The girl is awake."

The girl's frightened face flashed across his memory, sending a shiver down his spine. He pushed the image aside, hating himself for what he was about to do, and began making his way to the dungeon.

‡‡‡

Morning light filtered through the barred window, casting decrepit shadows over Keegan's body. She lay on the cot, blanketed in the sweet serenity of sleep. Sluggishly, she opened her eyes and still in a state of pseudo-sleep, yawned. She bolted upright with the realization she had overslept and was going to be late for class. It took her mind a moment to start racing in bewilderment as she glanced at her surroundings.

Where am I? Her eyes darted around the barren room, which appeared to be a dungeon cell. *Am I still dreaming?* She pinched herself. A disquieting feeling rose in her stomach like bile.

Warily, she stood up and walked to the door, holding back a wave of panic. Finding there was no way to open the door, she began pounding her fists on the wood and yelling. After several minutes with no response, she backed away and sank onto the cot, eyes wide, mind reeling, and a lump stuck in her throat. *Someone has to be here. They have to.*

3

Time slowed, each minute stretching into what felt like eons. There was no one word for what she felt—a pit of unease in her stomach that seemed to swallow her up, a blanket of shock that shrouded her in empty thoughts, a fear of the unknown that led to only one outcome: death. Waves of emotions threatened to break free from their cage and form into salty ribbons that would stream down her face.

No. She rose to her feet and began pacing; had to distract herself. *Breathe. Think of something happy: puppies, chocolate, diving... Oh, God, what if I die here? No. Focus. Snow, piano, reading on a rainy day...*

She was pulled from her thoughts when she noticed the opening set within the door. Standing on her toes, she was just able to look through the bars, and saw the backs of two men who wore black tunics underneath sleeveless shirts of chainmail.

What the hell; why are they wearing armor? "Hey," she called, "where am I?"

One of the men started to turn but the other gave him a hard look and he continued to stare forward.

About to repeat the question, the sound of footsteps echoing around the hallway staid her.

The guards moved aside to reveal a man standing before her. He was tall, easily reaching six feet in height—about a foot taller than her. His black hair was close-cropped and his eyes were a sullen blue, as if they'd given up hope. The thick, white outline of a scar followed the contour of the bottom of his left eye.

He inserted a key into the lock.

She scrambled away from the door, wandering what harm he intended and eyed the sword belted around his waist nervously. She desperately wanted to believe it was for show, but knew it was lethal. "Who are you? What do you want?"

He ignored her and stepped forward.

Keegan backed away, dread blossoming in her chest. Her eyes darted to the still open door; it was a long shot, but... she had to try. The muscles in her legs tensed and she rushed forward. As she ran past, the man wrapped his arms around her torso and swung her around until she was back where she had started.

"Stop," he commanded, pushing her against the wall. "Please, do not resist. I do not want to hurt you, but he will make me."

Keegan wasn't given time to consider his words as a second man emerged from the shadows. He had paling blond hair, stubble marked his square jawline, and his brown eyes stared at her cruelly.

4

The man holding her against the wall seized her arm and pulled her forward.

"What have I told you about showing kindness, Braxton?" the older man drawled.

Braxton said nothing, instead fixing his gaze on the floor.

Blood pounded in Keegan's ears. "Who are you people?"

The man turned his attention to her. "I am Caius Alagard. Who might you be?"

Keegan ignored his reciprocated query, focusing on prying the hand off her arm.

Braxton dug his fingers into her bicep, "Answer him."

"Keegan," she stammered, "Keegan Digore."

"Keegan Digore," Caius repeated, lifting her chin with the tips of his fingers, "you—"

"Don't touch me," she bit defensively, pulling away.

Caius grabbed her chin. "I shall do whatever I please."

With her free hand, she dug her fingers into the underside of Caius' wrist and wrenched his hand away. "Over my dead body."

Caius gave her a look of contempt before striking her.

She stared at him loathingly, her eyebrows knitted together in fury, as her hand rose of its own accord to brush her now stinging cheek.

"That can be arranged."

The malice in his voice sent spikes of fear through her as his lips pulled into an unsettling smile, leaving her with no doubt that he would live up to the threat gladly.

"You can't do this! I haven't done anything wrong."

Caius gave a maniacal laugh, walking from the cell and leaving her with Braxton.

Braxton released her arm. "Do not push him." Then locked the door behind himself.

Tears began sliding down her face. She wiped them away with a shaky hand but more kept coming and refused to stop.

‡‡‡

Braxton stood outside the cell again, this time, alone. Keegan was curled into a ball on the cot. It had been all too easy to see the terror on her face before and he hated himself for having taken part in its cause. Steeling himself, he pushed open the door. As it scraped across the stone floor, Keegan bolted up, the same expression already on her face.

5

He gently took hold of her arm, causing her to flinch. He could feel her trembling.

She stood when prompted and looked at him blankly before lashing out.

He quickly spun her around, wrenching her arm behind her back, and pushed her from the cell. As they walked, he could not bring himself to look at her.

Rounding a corner, he could see the two soldiers waiting for them outside the Red Room and the girl instinctively began fighting against him again.

"What took you so long?" one asked, an air of agitation in his voice. "He's been waiting."

Braxton understood the subtle warning, "I am here now."

As the soldiers opened the door, he pulled Keegan through. Waiting inside, as they had said, was his father, along with Kolt.

A chair sat in the center of the room and Keegan strained against him; it would have taken a blind man to overlook the gaping scars in the chair's wood and the deep red stains. Various instruments designed to cause pain hung around the walls and chains dangled from the ceiling.

Braxton did his best to hide his revulsion to the strong scent of iron in the air and forced Keegan to sit.

Caius told him, "You know better than to keep me waiting."

"I apologize, father," Braxton bowed his head.

Keegan looked between them, questions hanging in her eyes. Plucking up her courage, she asked, "What do y'all want with me?"

Caius went towards her. "Do not speak unless spoken to."

In a show of false bravado, she did not choose her words carefully. "Who died and made you king?"

Braxton saw anger pull at his father's face, but just as soon as it surfaced, it was pushed away.

Turning to Kolt, Caius asked, "Would you care to deal with this?"

Kolt smiled and Keegan paled as she realized the magnitude of her blunder.

"You will show us respect," Kolt yelled.

She responded to the verbal assault by covering her head and bringing one knee up to guard her torso.

"You are nothing," Kolt spat, placing his hands on the chair's armrests. "You will do as we say. Understand?"

Her eyes did not lift.

Kolt grabbed the front of her shirt and flung her from the chair.

She landed on her hands and knees and quickly tried to stand, seeming to know what was coming next. The kick caught her in the stomach, leaving her winded.

Braxton knew the beating would continue unless he stepped in. His brother was cruel—even more so than their father. He moved between them as Kolt brought his foot back to kick again. "Stop." The kick landed on his own shin and he winced. "She did not challenge you."

Kolt shoved him aside and knelt beside the girl. "Do you understand?"

She looked at him with watery hazel eyes and gave a slight nod.

Grabbing her arm, Kolt shoved her back into the chair then clutched her chin and drew closer to her. He gave a wicked smile, running his thumb along her lips before retreating to where their father stood.

Keegan hiccupped and took a shallow breath.

"Where do you hail from?" Caius asked with a knowing smile.

"Charlotte," she answered meekly.

Braxton was taken aback by her answer. Most times, Caius asked a question, made his way into people's minds, and answered himself to further mystify and baffle them. As a telepath, by simply making an inquiry, he could lead their thoughts to where he wanted them to go.

Frustration pulled at the corners of his father's lips and confusion knitted his brows. "Where is this Charlotte?"

"North Carolina."

Caius paused, something striking a chord with him. "North Carolina," he repeated, as if trying the words out. "How curious, I know of that place, but not of Charlotte."

There was no such place as Charlotte or North Carolina in Arciol; how could his father be familiar with the latter?

"It's not like it's the biggest city in the state," Keegan said sarcastically.

Caius snarled a warning, "Watch your mouth."

She looked away in compliance.

"Where are you from?"

"Charlotte."

"There is no such place."

"Yes, there is."

"Where are you from?"

There was a false calm about Caius, but Braxton knew the subtle signs, he was becoming increasingly agitated.

"Charlotte. But I go to school in Wilmington," Keegan offered.

"Tell me about Wilmington."

"Uh… It's a college town on the Cape Fear River."

Braxton stood quietly, waiting for Caius to move to the next question.

Do it, boy! he heard his father yell, clearly dissatisfied with the answer.

Glancing at Keegan and hating himself, he struck her.

Caius turned his back to them and was replaced by Kolt as the interrogator. "How did you get here?"

Keegan shook her head, "I don't know."

"You have to know how you got here," Caius said from the background.

"I- I don't."

"What do you know about the Lazado?" Kolt continued. "How were you planning to kill my father?"

"The who? And what?"

Kolt prepared to strike and she raised her arms in defense. Infuriated, he grabbed her hand and before Braxton could intervene, snapped one of her fingers.

Her cry tore at his heart. He clenched his fists and retreated within his mind; he had to, for his sake. Stealing a glance at her finger, he was relieved to see it was merely dislocated.

"Tell us what we want to know," Kolt demanded, placing his hand around the girl's throat.

"I am," she wheezed, kicking him back. She would rather endure pain than face death.

The screams she emitted were painful to hear and Braxton stared at the wall, refusing to look at what was happening.

By the time he returned her to the cell, she was compliant and seemed to care little about where he took her. Already a few cuts and quickly forming bruises marred her features. He let her walk into the cell of her own accord.

Without a sound, she rolled into a ball on the cot, staring blankly at the wall, the hand with the dislocated finger cradled against her chest. He stood and watched her until the guards made the evening rounds, bringing trays of what could barely be called food.

‡‡‡

Aron wandered past the cell slowly, peering through the small, barred window. The girl lay curled up and it appeared she was asleep. Dark bruises mottled her face.

As he made his way through the castle's corridors, his heart was tearing in two. He wanted to help the girl, but he feared his father more. His mind was dragged away from the girl as the dread of what he was about to face began to overwhelm him. Most evenings, he ate in the kitchen with the staff—at least they tolerated him. Because while he always had a place at the table as an Alagard, he was not truly welcome. He shuddered, recalling his three broken ribs from the last time he had dined with his family. The only reason he was braving the table tonight was because he wished to learn more about the girl.

Since birth, his family had found him to be nothing more than a nuisance—like a forever-present itch. As a child, he had struggled to understand why they disliked him, but at the age of five, Braxton had sat him down and explained; he was the reason their mother died.

Kolt, two at the time of their mother's passing, had not understood why she was no longer present but had realized it was Aron's doing—and had yet to forgive him. Braxton had been four, and while he too had been upset, he also understood Aron was not to blame.

As Aron grew, he began to look like his mother; it was one of the few reasons his father tolerated him to the extent he did, but also the reason he wanted nothing to do with him. Both were blessings.

While Braxton did not loathe him, he was being pulled in two different directions; he had lived long enough to be nurtured by their mother, but as the only elemental of the three boys, was under the cruel tutelage of their father. Never had Aron wished for the life Braxton led.

The dining hall's large double doors loomed ahead and the two guards outside gave each other enquiring looks as he approached. His brothers were already inside.

Braxton sat with his feet propped on the table, cleaning his nails with a knife. He glanced at Aron before returning absentmindedly to his task.

Kolt stared at him with disgust.

Aron chose a seat at the far end of the long table, well outside of Kolt's reach—or so he hoped. No one spoke and a strained silence fell around them. Time slipped by slowly until their father arrived.

When Caius saw Aron, he paused, then proceeded to disregard him as well. "Get your feet off the table," he snapped at Braxton, "you were not raised in the fields."

Food was brought out by servants. Aron ate slowly, more interested in what would be said about the girl.

"Keegan," Kolt started, "she is—"

"A problem," Caius finished. "I gathered that after I was unable to hear her thoughts."

"How were you not able to get past her wall?" Braxton questioned, genuine surprise and concern in his voice.

"Royik if I know," Caius answered, "But she *will* tell me what we want to know."

"She told us what we wanted to know," Braxton said quietly.

"Charlotte does not exist," Kolt barked.

"I am having some doubts," Caius said. "It has been well over two hundred years since my Nanagin."

Aron quickly recalled everything he knew about Nanagins, which was not a great deal. They were rare magical portals, requiring one to be in just the right place at just the right time, and transported a person to another world. In Arciol, it left behind a destructive blast. Throughout history, there were only a handful of occurrences where an Arciolan had been able to return. When they did, they boasted accentuated powers, well above the abilities of others. From what they could determine, the more time spent in the other world, the greater the augmentation.

"What does that have to do with anything?" Kolt snapped.

"Nanagins transport a person to another world," Caius began. "And I was taken to a port city called Wilmington in North Carolina. Quite a lot of time has passed; it is possible that much has changed."

"I am inclined to believe that is the case," Braxton agreed. "And she did mention Wilmington."

"You would be stupid to believe her," Kolt sneered.

"Either way, everyone has their breaking point," Caius uttered, ignoring them.

"Breaking point for what?" Braxton snapped.

Kolt commented, "With Braxton that could take months."

"Time is of no matter," Caius said, ignoring Braxton's question, "but if she is not broken within the week, you may take over if that suits you."

Kolt grinned sinisterly at the prospect.

"Of what importance is she?" Aron asked boldly.

Kolt looked like he was going to fly across the table and beat him.

"He poses a good question," Braxton remarked, shifting the attention away from Aron.

"Why?" Caius said. "Because she is the key to finding the Child of Prophecy."

The Child of Prophecy—or the bane of Caius' existence—was his father's obsession that spanned longer than Aron's nineteen years. Though Caius was the strongest elemental in the world, the Child of Prophecy was said to be stronger and the only person who could end his reign. While Aron, and most of the world, did not think that was such a horrible thing, Caius had devoted years to finding and destroying the child.

Aron stood up and quietly exited. It was best to leave while his father and Kolt were preoccupied with something other than him, and he had heard enough. Keegan would either reveal the whereabouts of the Child of Prophecy, or, she would die.

Leaning against a windowsill outside the dining hall, he gazed over the plains surrounding the castle. The sun had set, casting pink hues into the sky. While he wished no harm upon Keegan, to help her would mean a world of pain for him.

CHAPTER 2

Aron was still hiding in the shadows of an alcove outside the dining hall when the doors burst opened and Caius sauntered past, going towards the depths of the castle. He hesitated before following.

After a few minutes, he knew Caius was headed to visit the Blind Prophet, who usually knew the answers to the questions Caius asked long before he voiced them. Thus far, his predictions had never been wrong.

Caius continued until he came upon a plain wooden door on one of the lower levels, removed a key from around his neck, undid the lock, and slipped in.

Aron crept forward and pressed an ear against the wood.

"You know why I am here," Caius stated.

"As always, elder brother," came Alyck's raspy voice. "However, I cannot answer what you wish to ask."

"And why is that?"

"To know, I must first understand—and the girl remains *well* outside my realm of understanding."

"Then understand her," Caius yelled.

"An ant can no more understand the actions of man than a man can understand the actions of an ant. I cannot begin to understand without *seeing* her. And you know I need a name."

"Keegan Digore."

"Bring her to me."

There was a moment of silence before the door handle began to turn. Aron scrambled back into the shadows.

"The tide has returned, brother," Alyck said as the door creaked open, "and you shall be swept away in the undertow."

Aron watched as his father emerged and slammed the door in frustration.

Caius let out an irritated growl before punching the wall, then sucked in a deep breath, cradling his now misshapen hand. Enraptured in pain, he stalked away, forgetting to lock the door.

Aron stood in the gloom for a time before creeping forward and slipping inside.

"You are lucky tonight, Little King," Alyck said. "Anger has always made my brother forgetful."

"I suppose I am lucky in that sense."

His uncle sat in a chair, arms crossed loosely against his chest, knowing he had been eavesdropping. "You want to know about the girl."

Aron gave a curt nod.

12

"There is nothing you will not learn in due time."

Aron sighed, "Can you not be straightforward?"

"No, for nothing is."

Shaking his head, Aron reached for the door handle.

"Tsk, you give up too easily, Little King."

"Then are you going to tell me?" Aron asked, a hint of frustration in his voice. He had learned the only way to get information out of Alyck was to refuse to play his games.

"Contrary to what I told Caius, I know many things about her, but there are very few that *you* need to know currently."

Refraining from rolling his eyes, Aron asked, "And what would those be?"

"Firstly, she needs your help."

"Why would I do that? Should my father find out, I..." He shuddered at the possibilities.

"Because you need her help, too."

"How so?"

"That, you will discover for yourself."

Aron made to leave again.

"Help her, as right now she is the *only* person who can help us. You may go, Little King."

Aron eyed his uncle before taking his leave and crept through the castle's underbelly until he found himself outside his bedchambers.

Inside, a small fire burned in the hearth and the window was open, letting the chorus of night creatures drift through. He sat on the edge of the bed, torn. To intentionally go against Caius... was that something he was willing to do? That night, he tossed and turned until the morning birds began to chirp.

✠✠✠

Sleep did not find Braxton easily that night, and when it did, his dreams were unsettling. He was again surrounded by darkness, the world swallowing him up. Dark colors began to appear, painting a hazy scene. Keegan's face took form, her fear prevalent enough to transfer itself to him.

She pulled back and a set of indigo eyes appeared. Above them, a pair of black brows formed; he had seen them before. He focused again, trying to discern to whom they belonged. Words were being exchanged but he could not understand them. The pair of startling blue eyes began to move away, and Keegan followed.

13

He chased after them but found himself falling through oblivion, his breath sucked from his throat. He jolted awake and was momentarily disorientated, as the feeling of falling followed him into the realm of light.

Pale sunlight shone through his window and he realized it was morning. He would have gladly returned to sleep for a while longer, but the dream had his nerves on edge. Throwing back the covers, Braxton began to pace, his stomach tumbling.

What could this mean? Would it come to pass? He passed his mirror and stopped to look at his reflection. Stubble marked his jaw and he appeared worn. The scar under his left eye smiled at him cruelly.

He looked at his eyes. They were the same as the ones he had seen in his dream. Was he...? Pulling himself away from the mirror, he began to pace again. His mind keeping going back to the fact that he was going to be the source of Keegan's fear. But if the dream were to pass, would he not be the one to save her? Could he do that?

Finding himself only becoming more anxious, he went to his desk, pulled out a sheet of parchment, and a stick of graphite. As he drew, his worries melted away, presenting themselves on the page rather than in his head.

‡‡‡

Keegan was ready to make a bid for freedom as soon as Caius entered. She slid past him stealthily but as her foot crossed the threshold of the cell, she found her body froze mid-stride.

"Where do you think you are going?" he demanded.

Why can't I move? She struggled against the invisible bonds. "Let me go!" *What magical bullshit is this?*

Caius faced her. "Let you go; why not?"

Her body was released, and she careened into him.

He grabbed her wrist and began pulling her down the hallway like a misbehaving child.

She kicked at his knees and yanked her arm from his grasp then as she turned to run, hands on the back of her shoulders threw her to the floor.

Caius placed a heavy boot on her shoulder. "Did you *really* think you could escape?"

Defeated, she asked, "What do you people want with me?"

He grabbed an arm and pulled her to her feet without answering.

14

As they walked, she noticed he was taking her into the depths of wherever the hell they were and stopped outside a door along a weakly lit corridor. Unlocking it, he pulled her in.

From the shadows a dusky voice said, "Leave, brother, if you want your answers. She will not escape from here, if even I cannot."

Caius wavered, then released her and retreated outside.

A man stepped into the torchlight. "I mean you no harm, child. I only seek to answer your questions."

Keegan stood rooted in place, studying the man before her. Thin strands of greasy black hair, intermittent with gray, hung past his shoulders and framed a haggard face that once must have had chiseled features. She could just see the blue of his irises underneath milky white cataracts. Looking past the grime, he appeared to be in his late thirties.

She hoped he didn't notice her shaking. "Where am I?"

"Agrielha."

"Wh-where is that?"

"Agrielha is the capital of Arciol."

Keegan's eyebrows furrowed. "Those aren't real places."

The man moved closer. "Do you not wonder why my brother does not know where Charlotte is?"

"I-I don't– I don't know." She backed against the wall and prayed he wasn't cruel like the rest of his family. "Stay away from me!"

"You need not fear me, child."

Her heart pounded furiously. "Just… stay back. Tell me where I am. *Please*."

"I did."

"Those aren't real places!"

"Ah, but who is to say simply because they do not exist in your world that they do not in another."

"What?" Her mind was unwilling to grasp the concept.

"Exactly as I said."

"Are you trying to tell me I'm in a different world?"

He nodded.

"*Impossible*."

"What is possible and impossible is entirely relative."

She sank to the floor, running her fingers through her hair. *This has gotta be some kind of drug-induced trip.* And these people had already proven they weren't above it. Holding her hands along her temples, she muttered, "This can't be happening."

The man sympathetically placed a hand on her shoulder. "But it has."

"Don't touch me," she snapped, jumping to her feet.

"I have no intention of hurting you, Keegan."

Her gut clenched in fear. "How do you know my name?"

"I am the Blind Prophet. I know all, Keegan Ilene Digore. Or should I say Keegan T—"

"I just want to go home; what do I have to do to get there?"

"You are home," he said with an irritatingly smug grin.

"Please." Tears began to collect in her eyes. "Please, how do I go home?"

"You already are."

She groaned, "Why am I here?"

"To right the wrong."

"How the *fuck* am I supposed to do that?"

"Kill a certain man."

She didn't like the wicked grin he gave her and shook her head in dismay. "Why me? There's seven billion people in the world; why me?"

"No one else is powerful enough."

She motioned to herself, "And *I am*?"

"Not yet."

"And I'm supposed to do this alone?"

"Now, I never said that. Three shall join your plight. Brother in arms, brother in blood, brother in heart. Together, strong enough to move the stolid hearts of broken men; alone, forever cursed to remain nothing but a distant memory in the endless flow of time."

"What does that even mean? What the fuck is wrong with you?"

The Blind Prophet gave her another smug smile and slipped into the shadows.

"Answer me, Goddamnit!" Behind her, the door burst open.

She didn't resist as Caius took her back to the cell, her mind in disarray. She expected him to push her into the cell and leave, instead, he walked in and threw her up against the wall.

"What did he mean?" he asked.

"About what?"

"Everything."

"I don't know," she shrugged.

Caius delivered a backhanded slap, the ring on his finger scratching skin away on her cheek, "You feign ignorance."

She could feel blood gathering at the new seam and gritted her teeth. "I promise, I don't know. And even if I did, I damn well wouldn't tell *you*." She instantly regretted her words.

Caius grabbed her wrist. "What did he mean?"

16

She felt a burning sensation. "I don't know."

"Look at me," Caius growled. When she didn't, he grabbed her jaw and forced her to stare at him. "Tell me."

She clenched her fist; it was all she could do to stop herself from crying out. "I, don't, know."

"The sad thing is, I *almost* believe you."

Suddenly the pain was no longer a burning sensation nor was it contained to her wrist. It radiated across her body excruciatingly; the blood in her veins seemed to have turned to liquid fire. She could feel it coursing through her as her heart pumped. She wasn't even aware that a scream had escaped from her.

Caius began laughing wildly. "Tell me."

She sank to her knees as the blood reached her chest, feeling the fire circulating in her heart. "Make it stop."

Caius stared down at her.

"Please," she whimpered as the fire made its way up through her neck.

"Groveling suits you."

The blood found itself in her brain and the world imploded.

‡‡‡

Aron tried to walk inconspicuously down the row of cells, but the subconscious need to check over his shoulder made it difficult. He had almost reached Keegan's when Caius stormed from it, slamming the door shut. Quickly, he turned on his heels and hoped his father overlooked him.

"Coming to check on the girl?" Caius called.

Aron froze.

"Come see." Caius bore a nasty sneer. "Look at her."

He peered through the small window set in the door. Keegan lay against the back wall, one arm folded awkwardly under her chest while the other was cast haphazardly in front of her. Knowing Caius was waiting for a reaction, Aron tried to conceal his emotions, but disgust and hate flashed across his face.

"Does it make you mad that we have tormented her?" Caius taunted.

Clenching his jaw, he stared straight ahead.

His father pulled open the door, all joviality gone from his demeanor. "Go help her."

Aron stood still, unsure of his father's intentions.

Caius grabbed his shirt at the nape and pushed him into the cell. "Attend to her!"

He stumbled in and heard the door slam shut behind him.

Caius stood staring through the little window with a face like thunder.

Cautiously, he made his way to Keegan, wondering if she was even alive. As he got closer, he could hear her breaths. "I am sorry," he whispered, kneeling. "What is her crime?" he asked, glancing over his shoulder.

"She has committed none. Yet."

"Then why are you torturing her?"

"She knows where to find the Child of Prophecy."

A lump formed in his throat as he recalled Alyck's words. Gingerly, he scooped her up and transferred her to the cot. "And if she truly knows nothing?"

Caius chuckled. "Then you are not my son."

"She knows nothing," Aron said, his anger beginning to roil. "You are hurting an *innocent* person to satisfy your lust of bloodshed."

"Hold your tongue, boy. You know nothing of my whims or wants."

Aron gritted his teeth and glared at his father.

Caius started to walk away.

"Are you going to let me out?"

"If I am in a good mood I might instruct the guards to do so in a few days. This way, you get to spend some time nurturing that soft heart of yours."

He watched his father disappear from the window's small field of view, growing angrier with each receding step. When Caius was gone, he turned to the wall and met it with his foot. A dull pain formed in his toes as he sat back against the wall opposite the cot.

For too long had he sat by while his father had tortured, maimed, and killed people on whims. For too long he had been afraid... So where did the fear stem from?

Years before, Caius had let it slip that his mother had forced him to make a Death Deal; to break that vow meant Caius' own death. The deal was he could never kill or grievously injure her sons, nor could any being under his command.

Looking at Keegan, he finally knew what he was going to do. Time passed undetected as he began to scheme and he barely noticed the guards making the evening rounds. Eventually, he heard the jangle of keys and the click of the lock. Rising, he leaned against the wall casually.

The door opened to reveal Braxton. "Return to your room, Aron."

He surveyed his brother, who looked tired, worn, and remorseful.

As he walked past, Braxton placed a hand on his chest. "Do not push him; he will only hurt the girl to punish you."

Aron gave a slight nod and shoved past, making his way from the dungeon hurriedly, his anger threatening to boil over.

As he neared his room, he slowed, running his hand along the wall and stopping when his fingers found a divot in the stones. He looked at the wall; if he had not known it was there, it would have been impossible to find. The stone in question was a subtle shade darker than the surrounding ones and when he applied pressure, a hidden door opened.

Making sure no one was around; he slipped through the newly formed passage and closed the opening behind himself. The inside was dark as pitch, but he knew the way well enough to make the trip blind.

Three steps up and he took a large stride, knowing the fourth tread had been removed and dropped off into empty space. He had once tried to find where the hole led to by dropping a few items into it but had never found them again—much to his disappointment.

Tenth step up and he ducked; the ceiling jutted down to about his shoulders. Too many times had he hit his head on the low ceiling or walked face first into the obstruction. On one occasion, he had even managed to chip a tooth. He had blamed Kolt and the lie had been readily believed.

Step sixteen, he hugged the left wall as along the right-hand side a stone protruded at the average man's waist. When he had first discovered this passage at the age of eight, the stone had been at his shoulders. As he had grown, it had become increasingly painful to walk into.

At the twenty-ninth step, he turned right with the hallway. For the longest time, he had needed to proceed with hands outstretched to not run into the wall. It was not much farther now.

Twelve more steps and he came to a dead end. In the beginning, he had been disheartened this did not lead to some mysterious hideaway and had forgotten about it for a while. The next time he returned, he had come prepared with a torch and discovered another stone that needed to be pressed. He reached forward, pushing the stone into an alcove. A door gave way and he emerged into the cool night air.

Here, on top of the castle, high above the sentries, where the stars twinkled above like old friends, was his sanctuary. The gable was small, only about fifty feet in width and length, but it was all he needed.

A smile played on his lips as he spied someone standing near the edge, staring up at the night sky.

He crept towards her and she was too enraptured in the heaven's beauty to notice him. Taking a final step, he threw his arms around her.

She jumped, but relaxed as he leaned forward to kiss her cheek, and reached up to hold onto his arms, "Aron."

"Hello, Shiloh."

She turned in his arms to face him and he kissed her.

Even with his eyes closed he could recount every detail of her: the almost invisible freckles dotting her nose, the dimples that appeared when she smiled, the way her hair felt like silk when twirled between his fingers. "How was your day?"

"Oh, you know," she ran her fingers through his thick hair, "not nearly as great as my night."

He smiled and stared into her beautiful eyes that exuded love.

"How was yours?"

His smile faltered and he turned his back on her to hide a scowl. "I think… I *am* going to do something dangerous and unwise."

"Aron," Shiloh said softly, "you can't run away. How many times have we talked about this? Your father would tear the country apart looking for you. And once he found you, there's no telling what he would do."

"I wish it were that. Honestly, the results would be infinitely better."

Shiloh made him face her. "What are you planning?"

"I am going to help… someone. I am going to save her."

‡‡‡

Braxton eased the door open, wincing at the shrieking hinges. He did not come to this place often, then again, the only other person who had access was Caius.

"Hello, Uncle," he said to the man leaning against the shadow-shrouded wall.

"Hello, Braxton. It is not often I receive a visit from you. But I suppose these are… *unusual* circumstances. You are here to ask about your brother and the girl?"

"Yes, tell me Aron's future."

"I do not understand why you continue to ask that question."

"I need to know that nothing has changed."

"It has not."

"Say it, Alyck! Please, I need to hear it."

"Why?"

"Because I promised Mother I would look after him."

"Aron will live a long and prosperous life."

He felt himself calming. "Tell me about the girl."

"*Please*," Alyck scoffed. "She is the one who will shape the future. Her path is along the same road Aron will travel."

He felt his heart sink. "What can I do to help her?"

"It is imperative that you do absolutely nothing."

"But—"

"Absolutely nothing," Alyck repeated.

Braxton nodded and slipped quietly from the chamber. It was the dead of night, the perfect time for secret trysts and he had the feeling Aron had gone to see Shiloh. He knew of their relationship, but not where or how they had met. While he had no woman to hold, he had friendships of other sorts, and it was there he headed his steps.

Making his way to one of the upper levels of the castle, he looked for the indentation in the wall. Finding it easily enough, he pressed the stone, opening a small seam between the bricks. He slipped through and let it close behind him, casting him into darkness. Calmly, he climbed the stairs until he reached a dead-end. Pulling a lever, another door opened, spitting him into an anterior room. In the annexing chamber, he could hear rustling and clicking.

Braxton, came Myrish's voice, *tell us the goings-on.*

My father has the inclination he has found the Child of Prophecy, Braxton answered. *Or, at least someone who knows of its whereabouts.*

Torches on the wall cast a soft light over the twelve griffins. The magnificent creatures had the heads and wings of eagles and the bodies of immense cats. He made his way over to Niyth, one of the smaller ones, with a silver sheen to her feathers.

Humph, replied Niyth, *I doubt that. How many times has he found the Child?*

"Too many," he mumbled.

Then what makes this one different? Niyth shifted her large wings, causing a clinking of chains.

This one blew the throne room apart, Braxton said. *One moment she was not there and another it was a scene of chaos. And in the center of it all, there she was, unscathed.*

The griffins clicked their beaks, speaking in their beastly language that still eluded him. *Watch her,* Myrish instructed. *Watch her and protect her.*

CHAPTER 3

Stirring, Keegan recalled the events of the previous days. She rubbed the sleep from her eyes, feeling weary with the knowledge that today was going to be just as painful. She winced as her dislocated finger protested. She'd managed to get the joint back into place, but it was still swollen and sore. Closing her eyes, she took a deep breath as a tear trickled down the side of her face. Wiping it away, she swung her legs over the edge of the cot, wondering when someone would be coming for her. She wasn't kept waiting long.

"How are you?" Braxton asked softly as he approached, genuine concern in his voice.

She stood and looked him in the eye. "Why do you care?"

"I am not merciless like my father and brother—regardless of what others think."

"Coulda fooled me."

"Do you think I have a choice?"

"Yes."

A mix of shock and offence showed on his face. "No more talking," he growled, pulling her from the cell.

He took her to the same room as before and again forced her to sit in the chair in the center. She breathed a sigh of relief when she saw Kolt was absent. While Braxton did strike her, he did so in a way that allowed him to soften the blows. Kolt, on the other hand, reveled in causing her as much damage—physical and psychological—as possible.

"Where are you from?" Caius asked.

"Charlotte." She desperately wanted to add that no matter how many times he asked, her answer wouldn't change.

"How did you get here?"

"Don't know."

"What do you know about the Child of Prophecy?"

"The who?"

"Tell me what I want to know."

"I am. Or at least I'm trying to." Her response was met with a blow from Caius.

"What do you know about the Lazado?"

"The what?"

"This will stop if you tell me what I want to know."

"I have been," she yelled, clenching her fists. Her words became unchecked, "You're just too thick to get that." She saw Caius' fist coming towards her and remembered nothing more.

✝✝✝

By her count, three days had passed since she had first awoken in the cell, which would make that the night of April 24th—if she had her dates straight. Since arriving here, she had amassed more cuts and bruises than she cared to count. She lay on the cot unable to sleep, the cell dark, much like her prospects. She listened for the sounds of the night but heard little more than her own heartbeat. The clash of metal on metal and a dull thud outside the door caught her attention. Propping herself up, she listened carefully.

The door opened and a bright strip gushed forth. For an instant the light was blocked, then reappeared. As her eyes adjusted, she could just make out a figure approaching her. She remained still, unsure of what to do. Not for the first time, she wished she could melt away.

Keegan began to speak but a hand covered her mouth. Without thinking, she bit down, and instantly the taste of iron flooded her tongue.

A man muttered a strange curse, then whispered, "I am here to help you."

She sat up all the way. "What?"

"Shhh." The man found her hand in the dark and dragged her to her feet. "Come with me."

Keegan resisted. "Who the hell are you?"

He remained silent as he led her to the doorway.

Outside, two guards lay in pools of blood, a single arrow protruding from each of their chests.

She pulled away violently. "Who are you?"

The sound of footsteps echoed from further up the corridor. "Do you trust me?"

"No!"

"Too bad." He took her hand again and pulled her along.

While she had no idea who he was, he was helping her, and for the moment, it was enough. As they ran, she studied him.

His features were sharp, reminiscent of someone she'd seen before. Blue eyes, deep as the ocean, sat beneath heavy black brows, and shaggy, pitch-black hair covered the tops of his ears. She could feel rough callouses on his palm.

He led her through a warren of hallways to a worn timber door, pushed it open, and led her onto a grassy knoll.

Stars twinkled in the midnight blue blanket of the sky above and she breathed in its freshness, letting it fill her lungs. Looking behind, she stared up at a large stone wall. In the gloom, she was just able to make out turrets.

"What the…" She wasn't given time to question further as her companion didn't stop and the castle became lost in the darkness.

They ran across the expanse of grass, quickly reaching a low, wooden building with a thatched roof. Inside, was a long row of stalls filled with slumbering horses, who snorted at the disturbance. They went down the line, stopping outside a stall that housed a large, black stallion.

"Why are you helping me?" Keegan asked cagily as he began tacking up the horse.

"Does there need to be a reason?"

"Yes, I don't even know who you are."

"Aron."

"Okay, *Aron*, why are you helping me?"

"Because," he answered, adjusting the straps on the saddle.

"Cause what?"

"My reasons are my own."

She crossed her arms, "Not when they involve me."

"Would you rather I take you back?"

Her silence was her answer.

Aron finished saddling the horse and grabbing its reins, led it outside.

Once her eyes adjusted, she could see flickering torches in the distance.

"Get away from here as fast as you can," Aron said, helping her onto the animal.

"Where do I go?"

He handed her the reins, "Anywhere you like, as long as it is far from here."

"Aren't you coming with me?"

"No. Good luck." He slapped the stallion's flank, sending it running.

Keegan looked back; her savior already lost in the night. Turning around, she let the horse gallop into the unknown, her auburn hair streaming freely behind her.

‡‡‡

He was in darkness again then colors appeared, and he could tell he was in the castle's dungeon. The world around him was still and silent, like death. Two figures began to approach; one was Keegan. He turned his attention to the other person, hoping to discover his identity.

The same blue eyes were clear, mocking, and above them, dark brows. He reached up to touch under his left eye. Beneath his fingertips, he could feel the scar but looking back at the unknown person, he realized there was none; this was not him.

A banging awoke him abruptly.

He sat up groggily and yelled, while trying to orientate himself, "What?"

"The girl," a guard called, "has escaped."

Cursing, he threw back the covers. Dressing quickly, he grabbed his sword and opened the door. "Tell me what happened," he instructed as they started down the hallway.

"Someone helped her."

"Who?"

"We don't know, sir; no one saw him."

But he had seen who helped her—at least, a portion of his face. "Are they still in the castle?"

"No; they made it to the stables and stole a horse."

"*A* horse?"

"Yes, *a* horse," the guard repeated, unsure of the significance of the words.

"Then one of them is still here." He turned to the guard, "Tell Kolt to search the castle. I am going after the girl."

"Sir, your brother's already begun the chase."

"On horseback?"

"What other way is there?"

Braxton shook his head. "He will never catch her that way."

"Why?"

"He is an awful tracker when he can see; I do not expect him to get any better in the dark."

"Should you go after her?"

"Probably," Braxton muttered, marching past the man. "Search the castle and take into custody anyone who is where they should not be." Then he quickly made his way to the griffin stable, feeling strange to be doing so in plain view. He found the griffins awake and anxious, because although they were locked away, they could sense the broad feelings of the castle's inhabitants.

What is happening? Myrish asked.

The girl has escaped, Braxton told him, grabbing a saddle from the wall. He had never used one of those—was not sure anyone had—but how different from riding a horse could it be?

And you want me to help you find her, Myrish said bitterly. The griffin swung his massive head around and snapped.

Braxton dropped the saddle. *Myrish!* he said frustrated. *Have some faith in me.*

You would return our only hope to the hands of he who would cause her demise, Varley screamed, lunging at him, but restrained by the thick chain around her neck.

"No," Braxton snapped, stepping back to avoid another attack from Myrish. *I would have my father think that.*

The griffins calmed and twelve sets of black eyes scrutinized him.

But you still mean to take Myrish to look for the girl, Iwin said from the back of the chamber. He was the oldest and having once known the freedom of the open skies was loath to even consider Braxton an acquaintance, consequently rarely speaking to him.

But return empty handed, Braxton finished.

How can we know you speak your true intentions?

Look at his eyes, Varley said.

Iwin gave a snort and looked away from Braxton. *You speak truth, but the chance cannot be taken.*

‡‡‡

The castle was in confusion as Aron made his way back to his room, taking longer than he would have liked. No sooner had he returned and slid into bed, when Milo Sewth—Caius' personal guard—was banging on his door.

"Rouse, young prince, your father demands your presence."

Aron cursed and threw back the covers; he had hoped Keegan would have more time. He pulled on a shirt and a pair of boots and followed Milo, who led him to Keegan's cell. The dead guards had been removed.

"The king awaits inside," Milo said, impassively taking a place beside the doorway.

Aron nodded and stepped into the cell. On any given day, he despised, hated, and avoided his father, but seldom did he fear for his wellbeing, because while Caius could not kill him outright, there were countless atrocities he might commit to punish him. So, Aron had no doubt that should his father discover his involvement he could be certain of a torturous life that would only end when he himself took it.

Caius paced furiously across the cell while Braxton leaned against the wall.

"Where is Kolt?" he whispered to Braxton.

"Leading the search," his brother answered, eyes never leaving Caius. "Or a mockery of it."

Realizing Aron was there, Caius turned on him. "Did you have anything to do with this?"

"No, sir," Aron said, keeping his voice flat. "I was asleep."

Caius stared at him, fury in his eyes, then turned towards Braxton, lashing out. "She was your responsibility! You had best pray to Sola and Lunos that Kolt finds her."

Aron knew how this went; he and Braxton stood against the wall while their father paced. Occasionally, Caius would lash out at whoever he deemed to be the guiltiest. From experience, he would bear the brunt of it.

Night faded to dawn and dawn to day. When Kolt returned without Keegan in hand, it was he whom Caius assaulted.

When the tirade was finally over, Kolt said, "She is too far gone for me and my men to track."

Beside him, Braxton gave a snort. It was no secret that he was an inept tracker.

"Only the Vosjnik can do it now," Kolt continued.

"Milo," Caius roared.

The man came quickly.

"Fetch them."

Aron took a deep breath and let it out slowly. If the Vosjnik went after her, there was no chance she could evade them. But there was a still a chance—regardless how miniscule.

Kolt took a place along the wall as Caius resumed pacing.

Aron wondered if Kolt would continue to feel Caius' unbridled wrath because as his favorite, he rarely experienced it. Today was an exception.

Time passed and eventually the eight members of the Vosjnik filed in: Connery Sray, the telepath and leader; Dax Ockloun, the water elemental; Thahan Havidray, archery; Finlay Cralter, the fire elemental; Guthrie Urvent, the air elemental; Vitia Gorell, the life elemental and only female; Brennian Thandov, swordsman; and Kade Tavin, the earth elemental. These were the strongest, most ruthless, and bloodthirsty people in Caius' arsenal; they had to be, for to become a member the person previously holding the position had to die.

Caius gave orders, but Aron was not paying attention—he already knew what they were; find Keegan and bring her back *alive*. Killing was nothing to the Vosjnik, but alive… that was something they were not particularly great at. Aron studied their faces and began to lose faith.

27

While they were monsters due to their physical abilities, they were also monsters for blindly following orders. And while it was rare for one of them to think on their own, it did happen occasionally.

Aron recalled the story about one from before he was born. The man, Rosh Broyker, had been a spy for the Lazado, infiltrating the Vosjnik for six years before being discovered. He prayed there was a spy among them now. None looked like it, but if he were to place a wild bet, he would say either Guthrie or Finlay.

"Dismissed," Caius said.

As one, the Vosjnik responded, "Yes, sir!"

Caius turned to his sons and snarled, "Get out of my sight."

Aron needed no other cue and quickly made his way to his rooftop paradise. It looked different at dawn and he could see for miles. Grassland surrounded the castle from the south, west, and north. To the east was the sprawling city of Agrielha proper a mile away.

Shiloh was waiting for him.

"The deed is done."

Her countenance dropped. "You never listen, do you?"

"I do listen," Aron said, approaching. "I just find that it's best to listen to Alyck."

"*Alyck*; he's the last person you should take counsel from. Do you know what the other laundresses say about him? He's a snake that only serves the king."

"They are wrong."

"I find that hard to believe." Shiloh cupped his face in her hands, "But, it's done and the most we can do now is pray to Sola and Lunos that your father never finds out."

Aron wrapped his arms around her, pulling her close. "When I leave…"

She looked up at him uncertainly.

"I want you to come with me. Shiloh Laund, I love you; I will not leave you here with these… monsters."

Shiloh placed her head on his shoulder, "Just say when and we'll go to the ends of the earth."

He looked down at her surprised. "What changed?"

"I'm not staying behind."

‡‡‡

Kade followed Brennian from the cell, his heart racing.

28

"Be in the stable yard in an hour. Bring your armor. Cuirasses are to be worn when we ride," Connery instructed.

There were a few grumbles as they briskly made their way from the dungeon to the living quarters.

Once the door to his room was shut, Kade packed quickly. When done, he surveyed the small space that had been his home, a smile sitting upon his lips.

At the stables, Connery, Dax, and Vitia were already tacking up their horses. Kade made his way to his own horse, Arso, passing the stall that should have housed Caius' black stallion, Darkheart. He laughed to himself; the girl was braver than he'd presumed. He quickly saddled the dun and led him to where the others stood.

Vitia had pulled her long, black hair into a braid, making the tops of her horns visible. At a glance, she seemed human, but she was far from that; the woman was an Alvor.

"This damned girl," Dax grumbled, "I had plans today."

"Stop whining," Vitia said. "It's been too long since our last mission."

"We got back two days ago!"

There was a malicious gleam in Vitia's brown eyes. "Like I said, too long."

While all members of the Vosjnik were bloodthirsty killers, Vitia went a step beyond. She played with her prey before someone took pity on the bastard and put them out of their misery. She'd kept her last victim alive for weeks, breaking his mind and abusing his body.

Guthrie joined them.

"What's so important about this noxþ girl?" Dax asked.

"The king did not say," Connery answered, "and it is not our place to ask."

Finlay arrived and began playing with a small ball of fire in his hand.

"Put it out, Cralter," Guthrie said uneasily. "You'll burn down the stables."

"I will not," he argued, the flame reflecting in his pale blue eyes. "And it's Finlay; I hate being called Cralter."

There was a gust of wind and the flame disappeared. "Now, you won't, *Cralter*," Guthrie said coolly.

"Why must everyone spoil my fun? No one bothers Vitia when she wants to play with something."

"Stop moaning," Vitia said apathetically. "And I've earned it."

"Guthrie's right," Dax said, crossing his arms, "Things do tend to burst into flame around you."

"He's a fire elemental," Kade said flatly. "What do you expect?"

"For him to have some royiken control," Thahan said, joining the conversation.

They continued to banter until Brennian arrived.

As they led the horses from the stable, Cralter approached him, "Thank—"

"Don't thank me, Cralter," he snapped. "I only pointed out the obvious. However, I would suggest you quit acting like a child. Or have you forgotten that members don't just get replaced when someone stronger comes along?"

‡‡‡

"Two visits in almost as many days," Alyck said. "What is the world coming to?"

"You knew someone was going to help her escape," Braxton stated.

"Of course, I did. My brother does not keep me locked in this noxþ room for nothing."

"Is she safe now?"

"She will never be safe as long as Caius lives."

"And Aron?"

"As always, his fate remains unchanged."

"Is the girl really as important as my father believes?"

"Even more so."

"How?"

"Wait and find out. Is that all for today?"

Braxton considered telling Alyck about his dreams but decided against it, as it could easily be his subconscious trying to fulfill his desire to help the girl. "Yes," he said, turning to leave. The dreams were just that, nothing more.

As the door closed, Alyck said, "See you... soon."

Braxton made his way through the castle, heading to the griffin stable and finding himself strangely at ease. Standing at the open face of the wall, he could see far into the distance. Below, he watched the Vosjnik disappear over the horizon.

They sent the monsters after her? Varley asked, though it was more of a statement.

He nodded.

The griffins talked amongst themselves, sometimes in his language, other times in their own. He did not really pay attention.

30

The fates were decided long ago, Crowlin said soothingly. *No amount of worrying will change them.*

I know. Braxton turned away from the open wall and went to stand beside her, running a hand over her soft feathers. *But it is what humans do; we worry when we cannot control the outcome.*

Humans, such strange creatures. They keep themselves weak so they can claim they cannot change what will be.

Braxton sighed, she had given similar lectures before.

Thinking will get you nowhere; actions move you forward.

I know. But you must think before you act—lest you make things worse.

CHAPTER 4

During the day, the Vosjnik caught up to Keegan. As far as they could figure, soon after Kolt gave up, she had stopped to rest. Mostly, her trail led west towards Lake Romann.

Now, with the sun making its descent, they could see her on the horizon. Darkheart proceeded at a slow trot, indicating she had yet to notice them.

"Cralter, Thahan, Guthrie," Connery ordered, "flank her from the left. Kade, Brennian, Vitia, from the right. You know what to do from there."

"Yes, sir," they responded, spurring their horses.

Kade's hair whipped about his head as Arso raced across the grassland. The girl glanced back, and he swore she locked eyes with him. She stared for a moment, then realized the seriousness of the situation and frantically spurred Darkheart into a gallop.

Kade, came Connery's voice.

With a slight movement of his hand, Kade raised a column of earth in Darkheart's path.

The warhorse balked and Keegan pulled frenziedly at the reins.

He was surprised she managed to remain in the saddle but once control was regained, she quickly led Darkheart around the column. He was close enough to hear her yelling, "Go, go, go!"

Darkheart was a magnificent horse, but even he had limits, and ever so slowly, the three groups closed in.

"Vitia, go," Kade yelled.

"Who put you in charge?" the Alvor bit, a cutting smile on her lips. "Just go."

Vitia pulled ahead of the group and on the other side, Guthrie did the same.

Shadows grew longer as the rustic orange sun began sinking below the landscape. Kade knew Keegan understood what they were doing and had no choice but to move forward. Veering off to either side meant running into either he and Brennian or Finlay and Thahan, and turning back wasn't an option. Vitia and Guthrie were beginning to pull ahead and would soon turn to face her.

And thus it was done as the sun's form sank beneath the ground.

Keegan spun Darkheart around, looking for a way out. "Please. *Please.*"

Vitia laughed cruelly. "Stupid opida, what makes you think we would ever pity you?"

32

As tears welled in Keegan's eyes, a wind launched towards her.

Kade looked to Connery, unsure of what was happening.

"Hold your positions," Connery called to be heard.

As the wind intensified, the horses scrambled backwards to avoid being drawn into the gale. As a whistling began to sound from the strength of the squall, light exploded into existence. The wind reached a climax and shattered outwards.

Kade hunkered down on Arso, bracing for impact. The explosion was so intense that he felt the reverberations in his bones. Once his eyes readjusted to the darkness, he realized Keegan was gone and the area was coated in a layer of ash. The only thing that proved the girl had been there were tufts of upturned grass.

He stared in shock; he'd heard stories about Nanagins, but had never imagined witnessing one.

✠✠✠

The sun was just touching the needle-like tops of the pine trees when Jared Sieme arrived back at the clearing. He dumped his armload of sticks onto the ground, gazing about; trees surrounded a small expanse of grass no more than forty feet in diameter. Kneeling, he cleared away the debris at the center and grabbed a handful of leaf litter. Striking a piece of flint, he sent a spark jumping into the tinder. It began smoldering and he blew on it gently, letting it burst into flames.

He set the burning foliage down and placed small branches on top. As the flames grew, he added more kindling until he had a roaring fire. Satisfied with its size, he set about making a spit. Once completed, he retrieved a rabbit from his horse's saddlebag, which he skinned, gutted, skewered, and placed on the spit, leaving it to roast while he took the entrails to the edge of the clearing and buried them.

The smell of cooked meat wafted through the air, making his stomach grumble. Once it was done, he removed it from the skewer and ate ravenously, juices rolling down his chin. Cicadas and crickets chirruped in the background as the last rays of sunlight succumbed to the night. His hunger satiated, he leaned back against his hands.

Behind him, a branch cracked, and he jumped to his feet, pulling a knife from his boot. He waited apprehensively for a beast to emerge from the shadows; none did, and he sat back down, feeling on edge.

These royiken woods. He stabbed his knife into the soft earth. *Why did Lucas have to decide he's too good to run errands?*

33

Their mother was a seamstress in Suilenroc and although there were others who also qualified in the village, with even more in Tratoleck, she was the best and the well-to-do ladies of both paid highly for her work. Lucas, being the eldest, normally delivered items to clients in Tratoleck, or bought cloth and dye when needed. But he had suddenly decided Jared was better suited for the job. He tried to forgo the duty to his younger brothers, but Nico was too young and Carter irresponsible. Not having much of a choice in the matter, he had reluctantly accepted the role. This was his first trip, and thus far, he couldn't understand how Lucas had managed for so long.

The hustle and bustle of the city was overwhelming compared to the small village he was accustomed to. More than once someone had tried to pickpocket him, and the simple fact that he kept a hand on his purse had saved him. Once inside the foyers of the clients' homes, he was treated like filth by butlers and manservants. When forced back onto the streets, the smell of sewage and waste had assaulted his senses, threatening to make him sick. But despite all the city's downfalls, he preferred it to the forest that separated Suilenroc and Tratoleck.

During the day, the forest was unnerving enough; at night it worsened. The few times he had spent the night there, he had been relatively close to home, yet hated every moment. Everything about the place unsettled him, from the spindly, sickly-looking trees, to the ghastly creatures that dwelled within. The many stories of people venturing into the woods and never returning—the only evidence they had ever entered, demolished campsites—had not helped. The sounds of fearsome creatures often drifted over the treetops at night and sensible folk avoided it after dusk. Jared moved closer to the fire, its warmth making him feel protected.

Slowly, his eyelids began to feel the day's weight, and as they closed, his head dropped forward to rest upon his chest. The pop of a log brought him back from the brink of sleep. He tried to calm his nerves, but found his muscles tensing regardless. Another snap made him pull his knife from the earth and spring to his feet.

Gradually, he realized the entire forest was quiet, not even the cicadas thrummed. A light wind began to ruffle his hair, which quickly grew into a storm. There was a sound like thunder, and he was thrown backward, slamming into a tree. He sat slumped against the trunk, his head throbbing as pale blue and yellow spots floated across his vision. His horse, Brewer, pulled against the tether, braying frantically. After a few moments, his sight cleared, and he made his way to the large

Clydesdale to calm him. He quickly rebuilt the fire, making it larger than before to ward off this new, mysterious forest creature.

As he finished, the branches across the clearing began to rustle. It was then he realized he'd lost his knife in the blast and scrambled to find it as a dark horse pushed through the undergrowth. He relaxed at the sight of a harmless creature, but cautiously approached the pure midnight-black Friesian that reflected the firelight on its sweat-covered coat. The horse snorted and tossed its head as Jared grabbed the reins. It was then he noticed the young woman on the animal's back, lying slumped against its neck haphazardly.

The horse shifted, and the girl began to tumble. He dropped his knife to catch her, laying her gently on the ground.

She had a rounded face with freckle-dotted cheekbones. Possibly, she was quite pretty but the shallow cuts and dark bruises made it difficult to tell. He stared in disbelief, wondering who would be shameless enough to beat a woman. As he studied her, he realized she wore clothes he'd never seen before, along with shoes that appeared to be made of canvas with soles of a material much more durable than leather.

Gently, he checked her wrists. There were no markings of any kind. *She's not an elemental.*

The horse snorted and he went to tether it next to Brewer. Then retrieving his blanket from his saddlebag, made his way back to the girl, and unfurled it over her.

He sat beside her for a time, surveying her, questions running through his head then with a few movements of his fingers, he made the earth swell and cover her wrists, trapping them against the ground. *Who knows, she could be dangerous.*

He leaned against a tree, content to let his mind wander into the wee portion of the morning. Whoever she was, he got the feeling she was going to become someone important.

‡‡‡

She woke to the sound of a crackling fire and opening her eyes, found herself staring skyward, the branches of pines fringing the blue sky. Bolting upright, she remembered all was not right with the world—*especially* hers. She found she could only raise herself halfway as something pinned her hands to the ground. Looking down, she saw the earth had encased her wrists like manacles. "What the hell," she muttered.

Soldiers corralling her was the last thing she recalled. *They caught me*; it was the only explanation. She then noticed the young man tending the fire.

Even sitting down, she could tell he was of a decent height, around five-ten, with rich brown hair and matching eyes. He didn't appear overly muscular but might be stronger than his loose-fitting shirt and unlaced leather vest suggested. As she began pulling against the earthen restraint on her right hand, she realized he wasn't one of the soldiers.

"Take it easy," he said, raising his hands. "It's all right, I'm not going to hurt you."

She continued to pull against the cuff, noticing shallow fissures running through it. "Where am I?"

"Between Tratoleck and Suilenroc."

"How'd I get here?"

"I was going to ask you that."

She glanced down quickly; the cracks in the restraint had widened to the point it would soon crumble.

He approached slowly and knelt before her. "Will you tell me your name?"

She gave one last pull and her hand came free then swung wildly, aiming to catch the man with a right hook.

He caught her punch, and forced her arm back to the ground, using a well-placed knee on her bicep to hold her down. "Who are you?" he roared.

She didn't answer, struggling under his weight, and drove her knees into his back, sending him flying forward. Rolling over, she worked to free her other hand.

He quickly pushed her down again and earth rose to cover her arms up to the shoulders then sat on her chest, his knees squeezing her ribcage.

"What the hell did you do?" she screamed. "Get it off me!"

"Who are you?"

"Get it off me!" She could already feel herself beginning to shut down.

"Tell me who you are!"

She felt the cold steel of a knife against her neck. "Keegan Digore." Her heart raced—nothing made sense.

The pressure from the knife lessened. "Where are you traveling from?"

"I-I don't know."

"Where are you going?"

"I don't know." She could tell he was becoming aggravated by her lack of answers.

"How can you not know where you came from or where you're going?"

"I don't know. Please believe me!"

"Are you working for the king?"

"He's why I'm all beaten up." The words tasted like ash. "I would *never* work for that bastard."

He said nothing and stood up.

She eyed him for a moment. "Are you gonna let me go?"

"Why should I?"

"I haven't done anything to you."

"You tried to attack me."

"And you wouldn't've done the same thing?"

He walked back to her and began feeling around the waistband of her pants.

"What are you doing?" she blurted, instinctively jerking her knee up.

He stopped her knee before it made contact. "Checking for weapons," he said, running his hands down her legs.

She knew he meant what he said when his hands lingered no longer than necessary.

Satisfied, he walked back to the fire. As the earth covering her arms receded, he motioned for her to join him.

Keegan rose and looked over her shoulder. She might make it into the woods before he caught her... But then what would she do? She had no idea where she was headed and she'd lose the horse. She looked back to him; for better or worse, he was the only choice right now.

He handed her a piece of bread. "I apologize, but it's best to be cautious. I'm Jared Sieme."

Her face softened but when she didn't respond, Jared made his way to the horses and began adjusting the straps on his saddle.

Once done eating, Keegan quietly untethered her night-colored horse.

Jared surprised her by asking, "Do you have a place to stay?"

She gave him a searching look before shaking her head.

"Would you like a place to stay?"

"...Sure."

"You're welcome to stay with my family." He walked back to the fire and kicked dirt over it to smother the dying embers.

"Why would you offer such a thing to a stranger?"

"Looking at the state of your face, I'd say you could use some kindness in your life." He gave her half a smile.

For reasons beyond her understanding, it was comforting—even as she debated whether she should trust him. "Thank you."

‡‡‡

Kade finished untacking Arso and made his way outside to find Connery waiting for him. The sun was at its peak, blinding him slightly. He stifled a yawn; he was not fond of riding through the night.

"Ready?" Connery asked.

"No," Kade answered bluntly. "There's no good way to tell Caius what happened."

Connery nodded in agreement. "Be ready to become leader of the Vosjnik." With a failure such as this, there was a good chance Caius would imprison him—and that was thinking positively.

Kade followed him across the grass; as second-in-command he was privy to mission debriefings. From the battlements, sentries looked down at them, the noonday sun creating a halo effect around their heads.

Connery led the way to the throne room, the doors still missing from Keegan's explosive entrance.

A guard outside stopped them. "The king isn't here."

"I can see that," Connery growled. "Where is he?"

"Dining hall."

On the way there, Kade spotted Aron, who, when catching sight of them, paused and turned back to follow them. Of Caius' three sons, he disliked Aron the most; he was weak and yielding.

They finally reached the dining hall to only be stopped again. "The king isn't to be bothered unless it's urgent."

Connery shoved past. "I would not be here otherwise."

Kade followed and Aron slinked in after him.

The king and his sons sat at the far end of the table.

Caius stood, a smirk on his face. "I take it you captured her."

"No," Connery said, not one to prolong things.

Fury contorted Caius' face and he slammed his hands upon the table. "How did she evade you?"

"She experienced a Nanagin," Connery started, going on to describe the light, wind, and explosion that had preceded her disappearance.

Caius reached for the nearest object, which happened to be a metal water pitcher, and threw it across the room.

Water doused Braxton and the jug clattered across the floor, the sound echoing off the walls.

"Tell me why I should not have you executed?" snarled Caius.

Calmly, Connery answered, "I believe it is still possible to detain her; we simply need to consult your brother."

Some of Caius' anger dissipated as he headed towards the dining hall's doors, ordering, "No one leaves."

Aron scampered along the wall to avoid him.

Kade glanced at Connery and both pulled out a chair.

Braxton looked uncomfortable as water dripped down his face and body.

When Aron tried to take a seat, Kolt snapped, "Who said you could sit?"

Aron said nothing but looked at Braxton. The oldest Alagard boy stared back blankly. Slowly, Aron pulled out the chair. Kolt sprang up and made his way towards his brother, who did what any normal person would do to diffuse the situation by raising his hands and backing away. But Kolt wasn't normal; he struck out with a punch, catching Aron on the jaw.

As Kolt reared back to strike again, Braxton spoke up, "Let it go."

Kolt turned to face his older brother.

"Let. It. Go."

Kolt scowled at Aron and returned to his seat in a huff.

Aron leaned back against the wall, rubbing his jaw.

You would think by now Aron would have learned, Connery commented, pushing his thoughts out so Kade could hear. As a telepath, he could force his own thoughts into others' minds as well as hear theirs.

Hmph, Kade returned, *let them fight; fewer imbeciles to deal with.*

Be careful to whom you say that.

Kade smirked. *You feel the same.*

Connery shook his head. *Just be glad none of these* imbeciles *are telepaths.*

Kade put up barriers around his mind and laughed to himself; while Connery was an intelligent person, he had yet to realize Kade was also a telepath. Being part of the Vosjnik meant it was commonplace to shield one's thoughts.

Time passed slowly.

When Caius returned, he said, "Suilenroc," storming past them.

Connery said nothing, bowed, and exited.

As Kade neared the doors, Caius called, "If Connery fails again, you will be leading the Vosjnik."

Once his back was turned, Kade let a smile cross his lips.

‡‡‡

Jared led the way and Keegan quietly followed, her mind still reeling from recent events. Occasionally, he tried to strike up a conversation, but she responded curtly, wishing to be left alone.

"So…" Jared began again, "Where are you from?"

"Charlotte," she answered.

"Where's that?"

"Somewhere far, *far* away."

"Who… uh… did that to you?" he asked, pointing to her bruises.

"Caius."

"What was his reason?"

"He's a psycho."

"A psycho?"

"Crazy person."

"How did you escape?"

"I had help."

"Who helped you?"

"A guy."

"Does he have a name?"

"Yes."

At that point, he took the hint.

The sun was now close to the treetops and the forest was beginning to thin when Keegan could make out a small town nestled in the valley between several gently sloping hills. Seeing it made her worry Jared was about to take her through it, but he proved to be smarter than she'd presumed. As the sun dipped below the horizon, they climbed the last hill towards a picturesque two-story house. Jared guided them around back, approaching a brown, wooden barn. Outside the doors, he dismounted and heaved them open on groaning hinges.

Inside, the floor was littered with hay, stalls were filled with farm tools, goats and sheep occupied pens, and chickens roosted in the rafters. Towards the back were two empty stalls into which Jared tethered their horses.

While he untacked the animals, Keegan found a pile of hay that looked like a comfortable place to sit and plopped down, sending a puff of dust into the air. She would've easily fallen asleep if she weren't so nervous about meeting the Sieme family.

When Jared was done with the animals, she extracted herself from the hay, yawning, and followed him outside, pulling strands of straw from her rust-tinted curls. Outside, the sky was dark, a few stars twinkling high above. Rolling thunderheads obscured the horizon.

"Looks like it's gonna rain," she commented.

Jared glanced over his shoulder as he climbed the porch steps, "So it does."

The wooden steps creaked in slight protest under their feet and the stairs leveled out onto a wide porch. Jared pulled the door open and ushered her inside. She glanced at him for reassurance and with a deep breath, stepped over the threshold.

Inside, a family of five sat around a table with a single empty chair, plates of half eaten food before them. They seemed lively until they noticed her, at which time a tense silence settled over them.

Keegan looked uncomfortably at the floor, wishing she weren't the center of attention.

"Mother, Father," Jared said, approaching the table, "may I talk to you?"

His parents stood and followed him into the kitchen, giving each other nervous glances.

Keegan leaned against the wall by the door, crossing her arms, and continued staring pointedly at the floor.

Jared's brothers began whispering to each other, stealing wary glances at her.

She couldn't hear what they said, but assumed they were talking about her. The minutes ticked by slowly and finally Jared and his parents returned.

He motioned her over. "You can stay."

She breathed a sigh of relief.

"Would you like something to eat?"

She shook her head. "If you don't mind, I'd rather get some sleep."

"Give her Nico's bed," Jared's mother instructed.

She glanced over and saw the youngest boy start to protest; a look from his mother silenced him quickly.

Jared led her up a set of narrow, wooden stairs.

As she climbed, her vision began to distort. She blinked a few times until the world returned to normal clarity. It only worked for a second. Her heart started beating faster and when she reached the top of the stairs, she felt dizzy. Ringing began in her ears and she could barely see Jared further down the landing.

"Are you all right?" he asked.

41

She nodded, unwilling to admit she wasn't.

As Jared turned to continue, her legs became weak and she fell to one knee. She placed a hand along the wall to steady herself, but her body became like stone. The last thing she recalled was the cool feel of the grainy wood floor on her cheek and a muffled yell for help.

CHAPTER 5

Jared anxiously paced the hallway, up and down, the familiar creak of the floorboards having a calming effect. Waiting on Lucas, who had been sent to fetch the town healer after Keegan's collapse, was making him restless.

He started another round down the hallway when he heard the door slam shut. Rushing to the top of the stairs, he saw his mother and the town healer's son, Jameson, ascending.

Jared stepped aside, letting them by.

"I apologize for having kept you waiting, but mother is delivering Caara's baby and could spare only me," Jameson said. "Not that I minded; thought I was going to go deaf."

Jared was too anxious to even give a fake laugh.

Behind them, Lucas stomped up the stairs, his thick brown hair hanging in wet strands. "It's pissing down," he growled, shoving past them.

Jared watched silently as his older brother went to their bedroom, the door slamming behind him. He sighed, knowing he'd have to reconcile with him later, and entered Nico and Carter's bedroom.

Inside, Jameson and his mother stood next to the bed. Keegan lay beneath the covers, sweat beading on her brow. A single tallow candle on the bedside table offered light.

"Can you tell me what happened?" Jameson asked.

He gave a slight shrug. "She just... collapsed."

"You spent some time with her beforehand, is there anything else you can tell me?"

"She was like that when I found her," Jared growled, understanding the implication of the question.

Jameson nodded placidly and placed his hand on Keegan's forehead. "She has a fever. Fetch some wet rags, please."

Jared turned and left, pulling the door closed. Once in the kitchen, he began rummaging about for a cloth. Carter and Nico still sat at the table, talking quietly.

"How is she?" Carter asked.

"I don't know," Jared said without glancing up.

Lucas stomped in and Jared turned to look at him. He had changed into a dry pair of pants but wore no shirt. Lucas had a muscular body and a flippant attitude that made women fawn over him, much to everyone's annoyance. Jared returned to his task, doing his best to ignore him

Lucas poured himself a cup of water from a pitcher and leaned back against the counter. "How is she?"

"Don't know," Jared restated brusquely.

A tense silence followed.

"You shouldn't have brought her here," Lucas said ominously.

"Why not?" Jared asked defensively, finding a rag.

Lucas took a drink before answering. "You're endangering everyone."

"How so?" he bit, wetting the rag.

Lucas took another sip. "You hardly know her. She could be a spy for the king."

"Could be but isn't."

"How can you know that for sure?"

"I asked her."

"And if she lied," Lucas cautioned, setting the cup on the counter, "you and Nico'll be in a world of hurt."

Jared glanced at his wrist, the outline of the earth symbol stark against his light olive skin. He looked to Nico, who sat at the table, innocently watching. "I have more faith in people than you do," he said, walking away, not wanting Nico to see them fight.

Lucas stepped in front of him. "Faith has nothing to do with it. You've seen more of the world than just our little town. People lie and hurt others simply because they can."

Jared drew himself up, almost matching his brother in height. "Not her."

Lucas pushed him backwards. "You've endangered everyone in this house!"

He shoved Lucas in return. "I have not."

They converged on each other and, as they met, a force separated them.

Between them stood their father. "Enough," Jude roared, holding them at arm's length. "Both of you stop acting like squabbling children."

They scowled at each other.

"Lucas, quit being so cynical, people can be trusted. And Jared, you need to guard yourself more—you have too much confidence in the morals of others," Jude cautioned.

Lucas lunged at Jared but was stopped again.

"Enough! And wipe that look off your face, boy," Jude snarled, knocking Lucas upside the head.

Lucas stumbled and shot Jared a menacing glare before storming away.

Jared gave his father as innocent a look as possible.

Jude shook his head, walking away.

He made his way back upstairs and as he was about to enter the bedroom, stopped to listen.

"I can't imagine what must've happened to her," Jameson said.

"Is there anything you can do?" his mother asked.

"No. Neither the burn nor the cuts are infected. The only thing to do is to let the fever run its course. However, it may be possible she has a concussion."

"What could have caused this?"

"I'm not sure. I've never seen anything like this happen to an adult. I have some theories, but they're so fantastic I dare not say them."

There was a pause. "Will she live?"

"I can't say. She seems to be a resilient individual, but the body can only withstand so much. If her condition changes, please inform me."

"Of course. And thank you for making the trip here."

Jared heard them approaching the door and stepped back. "I have that rag."

His mother nodded, "Go on in while I show Jameson out."

He approached the bed slowly. Keegan's body was still, but her eyes moved rapidly beneath the closed lids. He placed the rag on her forehead, feeling the raw heat radiating from her. Grabbing a chair, he moved it to the end of the bed.

Outside, thunder clapped, and rain pelted angrily against the windowpanes.

✠✠✠

Aron crept down the corridors, the pads of his leather boots making minimal noise. This time of night, the only people about were the guards—and they had predictable paths.

In his hand, he held a key. A few years past, it had appeared in his room with a note saying, *Use wisely —Alyck.* Not knowing to what it belonged, he had placed it aside. A few months later another note had appeared. *Come see me —the Blind Prophet.*

He made his way down a flight of steps and a rat scurried nearby, setting his nerves on edge. Reaching the door, he looked around, making sure he was alone. There was a faint click as he pushed the key into the lock.

"Well, hello, Little King," Alyck said in a cool, derisive tone once he had shut the door.

45

Aron jumped again and took a deep breath before turning to see Alyck sitting in his chair expectantly. "Must you do that every royiken time?"

"Must you jump every time?"

"You knew I was coming."

"As always."

"Then you know what I'm going to ask."

"Have we been spending a tad too much time with Caius?"

"I will *never* be like *him*."

"One can only hope."

"Will you answer my questions?"

"Yes."

He waited expectantly. When Alyck said nothing, he asked, "Are you going to or not?"

"You must ask me something."

"Why did you tell my father where to find Keegan?"

Alyck's grin faltered. "It needed to be done."

"Why? By condemning her, you condemn us all."

Alyck laughed. "You do not know what the future holds, Little King. Only I do."

"Then tell me why."

"Actions are like ripples on the water. The smallest ones can turn into the biggest waves."

"Can you do anything but speak in riddles?"

"Of course, but where is the fun in that?"

Aron sighed and headed towards the door.

"I would not do that."

"Why?" Aron asked irately.

"Now is not the time to go gallivanting about the country with your fair maiden."

"How did you—"

Alyck rose from the chair and made his way over. "Have you not learned by now, I know *everything*." He held Aron's face in his hands. "Be patient, Little King. Your time will come and soon you will be free of Caius." After staring for a moment longer, he walked away. With a wave of the hand, he added, "Return to your room. And I would stay away from Shiloh."

‡‡‡

The world around him was blinding and Braxton shielded his eyes until it became tolerable. Studying his surroundings, he realized he was in his room. Everything seemed to be in place and he began searching for the glaring light. But as hard as he did, he could not find the source.

About to give up, it flashed behind him. He spun around and winced when the burst occurred again, his retinas slow to adjust. When they did, the flash came again, but not as bright—yet still enough to make him look away.

The light's intensity diminished slowly until he could discern its source; it came from the chest at the end of his bed. He fumbled with the keys around his belt and unlocked it. There was another flash as he opened the lid, making him cover his eyes.

The light pulsed weakly, emanating from a book. As it continued, he could barely see the details. He heard someone speak behind him and whipped around; no one was there. The voice came again, and he searched the room, frantically trying to find it. Annoyed and about to give up, he finally understood what the voice said: *Prophecy.*

He jolted up; everything around him was calm and in dawn's shadow. He was in bed and unsure how he had gotten there, as he was convinced he had been searching for something. But whatever he had been looking for completely eluded him now. Dreams, again.

Its vividness had him on edge as he slowly dressed, pressing his mind to recall what it had been about. As he was about to head to breakfast, a single thought resurfaced. Knowing the word *prophecy* meant something, he forwent breakfast and headed to the library instead; it was high time he learnt a little more about prophecies, besides the fact that Alyck made them.

✠✠✠

Jared had spent a sleepless night watching over Keegan, the drumming of the rain threatening to lull him to sleep. Now that the storm had broken and warm sunlight flooded through the glass panes, he sat in the chair at the end of the bed, feet propped up against the footboard.

The door opened and his mother entered. "Have you been up all night?"

He stifled a yawn.

"Get some sleep," Alessandra said, kissing his forehead. "I will watch her."

He merely looked up at her.

"Go."

47

Yawing again, he stood. "Wake me if anything happens."

Out in the hallway, Nico sat on the floor. "Is she going to make it?" He tousled his brother's hair. "I don't know, but there's no need for you to be concerned."

"You can't do that anymore, I'm fourteen." Nico said as he flattened his hair.

He laughed. "You're my little brother, I will *always* be able to do that."

Nico scowled and made an obscene gesture.

He returned the gesture playfully before making his way to the bedroom. Inside, lounging on his bed, was Lucas, who glared at him and returned to staring at the ceiling.

"I'm not going to fight with you," Jared said, sitting on his own bed. "I've done nothing wrong."

"You brought her here," Lucas responded darkly.

"I helped someone in need. What's wrong with that?"

Lucas sat up. "She's going to get us all killed. I don't even need to ask how you found her to know she's nothing but trouble. People don't beat women for no reason; she's done something to deserve it."

Jared pulled his boots off. "I may not know much about her or what she's been through, but I do know I did the right thing. She needed help."

"You're going to need help."

"I'm done arguing with you. I can't make you like her, but you do have to accept that she's here to stay."

‡‡‡

Keegan shielded her eyes from the splash and as Tommy surfaced, she sent a wave of water towards him, catching him in the face.

"No fair," her brother called, splashing back.

She laughed as they continued their war of sorts.

"Move outta the way," Char yelled from the top of the slide, shaking it impatiently.

Keegan looked to Tommy and they raced for the ladder. She reached it first and started the ascent but was pulled back into the water. Tommy climbed and stopped halfway up.

"Move your butt," Keegan said jovially, treading water.

"Nah, I'm quite comfortable here."

"Come on," she whined, giving his butt a poke.

"Nope."

"God, for a senior, you're such a kid."

48

He feigned hurt. "Me, a kid?"

She rolled her eyes. "Whatever."

Moving to an open part of the dock, she took a deep breath, and sank beneath the lake's surface. Her feet hit the sandy bottom quickly and getting as low as she could, she shot to the surface. As her hands broke water, she placed them on the lip of the dock and used the momentum to pull herself from the lake. Wiping away the water dripping down her face, she noticed the man standing on the dock. "Macerio!"

"Hey kiddo," he said with a smile.

"I'm not a kiddo."

"Sure, you are."

She ran forward to hug him. "Am not."

Macerio held her at arm's length, causing her to burst into laughter. She managed to get past him when he faltered because Char hugged him from behind. He tried to push them off with little success and in the background, Tommy laughed.

"Alright, alright," Macerio said, finally freeing himself, two large wet patches staining his otherwise immaculate clothes.

With a smile a mile wide, Keegan asked, "What're you doing here?" She grabbed a towel and wrapped it around herself.

He patted her head, "Come on now, little sis, I wouldn't miss this for the world."

Her grin widened.

"So, are you ready to start high school?"

She shrugged. "I guess. I'm kinda nervous cause I won't know anyone."

"You'll know me," Tommy pointed out.

"You don't count."

Tommy put his hands on his hips. "Well then."

"Oh, I'm supposed to tell you dinner is ready," Macerio added.

Keegan looked to Tommy.

"Race you up there," he said, taking off.

"Leave some for us," Char yelled after them.

"No," Keegan and Tommy hollered in unison.

They sprinted up the hill and the steps that led to the back patio of the large two-story house. Inside the screened-in-porch sat a plethora of people. It was just a few close family friends, but it was more than Keegan was accustomed to.

Chuck sat on Allen's lap and didn't look the happiest; she would've been the same if she were the one with an ear infection and doctor's orders were to stay out of the lake.

"Izarra," Keegan said, *"you didn't tell me Macerio was gonna be here."*

She gave her a smile. "I didn't think I'd have to."

"You know, Keegan," Allen said, *"you can call us Mom and Dad; you're part of the family now."*

Beside her, Mrs. Ashley gasped, "Oh, congratulations!" She came around the table and hugged Izarra. "When were you going to tell us?"

"Tonight," Izarra answered with a smile.

While everyone was busy giving their felicitations to her parents, Keegan approached her foster mom, Ilene Piscol, and gave her a hug. "Thanks for everything."

"You're welcome, baby girl," Ilene said and with a laugh added, "But don't think you'll be getting rid of me that easily."

"Of course not. I'm gonna come visit all the time."

"I'd like that."

"You should tell her what you did," Izarra chimed in.

Ilene's face became stern. "What did you do?"

"Well, since I don't have a middle name, when the adoption came through, we decided to make 'Ilene' my middle name, after you," Keegan explained.

"How on earth did you ever get so sweet?"

A small smile graced Keegan's lips as she turned onto her back, reveling in the warmth of the covers. Opening her eyes, she found herself looking up at a sloping ceiling. Past events flooded back, and she closed her eyes, dread washing over her. She wanted to be home, where the most she had to worry about was getting through college.

The door creaked and she allowed her eyes to open again. Nico slinked in and made his way across the room. He had fiery red hair, bright blue eyes, was as pale as an Irishman, and with just as many freckles. She would've said he was Irish had she not known better. She found herself going cross-eyed as she followed his movements. He stopped at the end of the bed and she realized there was someone else.

"Is she going to be all right, Mother?" Nico asked.

"I do not know," a soft voice relied.

Keegan propped herself up on her elbows. "I'm fine, Nico."

"How do you know my name?" he asked suspiciously.

"Your mom said, 'give her Nico's bed'. You were the one who got upset, therefore, you're Nico."

"Wonderful deduction," the woman remarked.

Keegan remained silent and her stomach released a loud gurgle.

"You must be hungry. Go on," the woman said to Nico, "get Keegan some breakfast."

Nico left dragging his feet.

"Cute kid," Keegan said after the door closed.

"Pardon?"

"He's adorable."

"Only if you catch him in a good mood."

Keegan studied the woman, who had mid-length, raven hair streaked with gray. Her brown eyes were soft and kind, extending a feeling of ease. "Thank you... uhh... Mrs.,"

"No need for formalities, Alessandra."

"Thank you for your hospitality, Mrs. Alessandra. Where's Jared?"

"He went to get some sleep."

"How long have I been out?"

Alessandra looked at her, unsure of how to respond.

"How long have I been asleep?"

"Just one night."

Keegan made to push herself upright and a dull pain shot through her arms. She looked down at her hands and saw five markings etched in white on the underside of one wrist. There was a leaf in a square overlapping four other squares that contained a stone, a water droplet, a flame, and a spiral. Her left pinky had been given a splint, which she was thankful for. "What..."

Alessandra made her way over, gently took her hand, and examined the wrist. "Why did you not tell us you are an elemental, and a unique one at that?"

"What the f— What are you talking about? What's an elemental?"

"Jared will explain." Alessandra walked quickly from the room, leaving the door open.

Keegan sat up, her mind unsure of where to go. Her eyes scanned the room, though not truly processing anything. She threw back the covers and made her way to the window. Her fingers gripped the fabric of her t-shirt, pulling her arms close across her chest. Outside, lush, green grass covered small hills out into the distance until they merged with a dark line of distant trees. The sun beat down, making everything seem bright and cheery. Three men walked away from the house; a dog, tail held high, bounded in front of them.

"You're up."

Startled, her head snapped to look at Jared.

He carried a plate of something that resembled pancakes and bacon. Sitting it on the bedside table, he took a seat on the bottom corner of the bed. "My mother said something about you being an elemental." He yawned, struggling to keep his eyes open.

She remained where she stood; it took all her willpower to not crumple.

Jared pushed himself off the bed and went to her.

Her eyes stared blankly at his chest, refusing to lift.

"May I?" he asked softly. When she didn't respond, he gently took her hand and turned it over. "Impossible."

Tears began to spill forth at his incredulity. Her knees buckled and she sank to the floor. Jared wrapped his arms around her, and she buried her head into his chest until she had no more energy left to spend.

CHAPTER 6

Books were piled high around Braxton like a wall. He had spent the better part of the morning searching and had finally been rewarded; two tomes seemed like they might be helpful. One was a thin volume, bound in dark moleskin that gave the origins of the Blind Prophets; on the front page, scrawled in his father's handwriting, was a spell. The other was nearly a foot thick with worn, yellow pages.

He focused on the latter.

Many of the later pages were blank, while the others recited the prophecies made by the previous prophet, Angela Alaga, and only a few from Alyck; it appeared Caius had seldom deemed a prophecy important enough to record.

He looked at the last entry from Angela, the words scrawled in tight script. He cursed under his breath; of course, it was in the Old Language. Not only that, but droplets of ink scattered the page, making the text difficult to read.

Jyken ey— —eki lunviyda — psod— ri ayþ drackyn, æa— woth viæn nuþ q—lx ayþ æyscs fayo eyar oywn þen. Nackh j—en eya casne, fackyon ictotm, —uh du woth unla ryo iruh ayþ adæmno. —od— woth yarv rhæpn casn— jappec eya. Qalx ayþ bu—a, qalx ayþ —aysne, qalx okæpyio, qa— ayþ payn ri luxyen, —æ ps—æ woth v—æn. Astæm egreþer —u woth ry— eyar oywn foylisha g—æ woth —olcan eyar haycl—n oh kævoka kunyi.

He transcribed the prophecy and set about replacing the books that made his wall. Leaving the library, he took the two tomes, not wanting anyone else to stumble upon.

In his room, he locked the books in the trunk at the foot of his bed. The day was still young, the sun having only just crossed over its highest perch. Deciding he had nothing better to do, he began making his way through the castle to visit the griffins. No one bothered him and he was glad; it was much easier than having to slink around like Aron.

Halfway to the griffins, he paused. Alyck was only a few years younger than Caius; maybe he knew what the prophecy said. When his father and Uncle were boys, it was common for the Old Language to be spoken. If not, Braxton had no doubt Alyck would find someone who could translate.

‡‡‡

When Keegan woke again, the room was still bright and airy from the sunlight streaming through the window. Jared sat next to the bed, head draped over the back of the chair, mouth wide open. She turned onto her side and his head snapped up.

"How are you feeling?" he mumbled, rubbing the sleep from his eyes.

She gave him a dejected look.

"We need to talk. Who are you really?"

"I told you."

"Then what aren't you telling me?"

"Lots of things, cause they don't matter."

"I need to know, if I'm to help you."

Keegan sent a puff of air from her nostrils. "I doubt anyone can help me."

"Regardless…"

Her naturally snarky disposition reared its head. "I'll let you know as soon as I do."

Jared shook his head.

"What did you mean by impossible?"

She could see sympathy oozing from his eyes. "You shouldn't be an elemental."

"Tell me something I don't know."

"You don't understand… One doesn't become an elemental overnight. You're one thirty-five days after birth, or not at all, and… you can't have more than one element."

"I don't know what to tell you; I have even less of a clue."

Jared squeezed his eyes together, then blinked a few times. "I'm too tired for this."

"Then get some sleep," she bit.

"Fine." He strode from the room, the door slamming behind him.

She stared at the door and drew her knees to her chest, feeling tears beginning to form. She pushed them back; they wouldn't help her survive—never had, never would. A grumble from her stomach reminded her of her gnawing hunger but the plate of food Jared had brought up earlier was nowhere to be seen. She threw back the covers and made her way downstairs. As she was about to turn the corner into the kitchen, she stopped.

"I don't like her," came a male voice.

"You don't like anyone," another jibed.

"Whether you like her or not isn't relevant," a man's deep voice retorted. "We need to decide what we're going to do."

"She needs to stay here, away from prying eyes," Alessandra said.

"I agree," the third man said, "but we'll be hard pressed to conceal a *third* elemental."

"If we turn her away," Alessandra said with a hint of anger, "we might as well cast out our sons."

"I didn't say it couldn't be done, only that it'll be difficult."

Keegan felt a tickling in her nose just before she sneezed. *Shit.*

There was a pause.

"Keegan," Alessandra called, "come join us."

"I was just, uh..." Abashedly, she came from behind the corner and felt five sets of eyes boring into her.

Jared's father motioned her over.

She slowly made her way to the table, tentatively sitting in the empty chair beside Alessandra.

"How are you feeling?" Alessandra asked.

"Better," she mumbled, staring at her lap as her stomach released an unearthly growl.

"Just a moment." Alessandra pushed her chair back and fixed a plate of food.

Keegan shoveled a few mouthfuls in before speaking. "I can understand if y'all don't want me to stay."

Jared's father said, "I can't say you'll always have a place here, but for the time being, you do."

"Thank you," Keegan murmured, "but I'd feel really bad if something happened because y'all helped me."

"Do not worry about us," Alessandra said, kindly placing a hand on her shoulder.

"Thank you." She wished she could offer more than just words. "If you don't mind me asking, why are you helping me?"

"Because," Jared's father said slowly, "if we stop helping those in need because we're afraid, then the king has truly won."

‡‡‡

"Can you tell me what this means?" Braxton asked, holding out the parchment with Angela's prophecy.

"No," Alyck said flatly.

"But... you know everything."

55

Alyck gave a small laugh. "While it may appear that way, it is not the case. I know everything about the future, but that, *that* is the past. And only half of it."

"But I think it has something to do with the future."

"That does not make it any less of the past."

He gave a frustrated sigh. "Who knows the Old Language?"

"Your mother did." There was a tinge of sadness in the words. "But she cannot help us now. I would recommend going to the place where you have that lovely little scrap of information."

"It will take me weeks to go through the library."

"It should not take you that long if you have any sense. Look for a book covered in purple stone with silver veins."

"A book covered in stone with silver veins?"

"Purple stone. And I promise it is exactly where I say it is."

Knowing Alyck would give him nothing more, Braxton left, slowly trudging back to the library. As he reached the doors, Milo Sewth appeared.

"Your father wants you."

Braxton groaned. "For what?"

"It is not my place to ask. Though I would assume it is important."

He took a deep breath and followed Milo. "It is always something important."

‡‡‡

Jared slept for the rest of the day, leaving Keegan with his family. She kept to herself while everyone went about doing this or that but through quiet observation, learned a little about each member of the Sieme family.

Jude was a tall man, towering well over Keegan. At least six and a half feet tall, he had bulging muscles, short brown hair, and a bushy, red-tinted moustache to match. Mostly, he was a quiet individual, but when he spoke, his word was gospel—even to her. He was a shepherd by trade, as were his sons.

But it was Alessandra, the only woman in the house, who seemed to keep the boys truly in line. Her voice was soft, yet Keegan could tell you never wanted to cross her. She spent most of the day somewhere within the house, though Keegan couldn't discern where. By late afternoon she re-emerged and began preparing dinner.

Lucas was twenty-one and did his best to avoid Keegan; obviously, it had to do with her being dangerous. Sadly, she agreed. In her world,

56

he would've been a heartthrob with his rich brown hair, electric blue eyes, and most of his father's height. And to top it off, he had spectacularly defined muscles and beautifully tanned skin.

Carter, at sixteen, looked up to Lucas, though also seemed to find him annoying. She was surprised there weren't regular fistfights. He had sandy brown hair and a small amount of peach fuzz on his upper lip that he was immensely proud of. He was a few inches shorter than Jared, not as muscular as Lucas—which was probably why he let Lucas win most arguments—and his eyes were a light amber.

Then there was Nico, his flaming hair and freckles completely out of place compared to everyone else's darker hair and somewhat tanned complexion. Exceedingly curious and observant, he spent most of the day talking to her. She tried to answer his questions simply, but he had a way of knowing which parts to latch onto.

Everyone gathered around the table just as Jared joined them. Dinner was an unexpected but pleasant surprise. She had anticipated a somber event and was taken aback when it was a loud affair, much like her own family dinners. She also noticed a new dynamic between Lucas and Jared. Lucas was constantly trying to emphasize his "elder brother dominance", but Jared would have none of it.

✝✝✝

A book covered in purple stone with silver veins. Braxton lay awake, staring into the darkness of his bedchamber. Since his meeting with Alyck, he had not been able to stop thinking about it. But as much as it weighed on his mind, he had not been afforded time to return to the library. And at this rate it would be next week before he fell asleep.

Sighing in frustration, he threw back the covers, dressed, lit a candle, and made his way through the dark hallways. At one point, he swore he saw a shadow emerge from a wall, but when he blinked it was gone. Of course, it might be Aron returning from one of his late-night trysts, but he ultimately chalked it up to his eyes playing tricks on him.

The bibliothecary had long since retired but his auxiliaries were still hard at work.

"Can we help you, sir?" one of the elder boys queried, seeming self-conscious.

"Yes," Braxton said, wondering how dull they would find him, "I am looking for a book covered in purple stone with silver veins."

The auxiliary stole a fervent glance to the other boys, no doubt wondering what punishment he would receive if he could not locate said item. "A book in purple stone... with silver veins?"

"Yes."

"There's no book like that here, sir. At least none that *I* know of."

"I presumed as much," Braxton told him, turning to leave. "Thank you for your help."

The boy seemed surprised at his acknowledgement and lack of anger. "If I were to find a book like that though, I... I'll let you know."

"At once," Braxton said, giving the teen a smile.

Back in his chambers, he extinguished the candle and crawled into bed. As he fell asleep, something struck a chord; Alyck loved riddles. He hoped he had not been given one, as more often than not, they left him stumped.

When he managed to fall asleep, he found himself going through the ritual of the blinding light. He did not waste time searching, knowing it was coming from his trunk, and quickly pulled the book out. It was familiar, but he could not remember what it was about, nor where he had seen it.

The scene changed and he found himself standing on a field with a purple-black sky behind him. Screams and wind buffeted him. Something tore at his chest and a single word rang in his ears, "Betrayer."

CHAPTER 7

"I wanna know about Caius," Keegan stated, watching Jared slosh buckets of water over the ground.

He paused for a moment, giving her an inquisitive look.

"Why do you want to know about him?" Nico asked.

"Know thy enemy, know thyself."

"What the nastor does that mean?"

"Language," Jared snapped, "there's a lady present."

Keegan laughed. "I'm by no means a *lady*. Honestly, I probably cuss more than y'all. But, if you know your enemy, you know their weakness, which can help you beat them. So, tell me about Caius."

Jared began, "Long ago peace was kept by the Council of Elders. They consisted of the most powerful elemental from each race."

"I'm gonna take a stab in the dark here, Caius was one of them."

"You would be correct."

Keegan crossed her arms. "Great."

"They kept the peace for centuries. Caius joined their ranks, and for a few years all was well. Then, he turned against the other Council members and crowned himself king. People were quick to rebel and form the Lazado. There was a battle for the city of Agrielha, but the Lazado weren't strong enough and Caius just about annihilated them. Those who survived fled to the Alvor city of Edreba. Caius tried to follow them, but the other races fought his advances. After about a decade of war, the Council of Elders sacrificed themselves to create the border that now separates the other races from us. The Lazado have remained in Edreba for the past 237 years. Those of us who have remained under Caius' rule have been living in fear that he'll find us if we're elementals."

"Why?" Keegan asked, "And how can he live that long? How old does that make him?"

"To answer the latter, 280. As for how he can live that long, no one knows."

"Wow, so helpful."

Jared straightened up and tossed the bucket aside. "Get in the mud."

"Why?" Keegan drew out the word. "And you didn't answer my other question."

"What was it?"

"Why are y'all afraid of being found."

Nico put it bluntly, "Because, if found, we either join him or die. Now, get in the mud."

Keegan cocked an eyebrow. "Uh, again, why?"

"Do you want to learn to be an elemental?" Jared asked.

"Yeah…"

"Then get in."

"Fine." She slipped off her shoes, rolled up her jeans, and slowly made her way into the mud patch, the sludge squishing between her toes. She crossed her arms, "What now?"

"Move the mud," Nico said, looking like he knew some secret.

She gave the Sieme brothers a blank stare. "Isn't that what y'all're supposed to teach me?"

"Yes," Jared acknowledged, "but some lessons are best learnt on one's own."

She placed her hands on her hips. "That doesn't apply here."

"I promise, it does."

"Just teach me."

"No."

"Teach me."

"No."

"Uhgg!" She snapped and felt a rush of energy triggered by her frustration. "Just freakin' teach me!"

"Fine."

"Good," she said, more pleased with herself than she should've been. "Wait, why'd your answer change?"

"Because you just proved you have the raw potential of an elemental. Turn around."

Turning, she saw a misshapen wall of mud had solidified behind her. "How'd I do that? Did I do that?"

"Magic," Nico answered.

She felt he should've said it sarcastically, or at least added a "duh".

"Now, you need to learn to control the magic," Jared said.

"And I do that… how?"

"Close your eyes and concentrate on the point between your brows. Look for a small knot of energy."

"What? I don't get what you're asking me to do."

"What don't you understand?"

"How to find this energy source thingy?"

"Do as I say."

"But that doesn't make sense. You can't… feel things in your brain." Jared stared at her confused.

Nico interjected, "Put your finger here," and tapped the spot above the bridge of his nose.

Slowly, she complied.

"Now close your eyes and look for something that shouldn't be there."

As she began to concentrate, she became aware of a slight pressure and the more introspective she became, the more the cause took shape in her mind's eye. It formed into an opaque gem with ethereal swirls. "Found it... now what?"

"Break it," Jared said.

"How the hell am I supposed to do that?"

Jared shrugged. "That's up to you."

Becoming introspective again, she gingerly took the gem in her hands; it sat on her palm like a stone, becoming a deep red color as it touched her skin. She readied herself and tried to crush the gem. Pulling away, she was dismayed to find it still whole. She tried again with the same result. "It won't break."

"Keep trying," Jared encouraged.

Biting the inside of her lip, she closed her eyes and returned to her task. After multiple failed attempts, she became exasperated. In her frustration, she threw the stone onto an imaginary ground. Time seemed to slow and she watched as it shattered, sending red shards flying away. As it broke, it felt as if electricity coursed through her body and she felt the same rush as before. She gasped and opened her eyes, the energy receding, then gave a little hop of excitement and had to steady herself. "Was that it?"

Jared smiled. "Yes."

"How did that help me control it?"

"You have to be able to freely access that energy to control an element."

"Oh, well, then I guess I've got the getting to it part down. So how do I do the actual controlling?"

"Once you have the energy, imagine the earth doing as you wish. You can use your hands as a guide."

Keegan closed her eyes but struggled to break the gem again. As her body buzzed, she took a deep breath and raising her hands, imagined a glob of mud rising. She opened her eyes, and to her surprise, the mud had risen. Releasing the energy in elation, she dropped the ball.

"You're unsteady, but that's good for your first attempt." Jared said, seeming to be holding something back.

Keegan smiled mischievously. "So, I guess I've got it."

"Not quite; you need to refine the skill."

"Okay. Oh, and what about the other elements? Can y'all teach me them, too?"

"We can't."

"Why?"

"Because we're earth elementals," Nico answered.

"So?"

"That means we can only control earth," Jared said, retaking control of the conversation.

"Then who *can* teach me?"

"That will depend on what element you want to learn," Nico said.

"I'll probably need all of them," she said, drawing out the syllables of the first few words.

"Each element is common to one race," Jared explained, pushing Nico into the mud. "Life to the Silver Tongues, earth the Torrpeki, water the Merfolk, fire the Dragons, and air to the Buluo. You'd have to go to each to learn their respective element."

Keegan looked at Jared like he had three heads. "All those creatures exist?"

Nico got up and threw a handful of mud at Jared, catching him in the face. "Yes. Why wouldn't they?"

"Uh, cause they're mythological."

"You little bwint," Jared said, wiping the mud off.

"Language," Nico chided.

Jared smacked Nico upside the head, then returned his attention to Keegan. "I assure you, they're real."

Nico took the opportunity to tackle his brother.

Keegan stared at them blankly before giving a sharp whistle. "Enough, dinguses."

They stopped to give her a perplexed look. Jared pushed Nico away and got to his feet.

"There's no way those…" she spoke with her hands, "whatever the hell you said, exist."

"Magic exists," Jared reminded her.

"Touché."

The two looked at her confused.

She clarified, "Good point. What about humans?"

"What about them?" Jared repeated, unsure of what the question was.

"What element's common to us?"

"None. We can be any element," Jared made a ball of mud rise. "Now catch." He sent the orb careening towards her.

She raised her hands to stop it but it hit her in the chest, knocking her into the muck. She sat up, spitting mud.

Nico gave a loud laugh. "You're supposed to stop it."

"It's not like I didn't try," she snapped, forming her own mud ball and launching it at Jared. He easily stopped it and made it levitate. Her scowl deepened and she crossed her arms.

Jared sent the ball back towards her; it crashed into her before she could react.

She snarled a curse at him, getting to her feet.

"Again," Jared said, sending another projectile.

She couldn't stop it and the exercise continued for hours. With each attempt, she got closer to impeding the oncoming strike. Then finally, just as the sun was beginning to touch the treetops in the distance, she stopped a ball and let it drop to the ground. She prepared to catch the next one, but none came. Glancing over, she saw Jared motion to join them. Shakily, she made her way through the mud, suddenly realizing how drained she was, and sat on the grass, "Why're we stopping? I could do this all day."

"It's time for dinner," Jared said. "And you have been doing this all day."

She shook her head, too tired to point out the missed sarcasm.

With a quick movement of Nico's hand, the dirt coating her body and clothes flew off and back into the mud patch.

Jared offered a hand and pulled her to her feet.

Grabbing her shoes, they made their way to the house.

✚✚✚

Keegan had been quiet during dinner and many times had needed to catch her head as it dropped forward. Now with dinner over and the table cleared, they lounged in their chairs. Alessandra stood by the washtub, cleaning the dishes. Keegan had offered to help but was refused. Crickets chirped in the springtime night and for a time the conversation pertained to nothing of importance.

Jared looked over and saw Keegan asleep in the chair, a hand against her cheek, mouth open.

"You worked her hard," Carter commented.

Jared shrugged. "No harder than Nico when I was training him."

"She must not've gotten very far then," Lucas said presumptuously.

"No, she was able to stop the ball by the end of the day."

"You act like that means something to me."

"That took me five months," Nico said, effectively quieting Lucas.

"There's something about her," Jared declared. "I can't place it, but she's something incredible—a force to be reckoned with."

"A word of advice," Jude said, "don't expect the world of her. She's only one person."

Jared nodded and shook Keegan's shoulder. "Let's get you to bed."

She looked at him groggily and yawning, blearily made her way up the stairs.

Jared followed, finding he'd become protective of her.

She crawled into Nico's bed and nestled beneath the covers. "Thanks," she said quietly.

"For what?"

"Helping me."

CHAPTER 8

Aron took a deep breath, filling his lungs, and the muscles in his arm tensed as he pulled back the bowstring. The fletching of the arrow brushed against his cheek and he moved his hand away. Exhaling, he released the string. The arrow shot forward, the string snapping back with a twang. He watched as it sailed through the air and hit the center of the target.

Beside him, Braxton shot and hit the outer ring. "You always were an excellent archer," he praised.

"I just practice," Aron commented.

"It's about the only thing you do."

"Father never would let me wield a sword." Aron notched another arrow, released, and it embedded itself flush with the other one. "So, this is what I do."

"He has his reasons."

Aron sent another arrow at the target and together they made a line. "And I have mine."

"Be careful when you say that. There is no knowing how father would take it."

"It is as it is, and he can take that however he royiken wants."

Braxton notched another arrow and let it fly. It clipped the target's edge and went tumbling off into the field behind. "Noxþ."

"Set the targets back a hundred feet," Aron said to the men standing nearby.

They jumped to do as directed.

"Why are you setting them back?"

"I need a challenge."

Braxton grumbled but said no more as they waited patiently while the boards were moved. The arrows that protruded like spines were plucked and returned to them.

"Do you think the Vosjnik have found Keegan?" Aron asked, running his thumb along the bristly feathers; it had been two weeks.

"We have not heard from them," Braxton answered, lazily loosing his arrow. It barely stuck to the target. "What makes you ask?"

Aron took his time shooting the next arrow and only answered when it was rooted into the board. "Curiosity."

"I think it's more than that." Braxton's next arrow missed the mark completely.

Aron chose not to respond.

"Move the targets back," Braxton called.

Aron glanced at him skeptically.

"But, sir," the men protested, "they're already at five hundred paces."

"Move them back," Braxton growled.

The men looked at each other but did as instructed.

Aron prepared his next arrow. "Getting a little ambitious?"

Braxton was quiet and as soon as the man moved out of the way, quickly loosed the arrow. "No," he said, walking away.

Aron stared after his brother, then looked at the target. The arrow was dead center.

‡‡‡

Braxton quickly located the book to stop the pulsing light and had a moment to examine it; the cover was a rich purple and the pages silver gilded. The surroundings changed and though he could see nothing, knew war and turmoil raged around him.

Purple dripped across the background, splattered occasionally with red. Wind began to buffet him and a single word echoed: betrayer. There was a screech and a searing pain ripped through his chest. He opened his mouth to scream but no sound escaped.

Another shriek pierced his ears and the world turned black. He could feel the covers over his body and the sweat dripping down his forehead; it took a moment for him to realize he was awake. He ran a hand across his chest, convinced he would find oozing wounds.

Throwing back the covers, he began to pace, his body too full of adrenaline to even attempt returning to sleep. As he walked, his heart slowed and his mind calmed. He recalled something else from his dream, a book. He understood Alyck's riddle now. The volume was not literally covered in stone; it was amethyst colored with silver gilded pages.

He slipped on a shirt and boots and made his way to the library. The auxiliaries looked surprised to see him but equally relieved as he amended his request.

As he returned to bed, a phantom pain manifested across his chest. It was hard to ignore, but after several hours of struggling, he succumbed to sleep.

‡‡‡

Night had fallen, but Aron was still wandering about the castle. Making his way through the passage, he found Shiloh waiting.

"Has there been any word?" she asked.

Aron could see she was tense. "No."

"I still can't fathom how you place so much faith in that snake."

"Because you don't know him as I do."

"And I never want to."

"He's helping us; I don't understand where this hatred comes from."

"It's not hatred, more a high distrust," Shiloh answered, giving a weary sigh.

"And why is that?"

"If you heard how the other girls talk about the Blind Prophet, you'd be wary of him too."

"If you had listened to them, you would never have fallen in love with the handsomest prince."

"More like the stupidest prince," she muttered.

Aron feigned offense, then pulled her towards him, kissing her gently. "Either way, you fell for me."

"That I did."

"When we leave, where shall we go?"

Shiloh glanced up. "To the stars."

"They say stars are the souls of the departed."

Shiloh scoffed, "That old wives' tale. Everyone knows it's not true."

"Oh, really?"

"Yes," she said matter-of-factly. "Stars are the lights of billions of distant suns."

"Who told you that?"

"My father."

They talked until the moon was low on the horizon. When he made his way back to his room, his eyelids were heavy, but his heart was very much alive.

CHAPTER 9

They had been traveling for just over two weeks and were finally reaching Suilenroc—which was normally a three-week ride from Agrielha. The town was nothing impressive, merely a collection of houses nestled between a few low-lying hills.

"Split up," Connery ordered. "If you receive any information on the girl's whereabouts, you know how to reach me."

Kade steered Arso away from the group and tethered the horse. He shook his head as the others began going around the main square; for the best fighters and elementals in the world, they weren't the brightest folk. He made his way down a side street until he reached the edge of town, where he about-faced, and headed back.

As he walked, he knocked on doors and talked to anyone he saw. The answer was always the same, no one had seen or heard of the girl. He was nearly back to where he'd started when he came across a man carrying what appeared to be jars of salves and creams.

"Have you seen a girl," he asked, "short stature, auburn hair, would've been wearing trousers."

The man's eyes narrowed. *That sounds like the girl Jared Sieme brought home,* he thought but said aloud, "No."

Kade smiled and walked on, while the man called after him asking why he was enquiring.

Closer to the center, he came upon an old woman sitting on a porch. "Do you know where I can find Jared?"

"You'll have to be more specific, dear."

"Jared Sieme."

"Oh, such a sweet young man," the woman said thoughtfully. "Hmm, his older brother though… Take forty years off me and I'd make him a man."

"Do you know where I can find Jared Sieme?" Kade repeated impatiently.

"Maybe."

Kade glared at her and reached into his purse, pulling out a bronze coin, and tossed it to her.

She pointed towards the back of the town. "On the hill."

Grinning, he walked away. *Found her,* he told Connery.

‡‡‡

"Ready to go?" Jared asked.

68

Keegan slipped on her shoes. "Yup."

From the kitchen, his mother called, "Be home early tonight, please."

"Yes ma'am," Keegan answered, as the door banged shut.

Jared saw her out of the corner of his eye and had to fully glance at her before his momentary confusion subsided. While he wasn't used to seeing women in trousers, he had grown accustomed to it with her—but it was still strange to see her in Nico's things. She'd begun to worry that "wear-and-tear" would ruin her pants—jeans as she called them—so his mother had lent her a set of Nico's clothes. Once hemmed, they fit well enough and she'd also shortened the shirtsleeves so they only came to her elbows. He thought it was indecent, but she seemed comfortable, and he'd learned you couldn't make her do anything.

"Why do we need to be home early?" Keegan asked.

"It's my birthday," Jared said. "She probably has a special dinner planned."

"Happy birthday!"

He chuckled, "Thank you."

"How old are you now?"

"Twenty."

"Damn it; you're older than me."

"You?"

"Nineteen. Today's May 11th, right?"

He nodded.

"I'll be twenty in a month."

"The eleventh?"

"Tenth."

In the two weeks Keegan had been training, the first had been spent practicing in the mud patch outside the barn. As the days progressed, she'd grown stronger and finally a rogue mud ball had hit the barn door, splintering a few of the planks. After that, they had taken to training near the forest's edge, far from anything they could break—other than themselves.

Jared led the way from the house to the barn. The sheep were gone, as Jude, Lucas, and Carter had taken them out to graze. Nico normally went with Jared but was helping their mother with a bit of cleaning. They made their way to the back of the barn and began tacking the horses.

Keegan struggled under the weight of the saddle but managed to get it on Bastille's back.

Earlier in the week, Nico had pointed out that her horse needed a name. She debated between Midnight and Bastille and chose the less stereotypical moniker for a black horse. He didn't understand what Bastille meant, but it sounded regal and fit the animal marvelously.

On the first day they'd moved location, Jared discovered Keegan didn't know how to saddle a horse and had spent an hour showing her how. She'd learnt quickly but always had him check her work. Leading the horses outside, they mounted.

Keegan spurred Bastille, flying past him, calling, "Slowpoke!"

He chased after her with a grin.

In the distance, trees that were at first no more than a hazy line, began to gain detail. As they neared, birds hopped to higher branches. Stopping at the edge of the forest, they turned the horses loose.

"What are we doing today?" she asked eagerly.

"Combat," Jared answered, rolling up his sleeves.

Keegan gave him an impish grin. "Any ground rules?"

That grin had him worrying. "No maiming. The point is to subdue the other."

"Fair enough," she said, causing the earth to encase his feet.

"Wait until I'm ready," he chastised, releasing himself.

"All is fair in love and war," she sang.

He ignored the comment and sent an earthen ball her way.

She swatted it away like she would a punch. "Come on, you've gotta do better than that to hit me now."

He sent her another orb.

This time, she stopped it and returned it to him, adding three of her own. While he was preoccupied with stopping the projectiles, she tackled him. Maneuvering herself until she had his arm in her grasp, she placed it between her knees and started bending it in the opposite direction.

"Argh," he yelped, feeling strain in his shoulder and elbow.

"Tap out."

"The royik?" He noticed she was no longer forcing his arm to bend, instead merely holding it in a position that left him with a solid ache.

"You give up by tapping either the ground or my leg."

He gritted his teeth and slapped her leg.

She immediately released his arm and rolled onto her knees.

"What the royik was that?" he roared.

"Me winning. And what does royik mean? I haven't been able to figure that one out yet."

"The point of this isn't to win," he growled, "It's to teach you how to use magic. And who taught you how to fight like that?" He rubbed his shoulder. "I think it's your version of fuck."

"Royik is definitely not an English word," she stated. "What language is it from?"

"The Old Language," he told her, still massaging his shoulder.

"Why cuss in another language?"

Jared shrugged. "Why use the curse words you do?"

"Touché. And, sorry, but winning is totally the point. And you learn to fight like that when you've got four brothers and we all do martial arts."

"What's martial arts?"

"Badass fighting. Shall we go again?"

Guardedly, he nodded and stood up.

✝✝✝

Silently, they made their way up the hill.

This could be the end of the mission, Kade thought. If he weren't in the Vosjnik, he could easily see himself settling down and starting a family here.

They rounded the back and dismounted.

"Be prepared for anything," Connery instructed. "Kade, with me."

Kade followed him up the porch stairs and Connery knocked on the door.

A woman opened it. "Can I—" She noticed the griffin emblem on their cuirasses and tried to slam the door.

"You should not have done that, Alessandra," Connery said, retrieving her name telepathically as he pulled her onto the porch.

She shrieked as he slammed her against the railing.

"Where is the girl?"

"Wh-what girl?" Alessandra stammered.

"Keegan."

"I do not—" she started as a rock smashed through the railing.

Kade shielded his face and as the debris settled, looked for the source. A redheaded boy stood behind the Vosjnik, several rocks suspended around him. *Another earth elemental.*

"His name is Nico," Connery said, hauling Alessandra down the steps.

The rest of the Vosjnik had already pulled out their weapons and the boy sent a rock towards Cralter. Kade reached for his power and let the stone sail harmlessly by.

Behind him, Alessandra screamed for the child to run.

71

Instead, the boy attacked Cralter again and his comrade reciprocated. Surprisingly, Nico managed to hold his own. Cralter sent a fireball towards him, which he dodged easily, and it sailed onto the porch, setting it alight.

"You should listen to your mother," Kade said.

Nico's scowl deepened as he charged.

Kade let the boy approach and before the fight began, had him pinned, even as he tried his hardest to fight back. "Stop," he hissed.

Connery dragged Alessandra towards them and forced her to her knees. "Tell us where she is."

Kade pulled Nico to his feet, twisting an arm behind his back.

"Say nothing," Alessandra instructed.

Kade grabbed a fistful of Nico's hair. "Tell us where we can find Keegan."

Neither responded.

He drew a knife and pressed it into Nico's side. "Tell us!"

Alessandra shook her head. "I do not know where she is."

Kade studied her face. "She's telling the truth."

Connery clenched his jaw. "What about you, boy, do you know where the girl is?"

Nico focused his eyes on the sky.

"You know something," Connery continued.

The boy wavered and glanced at his mother.

Growing impatient, Connery drew his dagger and prepared to bring it across Alessandra's throat.

"Say nothing," she implored.

Just before the knife touched his mother's flesh, Nico yelled, "At the tree line."

Connery paused and grinned, then looking the boy in the eye, sliced along Alessandra's neck.

Her body dropped heavily to the ground and Kade knew it had been a painless death.

Nico became hysterical, fighting desperately. While adrenaline pumped through his body, Kade knew he could become an actual threat. He wrapped an arm around the boy's neck and applied pressure.

Nico clawed at his arms in vain and slowly became limp.

Kade lowered him to the ground while saying to Brennian, "Toss me some rope."

"Just kill him," Vitia growled.

He bound Nico's hands. "No, he'll make an excellent addition to the king's army."

As he worked, Connery began giving orders, "Kade and Brennian, go look on the northern edge—"

Kade ignored the rest of the instructions; they didn't pertain to him.

✝✝✝

Jared landed with a thump and found Keegan sitting atop his chest. She kept her body low and placed a forearm against his neck. He reached up and tapped her side.

She shifted, placing her elbows in the crooks of his shoulders. Her hair gathered over one shoulder hanging down like a curtain, and she smiled mischievously saying, "You're easy."

"Hmmm," he responded, reaching up to tuck the hair behind her ear.

She gave him a probing look before hastily rolling over to lie on the grass.

He sat up, his body sore from her attacks, meanwhile, she had barely broken a sweat. They always began fighting using magic, but it never lasted long; each round ended with him receiving an onslaught of physical attacks.

She propped herself up on her elbows. "You've gotta learn to fight."

"I can fight," he snapped, insulted by the insinuation, "but I won't hit a woman."

She rolled her eyes and let her head fall back. "God, there's that stupid rule even here."

"Pardon?"

"The rule that guys can't hit girls. Y'all treat us like we're gonna break. I'm not a piece of glass."

"I never said you were."

She rolled her eyes again. "Yeah, you did, when you said you wouldn't hit a girl."

"I most certainly did not."

"Did too. You say you can't hit women, why?"

"Just… It… it's not– women are delicate."

Keegan got to her feet. "Who the hell decided *I'm* delicate? I'm about as far from delicate as you can get."

Getting to his feet, he took a step towards her. "You're taking this entirely out of context and proportion."

She shoved him back, "I am not."

Out of instinct, he raised a fist.

"Do it! Be a man; hit me!"

He clenched his jaw, staring at her angrily.

"Coward."

"I'm not going to hit you."

She began to rant.

He sighed; she was so incredibly hardheaded and hotheaded. Deciding to give in, he let his mind blank momentarily and his fist found its target.

She stared back at him, rubbing her jaw, then, with a wiry smile, said, "Good. Now we can have some fair fights."

Suddenly, the ground pulled itself from beneath his feet.

‡‡‡

Arso shifted his weight, forcing Kade to resituate himself in the saddle. Impatiently, the horse tossed his head, as Kade stared through the thin foliage that concealed them from their target. He didn't know who the man was, but doubted he'd be a problem. The two began talking after another bout of sparring, the man easily defeating her.

Arso shifted again, causing the foliage around them to rustle and Brennian's horse let out a soft snicker. *Blasted thing.*

The man jumped to his feet, "Someone's there."

Kade urged Arso through the underbrush, Brennian following him.

Keegan said something and the man moved protectively in front of her.

"Give us the girl," Kade said.

"Why should I?" the man asked boldly.

Kade saw through his pretense; he knew who they were and what they were capable of. He dismounted. "The king wants the girl and you're ill-equipped to protect her."

"You underestimate us," Keegan said, stepping forward defiantly.

Brennian laughed as he dismounted.

"It doesn't matter," Kade asserted. "You'll come willingly."

"Why the hell would I do that?" Keegan bit.

"You have nowhere else to go," Brennian answered brutally.

She paused. "Jared, where are the others?"

Kade could see the wheels turning.

"What do you mean?" Jared asked.

Keegan turned towards him, urgency in her voice, "Where are the others? Why are there only two of them?" She saw the smoke in the distance. "Oh god..."

Jared turned as well.

Fools, never turn your back. Kade walked forward, grabbed the back of Jared's shirt with one hand, his shoulder with the other, and threw him to the ground.

Brennian dealt with Keegan, drawing his knife and pressing it against her neck, wrapping his free arm around her shoulders. "You're coming with us," he hissed into her ear.

"Like hell I am," she said, bringing her foot up between his legs.

He grunted, loosened his grip slightly, and she tried to take advantage of the slack hold, but keeping his composure, he threw her to the ground.

Kade heard the breath knocked from her lungs and before she could get up, caused the earth to pin her down. He then focused on Jared, who was already fighting back. As he blocked the strike, one of his own rocks hit the back of Brennian's head, rendering him unconscious. Hopefully, when he woke up, he would assume it had been Jared's doing. Successfully blocking Jared's attack, he retaliated with an uppercut to the abdomen. As Jared doubled over, he grabbed his head and smashed it into his knee. Jared fell to the ground, stunned or unconscious—it didn't matter. Then he made his way back to Keegan, retrieving Brennian's knife along the way.

"You're an elemental?"

"Yes," Kade answered, kneeling beside her. "I'm going to release you; don't fight or try to run." He willed the earth encasing her to recede.

Keegan got to her feet slowly, a hard look in her eyes. She stared at him for a moment before beginning to move her hands.

He stepped aside just as a rock flew past his head. With a jerk of his fingers, earth rose, wrapped around Keegan's wrists, and pulled her hands to the ground.

She collapsed to her knees, hands held awkwardly against the grass. "Why are you doing this?"

He could tell she was already beginning to withdraw. "To keep you from Caius."

"Please, don— Wait, what? Why do you wanna keep me from Caius; you work for him."

"Revenge."

"For what?" Jared asked, shakily getting to his feet, blood dripping from his nose and mouth.

"Killing my parents," Kade growled.

"Understandable," Keegan said, some of the hatred and panic leaving her voice. "But how does kidnapping *me* accomplish that?"

"I'm trying to protect you. Caius knows where you are, so I'm taking you somewhere safe."

"And where would that be?" Jared asked.

"The Lazado."

"If that's true," Keegan said, "why didn't you just say that from the get go?"

"From the what?"

"From the beginning."

Kade motioned to Brennian, "I had to keep up appearances."

"Why should we trust you?"

"Trust me, don't trust me. I don't care." He released Keegan's hands from the earthen bonds and grabbed the front of her shirt, pulling her to her feet. "But you will come with me—one way or another."

"Don't hold your breath."

He let his fist connect with her nose.

Keegan hurled a strange curse at him. Blood trickled into her mouth and she turned her head to spit it out, flecking the green grass with red. "So, it's go quietly, or you beat the crap out of me?"

"If that's what I must do."

"Fine, we'll do it your way."

"There is no *we*. Only you."

"Like hell—"

"Show me your wrist," he instructed Jared. When Jared hesitated, Kade pushed the point of the knife into Keegan's neck, drawing blood. "Show me your wrist."

Scowling, Jared complied, confirming Kade's suspicion that he too was an elemental.

Kade withdrew the knife and pushed Keegan towards Jared. "Get ready to leave." He left them to retrieve their horses.

"Do we get a name to work with?" Keegan asked as he returned.

"Kade Tavin. Mount up."

"Not yet." She took a breath as if to gather up her courage. "I have a stipulation."

"What would that be?"

"We go help Jared's family."

Kade looked at Jared and noticed the resemblance to Nico and Alessandra. If he had any inkling Nico was still alive, it could—no, *would*—complicate matters. "By now, there's no one left to help."

Jared's face fell.

"What do you mean?" Keegan demanded.

"They're dead," Jared said in a hoarse whisper.

Keegan gave a subtle shake of the head. "No."

He shoved Darkheart's reins into her hand. "Now isn't the time to grieve."

"They can't be dead," Keegan said, almost pleading. "We can still save them."

"Stop," Jared said weakly.

Keegan turned to him. "How can you say that? This is your family!"

Jared pointed at Kade, "Do you see the star branded on the side of his thumb? That means he's a member of the Vosjnik."

"So?"

He put it frankly, "We're not known for being merciful."

"But... they didn't do anything!"

"They harbored you. Now, get on the horse before I'm forced to do something you'll regret."

"I'd love to see you try."

"As you wish." He let go of Arso's reins, approached her, and dropping a shoulder, placed it against her hip, allowing him to easily throw her over.

She yelped in surprise as he made his way towards her horse. Over the shock, she started beating against his back and yelling obscenities. Finding this achieved nothing, she grabbed a fistful of his hair and pulled.

He reached back and pried her fingers free as he shifted her onto the saddle.

Now that she had some leverage, she managed to get her foot between their bodies and kicked him back before sliding off the horse. Before she could go far, he grabbed her hands. She pulled against him, but his grip was unbreakable.

He took the reins and secured her wrists with them.

"UUARRG! Let me go!" she screamed.

He stepped back. "No."

"You bitch." Keegan lunged at him but the reins kept her in place. She noticed Jared hadn't moved. "Why aren't you helping me?"

"Because he's right," Jared answered. "There's nothing we can do."

"We don't know that!"

"Yes, we do," Kade snapped, becoming impatient. "Now get on the horse before I—"

"You already made that threat, and it *didn't* work."

"Get on the horse."

"Not until we help his family," Keegan repeated belligerently.

At this point, he knew he wasn't going to get her to go voluntarily. He marched over to Arso. "Get on the horse," he instructed Jared. When Jared didn't move, he roared, "Get on the royiken horse!"

He rummaged through Arso's saddlebag and pulled out two lengths of rope. When he returned, Keegan was attempting to pull the reins loose using her teeth. He grabbed her foot, hoisting her up, and forced her foot into the stirrup.

"What are you doing?" she shrieked, kicking at him with her free foot.

He tied her foot to the stirrup and stepped back.

She looked over her shoulder, trying to figure out what he'd done and realized he made it so she had no choice but to do as he wished. She glared at him with a look of utter loathing, then swung her leg over the horse and began trying to lift the reins over his head.

Kade lunged forward, grabbing the reins, "Oh no you don't."

"Let go," she said, jabbing her heels in. The horse started forward, but just pivoted around Kade.

He reached up and untied her hands.

At once, she began slapping at him.

He grabbed them again and taking the second length of rope, tied them to the saddle horn. A stream of oaths spilled from her mouth, all foreign to him. "I warned you," he said, taking the reins and securing them to Arso's saddle. "Follow me," he instructed Jared.

CHAPTER 10

A dark column of smoke marred the otherwise pristine sky ahead. His lungs burnt and there was a stitch in his side, but Lucas refused to stop running. He knew to expect the worst but prayed to Sola and Lunos for the best. He had never been religious, but he was shouting out to any god that was listening now. Behind him, he could hear the heavy breaths of his father and brother as they chased after him.

He reached the crest of the hill and froze. The house still blazed violently, there were deep gouges in the earth, and a body lay on the grass. An excruciating ache entered his heart and he raced forward.

Turning the body over, he stared into his mother's lifeless eyes. He knew he was screaming but could hear nothing. Hands pushed him out of the way and his father took his place. Jude sat there on the ground, gently rocking as he pulled his wife close against his chest.

Lucas turned away, anguish and anger rushing forth. He clenched his hands as the desire—the need—to hit something struck him. A sob sounded in his throat and he could feel his nails cutting into his palms, but he only clenched his fists tighter.

A rider approached.

"What happened?" Jameson asked, swinging down from the horse.

Lucas shook his head, covering his eyes with a hand. Hot tears rolled down his cheeks and mingled with the blood from his palm.

"Are any of you hurt?"

"No," Jude answered.

Lucas turned to look at his father. Tears still ran down his cheeks and into his moustache, but his voice conveyed composure.

"Have you seen Nico and Jared?"

"No. You need to leave."

Jude brushed a strand of hair from Alessandra's blank face. "Why?"

"This was the work of the Vosjnik."

Jude's head snapped up. "How do you know that?"

"They came through town asking about Keegan."

"Did you tell them anything?" Lucas demanded.

"Of course not!"

Lucas pulled back his fist. "Then how did they know to come here?"

"Lucas," Jude yelled, staying him.

"I'm not sure," Jameson told him. "Now, please, you need to go."

Jude wiped his eyes. "We bury her, then we leave."

"Where will we go?" Carter choked.

"East. It's where your brothers would've headed. I hope."

Jameson asked awkwardly. "Is there anything I can do for you?"

Jude stood and picked up Alessandra. "Tell the town we perished in the fire."

"Then you'd best leave now. The rest of the townsfolk will be here soon."

Jude nodded and sent Carter into the barn to retrieve a shovel and their packs.

Carter returned quickly and handed one of the packs to Lucas, tears still streaming down his face.

It suddenly struck Lucas that the only things to their names were the clothes on their backs and these few meager supplies.

"Come on, boys," their father said quietly, "we have a long walk ahead of us."

Lucas went to stand by his father and looked out over the hills. This land, once so familiar, was now soaked with sadness and blood. He followed his father down the hill. Come hell or high water, he was going to kill those who had done this to him—to his family. They would pay.

✚✚✚

The world was rocking; up and down it went in a steady motion. Nico's head rolled from side to side. Thud-ump, thud-ump went horses' hooves. He opened his eyes and saw tree trunks and leaves rushing past. He tried to turn, but arms that reached around him to hold the reins stopped him. He remembered what had happened and began to fight.

"Stop," growled a voice behind him.

"No," Nico yelled bringing his elbow back; it met a cuirass. His forearm and hand went numb.

"Halt," another voice called out.

The man behind Nico reined in his horse and it was now he noticed the rest of the party. Six men and a woman. He knew they were the Vosjnik, but it seemed they were missing a member.

The man dismounted, pulling Nico off with him.

He stared at the man, who had feathery hair so black it seemed blue, and intense eyes, pale as water. Black whiskers marked his triangular jawline and his skin was the color of tanned hide.

"Release me," Nico demanded, pulling hard. If his hands weren't bound, he would be using magic already.

"Silence."

"Drug him," another man commanded.

80

Nico assumed this to be Connery, the leader, who wasn't what he'd imagined. He was of average height, instead of the giant of stories. His hair was dark gray and in places stark white. Scars crisscrossed his face in deep lines and Nico had no doubt more covered the rest of his body.

"Who has the ether?" the man holding him asked.

"I do," the woman said, producing a bottle of jade green liquid from her saddlebags. After soaking a rag, she passed it on.

The man pressed it against Nico's mouth and nose.

He held his breath, but it only delayed the inevitable. The first breath was the worst; it felt like all the moisture was sucked from his throat. He began to cough, but it only made it worse. Slowly, his mind began to feel fuzzy and he was unable to access his magic.

"He has had enough, Dax," Connery said.

Dax withdrew and Nico collapsed onto the ground coughing and dry heaving.

"We will make camp here," Connery stated.

"We haven't found the opida yet," the woman sniped.

"And we have plenty of time to do so," Connery said, tethering his horse to a tree. "It will do no one any good to push too far. She is with at least one unwilling companion and they will be slow moving. Why hurry?"

"Because I want to kill the bwint."

"Our orders are to bring her back alive."

Glancing at Vitia, Nico could see she was fuming, and the horns protruding from her head only added to her fearsome appearance.

Noticing he had recovered, Dax pulled him to his feet and hauled him over to a large tree. "Sit."

"No," Nico said defiantly.

Dax pressed into the muscle in his shoulder. "Sit."

He winced but remained upright.

Frustrated, Dax kicked his legs out from under him.

His head hit the tree, sending spots dancing across his vision.

Dax walked away and returned with a long length of rope, which he wound around Nico and the tree. Done, he returned to his comrades and began setting up camp.

Nico watched the activities—wondering if he could name all members from the tales and rumors—while straining against the rope, which was tight and beginning to chafe his arms.

Based upon exchanges, he knew who Connery, Dax, and Vitia were. He found himself eyeing Vitia's horns suspiciously, wondering if they'd been grown magically. The man who lit the fire had done so with elemental magic so he was Cralter, the fire elemental. The former fire elemental had been something of a nuisance, thus, when replaced, his death was celebrated. He guessed the man with the bow strung across his back and bronzed skin to be Thahan, the archer. The other two, he didn't know. One had thin blond hair that seemed to be constantly blowing in some breeze. The other had a long sword that he held as tenderly as one would a woman.

The group ate, then lounged around the fire, while Nico's stomach gurgled loudly enough for them to hear.

Cralter noticed and asked, "Should we feed him?"

Vitia laughed. "No, I want to see how long it takes for him to grovel."

"I will never beg," Nico called, eliciting laughter.

"Better men have yielded," Vitia said with a cruel smirk.

Nico stared at them with a look of determination.

"Whatever helps you sleep at night," the man with the sword sniggered.

Slowly, they all retired, except for Thahan, who was unlucky enough to draw first watch.

✦✦✦

Night had settled, forcing Kade to let them stop.

Keegan waited agitatedly for him to release her.

He approached Bastille, beginning to undo the rope securing her foot to the stirrup. "I did warn you," he said, moving to the rope around her hands.

Free, she dismounted, then turned to Kade, making to smack him.

He caught her wrist. "I don't recommend that."

Scowling, she threw a punch with her other hand. Kade stopped her fist and swung her around, twisting her arms across her chest, then pushed her forward, sending her stumbling into Jared. She turned and before she could lunge at him again, Jared wrapped his arms around her.

"Let me go," she snarled.

"You need to calm down," Jared told her.

"I am calm." Even she knew she was lying.

"No, you're overreacting," Kade said, standing before her.

"You're under-reacting!"

Kade stared her down. "There was absolutely nothing *you* or anyone else could've done."

"There had to've been something!"

Kade declined to respond and they glared at each other icily.

Hurt, anger, and contempt exuded from her. She took several deep breaths and Jared tentatively unwrapped his arms from around her waist. Setting her jaw, she stormed away but didn't go far for fear of getting lost. She found a large pine tree and sank down against its trunk. Her emotions raged as she sat there, each one vying to be heard. Anger spoke the loudest and kept her cheeks flushed. That faded to sadness and tears leaked from her eyes. Defeat was the last to make an appearance and she realized Kade was right.

Goddammit.

Getting to her feet, she brushed away the dirt and wiped her eyes. Making her way back, she kicked at a pinecone heatedly. Back at the campsite, she took a seat beside Jared. Kade offered her a piece of bread, which she snatched from him.

They sat silently around the fire, Jared staring blankly into the flames, Kade sharpening his knife, and she eyed Kade. Now that she was doing that—rather than plotting his demise—she noticed his wavy, red-brown hair with a rebellious curl across his wide forehead. His eyes were a hard hazel with piercing shards of green and a muscular frame accented his strong jaw while freckles dotted his face and even made appearances on the backs of his hands. From her interactions with him so far, she knew they were going to be water and oil.

Kade stood, removed an item from his saddlebag, and threw it at her, saying, "Get some sleep, we have a long day ahead of us."

✢✢✢
✢✢✢

The quarter moon hung low on the eastern edge of the sky, giving them just enough light to see by. Jude placed the last shovelful of dirt on the grave and stepped back, tears gliding down his face.

He jammed the shovel into the earth and fell to his knees. "I wish I could've done better for you," he murmured, his fingers brushing the disturbed earth. "But I promise I'll give you a proper gravestone as soon as I can." With a whisper that Lucas strained to hear, he ended, "I will always love you."

They might not have been able to give her a proper grave, but Lucas knew his mother would've been satisfied. She rested beneath the boughs of one of the few oak trees in the forest and wildflowers were amok around her.

Jude turned to his sons, pulling them into an embrace, and there they stood, the shattered remains of the Sieme family lost in sorrow. No words were spoken and slowly they pulled apart.

Lucas shouldered his pack and stared into the dark forest. He'd learned to not dread it, but now it seemed to mock him, as all he felt was fear. He gazed down at the white cloth around his hands, red dots already pushing through like macabre daisies. He clenched his fists, sending shooting pain through his palms. It was a good pain; it would remind him to keep going, to kill the Vosjnik. He unclenched his fist and his fingertips were lightly bathed in crimson. Gritting his teeth, he stepped past the first line of trees.

Night truly overtook them now as the high branches blocked what little light there was from the waxing moon. They were slow-moving and their sullen footfalls snapped branches with shattering cracks. Time took on no meaning as they walked, the silence over them only intensifying the dejection.

Well into the night, long after even the night creatures had returned to their roosts, they stopped to make camp. They didn't bother to build a fire, and no one specifically stayed up on watch, but Lucas knew none of them slept.

‡‡‡

They are gone. Jared stared up at the dark underside of the forest. *They are gone;* that single unforgiving phrase repeated itself. *They are gone.* He lifted his head and looked around. *They are gone.* Keegan lay beside him, wrapped in the blissful serenity of her dreams. *They are gone.* He envied her. *They are gone.* The fire was low, casting little light. *They are gone.* Kade was leaning against a tree, eyes glazed over as they watched the flames finish their dance. *They. Are. Gone.*

Jared stood and slipped into the woods. *They are gone.* Ahead, the forest was pitch-black, only a few streams of moonlight pervading through the canopy. *They are gone.* He found his feet leading the way as his mind was overcome. *They are gone.* He was suddenly running, branches whipping him in the face and pulling at his clothes like angry hands. *They are gone.* Finally, he could run no more and sank down against the trunk of a tree, ragged, agonizing breaths shaking his body. *They are gone.*

Tears streamed down his face. *They are gone.* From somewhere far off, an anguished, animal-like cry broke the silence of the night. *They are gone.* The sound pulled at his heart, tearing it in two. *They are gone.*

84

He was no longer sitting. *They are gone.* He lashed out, punching a tree. *They are gone.* He kept punching until his exhausted body could spend no more energy. *They are gone.* He fell to his knees, sucking in the cool night air. *They are gone.* Warm blood ran between his fingers and dropped onto the dirt in heavy globules. *They are gone.* The pain in his hands was nothing compared to what he felt inside. *They are gone.*

But I am here. He rose from the ground. *I am here.* He kept repeating those words to stave off sorrow. *I am here.* Tears would do him no good nor raise the dead. *I am here, and they are gone.* As he re-entered camp, he noticed a few strips of bandage where he'd been lying. *I am here. I can make a difference.* He sat down, his body dropping like a rock. *I am here.* He wrapped his bloody knuckles, the cloth stinging as it touched the open wounds. *I am here.* He lay back, his hands folded across his chest. *They are gone. I am here. I can still protect Keegan.* He had taken her in to help her and that was exactly what he intended to do. *I am here. I* will *protect Keegan.*

‡‡‡

"I solved your riddle," Braxton told Alyck, and shut the door.

His uncle gave him a coy smile.

"You did not literally mean a book covered in stone, you meant it is the color of stone and the pages are silver gilded."

"I take it you found it then," Alyck said.

"Not yet, but I have the library's auxiliaries searching for it."

Alyck took a moment to answer. "You will never find it that way. This book is… ever-changing, showing each who holds it what they need most."

Braxton frowned. "So, I have to find it myself?"

Alyck rose from the chair. "Correct. And you have been given everything you need to do so."

"It will take who-knows how long to search the library."

Alyck placed a hand on his shoulder. "It is exactly where I say it is."

Braxton gave him a scowl before taking his leave.

The walk back to his room was shrouded in darkness, but before he knew it, he was there. As he opened the door, the pulsing light began and he made his way to the trunk, digging around until he found the book. He blinked and was no longer in his chambers.

Braxton looked around, perplexed and disoriented as he was still in the hallway outside the Blind Prophet's chamber. An uneasy feeling formed in his stomach and he cautiously began making his way back to his room.

As he walked, he thought about Alyck's words, trying to recall them exactly. Slowly, they came to him, 'I would recommend going to the place where you have that lovely little scrap of information.' *Have.* He began rushing through the halls.

Reaching his room, he dashed to the trunk and threw open the lid. Alyck had told him to look where he was *keeping* the books, not where he had *found* them. He grabbed the larger tome and stared at it, willing it to morph. After moments of nothing, he placed it on the floor, repeating the process with the thinner book, and getting the same result.

He sighed and was about to close the lid when a blotch of purple caught his eye. Moving an old cloak, a rich purple book revealed itself. Picking it up, he recognized it as a sketchbook Alyck had given him. Turning it over, he looked at the pages and was pleased to find they were gilded in silver.

It began to transform, and he dropped it in surprise then watched as the color slowly drained, leaving it a warm black. Cautiously, he picked it up and flipped the cover open. On the inside page, the title was written in neat script, *The Evolution of Language.*

CHAPTER 11

Someone was nudging her. Keegan extracted an arm from beneath herself and shooed them away. The bedroll was yanked away, causing her to bolt up. In the middle of the clearing, the campfire was running on fumes. Morning sunlight shone through the canopy, casting a greenish light.

"Time to leave," Kade said from above her.

She rubbed the sleep from her eyes. "What time is it?"

"Morning."

"No shit, Sherlock. I meant like what—oh, never mind; y'all don't have clocks."

Kade stared at her blankly for a moment. "Time to go."

"I got that part. We gonna eat breakfast?"

"No."

"Why not?"

"No food."

"God," Keegan mumbled, "you're as unprepared as Char."

"What did you say?"

"I said you're as unprepared as Char." She then noticed Jared, who had dark circles under his eyes and his knuckles were wrapped in bandages.

Seeing her gaze, he looked away.

"Who's Char?" Kade asked.

"My little brother." Keegan wrapped her arms around Jared and told him quietly, "It's gonna be okay."

Jared reciprocated the embrace and held her.

"What an odd name," Kade commented, untethering his horse, seemingly oblivious to Jared's misery.

"It's a nickname. His real name's Callum. And seriously, I'd've thought you'd've made sure we had food."

"It's not like I was able to prepare for this."

"How? You were looking for me. I'm sure you had to bring food."

"Yes, enough for me."

"Is it that much of a stretch to pack food for three?"

"It would've looked suspicious."

"Bull—"

"Enough," Jared interjected. "Please."

She scowled at Kade, but turning to Jared, let her face fade to a softer expression. "We'll need to stop at the next town."

"We were going to do that anyway," Kade said, adjusting a buckle on his saddle.

She sighed. "Alrighties then, let's get moving."

‡‡‡

They had been riding for no more than a few hours when Kade stopped in a clearing.

"We're stopping for the day already?" Keegan questioned.

"No. The next town isn't far from here," Kade replied.

"Isn't that a good thing?"

"Do you want to get caught?"

"No…" Her brows furrowed in confusion. "But how will going into town get us caught?"

"The townspeople will see you."

Keegan shrugged, "So?"

"When the Vosjnik come looking, they'll be able to tell them which way we went."

"People aren't gonna remember us."

"Maybe not Jared or I, but you, yes."

"Why would they remember me?"

Jared could see Kade was aggravated. But however, many questions Keegan had, they were valid.

Kade said, "You'll be staying here."

"Fine, whatever," she conceded. "Am I staying alone?"

"No."

"Who else is staying?"

"I am."

Keegan scrunched her nose. "I'd rather Jared stayed."

Seeing a potential fight about to start, Jared commented, "It's fine, I'll go. I just need some money."

Kade looked at him surprised. "Didn't you bring any with you?"

Keegan drew out the word, "No." Then added, "We're normal. And we didn't expect to get attacked by you twits."

Kade stared at her, as if debating on how to respond to being called a twit. "One should always be prepared."

She stared incredulously, "Says the man who didn't pack food!"

Kade started towards her.

Jared stepped in front of him, "Maybe your status as a soldier can help." When Kade glared past him, he added softly, "It's not worth the fight."

88

Kade's gaze lingered on Keegan for a moment longer before he walked away clenching his fists.

Jared gave a sigh of relief. With enough provocation, Kade would strike Keegan—repeatedly.

✝✝✝

Although he hadn't planned to be the one going into town, Kade appreciated the opportunity. It had been less than a day and already Keegan was wearing on him.

Before he emerged onto the road leading into the town—which was much closer to a village—he donned his cuirass; the sigil etched into the metal would give him credibility. As he passed between the small houses, people saw him and rushed inside, no doubt locking the doors. Children's faces peered through shutter slats, watching him with fearful curiosity.

As he dismounted, a middle-aged man approached. "Can I help you?"

"Do you represent the people of this village?"

"Yes, my name's Zandr Lype."

"Taxes are due."

"We just paid them. Two days past, I swear it."

"The king has increased them."

"Again? We barely have enough to live by."

"Taxes or conscripts," Kade offered. "Take your pick."

"Can you give us a few days?"

"No."

"Then we won't be able to pay."

"I'm feeling generous; give me any items of value and I'll sell them in your stead. You have an hour."

Zandr scoffed, "We have nothing of value here."

Kade knew Zandr was well-aware he was lying but the fear of retaliation made him co-operate.

He walked away and leaned against a house while Zandr made his way solemnly over to the townspeople, who had started emerging from their homes. Faces began to display anger and disdain but being with the Vosjnik for so long made him immune to remorse; he'd done worse—*much* worse.

He heard a giggle and looked around. To his right, a face disappeared behind the corner of the building he was leaning against. He turned back to study the people, watching the side of the house out of the corner of his eye. When it looked like he wasn't paying attention, the face returned; it belonged to a little girl with straggly blonde hair. He looked over and again she disappeared behind the corner.

"I know you're there."

No response.

"Come out."

The girl did as instructed.

She was around four years old and her eyes were a curious brown. Her face was covered in patches of dirt and she had her hands clasped behind her back.

"What's your name?" he asked, squatting down.

"Dayna Lype."

Zandr's daughter. "You shouldn't spy on people."

"Sorry, 'ister," Dayna mumbled, looking up at him and cocking her head to the side, "What your name, 'ister?"

"Ka—"

She interrupted. "Mamma says soldiers 're scary."

"Are you not afraid of me?"

She shook her head.

"You should be," Kade replied, standing.

"Why?" Dayna questioned.

"Because I'm a soldier."

She wrapped her arms around his thigh. "That not mean you be a bad person, 'ister Ka."

Kade glanced at her, lost for words; how was he supposed to react?

A woman began shouting the child's name and Kade pushed her away. "Go." He expected her to run off. When she didn't, he looked down at her again.

She held her hand out as if she wanted him to shake it. "Mamma says it polite to shake when you meet a new person."

Kade glared at her, then complied.

Dayna skipped away. "Nice to meet you 'ister Ka. I see you again."

Slowly, people began approaching him with a few coins or valuables in hand. By the end of the hour, he had acquired enough to buy what they needed in the next town.

He shouldered the bag he'd commandeered and was about to mount Arso when he paused. "My squad's beginning to run low on food."

"What do you want us to do about that?" Zandr asked irritated.

"Supply us with food," Kade growled.

"You'll have to pay for it."

Kade pulled out a few ill-begotten coins.

Zandr talked to one of the townsmen who left and shortly returned with several loaves of bread and packages of meat. "Will this do?" he snapped.

"Yes." Kade returned some coins to Zandr and mounted Arso. "Until next time."

‡‡‡

Keegan was lounging on the ground when Kade returned. He dropped the bag next to her head, making her jump.

"Geez," she exclaimed, sitting up, "whatcha got in there, rocks?"

"No."

She began rummaging through the bag. "Totally missed the sarcasm, dude."

"No," he said through gritted teeth, "chose to ignore it."

"Sure ya did."

"Keegan," Jared reproached.

She rolled her eyes. "I'll play nice."

Kade pulled his cuirass off and packed it away with the rest of his armor. Then, he took the sword that was attached to his horse's saddle and handed it to Jared.

Pulling the weapon from the sheath, Jared studied the blade. It was a long, thin sword with an angled cross guard.

Intrigued, Keegan moved closer.

"Ideally, you'd have an arming sword or claymore," Kade explained, "but and Estoc will do for now."

"Do I get a sword?" Keegan asked, reaching to take it from Jared.

Kade pushed her hand away, "No."

"Why not?"

"You're a woman."

"So?"

"Women don't carry swords."

"*So?*"

"You carrying a sword is a good way to get us caught."

"Seems like just about everything's a good way to get caught." Keegan stared at him for a moment before saying, "So, basically, I go weaponless?"

"No, you get this." Kade extracted a dagger from the pack and tossed it to her.

"I still need a sword."

"You're not getting one."

91

"Like hell—"

Jared interjected, "He's right. You shouldn't carry a sword; it would look strange. Why do you want one anyway?"

"I am strange, and it's something I'm going to need."

"How so?" Jared pressed.

"I– just– sword." She paused, trying to formulate an argument. "I still suck at this whole magic thing, and what happens when I need to defend myself?"

"That's what I'm here for," Kade said.

She laughed. "I promised I'd stop being belligerent, so I won't say anything about *that*."

"He's right," Jared said. "Both he and I are here to protect you."

"I can look after myself," Keegan stated, an air of bitterness about the words.

Jared sheathed the sword and tied it to Brewer's saddle. "You're in over your head here."

"I'm not gonna cower in a corner while y'all fight for me."

"No," Kade repeated stubbornly, tying the pack onto his saddle.

"Who gave you the right to tell me what I can and can't do?"

"I did, when I rescued you."

"You can hardly call that a rescue."

"Keegan," Jared said, "now isn't the time for this."

She seethed, "If now isn't, then when? When I've been caught because I couldn't fight back." There was a pause. "Or when I'm dead."

Kade gritted his teeth. "I'm leaving."

"No, you're not," Keegan spat.

"Who's going to stop me, you?"

She gritted her teeth and stared at him with a look of pure fury.

"You have two choices, be silent and come with me, or, strike out on your own. You'd better decide quickly."

She could see he instantly regretted insinuating they had a choice and gave him an antagonistic wave. "Bye."

"Do we have to do this again?"

Keegan balled her fists and stormed over to Bastille, muttering what Kade should rightly assumed were colorful choice-words and pulled herself up into the saddle. "I will get a sword, with or without your help. Mark my words."

‡‡‡

Lucas was surprised he'd slept, even if not for long. The same appeared to be true for his father and Carter. No one spoke and the silence was heavy. Carter's stomach gave a soft growl and Lucas rummaged through his pack, producing a few pieces of jerky.

Carter bit at the meat with little gusto.

Finally, Jude stood up, beginning the day. Their pace was slow, giving them all too much time to think.

Lucas could feel his anger welling up. Clenching his fists, he pushed it back down. Opening his hand, he saw more blood had risen to the surface of the bandages.

"You have to stop doing that," Jude told him quietly.

As he walked, he thought of what he was going to do to the Vosjnik. He would beat them into the dust, making their faces unrecognizable to even their mothers. He would flay the flesh from their bones, the whip cutting as deep as his laughter. He would watch as fire melted their forms, the yellow and orange flames turning red with their blood. He would let wolves tear them apart, as beast should destroy beast. He would drown them, the weight of their sins pulling them under.

Lost in thought, he barely noticed the passing of day. Time took on little meaning, and only hunger reminded him he was human. Soon enough, night found them again and they were forced to stop. A fire was lit and he watched the flames dance in the dark.

Fire gives light, but it also destroys. Something his mother often said, especially when he was angry. Had. As she'd explained it, a little bit of anger helped you push through, but you had to be careful to not let it consume you.

He started down at his hands. The blood staining the cloth had turned brown. He clenched his fist, turning the spots red once more. *So be it. I'll feed the flames and use them to destroy the Vosjnik.*

‡‡‡

Night was upon the castle, but that did not mean activities had ceased, at least not for Aron. He was headed to Alyck, but this was not going to be pleasant. That afternoon, he had found a note in his chambers. Though only two words—*See me*—a pit had formed in his stomach. While there was no signature, he recognized Alyck's handwriting.

Hesitating, he opened the door, the hinges protesting.

Inside, Alyck sat with his eyebrows furrowed in frustration. "Stay away from Shiloh."

Aron made to protest.

93

"You do not understand the reality of it."

"But—"

"There will be no happy ending!" he said then repeated in a whisper, "There will be no happy ending."

"You cannot know that."

"I cannot know that?" Alyck roared. "*I* cannot know that! I know more than you could ever hope to know, Little King. Now, please, listen."

"I love her."

"Then let her go. Or there will come a time when you wished you had."

Aron choked, "I cannot do that."

"But you must. Please, trust me."

"I love her," Aron reiterated.

Under his breath, Alyck muttered, "So did I." Speaking to Aron again, he said, "I cannot help you."

Aron began to stutter.

"Leave, there is nothing I can do for you at present."

"But I did not ask for help. You requested I come here."

"Leave!"

Aron set his jaw and slammed the door on his way out. He refused to believe his happiness with Shiloh was fleeting. The more distance from Alyck he made, the more his resolve solidified. They would be happy together—he would not entertain any other outcome.

‡‡‡

Nico awoke shortly after first light to the sounds of breaking camp—not that there was much to it. He didn't have to watch for long until the fire was all that was left.

Dax approached him, and scowling, began to undo the rope.

With the ropes slackened, Nico awkwardly pushed himself to his feet and tried to run.

Dax was faster and grabbed a fistful of his hair. "Pass me the ether," he snapped to Vitia. She gave him a soaked rag and he held it over Nico's nose and mouth.

He choked and what little magic he had regained overnight disappeared. He sunk to the ground hacking and heaving then yelped as Dax dragged him over to the horses and lifted him into the saddle. His hands were then bound to the saddle horn.

"Why do I have to look after the kid?" Dax grumbled loudly as he mounted.

"Because I say so," Connery answered, pulling himself up onto his brown destrier. "Move out."

Six horses followed the Commander as they made their way through the forest, no one talking, leaving Nico to his own thoughts.

The day passed slowly. Once, they had to double back because they were following the wrong trail. Another time, they stopped to relieve themselves, which was awkward for Nico with so many eyes upon him and his hands bound.

They stopped at dusk and again he was secured to a tree. His stomach gurgled loudly and Vitia asked if he was ready to beg. He remained quiet.

One by one, everyone retired, leaving Cralter on watch. Eventually, even he drifted off.

So much for that, Nico thought, beginning to strain against the ropes, holding back a cry of frustration when he realized the ropes were tight. Letting his head rest against the tree, it was then he noticed part of the rope had begun to fray where it had rubbed against the rough bark. His heart fluttered and he began moving his body in a sideways fashion to wear through the restraint further; a slow-going business as the rope around him and the bark against his back pulled at his body. Finally, he a strand snapped and from there he freed himself easily.

He eyed the horses and began creeping towards them. A branch cracked and he froze. Finlay stirred but didn't wake and he began slinking forward again. With care, he made his way through the sleeping bodies and had almost made it across, when a hand grabbed his ankle and he tumbled to the ground.

"Where do you think you're going?" snarled Dax.

Frantically, Nico felt along the ground, finding a rock. Grabbing it, he smashed it into Dax's face, who yelled out and released him.

The others roused and groggily drew their weapons, doing their best to not stumble over the uneven terrain.

Nico scrambled to his feet and took off running, branches whipping him in the face. Behind, he could hear the Vosjnik giving chase. Soon, his breaths became ragged and a stitch formed in his side—but he dared not stop.

A weight pushed him forward and he fell. Turning onto his back, he stared up into Dax's seething face, blood dripping from a gash in his cheek. He tried to wriggle free, but Dax sat atop his abdomen, pinning him.

"You're going nowhere!" Dax snarled.

Nico tried to feel around for a stick or stone lying within arms' reach.

Dax grabbed his wrists. "That's not going to work a second time."

Nico pulled against him, but his efforts were useless.

Dax looked around. "Where's that noxþox woman? Vitia," he called. When there was no response, he called again.

This time there was a faint reply.

"Over here," Dax yelled.

A few minutes passed and Vitia appeared from the shadows. Sidling over to them, she handed Dax a length of rope.

Nico let insults roll off his tongue.

Vitia kneeled beside him. "Look at this, the little whelp wants to talk like a man." She grabbed his jaw, "Silence."

Trying to continue his tirade, he found no sound escaped his lips.

Vitia stood, pulling her hair back, her hands awkwardly grazing her horns. Her brows creased as she looked at the sky. "Do you see that?"

"See what?" Dax questioned, standing and pulling Nico to his feet as well.

Vitia pointed up. "That."

Nico looked and saw the remnants of a trail of smoke.

"Vito," Dax murmured, sharing a look with her, before they took off running, pulling Nico along.

Bursting into camp, Vitia exclaimed, "We found them."

CHAPTER 12

Darkness had settled, forcing them to stop once more and after eating dinner quietly, the silence felt like a wet blanket, as Keegan was still irritated.

"How did you get all this?" Jared asked, referring to their food and everything else in the pack.

"Did what I had to," Kade answered cryptically, stoking the fire.

"That told us nothing," Keegan said. "And by that fact, you probably stole everything."

"It wasn't technically stealing."

"What exactly did you do?" Jared probed.

"I imposed a tax," Kade answered.

Keegan muttered, "At least you didn't kill anyone."

"Was there anything you weren't able to *obtain*?" Jared continued.

"Yes."

"We have food, what else do we need?" Keegan questioned tetchily.

Kade glared at her.

"Keegan," Jared sighed, "Just… go to sleep."

She frowned, "Fine." Then turned her back to them and lay down.

Relief appeared on Kade's face as he leaned against the tree behind him, hands behind his head.

"What weren't you able to get?" Jared repeated.

"Cloaks, water-skins, bedrolls, and a map." Kade yawned, "You're on watch tonight."

‡‡‡

Jared stared at the dying flames. Kade slept against a tree and Keegan was on her stomach underneath the bedroll. He grabbed a stick and stirred the embers. Knowing the fire would soon die, he added a few branches to its meager flames. As they burned, they sent up pale gray smoke.

The night air was cool and pleasant, and his body was beginning to numb. Owls hooted in the trees. There was a call. *Maybe a deer,* he thought, though, something didn't feel right. He heard the call again. Could he be imagining it? He listened carefully. The yell came once more and there was no doubt, it belonged to a man. He rushed to Kade. "Wake up."

"What happened?" Kade questioned, immediately alert, assuming the worst, and his sword already half drawn.

97

"Listen."

Kade listened and heard the yell when it came again. "It's them. Wake Keegan. *Now.*"

Jared nodded, went to Keegan, and shook her shoulder.

"Huh," she mumbled blearily, lifting her head. When she saw it was still dark, she put her head back down.

"Get up."

"Why?" she grumbled.

"The Vosjnik."

"Crap," she groaned.

Kade had already smothered the fire and was mounting his horse.

Keegan haphazardly bundled up the bedroll and tossed it to Kade, who shoved it into his saddlebag. They mounted their horses and spurred them after Kade.

As the sun began to light the sky, Jared turned to look at Keegan. She could barely keep her eyes open—not that he was doing better after riding for most of the night. "It should be safe to stop," he called to Kade.

"No."

"Can we at least rest for a few hours? Keegan looks as if she's about to fall out of the saddle."

"No."

"But we've put so much distance between us."

Kade reined in his horse. "That means nothing. This is the Vosjnik we're talking about; they are stubborn, determined people. It's noxþ near impossible for them to lose a trail once they've found it and I guarantee they all have a vendetta against me."

"If that's true, then why are we even trying to outrun them?"

"I said *near* impossible."

"What do we have to do to lose them?"

"Reach Suttan. It'll be possible to lose them in the city."

"Suttan's completely out of the way if we're headed to the Lazado and at least a week's ride from here."

"The *only* way."

"We'll never get there. We'll collapse from exhaustion at this rate." Jared looked back at Keegan. She sat hunched over in the saddle, her forehead resting against Bastille's neck.

"We don't have a choice. But if we can make it across the Tatat River, we may be able to gain some time."

"How far is that?" Keegan asked, drowsily straightening up.

"Half a day, give or take, depending on how many more needless stops we make."

She rubbed her eyes. "Then what're we doin' standin' around?"

"Are you going to make it?" Jared asked.

"I ain't got much of a choice, do I?"

"We've wasted enough time talking," Kade urged.

‡‡‡

Keegan was barely aware of where they were going—granted, it wouldn't've mattered if she was sleep-deprived or not. Heavy lids threatened to close and remain that way for a while.

Suddenly, Bastille stopped, causing her to jerk up. In front of her was a wide river, its waters a pale muddy brown.

"Where's the bridge?" she asked.

"There is none," was Kade's response. "At least not around here."

She rubbed her eyes. "Then how're we gonna get to the other side?"

Kade spurred his horse into the river. "Swim."

Jared followed, leaving her alone on the bank.

Bringing Bastille to the edge of the river, she watched as Kade and Jared made their way across. "Ya know, I'd really rather stay dry," she shouted as the boys reached the opposite bank.

"Get your arse over here," Kade yelled back. "I swear, if you make me come back there…"

She eyed the river, then steeled herself and spurred Bastille in. As the water hit her, she gasped; it was icy and the current gently pulled Bastille downstream. "Can we stop yet?" she asked, emerging from the water and shivering in the noonday sun.

Kade shook his head, "We should continue to put as much distance between us and them as we can."

She wrapped her arms around herself. "I thought we accomplished that by crossing the river."

Kade led the way forward. "No, we just bought ourselves some time."

This is just like that movie with all the dogs. What the heck's it called? Ugh, they did that thing where they erased their tracks and co… She sat open-mouthed for a second. "Oh, my god, we're idiots."

"Pardon?" Jared said, turning to glance at her.

"We're idiots. I know how we can lose them. We can erase the footprints and create a false trail."

Kade looked at her as if she'd lost her head. "There's no time."

"Oh, come on, all three of us are earth elementals; it shouldn't take that long."

99

"She's right," Jared acknowledged.

"Fine," Kade acquiesced. "Jared, erase our trail. Keegan, create a false path on this side of the river."

"Why're we doing all the work?" she complained.

"You're not. I'm going to create another trail on the other side of the river."

"Oh." She was silent for a second. "Have fun crossing the river again."

Kade glared at her and muttered something under his breath, then turned his horse and spurred him back across the water while she and Jared set about their designated tasks. Once done, they regrouped to continue.

‡‡‡

Nico jolted up, realizing he'd dozed off. Ahead, the trees were thinning, and he could hear running water. They emerged from the forest and the brown waters of a river flowed before them. In the loam, clear footprints could be seen following the riverbank east.

The man with the sword, Brennian, said, "They made our job easy."

"I would not be so sure," Connery responded. "Cralter, cross the river and check for footprints on the other side."

"Why m—" Cralter began.

"Shut your mouth and do as you are told!"

"Yes, sir," Cralter grumbled, spurring his horse into the water.

The rest of the Vosjnik waited patiently.

Cralter emerged from the river and his horse shook its hair free of water. They spun around and began searching. Soon, he came back to the bank. "There are footprints over here, too."

Connery cursed under his breath, "Thahan, join Cralter and follow that trail. Brennian and Guthrie, do the same on this side. If you lose the trail completely or it ends, come back here. Otherwise, keep going until you find them. After one team comes back, those of us here will regroup and catch up."

"Yes, sir," Brennian, Guthrie, and Thahan answered, heading off.

Vitia dismounted and pulled Nico from Dax's horse.

He sat on the ground, his legs bowed out in front of him and watched Vitia head into the forest to collect firewood while Dax took the horses to the river to drink. As he sat scowling, his stomach grumbled loudly. He tried to ask for food, but Vitia had yet to give him his voice back.

"Are you hungry?" Connery asked.

Nico stared at him confused but nodded.

Connery chuckled as he reached into a pack and produced a small loaf of bread. "I am a telepath."

Nico warily accepted the bread with his bound hands. He stared at the loaf before biting into it; it was stale, but he didn't care.

When Vitia returned and saw him eating, rage crossed her face. "Why'd you feed the boy?"

"Because he is just that, a boy." Connery answered. "Now, give him his voice back."

Vitia crossed her arms and glared at him.

"That is not a request."

She gritted her teeth, made her way over to Nico, hit him upside the head and stalked off.

"Forgive her. She can be a bit..." Connery trailed off, searching for the right word.

"Of an opida," Nico suggested.

This elicited laughter. "That is a man's word."

"I am a man," Nico asserted, as his voice cracked.

Connery smiled and shook his head as he struck his knife against a piece of flint, sending a spark jumping into a pile of tinder.

As dusk settled, Guthrie and Brennian returned.

"False trail," Guthrie announced, sitting by the fireside.

"Get some sleep," Connery said. "We leave at daybreak. Vitia, you have first watch."

Slowly, everyone drifted off and Nico realized they hadn't tethered him to anything.

Vitia stared at him, her brown eyes filled with hate. "You won't make it ten paces before I run my sword through you, boy."

Nico gulped, having no doubt she'd happily live up to her threat.

CHAPTER 13

Morning came all too soon, though Keegan wouldn't have called it that. The sun had yet to rise, and under normal circumstances, no one could pay her enough money to be awake at that ungodly hour. "Can't why sleep longer?" she mumbled. *Goddamnit.* Whenever she didn't get adequate sleep, her ability to speak coherently went out the window.

"Pardon," Jared yawned.

"Why can't we sleep longer?" she repeated correctly, untethering Bastille.

"Do you want to get caught?" Kade asked.

"If it means I get to sleep more, yes."

Kade glared at her but she knew he understood it was a joke.

"You can sleep in the saddle," Jared suggested. "I'll make sure Bastille doesn't stray."

"Easier said than done," she noted, as they left the clearing.

"What did you just call him?" Kade asked.

"Call who what?" she questioned, her brain struggling to follow even this simple conversation.

"Darkheart."

She furrowed her brows, "Who's Darkheart?"

"Your horse."

"Uh… his name's Bastille."

"Who gave him that name?"

"I did. It's a helluva lot better than Darkheart. What dipshit came up with that?"

"Caius."

"Makes sense; he is a dipshit."

"His name's Darkheart, so call him that."

"Uh, it's Bastille, so *you* call him that."

"It's Darkheart."

"Bastille."

"Darkheart."

"Bastille."

Exasperated, Jared snapped, "Can you two do anything without fighting?"

She held her hands up, "Hey, I didn't start it."

"Yes, you did," Kade snapped back.

"Did not!"

"What did I just say?" Jared barked.

After a few minutes of silence, she asked Kade, "What's your horse's name?"

"Arso."

She sniggered to herself; it sounded like he was trying to say asshole with a burnt tongue.

✢✢✢

The noonday sun was bright and blinding when Kade led them into another clearing. "We can stop now."

"Thank god," Keegan said, slipping off Bastille. She didn't bother to fetter the horse before leaning up against the nearest tree and falling asleep.

"How long do we have?" Jared asked.

"Not long," Kade responded. "The only reason we stopped is because we need those last few provisions."

"Who's going to go into town?"

"I am. Can I trust you to watch her?"

He nodded.

"Then I'll see you soon." Kade swiftly remounted Arso and rode away.

Jared grabbed Bastille's reins and tethered him to a log alongside Brewer then looked over at Keegan, wondering what was going through her head. Not being from this world, everything must be overwhelming, yet, she slept like nothing was wrong. So far, she'd taken every bump on the road in stride and it amazed him she had any fight left.

He'd been through hardship too, a different kind, and it'd broken him. Inside, he felt as if someone had smashed him into a million pieces and each bit hurt like a knife wound. But he kept it to himself; he didn't want Keegan worrying—this was his burden. He only hoped that time would put him back together and the pieces would stop hurting.

✢✢✢

Kade stalked through the market of Drath feeling less than amiable. Spending so much time with Keegan had put him in a foul mood and he almost regretted saving her—almost. Lack of sleep wasn't helping either.

What I really want—need—to do is... Bah, there isn't time. He looked up; the sun was just starting its decline. *Maybe. Maybe, if I'm quick about this.* He managed to sell the ill-begotten items swiftly, filling his purse.

103

In the market, vendors offered their wares: fruits and vegetables for the common folk, meat and fine wines for the servants shopping for their masters, and silks and jewelry for the rich merchants and tradesmen. He ignored most until he came upon a stall hawking what he was looking for. The mercer stood behind a little table, cloaks hanging from strings slung between posts while dresses and lavish fabrics covered the table.

As he approached, the man called out, "Maybe a few yards of fine velour for your beautiful wife to make a gown."

"No."

"A shame," the man said. "I sell the finest velvet in the city. Come, feel this. See how soft it is on the skin." He held up a piece of rich, red fabric.

Kade glared at him.

The man slowly placed the bolt back on the table and stared back silently, his eyes darting about. No doubt, he was unaccustomed to irritable customers. "Is there—"

"I need two cloaks," Kade said.

Regardless of the attitude, his eyes regained their gleam as he realized he was going to keep Kade's patronage. "I have many cloaks. This one has rabbit fur lining; wonderful for warmth and beaut—"

"Stop talking," Kade growled; Keegan had worn down his patience and this man was treading on thin ice. "I want two woolen cloaks. Those ones there." He pointed to two simple, black cloaks hanging at the back of the booth.

"Are you—"

"Yes."

The vendor warily took down the cloaks, folded them neatly, and set them on the table. He stood away from the edge of the booth, almost as if he were afraid Kade was going to bite. "Two gold coins."

Kade guffawed, "They're hardly worth that."

"I sell the fines—"

"Everyone says that. Lower the price."

The man stammered for a moment before gathering his mettle. "No."

Kade was about to continue arguing when he paused and picked up an emerald green dress. "Fine. Two gold coins for two cloaks and a dress."

"I can't do that; I'd be cheating myself."

Kade pulled out two coins and made to hand them over. He needed to hurry this along, so he made sure the man saw the star branded on his thumb.

"Tw-two gold c-coins will suffice."

Kade sneered, tossing the coins onto the table, and grabbed the items. He shoved them into his bag and walked away, leaving the man with sweat beaded on his brow.

Acquiring the rest of the supplies was a simpler task. No one argued with him over prices or tried to sell him unneeded luxuries. He had a feeling word of his presence preceded him.

He leaned against a building, repacking the bag so everything sat nicely and glanced at the sun. It had barely moved from its high perch. He smiled to himself; there was still plenty of time to scratch one of his ever-present itches.

Where should I go? He knew little of Drath, never having been in the city before. Brennian was from Drath though, and always bragged he knew the best haunts. There was one bagnio he'd talked about often, owned by Clark Idar.

He turned back towards the market and eyed the merchants, wondering who was sordid enough to frequent the establishment he was looking for. He approached a wine-seller. "Do you know where I can find Clark Idar?"

The man smiled, revealing discolored teeth. "Take tha' side street ov'r there," he pointed. "Turn down the third street 'n the left and then the alleyway 'n the right."

He nodded his thanks and found his way easily enough. When he turned down the alleyway, it smelled of piss and he had to be careful to avoid stepping in the large puddles that littered the uneven ground. A mutt hugged the wall and picked at a bone between its paws. Further ahead, women leaned against the wall of a building and pulled at any man who passed by. Their dresses were hardly more than thin chemises, leaving little to the imagination.

They saw him and a thin brunette with her hair pulled back into intricate braids approached. She bore a flirtatious smile and cunning gleamed in her eyes. "Is there anything I can do you for?" she asked sweetly.

Kade let a grin cross his face as his answer.

She grabbed his hand and pulled him through a doorway.

The inside of the building was nothing grand. A tatty couch and ottoman were pushed up along one wall, a few uncomfortable-looking chairs sat idly about, and an iron chandelier with half melted candles hung from the ceiling.

The girl pulled him along into the depths of the building and as they passed a tall man dressed in rich velvets with rings hugging every finger, she said, "Hello, Master Clark."

The man gave a slight nod with a toothy smile. "Making money today I see, Marka."

"Yes, sir," she answered without turning back.

Marka led him down a long hallway, passing few others, and drew him into a room at the end, which was just as sparsely furnished as the foyer. There was a bed with thin linen sheets, covered in a musty duvet, and a few pillows at its head.

Kade dropped his bag by the door, did the lock, and turned his attention to Marka, who sat patiently on the edge of the bed.

"Off with it," he said, undoing his belt buckle.

While he was busy pulling off his own clothing, Marka let her dress drop to the floor. She stepped out of it and he stopped to look at her, his shirt in his hands. There was a calmness in her dark eyes and her head was held high like a noble lady. Her breasts were wanting, and a flat stomach gave way to rounded hips.

She came forward and began to kiss along the side of his neck. Kade felt her teeth pull gently at his skin and at this, he pushed her back onto the bed and crawled atop her. He started slowly, wanting to enjoy it; who knew when he would get the chance again. Marka let out a soft moan. Wanting to get his worth, he reached forward and groped her breasts, which were soft underneath his calloused hands.

Beneath him, Marka feigned pleasure. He felt a twinge in his ego and changed his strokes; her tone changed, too, and he grinned. Being one to make a point, he rolled over onto the bed, sitting Marka atop of himself and watched her face contort into one of pure ecstasy.

Sweat covered their bodies and in the final throes of passion, he let out a grunt of euphoria as his muscles relaxed. With a heavy breath, Marka rolled over onto the bed beside him.

Without so much as a glance towards her, Kade pushed himself off the bed and began to dress. He grabbed his sword, buckled it around his waist, and made for the door, shouldering the pack.

"Aren't you forgetting something?" Marka said, sitting up on the bed, still baring all.

He callously flipped her a silver coin, which landed on the bed beside her and strode from the room. Once outside the bagnio, he looked up at the sky. The sun was a few hands widths from the horizon. *Perfect.*

‡‡‡

Someone was kicking her leg.

I swear, Keegan thought sleepily, *I'm gonna kill him.* "What?" she growled, opening her eyes, expecting to see Kade; instead, she looked up at a steely-eyed man, who pointed a sword at her. "What the hell?"

She scrambled to her feet, keeping her back against the tree. She then saw the other soldier holding another sword against Jared's throat across the clearing. "What do you want?"

The man smiled and pulled her away from the tree.

She noticed a branch on the ground and feigned tripping to land beside it. As the man reached to pull her up, her hand closed around the stick and swung it, rolling onto her back. It caught the man in the face, surprising him, and she brought a foot up between his legs. As he groaned and dropped to his knees, she grabbed his sword and placed it against his chest. "Let Jared go," she told the other soldier.

The man laughed and dug the point of the sword into Jared's neck, drawing a ruby droplet of blood. "I think not."

"I'll kill him."

"I don't think you will."

Keegan looked at the man holding Jared, knowing she'd seen him before. "Let him go. And what do you want with us?"

"To take you to Caius."

Shit. "Well, you're not gonna."

He threw his head back and roared with laughter.

"You should listen to her, Cralter," Kade said, riding into the clearing.

"It's Finlay, you bwint, and we were wondering where you got to," he said, turning his head to look at him. "Thahan, how long do you think it'll take me to run my sword through the boy?"

"About as long as it'll take me to do this," Thahan responded, springing forward and throwing Keegan to the ground. He sat on her chest, wrapping one hand around her neck, the other pinning her hand that no longer held the sword.

As she struggled against him, he glanced at her wrist. It was an impulsive action and she watched confusion knit his eyebrows together. His hand covered most of the markings, but the edge of the earth symbol was visible.

"You almost fooled us with those false trails," Thahan said.

"If that were true, there'd be more of you here," she challenged.

Keegan gasped as he started cutting off her air supply. Knowing she only had one chance, she brought her free arm to the inside of his elbow, loosening his grip, and punched him in the throat. His hand released instantly. She grabbed the neck of his shirt, flung him over, reversing their positions, and quickly punched him in the throat a few times to make sure he stayed down.

When she looked up, Kade had the point of his sword against Finlay's neck. "Go help Keegan," he told Jared.

"Are you all right?" Jared asked, kneeling beside her. He tried to wipe away the blood on his neck but only succeeded in smearing it across his skin.

Coughing a bit, she nodded. "What'd we do now?" Though Thahan was unconscious, she kept her attention on him. When Jared remained silent, she looked up and stared at Kade in shock. His sword's blade was bathed in red and Finlay lay on the ground, his throat slit. Jumping to her feet, she yelled, "Why'd you do that?"

Kade wiped his blade on Finlay's shirt. "He would have told the others where we are."

"There must've been another way."

"There wasn't. And we need to leave, now. Before the rest of them realize these two are missing."

"Oh, my god," Keegan muttered, her face paling as she ran her hands through her hair. "You killed him."

"If you're going to be sick, do it quickly."

"What the hell is wrong with you? You just killed someone!" He made his way over to them. "And you killed Thahan."

"What? No, I didn't!"

"He's not breathing."

Keegan knelt beside Thahan, stuck her hand above his nose and mouth, and sighed with relief. "He's breathing."

Gripping his sword tighter, Kade started towards Thahan.

"What're you doing?" she questioned. When he didn't respond, she asked again, "What are you doing?" Realizing his intentions, she stood between him and Thahan. "I won't let you."

Kade's voice was unnaturally even, "Move."

"No."

"Let him do it," Jared said, trying to pull her out of Kade's path.

"No."

"Do you really want to do this?" Kade asked warningly.

"Yes," Keegan gulped. "It's what's right."

Kade stared at her for a second longer, then shoved her aside.

She tried to remain in place but was no match for his strength. She stumbled and watched as the sword neared Thahan's chest. "No," she cried, subconsciously reaching for the energy that would allow her to move mountains. A rock pulled itself from the ground and hit Kade on the side of the face and rather than the sword going through Thahan's chest, its point went harmlessly into soil.

Kade stared at the ground, stunned, before toppling over.

"What did you do?" Jared yelled.

"I-I don't know," she said in as much shock as Jared. Her eyes darted between Kade and Thahan. "What... do we... do now?"

"Leave. Grab his sword."

She pulled it from the earth and stepped back while Jared grabbed Kade and somehow managed to get him onto Arso's back.

Unsure of what to do with the sword, Keegan put it back in its sheath belted around Kade's waist. "Do you know where you're going?"

"No, but I know the general direction," Jared responded.

"O-okay. Lead the way."

‡‡‡

At sunrise, the Vosjnik packed up camp and crossed the river. The water was cold and chilled Nico to the core. As the sun rose higher, they followed the second trail.

Around mid-evening they arrived in a clearing, finding Cralter with his throat slit to the bone and Thahan lying nearby on the ground; Nico couldn't tell if he was alive.

Vitia jumped from her horse, rushed over to Thahan, and began working her magic.

He awoke coughing and sputtering curses.

"What happened?" Connery asked grimly.

"Kade," Thahan bit. "Royiken Kade Tavin happened."

Dax cursed under his breath. "This entire mission has gone to the dogs."

"How exactly did you and Cralter get yourselves in this situation?" Connery pressed.

"We found Keegan and Jared," Thahan started.

At the mention of his brother, Nico's attention snapped to Thahan.

"Kade was nowhere to be seen, so we assumed they'd snuck away. Cralter dealt with the boy and I grabbed the girl. The insolent little opida fought back and managed to get my sword, but not for long. Then Kade showed up and that's when this happened."

"Who killed Cralter?" Guthrie asked.

109

"Why do you care?" Thahan accepted a water-skin from Vitia. "You hated him."

"Doesn't make him any less of a comrade."

"I don't know." Thahan confessed, "The bwint knocked me out."

Vitia roared with laughter. "You let that weak, little opida knock you out?"

Thahan got to his feet unsteadily, "She's not as weak as she appears. And she's an elemental."

"That cannot be," Connery said. "The king himself confirmed she was not."

"I saw the mark."

"I told you!" Brennian exclaimed. "I wasn't imagining that I saw her practicing magic."

Connery was silent, his face hard and his eyes filled with fury and a flicker of worry.

Nico had no doubt that if he couldn't salvage the situation, he wouldn't have his head much longer.

"Burn the body," Connery said rigidly. "Then we move out."

CHAPTER 14

Lucas's foot fell on a branch, snapping it in two. The sound was like thunder compared to the silence he'd become accustomed to. Today was their third day walking—it felt like a lifetime; from experience, he estimated they'd reach Tratoleck before nightfall.

Though his father had said they would head east to chase Jared and Nico, they'd decided to first go to Tratoleck, as they had friends there and needed horses, food, and other necessities for a long journey.

While Jude did his best to not show it, Lucas could see how much their mother's death was hurting him. Jude was normally quiet, but he'd become despondent. Lucas understood—they were all aching in the worst way.

As the sun made its descent, they came upon the gates of Tratoleck, the guards ignoring them as they entered. Earlier, it'd been decided they would go to Virgil and Laiyla Fulpe, who had been friends for years—and their daughter was an elemental. Laiyla had grown up in Suilenroc and was—had been—Alessandra's closest friend.

Lucas led the way and they soon reached the Fulpe house in the inner quarter of the city. Their home was tall, reaching three stories, its surface made of dark brick with a few windows looking over the street.

They climbed the steps and Jude knocked on the door.

Alivia, the Fulpes' daughter, opened it. Her face lit up when she saw Lucas, then turn to worry when she noticed Jude and Carter. "Mama, Papa," she called into the house before inviting them in.

As she closed the door, Virgil descended the stairs.

"Jude," he said cheerfully. "It has been quite some time since I last saw you. And this must be Carter; my, what a handsome young man you are turning into. Where is the rest of that motley crew of yours?"

"We've had a bit of… misfortune," Jude told him.

Virgil's face fell. "You need a place to stay; of course, you will stay here."

"Thank you. You don't know what that means to us."

Virgil turned to his daughter, "Alivia, get Carter and Lucas settled in. I believe I have some things to discuss with Jude."

"Yes, Papa," Alivia said, starting up the stairs.

Lucas and Carter followed her, the faint smell of honey wafting from her. The upstairs hallway was lined with doors.

Alivia opened one and said, "Carter, this will be your room."

Carter gave Lucas a look of uncertainty but entered anyway.

Alivia continued down the hallway, saying, "Lucas, this one is yours."

As he entered, he mumbled a thank you.

"If you need anything at all," Alivia told him, gently placing a hand on his shoulder, "my room is right across the hall."

Lucas gave her a small grin, though it must've looked more like a grimace, and shut the door. She was still enamored with him, regardless of the fact he'd turned her down on multiple occasions. It was the primary reason why he'd made Jared take his place on errand runs.

The room was simple to those who'd grown up in the upper echelons of society, but for him it was luxurious. A large bed covered in colorful pillows was set against the wall. There was a writing desk pushed into one corner and opposite the bed was a full-length mirror. He dropped his bag and made his way over.

The reflection that stared back at him seemed empty. There was no life in the blue eyes, only sorrow and anger. Coarse hairs had begun to form a dark shadow along his jaw. A knock at the door pulled him away from the reflection. Before he could reach the door, Carter burst in.

"What do you think of this place?" Carter asked, quickly closing the door.

"It's exceedingly temporary."

"Are you sure?"

"What do you know?" Lucas asked, anger rising; he clenched his fists, daring the wounds to reopen.

"I overheard Father and Virgil talking; we might be staying longer than we thought."

"How much longer?"

"Indefinitely."

There was another knock on the door and Jude entered.

He took one look at Lucas. "Carter already told you what little he heard."

"Yes," Lucas said sourly.

Jude sighed. "Boys, we are in a very difficult situation and there's little we can do."

"The—"

"Let me finish. There's little we can do, but we'll make it count. Lucas, I know you want to go after the Vosjnik, but that's suicide. Our best course of action is going to the Lazado. Now, I've talked with Virgil and they are planning to flee, too. When they leave, we're going with them."

"When will that be?" Carter questioned.

"Soon, hopefully. Until then, Virgil recommends we find work to occupy our time. Lucas, he's going to introduce you to one of his friends in need of an assistant. And Carter, you and I will go out tomorrow and see what we can find." When they didn't respond, Jude took his leave. As the door closed, he said, "Dinner will be in an hour."

‡‡‡

Jared took a bite. Since the Vosjnik were still on their trail, Kade refused to let them make a fire large enough to cook over, which meant half-stale bread as a meal. Kade had regained consciousness relatively soon after they took off, a dark bruise marring his face. He was rightly mad, but Jared knew Keegan never intended to hurt him; the magic had come forth from an instinctual source, as at its core, elemental magic was a tool of survival.

"Hey... uhh..." Keegan mumbled awkwardly, "you've got some dirt on your neck."

Kade glared at her but reached up regardless.

"Other side."

He rubbed his neck. "Did I get it?"

"No. It looks like it may be a bruise." She eyed him for a second. "If I didn't know better, I'd say it was a hickey."

"A what?" Jared asked.

"A hickey. You get them when someone sucks or bites your neck when things get... passionate."

Jared stared at her at a loss for words.

She stared at Kade; an eyebrow raised. "You gonna say something?"

"No."

She rolled her eyes and mumbled audibly. "Man-whore."

"Excuse me?"

"You heard me."

They stared at each other.

"How many of you were in the Vosjnik?" Jared intruded, aiming to break the tension.

Kade was slow to answer. "Including me? Eight. Six now." A log popped. "It should've been five."

Owls hooted in the background to fill the silence.

"I can make it five," Keegan muttered.

"Keegan," Jared snapped.

Rolling her eyes, she asked sourly, "Anything we should know about them?"

"Avoid them at all costs; they're monsters," Kade said.

"What does that tell us about you?"

He was silent for a moment. "The lengths I'm willing to go to deliver you to the Lazado."

"Is there anything *else* we should know about them; god forbid we get caught?"

"No. If you're caught, nothing but death will help you."

"We're screwed."

Jared pressed, "What can you tell us about them in general?"

"There's a life, water, fire, earth, and air elemental, a telepath, an archer, and a swordsman."

"Which one were... are.... were... is... you," Keegan asked, making faces as she spoke.

"Earth," Kade said.

"Oh yeah, I knew that. What about Finlay?"

"Fire."

"Thahan?"

"Archer. How do you know their names?"

"They were said earlier."

"Were they?" Kade asked Jared.

"Maybe," Jared rubbed his nose.

Kade turned to Keegan. "Hmmm?"

"I don't know what you're thinking," Keegan started, "well, I have an idea, and you're wrong. I'm just really good with names, faces, and weird facts."

"I find that hard to believe."

"The only thing hard around here is your head." There was a moment's pause before she burst into laughter.

"What's so funny?"

"Nothing you would understand," she told him, her laugh dwindling to a chuckle.

Jared steered the conversation away from an argument, "Who's the leader?"

"Commander," Kade corrected, still hung up on Keegan's comment. "Connery Sray."

"Which one's he?" She enquired.

"Telepath."

"Ah, that's so cool! Man, I wish I could read minds."

"I'm not sure it's what you think it is," Jared disputed. "And it'd be annoying always hearing everyone's thoughts."

"I'm sure there's a way to block it out and stuff," Keegan shrugged. "Any light you can shed on the matter?" she asked Kade.

"Not at the moment."

"We'll just have to ask a telepath when we see one."

"No," Jared bit.

"Why?"

"Avoid telepaths; they're snakes."

"Okay…" She turned to Kade, "Did you get what we needed?"

"Yes." He stood up, removed several rolled items from his saddlebag, handed half of them to Jared, and threw the rest at her.

She caught the bundle with her face.

Jared opened his and found there was a bedroll, a cloak, and an empty water-skin.

"Why do I need this?" Keegan asked, holding up the dress.

Kade sat down again. "Women don't wear trousers."

"I do."

"But you shouldn't; it looks peculiar."

"I'm a peculiar person."

"Keegan," Kade said sternly, "just wear the royiken dress."

Jared could tell she was momentarily confused by Kade's vernacular.

Surprising them, she stood, sighing, and said, "Fine."

"What, no further arguing?"

She turned her back to them, grabbing the bottom of her shirt. "Honestly, I'm too damn tired to."

"Whoa!" Kade and Jared yelled, causing her to stop.

She turned back to face them, the bottom of her stomach showing. "What?"

"You should… uh… be more modest," Jared stuttered.

"Oh, chill," Keegan chided, turning again and pulling her shirt off.

Jared looked away quickly, feeling his cheeks reddening.

She laughed when she noticed his flushed face. "I assume you don't have much experience with women."

He looked up, forgetting her state of undress. The dress had just finished falling over her hips. "No," he admitted self-consciously.

"Talk to Kade," she grinned, taking a seat. "He can probably give you some tips on how to get laid."

"Get what?"

"Laid—have sex."

Jared stared at her mortified. "Why would you even say something like that?"

She rolled her eyes. "It's a joke, calm down." Giving a shrug, she added, "Though, there's probably some verity in it."

"How could there possibly be *any* truth in that?"

"I'm willing to bet Kade's been to a few brothels."

"More than a few," Kade commented casually.

She motioned at him, "There ya go."

"You forgot to remove your trousers," Kade pointed out.

"Yeah, those ain't coming off."

"The whole point of wearing a dress is so you don't need to wear pants."

"You can't see them, and I've already done as much compromising as I'm gonna do."

Jared attempted to stifle a yawn.

"Get some sleep," Kade said. "Keegan, you have watch."

‡‡‡

The air was pleasant now that it was late spring and a light breeze sent Aron's hair skittering. In the winter, the winds were biting, keeping their meetings short. But it was a clear night with a new moon forcing the stars to illuminate the gable. The torches below stood out like candles in a dark room.

He heard Shiloh making her way up the last few steps and turned to greet her. Her long, blonde tresses were piled in a loose coil on top of her head.

Meeting her with a passionate kiss, he announced, "We will leave on the next new moon."

Shiloh leaned forward and gently kissed his lips. "I can't wait."

Hand in hand they made their way to the edge of stones and stood staring out over the darkness, the breeze sending wisps of golden hair dancing about her face.

"Where shall we go?" she asked, her voice floating in the draft.

"Anywhere we like," Aron said, wrapping his arm around her shoulders, "as long as we are together."

She rested her head against him. "I've always wanted to see the Merfolk."

"Then that is where we shall go."

"Have you thought about how we're going to get out of the castle?"

"Not extensively. But I am thinking we can stow away on a wagon at the end of the day."

"I love you," Shiloh whispered.

"And I you." Aron turned to look at the sky and, for the first time, felt as if the misery of his family was lifting. But Alyck's words replayed in his head, 'there will be no happy ending'. *Yes, there will.*

‡‡‡
‡‡‡

It would be great if the book gave a direct translation of the prophecy, but Braxton was not that lucky. The book was a dictionary of sorts that gave translations of words from the Old Language. Thus far, he had managed to translate most of the first line: 'While you have slaughtered — children of the dragon, she will rise again from the ashes by your own...'

He flipped through the pages looking for *pen*. It translated to 'doing'.

Braxton leaned back in the chair and was suprised that darkness had fallen. He stood up, streching his muscles, and considered pushing through the night. Eventually, he decided against it; translating was slow work and he had made considerable progress.

Blowing out the candle, it took his eyes a moment to adjust to the dimness, the only guiding light coming from the stars shining through the open window. Yawning, he pulled off his clothes and crawled into bed, the blankets enveloping him in a welcoming embrace.

His night visions were filled with slick, purple blood covering the ground. His sword similarly coated. Painful screams assaulted his ears.

"Haxnug," he cried to his mind's foe.

"Betrayer!" voices shrieked in return.

Wind buffeted him, throwing his sword from his grasp as long talons reached towards his chest. As they were about to touch him, he bolted up, his heart beating against his breastbone.

The room was only half-lit by the rising sun.

Taking a deep breath, he lay back down and returned to sleep, muttering, "Only a dream."

CHAPTER 15

The clang of metal on metal rang throughout the shop as Lucas stood beside Virgil. They'd been in the city for five days and Virgil was now finding time to take him to the blacksmith, who would hopefully become his new employer.

"Waylan," Virgil called out.

No response.

"Waylan," Virgil called louder.

The noise stopped and a surly, black-skinned man came from the back room. He was taller than Lucas by several inches—something Lucas was unaccustomed to from anyone aside his father. A wiry black beard covered the smith's jaw and, in his hand, was a large hammer.

Setting it down, the blacksmith greeted Virgil with a hardy handshake. "Virgil, how's that chandelier holding up?"

"Quite well. Laiyla loves the noxþ thing."

"Well, what can I do for you today?"

"You are still in need of an assistant?"

"I am. Ya got one for me?"

Placing a hand on Lucas' shoulder, Virgil said, "I do, if you are willing to give him a chance."

The smith introduced himself, "Waylan Piscol."

"Lucas Sieme," he reciprocated.

"Have you ever apprenticed for a blacksmith, boy?"

"No, sir."

"Then I doubt you'll be of use."

Virgil stopped the smith as he made to return to the back of the shop. "The boy may not have experience, but he is strong and willing to learn. At least give him a chance; it cannot hurt."

Sighing, Waylan answered, "Fine. Your wage'll be a copper a day until you can prove your worth. At which time, we'll renegotiate."

"Thank you," Virgil said.

"Be here an hour after dawn the day after tomorrow," Waylan told Lucas, walking away.

"That went better than expected," Virgil said once they'd left the shop.

"Is there something you haven't told me about my employer?"

"Waylan… he can be a *tad* prickly and hard-headed at times. But he means well," Virgil promised.

‡‡‡

118

The last four days of travel had been grueling; continued lack of sleep made them short-tempered and the littlest things were certain to spark a fight between Keegan and Kade. Jared did his best to not get involved. Although they were certain the Vosjnik were still trailing them, Kade felt there was enough distance between them to stop for a few hours every night.

"Put your cloak on," Kade instructed on the fifth morning.

"Why?" Keegan asked, pulling the cloak from her saddlebag.

"It'll help conceal your face."

"Oooh, are we gonna reach the city today?" she asked excitedly.

Jared could tell she immediately regretted the needless over-expenditure of energy.

"Yes. And whatever you do, say *nothing*."

"Why?"

"Is that your favorite question?"

"No... Yes... I don't know. Why?"

"Just, do as I say."

"Sir, yes, sir," Keegan said, feigning indignation as she did the cloak's clasp.

They rode for a little longer before emerging onto a wide dirt road. A few weary travelers walked along the sides. In the distance, the high walls surrounding Suttan could be seen in the hazy, mid-morning sky. Behind the city rose tall mountains.

"I didn't know there were mountains nearby," Keegan commented.

"Those are the Westerlies," Jared told her.

"Wow, such a creative name. What's on the other side?"

"Nothing," Kade answered. "This kingdom ends where they begin."

"There has to be something, the world doesn't just drop off like a cliff."

"I didn't say that. I said that we don't know what's on the other side."

"No, you didn't," Keegan argued, "you said 'nothing' which isn't the same thing as 'we don't know'."

"Th—" Kade started then shook his head and became quiet; apparently, this wasn't worth fighting over.

"Why doesn't anyone go explore?" Keegan queried. "It might be a way to get away from Caius."

"People have," Jared provided, "but it's said that few came back, and those who did vowed to never cross the mountains again."

There was a gleam of curiosity in her eyes. "Why?"

"Something about giant, horned men—if I remember the story correctly."

As the walls grew closer, more travelers appeared on the road.

Nearing the gates, Jared eyed the sentries nervously. Neither paid them much attention, but as they started through the entrance, there was a clang and his heart dropped.

"Halt," one of the guards called.

Jared turned and saw that one of Kade's saddlebags had worked itself loose and was now lying on the ground.

Kade pulled Arso around and hissed as he passed, "Keep going."

Keegan gave Jared an uneasy look and pulled Bastille to a stop.

As Kade slid down from Arso, one of the guards was already picking up the bag and opening it.

"What are you doing with a set of the king's armor?"

"I'm one of the king's men," Kade returned, reaching for the bag.

The guard pulled it away. "A slack jaw like you would never be allowed t' serve in the king's army. You stole this."

Kade grabbed at the bag, placing his hand so his brand faced upwards.

The guard glanced down and his face paled. "M-my deepe-est appologies… sir. I-I didn't know."

"Obviously," Kade snarled, as the man released his bag.

The guard continued, "If you don' mind me asking, what 're you doing with these villeins?"

"That's none of your concern. Oh, and should you tell anyone we're in the city, I can assure you that you won't live to see the new week."

The guard ashamedly retook his post with a pale face.

After re-securing the bag onto Arso's saddle, Kade led the way into Suttan. Within the walls, the buildings grew steadily in size as they converged at the city's castle in the center.

"Where do we go?" Keegan asked.

"To see a friend," Kade said, leading them through the gate's square.

"How do you know where you're going?" Jared asked.

"I used to live here."

Both Jared and Kade paused, waiting for Keegan to say something. When she didn't, they turned to look at her. She seemed distracted; her eyes darting about, following random pedestrians who milled around them.

"Keegan," Jared said to get her attention.

"Yeah," she responded, still looking around absentmindedly.

"You all right?"

"Mhmm," she nodded airily.

✛✛✛

She was sweating in the midday sun; however, it wasn't the heat causing her to perspire. Since they'd begun encountering people on the road, she had started hearing voices. At first, they were faint, barely whispers, but as they neared the city and the number of people increased, so did the babble—and it was growing louder.

Now that they were inside Suttan, it was like a concert in her head. Voices of men, women, and children flooded her mind. She looked around, trying to discern to whom they belonged, but they were never present long enough for her to pinpoint.

I need to buy—
Hmm, he's quite—
—stay away from that.
Pass—
—not to him.

Jared glanced at her, noticing her discomfort. She stopped looking around, instead focusing on Bastille's neck.

Left up ahead, then—

Kade took the next left and led them towards the inner section. The central streets weren't as crowded and they were able to move faster, but the voices didn't lessen.

—can't be preg—

She had underestimated how large the city was, expecting it to be something that even she could easily navigate; it was like a maze. Without Kade, she and Jared would've been hopelessly lost.

—late. I must be getting home.

Kade stopped outside a haggard-looking building and dismounted. A crooked sign above the door read 'Gydrick's Inn and Tavern'.

I cannot stand h—

"Are you sure we should stay here?" Jared asked.

"Yes," Kade answered, almost happily. "Gydrick's has the best ale in the city."

Keegan rolled her eyes.

—needs a bath.

They dismounted, handed their reins to a stable boy, and followed Kade into Gydrick's. Inside, tables crowded the room, at which a few patrons sat, some already evidently drunk.

Anuhher rund!

121

Kade headed to the bar, "Wait here."

Jared pointedly watched him while Keegan leaned against the wall.

The voices were constant. It wasn't as if they were simply one after the other, but all at the same time. It made focusing on any one voice—or anything really—difficult. Her head was beginning to hurt from trying to go in so many directions.

Where's my ale?

Jared leaned over and whispered, "Are you sure you're all right?"

She realized she'd been scowling. "Yeah."

Kade approached them, a key in hand. "Room eight."

The stairs to the second floor were narrow, forcing them single file and to hug the wall when another patron came down. The landing hallway was only slightly wider. Doors lined the walls with numbers in the center.

Kade unlocked the door with a crooked '8' to reveal a small room. There was only one bed pushed against the wall and a grimy window to filter the sunlight.

Tentatively, Keegan entered and made her way to the bed.

La ladi da di di da—

The lumps in the mattress were large, but after a week of sleeping on the ground, it felt like a cloud. She swung her feet up and lay back.

Look at the p—

When Kade shut the door, the voices became muffled. While she didn't understand why they were muted, she was glad. She took a breath, feeling like a weight had been lifted, and mumbled. "Who gets the bed?"

"You," Kade answered, dropping his bag on the floor.

Do not touch—

"You sure?" Keegan asked, closing her eyes. "We can rock, paper, scissors for it."

"Pardon?"

"Never mind." Given the chance, sleep would come quickly.

AAAHHHH!

Keegan jolted up in a state of panic and tumbled to the floor. As she lay there, it felt as if someone was taking a hammer to the inside of her head. Whatever was happening was going to relieve her of her sanity—what little of it was left.

Jared rushed over. "What happened?"

She pushed herself up, her eyes glazed over, and was barely aware of him kneeling beside her. *Breathe. In, out. In, out.*

Jared called her name.

She brought her attention back to him, "Yeah."

"What's wrong?"

"Nothing."

Across the room, a frown graced Kade's already naturally harsh features. "Jared, go check the horses."

Jared turned and looked at him confused. "The horses are fine."

"Go check."

Quietly, Keegan told him, "Just go, I'll be fine."

Kade shut the door behind Jared and there was the faint click of the lock.

Something wasn't right; all the voices had vanished. "Why'd you lock the door?" she questioned.

"I don't want to be interrupted," Kade said darkly.

She regretted having told Jared to go. "What're you planning?"

"You tell me."

She got to her feet. "I don't know; I can't read minds."

Or can you?

"I can't."

"You just did."

"No, I didn't."

Watch my lips, they don't move, yet you hear me speaking.

Keegan stared at him blank-faced. "You've gotta be freakin' kidding me."

"How long have you been hearing voices?"

"How do you know I've been hearing voices?"

"I'm a telepath."

"So, every telepath goes through this?"

Kade nodded.

"Why didn't you tell us?"

"There was no need to."

"I beg to differ."

"Would it have changed anything?"

"I don't know—it could've. We're gonna have to tell Jared."

"No," Kade growled.

"He's gotta deal with us, he has a right to know."

"No."

She crossed her arms stubbornly. "Too bad, I'm telling him."

Anger crossed Kade's face. "I don't recommend that."

"What're you gonna do? Jack shit."

"Haven't you learned anything?"

"I've learned you're an asshole. You don't scare me."

Kade started towards her when the door handle turned and there was a thump.

Jared called, "Why's the door locked?"

"Say nothing," Kade ordered in a threatening voice.

"The horses are fine," Jared told him, walking in.

"Jared, Kade's a tele—" Keegan started. It suddenly felt like a million white-hot nails were digging in her head. Screaming, she dropped to her knees and hunched over.

Jared rushed to her side, frantically asking what the source of her agony was.

She took gulping breaths and managed to steal a glance at Kade through watery eyes. He had a face like thunder, and she realized this was his doing. "He's a telepath," she managed in a voice that felt incredibly small. The nails dug in deeper and she compressed her body even more.

Jared turned on Kade, drawing the knife he kept in his boot. "Stay away from us."

Kade laughed and with a flick of the wrist sent Jared's knife flying. It embedded itself into one of the wooden panels of the wall.

"No," she said, "we need him."

Jared shook his head. "We don't need this manipulative bwint."

"I'm a telepath."

Jared crouched before her. "Then give me one good reason why I shouldn't wash my hands of you—*both* of you."

She raised her eyes to look at him pleadingly. "I just found out. And, really, what's so bad about telepaths?"

"I'll let Kade explain."

She looked to Kade.

"Telepaths are notorious for being informants for Caius."

"So?" Keegan shakily got to her feet. "That doesn't mean we are."

"Maybe not you, but Kade's already confirmed the stereotype," Jared snapped.

"Does the good not outweigh the bad here?" she argued in Kade's defense, pausing in surprise that those words had come from her.

"I don't believe so."

"So, what're you gonna do; leave?"

"Yes. Grab your things, *we* are going."

Kade drew his sword, "You're welcome to go, but she stays."

"What kind of person would I be to leave her with a monster like you?"

Kade placed the point of the sword against Jared's sternum. "She stays."

Keegan looked helplessly between them. "Kade, would you go downstairs so I can talk to Jared?"

"How do I know you won't run?" Kade countered, eyes locked with Jared's.

"I have nowhere to run to, nor do I even know *where* to go."

Kade's gaze fixed on her for a moment. Pulling his sword away, he sheathed it, and slammed the door shut behind himself.

‡‡‡

Kade stomped down the stairs, muttering curses under his breath. Reaching the tavern, he wished someone would pick a fight because he *really* wanted to hit something.

Approaching the bar with a deep scowl, he barked, "A pint."

"Comin' up," the barman said cheerfully, grabbing a glass and filling it from the tap. Amber liquid flowed, topped with a layer of foam.

Kade slid him a copper coin. He thought about listening in on the conversation upstairs but doing so would only further the stigma and, as far as he was concerned, it wouldn't change the outcome; Keegan was going with him. He took long a gulp.

A woman sidled up next to him. "Is there anything I can help you with?"

He ignored her.

She ran a hand down his back. "A big strong man like you must need something."

"There are many things I need," he began without looking at her, assuming a smirk had crossed her face. "But I don't need a filthy hynak like you." He turned to face her.

She stared at him open-mouthed, revealing just a few yellow teeth stuck in her gums and looked like she'd been dragged behind a horse through the city.

He added, "Nor would I want to associate with an old hag."

Her hand moved across his face.

He sat calmly for a moment, then stood, towering over her.

She stared at him, fear in her eyes.

"Never touch me again," he growled, "you filthy, sti—"

Someone smacked him upside the head.

"Shut up, dumb ass," came Keegan. To the woman, she said, "Get outta here."

The woman pushed past them hurriedly.

He started to say something.

Keegan cut him off, "Shut your face. Now, Jared has agreed to stay under the stipulation that you answer *all* our questions. Understood?"

He glared at her.

Taking his silence for agreement, Keegan said, "Come on then. Oh, if you ever do that mental torture shit again, I'll listen to Jared."

He followed her to the table where Jared sat, scowling as he nursed a tankard.

Keegan took a seat on the bench and Kade sat beside her. "Do we wanna get some food?"

Jared's stomach grumbled.

"I'll take that as a yes. Mr. Money Man, would you care to order?" When no one moved, she fixed her gaze on Kade, "That's you."

He stood and made his way back to the bar, ordered, and returned to the table as Jared downed the rest of his ale.

"First and foremost," Keegan said, rubbing her temples, "how do I block out the voices?"

"Put up a wall," he answered.

She looked at him unamused. "And how, pray tell, do I do that?"

"I can't explain the minutia of it. It was a skill I picked up as a child."

She dropped her head onto the table. "So *fucking* helpful."

He sat for a moment, then slowly expanded his own wall to encompass her mind.

It took her a few seconds to realize the thoughts were being blocked. "Why can't I hear voices anymore?"

"I'm shielding you," Kade said as the barmaid brought them food and drink. "I remember going through the same thing." He took a gulp of ale, "Except no one was there to help me."

Keegan stared at him, shocked. "Are you actually being decent? Holy crap. Where's the real Kade?"

"This is a one-time thing."

"And there's the Kade we know and tolerate."

"What's your motivation?" Jared finally spoke.

Kade bit into a piece of bread. "To kill those who wronged me."

Jared scowled at him and downed half his pint.

"Slow down," Keegan told him. "That's your third one; I don't wanna be lookin' after your drunk ass."

Jared glared at her, and spitefully, emptied the tankard, slamming it onto the table in a show of bravado. "Another," he yelled to the barmaid, who came quickly.

Keegan turned to Kade. "How exactly do you make a shield for someone else?"

"Again, it's not something I can explain."

"You h'd better start giving us some real answers," Jared snapped as the barmaid returned with his drink.

"Then ask questions I can capably answer."

"Why was it when you shut the door, the voices... thoughts, became muffled?" Keegan enquired.

"Solid objects interfere with reception. Being underground will completely block thoughts from the surface. Though, anyone underground can be heard just fine."

Keegan knitted her brows together. "What?"

Kade sighed and clarified, "If you're underground, you can't hear someone who's on the surface nor can they hear you. Anyone who's underground with you can be heard just fine."

"Okay, so it's like an internal walkie-talkie."

Kade and Jared looked at her perplexed.

She shook her head, "I'll explain once I've explained the three billion other things y'all need to understand to get what the hell a walkie-talkie is."

Jared downed the ale and slammed the tankard down on the table again. "How 'id you find us?"

"The Blind Prophet."

"How did you know to look for us at the forest's edge?" Keegan pressed.

The barmaid collected Jared's tankard once more.

"You," Kade lied. Even if Jared wasn't well on his way to getting drunk, he'd never tell them what had occurred.

Keegan stared at him with a look of confusion as he took a swig.

"Your thoughts are unusually loud." While that wasn't how he'd found them, it was a true statement.

"How? Wouldn't all thoughts be at the same volume?"

"No. Some tend to be louder than others."

"How does that make it easier to find a person?"

"It's the same as if someone is actually speaking. The louder someone speaks, the easier it is to find them in a crowd."

Keegan nodded, "Okay. Wait, wouldn't you have to know what my... Do voices and thoughts sound the same?"

The barmaid set another mug in front of Jared.

"I don't understand your question."

Jared reached for the tankard's handle.

Keegan slapped his hand away and pulled the drink to their side of the table. "You've had enough."

Jared frowned, then took her cup and downed it.

She sighed, clenching her fists, and continued with the conversation. "Does a person's voice and thoughts have the same voice, I guess is the way to put it."

"Yes."

The barmaid made her way back to their table. As she reached for Jared's tankard, Keegan told her, "He's cut off."

The barmaid looked at her puzzled.

"No more for him." Then, once more, jumped back into the conversation, "Huh... interesting. Okay, so how did you know whose voice to follow when you were looking for us?"

"Again, I don't understand."

"When you were looking for me in... wherever the place Jared lived—"

"Suilenroc," Jared slurred, grabbing the drink Keegan had taken from him and swallowing it before she could scold him.

"Yeah, Suilenroc," she continued, "How did you know which voice was mine?"

Kade finished his drink. "The Vosjnik almost captured you a couple of weeks prior."

"That was y'all? No wonder Finlay and Thahan looked familiar. Damn, I'm losing my touch."

"How d' you do that?" Jared said, his slur worse.

"I'm good with names, faces, birthdays, things like that; I told y'all this before." Keegan sighed and turned to Kade, "I'm gonna take him upstairs; he's gone."

"He's right there," Kade said.

"No, I mean he's drunk." Once she got Jared to his feet, she asked, "You comin' or stayin'?"

"Staying."

Steering Jared towards the stairs, she added, "Oh, and don't think we're done asking questions."

Kade ignored her and called out to the barmaid, "Another ale."

‡‡‡

She pushed Jared forward, "Come on."

128

They made it up the steps without too much difficulty and moved towards the room. Jared took the door handle, turned it, and found it locked.

"Stay here, I'll get the key," she told him and made her way downstairs, pushing through the crowd to get to Kade.

He was still sitting at the table, gulping down ale like water.

"I need the key."

He pulled it out of his pocket and placed it on the table without breaking away from the tankard.

"Thanks." She hurried back and found Jared sitting on the floor, arms crossed, and scowling. "Up ya get."

"I ca n't. My 'ead feels funny."

She offered him a hand. "Yeah, that happens when you get drunk."

Taking her hand, instead of her pulling him up he pulled her down. Her knee drove into the floor and her forehead went into the wall. She knelt back, groaning and rubbing her head.

"I um surry," he said, placing his hands on her cheeks.

She scowled at him and sighed.

He gave her a wet kiss on the forehead. "To make better."

Keegan grabbed his forearm and elbow, helping him to his feet, and after unlocking the door, led him inside. "Can you stand on your own?"

"Sur'."

She let go of him to shut the door and once it was closed, his hand grabbed the back of her dress and pulled her to the floor again. She rolled away. "What the hell?"

"Los' ma balance."

She got him on his feet again and half-dragged him to the bed.

"You 're supposed to be in the bed," he said, pouting childishly.

"I know." Kneeling, she undid the lacing of his boots, pulled them off, and tossed them towards the end of the bed. Looking up, she saw he'd removed his shirt.

He undid his belt and handed it to her.

She placed it on the floor. "You good?"

He nodded.

"Then get some sleep."

As he lay down, he asked, "How 're are you s' gentle now, yet always fighting with Kade?"

Once he succumbed to sleep, she responded. "Where to even begin?" She took the bedroll from her pack and set it beside the bed. "For starters, I don't really mean to fight with him. He just gets under my skin and my mouth has a mind of its own. It's a habit I really gotta break."

129

Taking a seat, she continued, "As for being 'gentle' with you, it's cause I care about you. You're my friend and once I've deemed you as such, I'm loyal to a fault."

She was quiet for a second and a tear rolled down her cheek. "I don't know if you know this, but…" she whispered, wiping her eye, "I'm scared shitless. I'm afraid of a lot of things right now, but what worries me the most is that you might get hurt. I know I'm a goner—I've kinda come to grips with that, also kinda haven't—but I can't stand the thought of something happening to you. I refuse to let my friends get hurt. But I can't protect myself, so how in the hell am I supposed to protect the people I care about?" She slumped down. "I can't, and that terrifies me."

‡‡‡

In the four days since they'd found Thahan, the Vosjnik had seldom stopped. Yet, they seemed to gain little ground on their quarry. They knew enough about Keegan and had a plethora of knowledge on Kade, but the only thing they knew of Jared, was his name. And Nico had no intention of saying anything to incriminate his brother. Connery seemed to believe they were headed to Suttan, reasoning that Kade knew it'd be almost impossible to find them there.

On the fourth night, Suttan appeared on the horizon like a haze.

Connery was sullen and silent as they rested for a few hours. The others were quiet simply because they were in awful moods. Little sleep and the aggravation of being a step behind had worn them down.

"We will enter the city in the morning," Connery said, staring at the fire.

"Why?" Vitia snapped. "We'll never find Kade anyway."

"I have no doubt that they are already in the city, and honestly, I doubt we will ever find them. The most we can hope for is for them to get caught by the city guards."

The Vosjnik stared at him with blank expressions.

"Get some sleep, I will take watch."

Slowly, one by one, they lay down and left Connery to himself.

130

CHAPTER 16

Nico watched the Vosjnik pack camp silently. Connery led the way towards Suttan slowly, no longer finding any need for haste. People on the road saw them and scurried away. Under most circumstances, the only way to discern a member of the Vosjnik was to see the star branded on their thumb, but the griffin emblem on their armor dignified them as king's men, ensuring people steered clear.

They were stopped at the gates. "What be yer business?"

"We are chasing fugitives," Connery announced. "Have you perchance seen two men traveling with an odd-looking woman?"

"We see many people passin' through 'ere 'evryday," the other guard sniped, "most of 'em strange lookin'. What makes ya think these three would stand out? And even if someone 'ad seen 'em, it'd be neither o' us; we were up on the wall 'esterday."

"Who was here yesterday?"

"No idea. You 'ill have ta ask the Captain of the City Guard," the first man said.

"Where can I find him?"

"In the castle wi'h the lord."

"Send a runner to inform them we are coming."

The second man guffawed, "Who 're you ta give us orders?"

"Commander of the Vosjnik."

Both of their faces paled.

"We 'ill get right on that, sir," the first soldier said, scrambling away.

Connery looked angrily at the second man, then urged his horse through the gate.

Inside, the city bustled, and the horses made their way through the crowd slowly, even though people pushed to get out of the way. As they traveled farther from the wall, the crowds lessened. High above them, the castle loomed over the smaller houses and soon its shadow engulfed them.

The gates were open, and four guards stood at attention. Upon seeing them, one man rushed inside. The other three stood stock-still as they passed. The courtyard was cobbled and, on the steps, stood several men.

Connery dismounted and handed his reins to a frightened-looking stable boy.

"Welcome to Suttan, Commander," a man in dark blue silks called out.

131

"I need to speak to the Captain of the City Guard, Lord Seignour," Connery said coarsely.

"Present," another man said, stepping forward. He was a short, middle-aged man with the hair around his ears beginning to lose its color. Two swords were belted around his waist, one on each hip, and the point of a dagger's sheath protruded from the back of his belt. "Sir Faryis Mettero; how can I be of service?"

"I need to speak with anyone who was on duty at the North gate yesterday and the day before."

"Of course," Sir Faryis gave a slight bow then turned on his heels and walked across the courtyard.

The other men were silent.

Taking charge, Lord Seignour said, "Is there any other way I may be of service?"

"Yes," Connery stated, "my men need room and food, and see to it that their horses are fed and stabled. I need a hall to conduct interviews, and the men who guard the gates are to account for *everyone* entering and exiting the city. I also need access to your Looking Glass."

"For how long?" Lord Seignour asked, taken aback by Connery's brusqueness.

"Until we find who we are looking for."

Lord Seignour nodded, then snapped and a page scrambled forward. "Tell the servants to prepare.... one, two..." he mumbled a bit, "seven rooms."

"Six. The boy will be staying in a cell."

Lord Seignour could tell they were growing restless. "Let us continue talking inside, Commander. I am sure your men are weary, and some matters are best discussed behind closed doors."

Connery motioned for him to lead the way.

To the Vosjnik, Lord Seignour said, "Stefan here will show you to your rooms. If you have any wants, let him know. I ask only one favor, leave the lad his life; it is ever so hard to find a decent page."

Dax dismounted, pulling Nico down with him, and handed him over to two guards in breastplates and leather armor.

Nico strained against them, but they yanked hard and dug their fingers into his arms, leading him into the depths of the castle. The cells were mostly empty but a few housed grungy-looking men with scraggly beards. They came to the end of a row and threw him in, hands still bound.

The barred door slammed behind him and he turned to ask them to release his hands, but the guards were already walking away. He grabbed the bars and watched forlornly as they disappeared. When they were no longer in sight, he surveyed the cell. It was small, maybe ten feet in width and length. A pile of hay was pushed into a back corner and a chamber pot sat in the other.

He plopped down onto the hay and began undoing his bonds. It took some time, but they finally came loose. He shoved the rope under the hay; it might prove useful later. Slowly, the reality of the situation and all that had ensued sunk in as he was given time to think. The surrounding's bleakness only strengthened his feelings and finally, distress broke forth as he buried his head in the straw to hide his tears.

✠✠✠

Braxton read the translation, "While you have slaughtered — child of the dragon, she will rise again from the ashes by your own doing. Rule while you can, false lord, for it will only be for the moment. A child will come—" In four days, this was all he had managed. So far, everything corresponded with what was already known about the Child of Prophecy.

He glanced up and was shocked to find the room bathed in light; day had come without him realizing it. A weight pressed over his body as exhaustion sank in. He blinked, trying to hold back the desire to fall asleep where he sat.

Slowly, he cajoled himself into making his way over to the bed. It did not take him long to sink into a state of nothingness.

He stood on a ground covered in blood, the sword in his hand stained a dark purple, and angry voices yelled at him, "Betrayer! Marmarda! Soucer!"

Talons materialized and reached towards his chest. He could feel them scraping at his body, turning the flesh to ribbons.

He awoke suddenly, breathing heavily, his face covered in sweat. As his heart rate calmed, he began to think more clearly. Trying to recall the dream, he discovered he could not recount a single detail.

✠✠✠

He had gotten drunk. Jared awoke with a pounding headache and found most of the previous night was a hazy memory; what he remembered was sitting at the table drinking—and Keegan telling him not to.

He opened his eyes blearily, the light pouring through the window hurting them. Groaning, he attempted to sit up. His head felt light and he slowly lowered himself again, sinking into the pillow. It was then he

133

realized he was in the bed. Turning his head, he saw Keegan curled up on the floor underneath a blanket. Looking around the room, he noticed Kade was nowhere to be seen.

He forced himself upright. *Son of a—* he thought, swinging his legs over the side of the bed. His eyes swam and he felt nauseous. Berating himself, he held his head in his hands. The door opened and he looked up.

Kade held a water-skin and half a loaf of bread. He swung the door shut heavily.

To Jared it sounded like a painfully loud clap of thunder. "Quietly."

Kade walked across the room and threw the water-skin on the bed. "Drink up."

Jared tentatively took a sip. The water was cool as it ran down his parched throat and he took another small gulp. "Why's Keegan on the floor?"

"You'll have to ask her that yourself," Kade handed him the bread. "I would've left you downstairs."

Jared took the bread and ate quietly while Kade rummaged through one of the packs.

"Get dressed," Kade said finally, "we have business to attend to."

Jared looked down and realized he was only in his trousers. "Where's my tunic?"

Locating it at the foot of the bed, Kade picked it up and threw it at him.

He pulled the coarse woolen garment over his head, then found his belt at the head of the bed. When he stood, the world swam before his eyes and he had to steady himself against the bedpost.

"Stop being such an aunig," Kade said.

Jared buckled his belt. "Do you want to wake Keegan?"

"No, she had a rough night."

Jared sat back down on the bed to pull on his socks. "And whose fault is that?"

"Yours actually."

Jared stood up, "How—"

"Both of you shut up," Keegan mumbled. "Jared, you made last night difficult, Kade, you're making today difficult; so, if y'all're gonna fight, do it somewhere else." She pulled the blanket tighter around her shoulders. "Jared, Kade still owes you answers, so do that while y'all're out."

"I will." Jared knelt beside her, put a hand on her forehead, feeling a knot, and wondered about its origin. "How are you feeling?"

"Like shit," she answered, blearily opening her eyes. "The voices kept me up most of the night."

"Try to get some sleep."

"No, I'm gonna stay up and throw a rager."

"A rager?"

"Big ass party."

Kade stood impatiently by the door. "Let's go, we have much to do."

Jared looked over his shoulder at him, then back at Keegan. He scooped her up in his arms but halfway up, he collapsed onto his knees, making her gasp in surprise.

Squirming out of his hold, she muttered, "I got it," and shuffled over to the bed, the blanket draped around her like a cloak. She nestled into the mattress.

Jared kissed her forehead. "Sleep well."

"Mhmm," she murmured in return.

Kade waited impatiently for him with crossed arms. Once out in the hallway, he asked, "Was that necessary?"

"Yes."

Kade locked the door.

"Is that necessary?"

"Yes."

As they made their way down the hall, Jared steadied himself against the wall, his legs still weak at the knees.

Halfway down the stairs, another patron stumbled upon them; an older man with graying hair, lips pulled back into a sloppy, drunken smile, and mumbling to himself.

Kade and Jared hugged the wall to let him by.

Unsteadily, the man lurched into Kade then began apologizing profusely in slurred speech, while steadying himself.

The smell of alcohol emanating from his breath made Jared's stomach churn.

Pushing past the man, they descended into the tavern, which was mostly empty. Kade strolled casually out onto the street but Jared stopped on the doorstep, hiding in the inn's shadowy innards.

"I don't have all day," Kade called.

Taking a deep breath, Jared stepped over the threshold. The light was blinding, causing his pupils to dilate painfully. Squinting and gritting his teeth, he followed Kade. "Where are we going?"

"To see a friend."

"Why?"

"To save Keegan."

He grabbed Kade's arm. "I told you to stop giving us vite answers."

Kade jerked away. "Learn to ask better questions if you don't like my answers."

"That's exactly what a telepath would say."

"That's exactly what an idiot would say."

Rage welled up but before he had time to react, he saw Kade's countenance turn to worry.

Kade patted his pockets and when he couldn't find what he was looking for, sprinted towards the inn.

"Where are you going?" Jared called after him.

✝✝✝

Only a few minutes had passed when Keegan heard the door open and close again. She took a deep breath, repositioning herself to face the doorway. Hopefully, the boys would keep the noise to a minimum. She heard the pads of leather boots on the wooden floor, then nothing.

As she was beginning to question the silence, someone grabbed her wrist.

Her eyes snapped open and looked straight at Kade. "What're you doing?" she asked, pulling her hand away.

"I, uh, forgot somethin'," Kade stammered.

"Yeah, your head. Where's Jared?" she asked, noticing his absence.

"Hmm? Oh, he 's runnin' a few errands."

Keegan eyed him suspiciously. His manner of speaking was drastically different from normal. "Did you find us a boat?"

"Yes."

"Great, when can we leave?"

"In a week."

She nodded, smiling lightly, before letting her face became flat. "Who are you?"

"Pardon?"

"Who are you?" she growled, getting to her feet.

Kade stared down at her in shock.

"You're not Kade; now tell me who you are."

The impersonator could see the ruse was up. "D' you really want t' know who I 'm?"

Keegan glared at him.

"I 'm a thief."

She crossed her arms. "We don't have anything valuable, so save yourself some time and *leave*."

136

The man began to circle her. "Now that can n't be true. I wonder 'ow many gold coins the king would pay for you. Maybe 'e would make me a lord."

She began to feel uneasy. "Why would Caius want me?"

He tucked a strand of auburn hair behind one ear, making her flinch. "I 'ave never seen a quintuple elemental 'fore; I do n't believe anyone 'as."

The door burst open and Kade—the real, very angry one—stormed in. He saw the imposter and for a moment hesitated, before flinging himself at him.

In the time it took for them to fall to the floor, the impersonator transformed. He now had stark black curls covering his head. His skin became sun-kissed and his eyes turned to a stormy gray. Running diagonally from the top of his forehead across his face was a thin white scar.

Jared joined them, standing in the doorway out of breath.

"Raven Broyker?" Kade said, stopping his fist mid-punch.

"*Reven*," the man responded. "You never could get it right."

Kade's face remained blank, then slowly pulled into a smile reserved for old friends. He reached down and grasping Reven's hand, pulled him to his feet.

"Have n't seen your face 'round these parts for a while," Reven commented, brushing himself off. "It 's made the whole city all the more pretty. Though, I 'ave to say, your mug 'as gotten much uglier, with that nasty bruise an' all. Or maybe that 's an addition."

Kade was smiling all the while.

"Where 'ave you been?"

"Here and there," Kade answered nonchalantly.

"Doin' this an' that an' the occasional whore." Reven embraced Kade, clapping him on the back.

Kade reciprocated the gesture. "More than the occasional whore."

Reven laughed.

"Do you still hang around Downy's alley?"

Keegan looked to Jared, who was as confused as she and queried, "Y'all know each other?"

Reven and Kade laughed. "Yeah."

"What the hell is wrong with you?" Keegan barked.

Reven shrugged, "Man 's got to get his kicks somehow."

She clenched her fists.

Seeing her anger, Reven sought to placate her, "Calm, little lady, I jest. There 'ave been rumors 'bout an elemental the king 'as been searching for. As I was enjoying a fine pint o' ale last night, I sensed you."

She crossed her arms.

"Your being was strange an' foreign t' me an' I wished t' find out more."

"So, you break into our room and threaten to hand me over to Caius?"

"No, I find out what kind o' person you and your companions 're. And they 're good ones at that."

"You still threatened to do it!"

"An empty threat."

"What do you mean by sensed her?" Jared asked, finally shutting the door.

"I 'm a life elemental," Reven said, pulling back his shirtsleeve.

"How does that work exactly?" Keegan questioned, suddenly intrigued.

"You'll have to ask a Silver Tongue. I can n't explain it."

Keegan rolled her eyes. "God, you and Kade both suck ass at explaining things."

Reven's eyes flicked to Kade.

Kade shrugged.

"Never mind," Keegan mumbled.

The four of them stared at each other silently.

"So…" she encouraged.

Reven turned to Kade, "I suppose you need to see Thaddeus."

"Yes," Kade said in a low voice.

"Who's that?" Jared asked.

"The man who raised me after my parents died," Kade responded.

"Well, have fun." Keegan sat back on the bed and swung the covers over her legs.

"You're coming, too," Kade said.

She pursed her lips. "Why?"

"I don't trust you alone."

She glared at him.

"No amount of dirty looks is going to change anything." Kade picked up her shoes and handed them to her, "Now, be a good girl and do as you're told."

✝✝✝

Keegan had been reluctant to go to Thaddeus' but was smart enough to realize arguing wouldn't change Kade's mind. As for Reven's actions... she had some choice words for him but smartly kept them to herself.

"How did you know I was in trouble?" she asked as they walked down the street.

"I felt you getting nervous," Kade answered.

"How?"

"What do you mean *how*?"

"Feeling nervous is an emotion, not a thought."

"Emotions are thoughts."

Keegan paused. With a slight sideways nod of the head, she said, "Okay, I can roll with that; emotions are thoughts on a basal level." She peered over at Reven, "How did you not recognize Kade?"

"I 'ave n't seen 'im in almost five years."

"Still, wouldn't you recognize him? From what I've gathered, y'all were pretty good friends."

"People change quite a bit in five years," Kade commented.

"An' with my bad eye, you 're lucky if I can tell a man from a dog," Reven added.

"Is it really that bad?" she asked suspiciously.

"No. I 'm only half blind in tha' eye. Still makes seein' a bit diff'cult."

"Speaking of which," Kade said, "how did you get that lovely addition?"

"Disgruntled fighter. Thought I cheated, so 'e swung a knife at me. Last time he 'ill do that," Reven promised.

"...you killed him?" Keegan said with a half-cocked eyebrow.

Reven laughed, then feigned offence, "D' you really think I could kill a man?"

"Wouldn't put it past you."

Reven gently elbowed Kade in the ribs. "This one 'as fire in more than just 'er hair."

"Don't remind me," he muttered.

"Keegan, where 're ya' from? I do n't think I 've heard an accent like yours 'fore."

"Uh..." Keegan fumbled, "The South. I'll explain later."

"I 'll hold you to it. Well, here we 're."

"Where's *here* exactly?" Keegan asked, looking skeptically at the two-story brick building.

"Come inside an' see."

The interior of the shop was exactly as Kade remembered—a warren of bookshelves. Dust hung suspended in the air, making Jared sneeze. Keegan bore a childlike grin as she beheld the seemingly endless number of books.

"D' ya' remember the way?" Reven jibbed.

Kade gave him a sideways glance and started through the store. Every so often, he took a wrong turn, making Reven snicker. At one point, they had to backtrack to find Keegan. When he found her, she held a book open in her hands. "Stay with us," he told her, grabbing the book and shoving it onto the shelf.

After a few more turns, the shelves gave way to a cleared space where the counter was. Behind it stood Thaddeus. His brown hair had turned gray, but the same kindness and warmth exuded from his eyes.

"Kade, my boy," Thaddeus said with a wide smile. "Too much time has passed since we last saw each other." He came from behind the counter and embraced him in a one-sided hug.

"I need to know how to get to the Lazado," Kade said abruptly.

"What, no pleasantries for an old man?" quipped Thaddeus.

"No time. I need to get someone to the Lazado."

"Is he an elemental?" Thaddeus asked, nodding to the person behind Kade.

"Yes, he's a... *He*?" Kade spun around. "Where's Keegan?"

Jared also turned. "I don't know; she *was* behind me."

"Keegan," Kade yelled. Nothing. "KEEGAN!"

"Whaaat?" came a faint reply.

Kade started to make his way back into the store.

"It is fine," Thaddeus said with a small smile. "Leave her be, I can meet her later. But you, you must tell me all that has transpired in these last five years."

"I don't have time."

"Of course, you do."

Kade frowned as he was led into the back room.

140

CHAPTER 17

She had meant to follow them, but the temptation of the books was overpowering. First, she'd stopped to look at a title, then, before she knew it, she was sitting on the floor enthralled in its pages. The book she had in her lap was entitled *The Peoples of Arciol*; the first chapter gave a brief history of this world.

The origins of most of the races can be attributed to the Merfolk. They are humanoid creatures with certain fish-like attributes, such as webbed fingers and toes and dorsal and pectoral fins. The Merfolk reside beneath the waves of the Eastern Ocean. No one is certain how long they called the seabed home before rising from the depths and taking their first steps onto land. The Merfolk are the first of the humanoid elementals and are most notably known for their control of water.

The first Merfolk to emerge from the sea stayed for only short periods, never venturing far from the waves. Over time, they grew accustomed to the land and began wandering farther, at which time they came upon the Illeria Mountains. A few took residence within, beginning their excavation. After several generations, the Merfolk lost the ability to live on land and sea. They lost the webbing between their fingers and toes, and their fins. They also became much larger, towering over their oceanic brethren. Small horns sprouted from their skulls and their skin turned to a dull gray. In time, what was once control over water, became control over earth. This new race was deemed the Torrpeki.

Over the next century, the Torrpeki excavated a series of cities and tunnels through the mountains and preferred their subterranean dwellings. After several centuries of underground living, the desire to explore arose once more. Exploration parties left the mountains, heading west into the Yarav Forest, where they discovered an untouched forest with trees larger than twelve Torrpeki in circumference.

Some fought to preserve the forest while others began to tear it down to make way for great cities. A rift formed between the two sides and eventually those who wished to tear it down were driven further west, where they have disappeared from our history. Those who remained worked to create a harmonious existence between the wild and tame. Over generations, their physiques and magic evolved once more, as did their name. The Alvor lost the immense girths they had possessed as Torrpeki and became graceful beings. They also gained navels and their tongues took on a silvery hue. The small Torrpeki horns morphed into large curling ram's horns that grow with the Alvor throughout their life.

Their magic became what is now classified as the element of life. Some Alvor sought to fuse themselves with nature and began changing themselves into beasts. Some permanently became beasts, while others could transform between Alvor and beast at will. Those who did this were seen as abominations and were driven east into the Glensung Plains. Some retained the abi—

Someone was calling her. She looked up and yelled, "Whaaat?" Hearing nothing more she continued reading.

Some retained the ability to shift, while others permanently reverted to their Alvor shapes. Those who continued life as shifters were dubbed Werewolves, as their preferred shape was that of a wolf. Now, a wolf is the only thing they can shift into. These two, now very different races, continued to travel together and made their way across the Glensung Plains. Though these peoples would eventually split into different tribes, they have all remained nomadic.

Gradually, the Werewolves lost the ability to be elementals while the non-shifting Alvor gained the ability to control air. With this new evolution, they became the Buluo. These people's physiques also changed, becoming rugged and stout, and their skin darkening until it was a rich red brown. With continued movement north, the Buluo discovered the dragons, who resided in the Averit Volcanoes. The dragons refused to communicate with the Buluo, despite being sentient, and fighting between them ensued.

It was here the world discovered dragons could breathe fire, which led to their classification as fire elementals. The Buluo were pushed south, though they continued to seek a way north. This war was not over lands but principle and respect. Returning to their roots, the Buluo requested the help of the Alvor, Torrpeki, and Merfolk. At first, all refused, but as the dragons pushed further south and discovered the other races, they began ravaging the Yarav Forest and Illeria Mountains. The Merfolk still refused to join, safe in their watery domain. Fighting continued for near a century.

Finally, after so many years of bloodshed, the Merfolk could take it no longer and called a meeting between the leaders of every race. This meeting was deemed the Council of Elders. A treaty was drawn up and stipulated that while any person of any race could walk through the lands unhindered, as a people, each race would not seek to push the boundaries of their territories. Each race was given no more and no less than what had been their original territory. The Alvor were given the forest, the Torrpeki the mountains, the Buluo the plains, the dragons the volcanoes, and the Merfolk the oceans. To further unify these newly formed "nations", the Council of Elders combined the existing five elements and created humans.

Due to them being a combination of the existing races and their elemental abilities, there is no one element that presents itself more often than another in the human race overall—although, there can appear to be oversaturation of one element in a generation. The Council of Elders was set to meet once a year or when they were needed to settle a dispute between the races. The members were to consist of the single strongest elemental from each race, regardless of the type of magic they wielded.

For a brief time, humans were subservient to the other races which was ended by The Dragon King. Humans were given the lands west of the Yarav Forest and a seat on the Council of Elders. Progressively, many humans lost the ability to control an element, thus, only a small proportion of the current population are elementals. For the other races, the majority of their numbers are elementals. While each race is known for controlling a certain element, it must be noted that there are exceptions to this rule in abundance.

The text then went into further detail about each race's history, cities, and abilities but Keegan put the book back on the shelf and was about to begin wandering around when Reven appeared.

"Kade wants you."

She got to her feet. "I'd've thought y'all 'd've sent Jared to get me."

Reven stared at her for a second before managing to parse her words. "Kade wanted t', but then we would 'ave had to find two people instead o' one."

"I told you to stay with us," Kade said crossly as she entered the back room.

He and Jared sat at a square table. Across from them was a man with dark gray hair and deep brown eyes, his skin a series of mountains and valleys. She presumed him to be the owner.

As he scrutinized her, she saw surprise, confusion, and worry blemish his features.

"Eh," she shrugged, "close enough."

Kade made introductions, the irritation in his voice noticeable.

"Hi," she acknowledged Thaddeus with a rigid wave. "Whatcha want, Kade?"

"Thaddeus wishes to speak with you."

She crossed her arms. "Okay…"

"Tell him about... yourself," Kade instructed, waving a hand towards her.

"I thought *he* wanted to talk to me."

"He does."

"Then why hasn't he said a word to me?"

Kade was about to respond when Thaddeus said, "You must stay with us while in Suttan."

"No, we—" Kade started quickly.

"I insist. Reven, take them back to Gydrick's to retrieve their belongings while I talk to Keegan."

Kade yielded with a scowl, his chair scraping against the floor. He stomped from the room, pulling Reven and Jared out by the fronts of their shirts.

Thaddeus motioned to the now empty chair.

Guardedly, Keegan took a seat. "I've never seen him listen to anyone."

"Neither have I," Thaddeus revealed lightheartedly. "May I see your hands?"

She set them on the table, palms down.

Thaddeus gently picked up her left hand, turning it over and running a finger over the marks on her wrist.

A shiver coursed down her spine.

"Kade was not lying."

She pulled her hand away. "About what?"

"You, possessing all five elements."

"Why is everyone so shocked by that?"

"Do you know why a soul can only innately control one element?"

"No."

"When two elements are selected by a body—"

"Wait, you can pick what element you want?"

"No, it is randomized. When I say selected, I mean the specific element that will present itself. When two manifests, they battle each other, tearing apart the person from the inside. Yet, inexplicably, they are in perfect harmony within you."

She shrugged, "I don't know what to tell you." They were silent for a moment. "Why do they react like that?"

"The elements counter each other like water and oil."

"Why?"

Thaddeus's eyes twinkled as his lips pulled back into a small smile. "You will have to ask someone more knowledgeable than I."

"If people can't have two elements, how do you know having two will kill you?"

"On very rare occasions, a child is born with two elements. None of them have lived longer than a few months."

"I haven't been an elemental that long, it's possible this could still kill me."

"I doubt it."

"Why?"

"Have your organs begun to fail?"

"No."

"Then you shall live."

With a grimace, she commented, "I wouldn't bet money on that."

"You underestimate yourself."

"No, I'm realistic."

Thaddeus leaned back in the chair. "You seem—" he broke off.

"I'm what?"

Thaddeus rose to his feet. "All in good time."

Keegan eyed him but decided not to press. She watched as he ascended the stairs in the back corner of the room.

A few minutes later he returned and walked out into the body of the shop. "You are more than welcome to wander around until the boys return."

‡‡‡

Aron stood in the chamber that housed the Looking Glass. The surface of the full-length mirror rippled, and Connery's image replaced Caius'. He and his brothers stood behind their father, half listening to what was being said—feigning inattention in his case.

"We followed them to Suttan, but have not found them," Connery reported. "I have enlisted the help of the city guard. So while they made it into the city, they will not make it out."

"Who is 'they'?" Caius growled.

Connery paused. "Kade and another man identified as Jared Sieme."

Rage contorted Caius' face. "I sent you on a simple mission! How hard is it to capture one girl?"

"We might have succeeded had we known she was an earth elemental and prepared accordingly."

Caius froze. "She is not an elemental; I checked myself."

145

"Brennian saw her practicing with Jared, and Thahan confirmed it when he saw the mark. He and Cralter caught up to them outside of Drath."

"If they found them, why are they not in custody?"

"Kade killed Cralter, and the girl was able to disarm Thahan."

"When you return, you will answer for your incompetence."

"We did manage to capture an elemental, a boy by the name of Nico Sieme, who was able to stand against Kade for a time; he will make a wonderful addition to your army."

"I do not want him; I want the girl. Find her!" Caius roared and stormed out, completely ignoring his sons.

Braxton, Kolt, and Aron waited cautiously for a moment before they too made their way from the room.

‡‡‡

With the horses boarded in a communal stable, they headed back. Jared and Reven made small talk, while Kade remained silent. Reven led the way through the shop, lest Kade, who had never understood why Thaddeus made it so difficult to get through the place, got them lost again.

Thaddeus was behind the counter again. "Your friend is in the back."

Jared and Reven ambled past and greeted Keegan.

As Kade walked by, Thaddeus grabbed his arm. "There is something you need to know."

Kade rounded the counter and waited patiently.

Thaddeus hesitated.

"Well? Say it already."

Reaching into his vest, Thaddeus produced a yellowed envelope, which he sat on the counter and slid across. "Do what you will, but you impart this upon others when the time is right."

"What does that mean?"

"You will understand once you have read it." Thaddeus patted him on the back before walking away.

Kade stared after him, then returned his attention to the letter. The parchment was browned from age and worn where it had been unfolded and refolded countless times.

Carefully, he opened the page.

Dearest Father,

146

If you are reading this, then I have likely perished at the hands of those I called comrades for the past six years. Granted, in their eyes, it is justified as I have deceived them. But do not think less of me; I have betrayed no one, only always stood against. These six years you have seen me not I have been a member of the Vosjnik, as a spy for the Lazado.

For the most part, my time with them yielded standard information that I passed on, but recently I had to act. The Blind Prophet Alyck, for the first time, made a voluntary prophecy to Caius on the twentieth of April. 'A child is about to be born who shall play a part in your demise. Search high, search low, but look no further than Suttan. Find it if you can, but know this, as long as it remains in this world, your tale is drawing to a close.'

Caius immediately ordered the Vosjnik to find the child. But before we left, Alyck found me, strange in itself because Caius keeps him locked away in the castle's belly. He implored me to find the child before the others. When I asked why, he said, 'Because this is the one who begins and ends it all, the center upon which the revolution will circle, the conduit of our freedom. I know who you are, Rosh Broyker; I know you yearn to change our fate. This is the chance for you to do so, but only if you are quick. Caius has chosen the path that the prophecy will take so do as he says and travel to Suttan. The child will be fathered by Kagen and mothered by Korissa. Bring it to the center of the Mountain of Marble. But remember this, you can only save one.'

Kade paused; Kagen and Korissa were his parents' names. He leaned against the wall and let himself slide down until he sat on the floor.

He was right; I do want to change our future. We arrived in Suttan on the fifth of May and the Vosjnik wasted no time beginning their search. Any infant found to be less than thirty-five days of age was killed, no exceptions. Any child older than thirty-five days and not an elemental was spared. Any elemental found, regardless of age, was to be escorted to the city's castle to be dealt with later. After we cleared a house, we chalked an 'x' above the doorframe.

It took me over a month to find them and when I did, Korissa had just given birth. At first, Kagen and Korissa resisted relinquishing the babe to me, as they assumed I was working for the king.

His heart pounded against his breastbone. He had grown up with his parents; how was this possible?

After I explained the situation and with much persuading, they agreed with heavy hearts to relinquish their daughter to me.

Kade's head reeled. *Daughter?*

Before I left, Kagen scrawled a few words onto a piece of parchment. 'Give her this,' he said, 'Let her know we love her.' He had written four words: Her name is Keegan.

Kade's breath caught in his throat. Could it be... was Keegan his sibling? *No.*

With the child, I fled. We are currently halfway to our destination, the Mountain of Marble—or, the castle of Agrielha. For a babe, Keegan is remarkably well behaved. Seldom does she cry, preferring to stare at me inquisitively. I regret taking her, as she needs a mother's milk, but it could not be avoided. As a life elemental, I have found a way around this by transferring energy to her whenever she screams for food, but I fear it may stunt her growth.

By now, you must be wondering why I am telling you this. First and foremost, you are my father and deserve to know what happened to your only son. Second, because you are one of the last Keepers of Prophecy. Third, because I request that you help my wife and unborn child with whatever they need. Finally, because I must ask another favor. Korissa gave birth to a second child, a boy they named Kade. I ask you to look after him. I would do it myself, but I suspect my time in this world is about to end.

Forever and always your son,
Rosh

Kade reread the last few lines again, then shakily lowered the letter from his field of vision, understanding at last; he and Keegan were twins. He jumped up and stalked into the warren of shelves, with each step his fury growing until he could contain it no more.

The muscles in his arm tensed and his fist met the hard wood of a shelf. There was a splintering crack and he stared at the end of the shelf; there was barely a dent. He looked down at his fist and saw blood dripping from his broken hand.

Raven, he thought.

His friend replied, *Yes?*

148

I need you.

Where 're you?

Figure it out. He leaned against the wall and waited.

It wasn't long before Reven arrived.

"Heal this," he said angrily.

Reven examined the hand. "What did ya get int' a fight with?"

"Bookshelf."

"Can I ask why?"

"No."

Reven took a deep breath and began to heal his hand.

It began to tingle as the splintered bones became whole again and the skin stitched itself together.

"What d' you 'ave there?" Reven asked, noticing the letter.

Kade tucked the parchment into his tunic. "Nothing."

"He gave it to you," Reven said quietly.

"Pardon?"

"Father's letter."

Kade eyed him. "How do you know about that?"

"I 'm a Keeper o' Prophecy, too; it 's my job to know 'bout that."

Kade gritted his teeth.

"Do n't worry, I 'ill not tell Keegan. Come on now, Grandfather wants us in the backroom."

"For what?"

"He did n't say."

‡‡‡

Braxton exited the darkness that surrounded him and came into the anterior room. From the clinking of metal, he knew the griffins were awake. He took a torch off the wall and brought it into the stable.

The twelve griffins stared at him, hardly balking at the sudden brightness.

Any word? Crowlin asked.

"The girl continues to evade the Vosjnik," Braxton informed them.

A sense of ease overcame the griffins.

Braxton made his way over to Iwin. "You speak the Old Language." It was said as a statement but possessed the elements of a question.

I do, Iwin answered, his glossy eyes giving no hint of what he was thinking.

"Will you help me translate something?"

149

No. The answer was simple but stung. *I would sooner break my wings than give you information to further enslave the world.*

The silence from the other griffins told Braxton that while they agreed, the malice behind the words was unfounded. Having to swallow the hurt, he made his way through the stable to the hidden passage.

Just as the door was closing, Myrish spoke to him, *Alyck knows the Old Language.*

He paused. Why would Alyck make him get the translation when he could do it himself? He headed back to his room to retrieve the key to the Blind Prophet and made his way over, running his thumb over the key absentmindedly. Inside, he found Alyck waiting for him.

"Why?" he asked.

"Why what?" Alyck parroted.

"Why make me work when you know the Old Language?"

"Why not? It will not harm you to learn it."

"Tell me what it says."

"Oh, come now, you are over halfway done, finish it yourself."

"Translate it."

"No."

He eyed his uncle angrily and turned to leave.

"Oh, just as a reference, it is plural."

"What?"

"Finish translating and you will understand."

Braxton let the door slam behind him and stomped to his room in a foul mood; Alyck always knew how to get him into a state.

At his desk, he pulled out the *Evolution of Languages* and began trying to parse the prophecy again. 'While you have slaughtered —child of the dragon, she will rise again from the ashes by your own doing. Rule while you can, false lord, for it will only be for the moment. A child will come who can challenge you. From the fire, from the earth, from adversity, from the...'

It was mostly complete, but after what Alyck said, there must be something he was mistranslating. He let the book fall open heavily and rested his head on a hand. Angrily, he turned the pages, struggling to find the translation for *payn*. Eventually finding it to mean 'path'.

He moved onto '*ri luxyen*'. It meant 'of exile'. By the time he finished the fourth line, the sky was pastel colored with the sun halfway below the horizon.

‡‡‡

In the back room, Reven took the last empty seat, forcing Kade to stand against the wall.

"I suppose it is time I tell what I know," Thaddeus said, more to Reven and Kade than the others.

Keegan had a pained look upon her face. "Why do I get the feeling I'm not gonna like what you're about to say?"

Thaddeus ignored her comment, "A few days before the rightful ruling queen, Seleena Vælar, was dethroned, a prophecy was made."

"How does this have anything to do with us?" Keegan asked. "From what I understand that was like two hundred years ago."

"237," Jared corrected.

Thaddeus looked at her knowingly. "It has everything to do with you."

"Okay…" Keegan said, "I'll play along. Who made this prophecy?"

"The Blind Prophet Angela Alaga."

Keegan stared at him confused.

"With each ruling bloodline, a prophet is designated. While someone of immediate relation to that bloodline remains on the throne, that prophet can live indefinitely. In exchange for their sight, the prophet gains the power of foresight. The pro—"

She interrupted again, "How could you know about this prophecy? Cause again, hasn't Caius ruled for like, two hundred years?"

"237," Jared corrected.

"Thank you, Jared," she said through gritted teeth.

Thaddeus continued, "With each Blind Prophet, comes a Keeper of Prophecy, though we have a normal lifespan. My ancestor was training to become the next Keeper when the prophecy was made, and we have passed it down through the generations."

Kade stared blankly at the wall, only half listening.

Thaddeus began to recite, "Four children shall defeat the despot. To rouse, drive, intercede, and assuage his companions is one's self-given duty. A life of displacement one must lead. To right the wrong is one's ambition. To sit upon the throne is one's right by ancient blood. Black and white yet compelled to stand in spite. To each their own misfortune; the lies of the mother shall condemn the first, the light before the thunder shall be the second's demise, the steel of the blade shall cast down the third, forbidden love shall be the ruin of the fourth. Twenty fingers from their birth must we count until revolution is sparked by the one of all elements."

Keegan rested her head against her hands. "Great. Anything else I should know?"

The words caught Kade's attention and he was glad her back was to him.

Noticing Thaddeus' quick glance to him, she turned. "Do you know something?"

Kade remained silent.

Her frown deepened and she stood, the chair scraping against the floor. "Well then."

"Where 're you going?" Reven asked.

"Anywhere that isn't here," she flared, storming away. "I can't deal with this right now."

"What 's there to deal with?" Reven questioned.

"The fact that there's a pretty good chance I'm gonna die—painfully—I'm involved in some crazy war, oh, and let's not forget that a bat-shit crazy king wants me dead!" When nothing more was said, she made her exit.

"Follow her," Thaddeus requested.

Kade bit, "How do you want me to do that?"

"You know how."

CHAPTER 18

Jared's mind was still processing things. Keegan was right; their lives were about to become filled with even more difficulties and hardships. He took a deep breath, letting it out slowly.

"Take a seat," Reven said to Kade.

"Thaddeus spoke of four children, yet there are only three of us," Jared stated.

"Right you 're," Reven said, "there's a fourth who 'ill join you, though I do n't know who he 's."

"Some forgotten, bastard royal by the sounds of it," Kade answered.

Jared studied him; something was off. His eyes were glazed, his expression completely blank, and his skin slightly sallow. "What's wrong?"

"Nothing," Kade responded meekly.

Jared changed his mind about wanting to know; if the information affected Kade as it did then he had no desire to be encumbered by it either. "Where's Keegan?"

"Front door."

They sat in silence.

Out in the body of the shop, they could hear Thaddeus shuffling around. Then, with his work done, he bid them good night. "Do not stay up too late and *do try* to keep out of trouble."

"Yes, Grandfather."

Silence once more.

Trying to let his mind wander, Jared glanced at Kade, who was sitting as stiff as a board, a worried, unsure look upon his face. "Is everything fine?"

Kade shook his head, his eyebrows creasing further. With a scowl, he muttered, "Noxþilk, Keegan, just couldn't stay out of trouble."

"What are you talking about?"

"She got herself kidnapped," Kade griped.

Jared jumped to his feet. "By who?"

"No idea; her thoughts are too muffled to tell."

"Muffled by what?" Reven asked.

"Walls I presume," Kade answered harshly. "Vitt, I can't sense her at all now."

"What does that mean?" Jared pressed.

"She must've been taken underground."

Jared let out a stream of curses.

"That door still in Downey's Alley?" Kade asked Reven.

"Yeah. Why?"

"That's where she was. You two stay here, I'll go *retrieve* her."

Reven laughed, "Good luck getting int' the underworld. It 's been five years since anyone 'as seen your royiken face; they 'ill not rem'ber you."

Kade gave a sly grin. "Just don't get in my way."

They left before Jared could protested at being left behind and he began to pace anxiously.

He lost track of time and it could have been hours or days—or moments. He snapped out of his mind, thinking he'd heard the front door close and his heart skipped a beat. It wasn't long before Reven and Keegan appeared from between the bookshelves and he sighed in relief.

Blood covered Keegan's nose and mouth and from the way Reven supported her, there were other injuries.

"Let 's get you cleaned up," Reven said.

"I'm fine," she asserted.

Reven gently placed a hand on her side making her wince. "You sure 'bout that?"

"Where's our stuff?"

"Upstairs. What d' you need?"

"My t-shirt."

"Your what?"

Tiredly, she explained, "Black shirt."

Jared sat in the chair beside her. "What were you thinking?" When she didn't respond, he snapped to get her attention.

"What?"

"Is everything all right?"

Through gritted teeth, she answered, "Yes."

"What were you thinking?"

"Wha'do you mean?"

"Why'd you leave the shop?"

She avoided his gaze, mumbling, "I dunno."

"Keegan."

"I wanted out."

"Why?" Jared asked, wiping away some of the dried blood from her face.

"I- I just don't- I don't wanna be here. I don't wanna deal with any of this." She flinched and took the rag from him.

"And Kade and I do?"

"No, but you're used to this world."

"What are we going to do with you?"

154

She gave him a depressed look and shrugged.

Reven returned and tossed her the shirt. "That's very revealing."

"Not really," Keegan said, catching it and resting her head against the back of the chair.

Reven squatted in front of her. "Are you all right?"

"Tired, sore, beat to hell, and sick of y'all asking me if I'm okay," she answered grumpily.

Reven turned to Jared, "Why do you n't head up t' bed?"

Jared crossed his arms. "Why should I?"

"I 'm just going t' tend to her bruises; no need for you t' stay up 's well."

"Fine," Jared said, heading towards the stairs. "No more running away."

"Hardy har har," was Keegan's response.

"Take your pick of the beds," Reven told him.

Upstairs, a single candle on a dresser provided light. The room was furnished sparsely with two dressers and two beds, which were pushed against opposite walls, a door set between them. He assumed the door led to Thaddeus' room.

Keegan, he thought, wondering if she would discern his voice from everyone else's.

I swear to god, if you ask me if I'm okay, I'm gonna come up there and slap you.

Then you'll have to do so. Are you all right?

For the umpteenth time, yes. Now stop asking!

For some reason, her words hurt. *Good night.*

There was a pause, *Night. And thanks for checking up on me; as much as I bitch 'bout it, I do appreciate it.*

‡‡‡

Reven stared at her for a moment before situating himself in the chair next to her. He reached forward and placed his hand on her cheek.

"Wha—"

"Hush."

Unsure of what to do, she sat still and began to feel a tingling in her cheek—not a painful feeling, but one that made staying stationary difficult. Reven pulled his hand away and the sensation disappeared. She ran a hand over her skin. "What'd you do?"

"Healed you."

"How'd you do that?"

155

"I 'm a life elemental, remember?" He extended a hand towards her face again, placing it over her eye this time.

She felt the same sensation as before and when he removed his hand, asked, "So that's what life elementals do, heal?"

"'Mongst other things." He casually placed a hand on her collarbone and the side of her neck.

"What else can y'all do?" she asked, rolling her shoulders.

"Sit still. Healing, obviously, make things grow, control living things, and change our 'ppearance. There 's much more you can do, but those 're the big things."

"That's how you were able to look like Kade."

"Yes."

As his hand fell away, Kade came through the doorway.

He glared at her, arms folded across his chest, blood splattered across his torso and face. "Can you not stay out of trouble?"

"It's not like I went looking for it," she responded defensively.

"I swear, you—"

"Not now," Reven said, standing. "We 'ave all had a long day; this can wait till the mornin'."

"Normally, I'd agree," Kade opened, "but I don't know what asinine thing she'll do overnight."

"It 's fairly hard t' get into trouble while sleeping."

Kade stared blankly at his friend. "You haven't spent that much time with her; you'd be amazed."

"It can wait," Reven said, placing a hand on Kade's shoulder then returned his attention to Keegan said, "It 'ill take me a while to heal your ribs; can I do it in the mornin'?"

"Sure," she groaned, pushing herself from the chair, and beginning to make her way to the stairs.

"Where are you going?" Kade demanded.

"To bed. I'm tired and don't feel like getting bitched at."

"Bitched at?" Reven asked.

"Yelled at," Keegan explained. Over her shoulder, she said to Kade, "You coming or not?"

"It doesn't appear I have a choice."

"You don't *have to*," she pointed out. "You could go do something else. Or someone else." Halfway up, she turned and headed back down.

"Where are you going?" Kade demanded, blocking her way.

She pointed to the table. "To get my t-shirt."

Kade eyed her for a second, then let her by.

"Y'all head up," she said, noticing neither he nor Reven had moved.

"What are you planning on doing?"

"Changing." With a small smile she added, "I mean, y'all're more than welcome to watch, but then I'd have to kill you."

Reven stared at her, obviously surprised by her brass.

Kade began pushing him up the stairs.

"Stop that."

"Trust me, not worth it," Kade said as the second floor swallowed them.

She tossed her shirt onto the table and began removing the dress, quickly finding there was no good way to pull it off without causing her ribs to smart. And putting the shirt on didn't prove to be any easier.

She blew out the candle on the table and blindly made her way up the stairs. Upstairs, she shuffled along in the darkness, accidentally kicking Kade.

"Watch it," he grumbled, slapping her leg.

"Sorry," she whispered, stepping over him and putting her hands out.

Sitting on the edge of the bed, she kicked off her shoes then gingerly swung her legs up and laid back. Sleep came quickly.

‡‡‡

Wind buffeted him, making it hard to stay on his feet, and the sword in his hand was bathed in purple blood.

An angry voice screamed at him, "Betrayer! Marmarda! Soucer!"

He could not tell where it came from and it seemed to echo about.

"Az ryla sarig," he cried. "Plazde, haxnug!"

"Betrayer! Marmarda! Soucer!" the voices repeated relentlessly.

Talons reached towards him, scraping at his flesh, making pain radiate across his body. The world turned black, darkness coating him like a blanket while voices began to call out from afar.

Three men emerged from the darkness and he recognized two of them: Aron and Kade. The third, was a stranger. His hair was brown like mud, and he had eyes of a similar shade. His jaw was squared and there was a slight upturn to the corners of his eyes.

"Jyken eya meki lunviyda zæ psodæ ri ayþ drackyn, æay woth viæn nuþ qalx ayþ æyscs fayo eyar oywn þen," Aron said.

"Nackh jyken eya casne, fackyon ictotm, iruh du woth unla ryo iruh ayþ adæmno," Kade added.

Braxton tried to speak, but no words came forth. He had no choice but to listen.

157

Together the three spoke, "Psodæ woth yarv rhæpn casne jappec eya."

The man he did not recognize said, "Qalx ayþ buna, qalx ayþ waysne, qalx okæpyio, qalx ayþ payn ri luxyen, zæ psodæ woth viæn."

Suddenly, he was awake. Confused, he tried to stand and realized he had become tangled in his sheets. Once he had extricated himself, he paused to think. The dream's details were fuzzy, but there was one thing he recalled perfectly—pain.

CHAPTER 19

Lucas walked down the now busy streets; an hour after sunrise there had been few souls about. The morning had been long, but surprisingly, he hadn't detested the work as much as he'd presumed. What Virgil had said about Waylan was true—he was prickly and stubborn but meant well.

Waylan had spent the better part of the morning teaching him the tools of the trade. A plethora of instruments hung on the back wall of the shop or rested on tables. Waylan had told him the name and use of each.

There was an assortment of hammers, tongs, and punches, whose uses were self-explanatory, but other items, such as the fullers and swages, needed clarification. He'd learned their functions quickly, which seemed to please Waylan. At lunch, he was sent home so Waylan could get some work done.

Lucas climbed the steps to the Fulpe house and entered. He'd stopped knocking, as, for the foreseeable future, this was also his home. Inside, all was quiet, and he headed upstairs.

Alivia poked her head out from the drawing room. "Oh, you are home," she said excitedly. "Come join me for lunch."

"I'm not particularly hungry," he dismissed.

"Just a little snack then."

He sighed; she would find a way to refute all his excuses. Acquiescing, he made his way to the drawing room, which was light and airy. There was a black divan, a couch, and a few plush armchairs. He went to sit in the armchair, but Alivia pulled him over to the divan. On the table in front of them was a plate of lemon squares.

"Help yourself."

He took one.

"Are they not just lovely?" she asked.

He declined to respond; it was too sugary for his liking.

Alivia reached for one, making sure to situate herself closer to him. "So, tell me, what is it like working for a smith?"

"I haven't worked there long enough to form a true opinion," he said, moving down the divan.

She placed a hand on his leg. "A first impression then."

Slowly, he told her, "I think it'll be fine."

"Only fine?" she asked, leaning in.

He jumped up. "Alright, let's get one thing straight. Alivia, you're a lovely girl, but I have absolutely no interest in you." Lucas walked away before she could respond.

‡‡‡

Keegan yawned and groaned as she stretched, feeling the soreness in her side. It was hard to tell what time it was in a room with no windows, but she guessed it was probably early afternoon. She sat up and carefully got to her feet. Thanks to her socks, she managed to slide over the wooden floors.

On her way downstairs, she noticed a mirror and lifted the shirt to look at the bruising on her side. The area around her ribs was dark. She was no stranger to bruises, but to see one so large and dark was unsettling. She ran her fingers lightly over the edge of the bruise and clenched her jaw in discomfort.

Letting the shirt fall, she looked at her reflection in its entirety. Even though her borrowed pants were black, she could see patches of dirt. Her face was devoid of bruising, thanks to Reven. She reached up and ran a hand through her hair; it was slick with grease. Quickly, she pulled it into a bun and began to slowly make her way downstairs.

From the top of the stair, she saw the boys sitting at the table. Kade and Reven were talking while Jared read from a thick, leather-bound book. As she descended, she noticed voices beginning to mingle with her thoughts. It wasn't that they hadn't been present upstairs, but up there they were soft, and she barely noticed them.

"So nice of you to join us," Kade said, hearing her groan with each step.

"Yeah, yeah, yeah."

"What were you thinking?"

"Oh god, we're starting with this already?"

"Yes, because apparently, it's something we need to talk about."

She made her way to the table. "What is?"

"You shouldn't run off."

"I goofed," she shrugged. "Sorry, I shoulda known some asshats would try to sell me as a hooker."

"Yes, you should have."

"That was sarcasm."

"I can heal your ribs now," Reven interjected.

With a look of relief, she said, "Yes. Please."

He pulled his chair closer to her then was silent, as if waiting for her to do something.

"Right, you need me to pull up my shirt."

Kade said snidely, "Seems you'll lift your shirt for any man."

She knew he meant to get a rise from her. "At least I won't drop my pants for any man like you."

Reven snickered as he placed his hands on her side.

She leaned against the back of the chair, letting him work his magic. "What time is it?"

"Midafternoon," Jared answered without looking up from his book.

Keegan gave a small nod. "Figured. Haven't slept that late in ages; I'm usually up by like ten, eleven, at the latest."

Reven looked at her confused. "What 're you talking 'bout?"

She shook her head. "I keep forgetting y'all don't have clocks. It's like mid to late morning."

"Oh."

She looked to Kade, "So… can you explain how to put up that wall thingamajig?"

"I told you," he said, "it's just something I picked up."

"Well, help me pick it up." She shifted in the chair.

"Sit still," Reven instructed.

"Practice," Kade said bluntly.

She glared at him. "No shit, Sherlock. But I kinda have to understand what I'm doing before I can practice said thing."

Reven gave her a baffled look, trying to work out her first phrase.

"Fine," Kade said gruffly. "Keep me out."

Keegan realized all voices but her own were gone, "Wait, what're—" then noticed another entity in her head. The feeling was strange, like ice water rushing through her mind.

Push me out, Kade told her.

Closing her eyes, she gathered her thoughts and pushed back against him. It was like running into a brick wall. She threw herself at him again. This time, he moved slightly. Repeating the action, she slowly pushed Kade out. Once he was removed, she opened her eyes, surprised at how much energy it had taken.

Kade sat in his chair like nothing had happened. "It's a start. Again."

She jolted, feeling the icy tendril again. Over the initial shock, she sent her consciousness at his like a battering ram and slowly pushed him towards the edge of her mind. As he neared it, he slipped past. She gritted her teeth and started over. Again, once she had him on the outskirts of her mind, he slipped back in.

"Stop doing that," she snapped.

"Make me," Kade said snarkily.

"That's my line."

She closed her eyes and tried to force him out again but several more times he played a game of cat and mouse. Finally, her frustration boiled over and her consciousness grabbed the tail of Kade's tendril and dragged him out.

Once he was removed, Keegan retreated to the innards of her mind, though she could still feel him testing her, trying to re-enter. Her frustration acted like a barrier to keep him out.

"You managed to put up a wall," Kade said.

She smiled. "Really?"

Her guard lowered and he slipped back in.

"Goddamn it."

"Don't let your guard down."

She reached over and slapped Kade upside the head and his presence disappeared.

"Sit still," Reven chided.

Kade glared crossly at her.

"Well, at least I've kinda got it," she said.

"Would you sit still," Reven said irritated as she continued to wiggle.

"Sorry. How much longer is this gonna take?"

"A while," Reven answered unenthusiastically.

"Ugh." Keegan let her head drop forward. "Can I get a book or something?"

"No, just sit still."

"You'd best let her," Kade spoke up.

Grumbling, Reven leaned back in the chair. "Fine."

"Back in a jiffy. Erff," she complained, popping out of the chair. Excitedly, she walked into the bookshop. Striding past the counter, she overlooked Thaddeus and another man with him.

Thaddeus called her back. "How are you feeling? I heard about last night."

She bit the inside of her cheek. "Fine."

"Ah, where are my manners? Taite, this is Keegan Digore. Keegan, Taite Ault."

She glanced at the man beside her, who was barely taller than she, and gave him a once over. He was stocky, with slightly greasy brown hair and jade green eyes. Based upon appearances, he seemed like he'd be a somewhat decent person, but something was off. "Uh, nice to meet you," she said, holding out a hand.

Taite looked at her blankly, then turned back to Thaddeus. "I'll need a week. There are some matters I must attend to before I can take them."

"Thank you," Thaddeus said, smiling.

"By them," Keegan remarked, "I hope you're not referring to Jared, Kade, and I."

Taite ignored her and continued his conversation with Thaddeus. "Not a problem, old friend. I'll see you in a week."

Aggravated that she was being ignored, Keegan snapped, "Are you deaf or just stupid?"

Taite started towards the door. "Women should be seen, not heard."

Open-mouthed, she stared after him. "You son of a—"

"Keegan," Thaddeus cut her off, knowing how the sentence would end.

‡‡‡

After Keegan left the room, Reven asked, "Is she always that..."

"Annoying," Kade offered.

Jared proposed, "Stubborn."

Reven thought for a moment, "Both."

Shrugging, Jared answered, "That's just the way she is. Though, I'd say Kade's just as stubborn."

Kade glared at him. "I'm only as stubborn as necessary."

Reven burst into laughter.

Scowling, Kade kicked the chair out from under Reven, sending him tumbling to the floor.

Reven used his magic to send Kade flying backwards.

"Stop fighting," Thaddeus called from the bookshop.

Slowly, they got to their feet. Gradually, Reven's glare transformed into a smile following with a hearty laugh, which Kade joined in. They righted the chairs and retook their seats.

Jared reopened his book and hoped neither noticed him chuckling.

"What 're you reading?" Reven asked.

Jared showed him the spine. "Earth Elemental Techniques."

Kade nodded his approval. "If you see any techniques you want to learn, let me know."

"Sure," Jared answered with a look of uncertainty.

"Kade 's mastered just 'bout every skill in that book. Learned 'em so he could join the Vosjnik," Reven said sourly.

"Can we move past that?" Kade said gruffly. "It was five years ago."

"This one," Jared said, flipping the book around so Kade could see.

"The Rimor. Not the easiest skill, but also not the hardest, and it's fairly useful."

"What is it exactly?" Reven asked.

"An immobilization technique," Jared answered.

"Just so you know, you'll never stop the Vosjnik with such a weak technique." Kade told him. "Something along the lines of the Zoutsi's what you need."

Jared crossed his arms, "Never heard of it."

"You probably don't know the name of any techniques," Kade responded. "And not many humans have heard of the Zoutsi."

"How do you know of it then?"

"The Vosjnik captured a Lazado earth elemental once. I learned it by analyzing his memories and he learned it from the Torrpeki."

"Can you teach it to me?"

Kade shook his head. "You're not at a level that you can do it. I'll let the Lazado teach you."

"I have no intentions of waiting that long to kill—" Jared started, cutting himself off as Keegan returned.

"Okay, good ta go," she said, dropping a book on the table. She rolled up her shirt, and taking a quick look at the bruising, it wasn't as bad as before, all areas of blue having faded to a deep yellow. Turned to Kade she said, "Taite seems like a real asshole."

Kade raised an eyebrow. "When did you meet Taite?"

"Just now. By the sounds of it, he's taking us to the Lazado."

Kade strode from the back room, slamming the door shut.

"I guess I'm not the only one who doesn't like Taite," Keegan said slowly.

"I guess so," Jared said, returning to his book.

‡‡‡

Kade stormed into the body of the bookshop and slammed his hands on the counter. "No," he said furiously. "Absolutely not."

"No?" Thaddeus repeated.

"Taite is *not* taking us to the Lazado."

Thaddeus moved from behind the counter, and taking a stack of books, headed towards the warren of shelves. "And why is that?"

"I don't trust that rat." Seeing him struggle with the weight of the books, Kade took them.

Thaddeus began placing books on a shelf. "I am sorry you feel that way."

"W—"

"You need Taite. Do you think it is easy to get to Edreba?"

164

"Yes," Kade answered exasperated.

Thaddeus grinned. "There is a reason Kojotes exist."

"We don't need him."

Placing the last volume on the shelf, Thaddeus said, "You do. There is much about reaching the Lazado you have not accounted for."

"Such as?"

"Do you know how to get there?"

"That's why we came to you."

"Getting there is only half the battle. They do not readily accept strangers into their stronghold."

"You can vouch for us."

Thaddeus placed his hands on his shoulders, "These old bones of mine cannot make that long journey."

"We will—"

"For once in your life, trust me. Taite will not lead you astray. Now, end of conversation."

Kade started stammering.

Thaddeus added, "You leave in a week," before walking away.

CHAPTER 20

Reven spent a large part of the afternoon healing Keegan's ribs. Often, he needed to yell at her to sit still, so when he was finally done, he seemed relieved, and exhausted.

"Try not to' break any more bones," he told her, devouring a loaf of bread. "Healing takes so much out o' me."

She nodded. "Thanks."

"D' you want t' get Kade? Grandfather should 'ave dinner ready shortly."

On the second floor, she found Kade sitting on one of the beds looking at something unfamiliar to her. "Whatcha got there?" she asked, surprising him.

"A portrait of my parents," he answered.

She took a seat beside him. The portrait was no more than a few inches long, small enough to fit in a pocket. The couple in the painting looked strikingly like Kade, or rather, he looked very much like them.

The woman had rich brown hair that fell in gentle waves over her shoulders. Her nose was small, giving it a button-like appearance. Pale, sea green eyes gave Keegan a yearning for the ocean.

The man stood above the woman, a hand on her shoulder. He bore a cheeky smile and his red hair stood out in relief like a spark. Light freckles dotted his features and matched the hue of his brown eyes.

She had to stop herself from laughing at his large forehead. "Your dad looks like a real character."

"A what?" Kade questioned.

"Like he was a fun person."

Kade smiled sadly. "He was. He Always found something to get into. Mostly trouble."

"What were their names?"

"Kagen and Korissa."

"They really liked 'k' names, didn't they?"

"It was a tradition on Father's side. Mother just happened to fit the pattern." Kade looked back at the portrait longingly.

"Were they elementals?"

"Yes. Father was an earth elemental and Mother was water."

From downstairs, Thaddeus called, "Dinner."

Keegan laughed. "That's what I came up to tell you."

‡‡‡

Kade reflected on the earlier moment with Keegan; it felt strange to show her a side of his life that few had seen. It was even stranger to think she should've been part of it.

Dinner passed quickly and afterwards Thaddeus retired for the night.

"Can we get some earth training in?" Keegan asked. The inflections were different from how she normally spoke.

"Absolutely not," he said.

"Goddamnit. Reven said the exact same thing."

"As he should."

"Ugh, do y'all not trust me?"

"No," Raven and Kade answered together.

She looked offended. "Why not?"

Kade gave her a look, "Really? After last night, you shouldn't need to ask."

"But you'll be with me."

"*No.*"

"Then what am I gonna do for a week?"

"Train."

"You just said I couldn't."

"I said you couldn't practice earth magic," Kade explained. "Nothing was said about telepathy and life magic."

"I'm not gonna get to see the sun this week, am I?"

"With any luck, no."

She gave them an annoyed glare before stalking upstairs.

"Do you really intend to keep her indoors all week?" Jared asked.

"Yes. The Vosjnik are probably in the city, and there's no need to increase the chances of them finding us. I can't stop you from training," Kade continued, "but if you do, I recommend doing so at night and having Reven as a lookout."

Jared nodded then looked to Reven. "Are you up for it tonight?"

"As long as it 's a short session," he answered tiredly.

"Let's get started then," Jared said, heading to the back door.

Give me a head's up 'fore you volunteer me for somethin' next time, Reven complained.

Upstairs, Kade found Keegan lying on a bed, staring at the ceiling. "Are you going to be bitter all week?"

She sighed, "No, I just wish y'all wouldn't treat me like a kid that's gonna screw everything up."

"Then stop acting like that."

Her fists clenched and she rolled over to face the wall.

He crossed his arms, hearing her thoughts, which contained many harsh words directed at him. "Say that to my face."

"Get out of my head."

"Make me."

She turned to scowl at him. "I'm *really* not in the mood."

He extended his thoughts and was met with a thick wall of anger. "We'll begin in the morning."

"Whatever."

He heard Reven, *Can we borrow you? Jared needs a target to practice with.*

Kade took a deep breath, *Sure.*

As he made his way downstairs, he stole a glance at Keegan. To help her keep up a wall, he was going to have to keep her angry. While it was the best learning tool, he didn't want to deal with her moodiness all week. *Someone help us all.*

‡‡‡

Jared sat on the stoop with Reven. Behind the shop was a small walled-in garden, enclosed on three sides by buildings and a tall wooden fence on the fourth. They were lucky no windows looked out onto it.

When Kade arrived, he asked, "What do you need me to be a target for?"

"Not so much a target as a victim," Reven answered.

Kade's face took on a highly unamused look, "Let's get this over with. What move are you trying?"

"The Rimor," Jared told him.

Kade stood across the way from him, arms folded.

Jared took a deep breath and reached for his magic. With a jerky movement of his hands, he made the earth rise. Instead of it rising to Kade's knees on both legs, it shot up to his hip, encasing only one leg.

Kade's eyes widened drastically. "Careful there."

"'Pologies," Jared said, lowering the earth.

"Start slowly. This is just practice."

He gave a curt nod. Again, the ground rose only on one leg. Seeing this, he directed more magic to the other. Now it went up the other leg. Several times he tried to correct the imbalance, but it just shifted from side to side.

"You don't do many precise techniques," Kade asserted.

"No."

168

He tried again and had Kade's leg encased up to the middle of a shin when he shook the dirt off and started towards him.

"Best thing to do is work on controlling two very different pieces of earth that require precise dimensions. I would start with a block and an orb."

"Why not continue practicing this?"

"The concept spans many techniques. While you might master this eventually, you'll still struggle with the others. Get the building blocks and the rest comes easy." Kade gave a yawn and headed inside.

Jared crossed his arms, not finding verity in the philosophy.

"I 'd give his way a chance," Reven spoke up, also heading in. "Kade may be a bit of an arse, but 'e knows what 'e 's doing."

CHAPTER 21

"Ready?" Kade asked from across the table.

"I guess," Keegan responded.

While she was still annoyed with him, she managed to keep it from being overly apparent. And he only knew her true feelings because he was already in her head.

She constructed her wall, under the pretense he had yet to attack.

It was flimsy, but it was a good start. In fact, quite impressive given that only yesterday she hadn't been able to construct one consciously. She learnt at an incredible rate, far beyond even Caius' most skilled elementals—far beyond him, and he was said to learn at a lightning pace.

"You gonna attack or just sit there?" she asked, bouncing her knee rapidly.

I already have.

Damn it, she snapped, more at herself than him. *How long've you been in here?*

Not long, he said, removing himself.

"Why didn't I feel you just chillin' out inside my head?"

"If you're not being actively invasive, it's easy to go unnoticed. You'll have to learn to pick up on the subtle changes of someone being passively intrusive. What I'd like to know is how you're learning so fast? Is this part of your powers?"

She bit her lip. "I don't think so. Jared noticed the same thing when he was teaching me earth magic, but even back home, if I really wanted to learn something, I picked it up almost instantaneously."

"Interesting."

She shrugged. "Let's try again."

He gave her a moment to put up a wall then placed a hand on it. It crumbled; it was weaker than the first one. "Are you even trying?"

"Yes," she answered in what might be described as a half-whine.

"Is this something you want to learn?"

"The principles behind it are cool as hell, but... I don't know, I haven't really got an answer for you on that one."

He raised an eyebrow and was about to have her put up a wall again when Reven came through.

"How 's it goin'?" he asked.

She slouched her shoulders, "Lousy."

Knowing he'd probably regret it, Kade revealed one of her thoughts. "Did you know Keegan thinks you're... cute." He didn't need to look at her face to know how she felt; her emotions came rolling like storm waves.

"Cute?" Reven questioned.

"Oh, you know…" Kade started, looking to Keegan. The muscles in her jaw were tight. "Help me here, what's the word I'm looking for?"

Her eyes shot daggers at him.

"Ah, yes, handsome."

Reven gave a small, cocky smile as he walked away. "Why, thank you."

Examining her wall, he found it was much sturdier, having to push and batter before it gave. "Better, but you still need work."

She silently glared at him.

"Are you going to say anything?" He wanted to smile but knew it might push her over the edge.

"You can't do shit like that," she growled.

"Of course, I can."

"No," she said in a calm voice that only emphasized her anger.

"Until you can stop me, I can, and I will."

‡‡‡

The falcon sat heavily on Braxton's arm and the sun was warm on his face. While he had not been fortunate in the hunt, it was still liberating to be outside the castle walls; it was not often his father allowed him to leave the grounds. While Kolt had a little more leeway, it was still not much. However, it was far better than what Aron got; he was fairly certain his youngest brother had never left the castle.

The resident falconer reached up to take the bird from him, and with it gone, he jumped down from the horse. Shading his eyes, he looked up to the roof of the castle and saw what might be a person. Sighing, he made his way across the grass, the men who had gone hawking with him following, grumbling about the day's failure.

He considered going to the bathhouse but decided against it, ready to have some time alone after having to spend the day with the superficial nobles. When he reached his chambers, a servant was still in the process of changing the sheets.

"I apologize, sir," she said flustered. "I'll be done momentarily."

"Take your time, Shiloh," Braxton said with an easy smile.

She gave him a nervous grin, returning to her work. In an attempt to make idle talk, she asked, "How was your day of hawking?"

"Wonderful."

171

"I take it you caught quite a bit then."

"No," he said with a light laugh, "nothing at all."

She seemed confused by his answer, but her work completed, took her leave.

He could tell she wanted nothing more than to be far away from him. As she left, he told her, "Tell your father I really enjoyed his stuffed quail last night."

"Of course, sir," she answered, closing the door.

Alone again, the sun seemed to shine less brightly, and colors became drearier. This was one of the times he wished he had a friend— a true friend, not one of the nobles' sons he was forced to interact with. Of the three siblings, Aron was the only one who had managed the feat.

About a decade ago, Aron had befriended one of the cook's daughters and managed to keep it mostly hidden. Braxton was almost certain he was the only person who knew of the girl, which had occurred by pure happenstance one night when he saw them coming from the secret passage that led to the roof on one of his secret visits to Alyck. He smiled to himself; just knowing Aron had someone with whom he willingly spent time made the day regain some of its brightness.

He went to his desk and pulled out a sheet of paper. It had taken time, but he had finished translating the prophecy. It read, '*While you have slaughtered — child of the dragon, she will rise again from the ashes by your own doing. Rule while you can, false lord, for it shall only be for the moment. A child will come who can defeat you. From the fire, from the earth, from adversity, from the path of exile, this child will rise. But know it will be your own foolishness that will seal your fate, oh wicked king.* '

He had been able to fill in the gaps in most of the places where inkblots had obscured the words, however, he still felt he might have mistranslated something. He kicked off his boots and pulled out a leather notebook from a drawer in his desk. He had spent enough time worrying about things others wanted him to do; he needed time for himself. Taking a stick of graphite, he opened the cover of the sketchbook to a blank page and began to sketch a falcon in flight.

‡‡‡

Earlier, in passing, Shiloh had requested they meet that night. It was unusual for her to set up a meeting in such a manner, but something in her voice implied importance. Now, he stood on the roof as the sun set, casting oranges and pinks into the sky.

When she arrived, she rushed into his arms, pressing her head against his shoulder.

"What is troubling you?" Aron inquired.

"Braxton," she told him, "he knows something."

"How could he possibly know anything?"

"I... I'm not sure. He told me to tell my father that he enjoyed the stuffed quail."

"So?"

"Braxton has never set foot in the kitchens, so how does he know my father is a cook? And, he knew my name."

"None of that is cause for concern," Aron reassured her, tucking a strand of golden hair behind her ears.

"Aron, something's not right."

There will be no happy ending.

He pulled her close. "We are leaving soon and then it will not matter. Neither Braxton, nor anyone else will be able to hurt us. *Ever.*"

Shiloh remained silent then after a moment, she pushed away from him. "I should be getting home. Father will be worrying."

She took a few steps before Aron pulled her back and kissed her. "You are going to be fine. I am not going to let anything happen to you."

"I know." There was something sad about the way she said it, almost as if she did not believe him.

He let her go and was alone on the gable as the stars awoke. Looking up, he muttered to the heavens, "There will be a happy ending." By Sola and Lunos, he swore, there would be a happy ending.

CHAPTER 22

The floor was hard but, compared to the snow and forests he was accustomed to on missions, was considerably better. He'd been training Keegan for four days now and was duly impressed. The wall she could construct was much sturdier, although, she still had trouble maintaining it. Often, she needed help fortifying it and to do that, he divulged some of her inner thoughts. A tricky proposition as he had to choose thoughts that did little harm besides embarrassing her when they became known. But he'd done well at finding that balance.

Beside him, he could hear Keegan breathing softly. Dreams were one of his favorite things to observe; they revealed much about how a person rationalized the world. He slipped into her mind and watched as she reached into a cabinet.

He looked around the room; it was large and airy, and he sat on a high countertop made of dark black-blue granite. Cabinets lined the walls and made up the base of the counters. There was a large sink set within the countertop, halfway filled with dishes. Large items he could not name interrupted the cabinets. One was quite tall and seemed to be made of metal; two handles divided it and there was a quiet whirring coming from it.

Keegan turned and froze upon seeing him. "What're you doing here?" she asked uncharacteristically pleasantly.

"Observing." He pointed to the structure behind her, "What's that tall thing?"

"A fridge. How do you not know what a fridge is?" She began to scrutinize him.

"What does it do?"

"It keeps food cold…"

He watched as the pieces fell into place.

"Son of a bitch. You're invading my dreams now? Seriously, Kade, what the fuck?"

"What a useful device. How does it work?"

"I– I don't know the mechanics of it," she said, giving him a puzzled look. "Why are you in my dreams?"

He looked around. "I'm not sure this is a dream; the details are too crisp. I'd say this is a memory."

She crossed her arms. "Whatever. Either way, you're not supposed to be here."

"I know."

"Then get out."

"Make me and put up a wall."

"Dude, I'm asleep; I can't even control what I'm dreaming about. Or remembering…"

"It's something you'll have to work on." He could feel her anger solidifying into a wall. It was weaker than anything she'd created while awake but was a fair start.

She reached out and slapped him.

There was a sudden pressure on his throat, and he pulled himself from her mind. In the dark, he lay on the floor coughing and spluttering curses. In her sleep, she'd managed to hit him in the throat.

From the bed, she mumbled, "Serves you right."

✦✦✦

She awoke with the feeling that something was amiss but couldn't pinpoint what. Shrugging, she went downstairs. At the table sat Jared, his nose in a book, Reven, and Kade, nursing what appeared to be a steaming cup of tea.

"I didn't take you as a tea person," she commented, taking a seat.

Kade gave her a harsh glare.

"Jeez, what crawled up your butt and died?"

Reven laughed unabashedly.

"Don't you remember?" Kade asked, his voice slightly hoarse.

She shook her head.

"You hit him in the throat," Reven said. "Actually, I 'm impressed 'cause it 'ppears you did it in your sleep."

"She wasn't aiming for my throat though," Kade snapped.

"Or was I," she teased.

Kade's scowl deepened.

"If I wasn't aiming for your throat, where was I aiming for?"

"My face."

"What'd you do to warrant that?"

"I was in your dream," he told her with little remorse.

Her smile faded. "Serves you damn right."

Kade gritted his teeth, clearly doing his best to not give a snide retort. "Work with Raven today; I'm done with you."

"Gladly. At least Reven isn't a blabber-mouth."

The boys looked at her blankly.

She elaborated, "Someone who can't keep a secret."

Rolling his eyes, Kade stood up and walked away.

Turning to Reven, she said, "So, where do we start?"

175

"Healing," he answered. "Cuts and bruises for now, maybe major injuries later, depending on how you do."

‡‡‡

Jared watched as Reven endeavored to teach Keegan life magic. At first, he paid little attention, but as time wore on, he found her to be almost comical. They'd been working for a few hours now and she had yet to perform any act of life magic. He could see how frustrated she was becoming after earth magic had come almost naturally.

She leaned back in the chair, crossing her arms. "Ugh! Why can't I get this? I'm doing everything you tell me to. I break the gem, then focus on the bruise, but nothing happens."

Something dawned on Jared. "Are you accessing earth or life magic?"

"There's a difference?" she asked, her frustrated expression softening.

Reven laughed. "I s'ppose this 's my blunder. For each magic there's a different paika."

"A what?" she questioned.

"A paika. It 's the source of your magic."

"Ohhh, you mean the gem thingy."

"Yes, the gem thingy."

"So, I've been breaking the wrong one for like, three hours?"

"It 'ppears so. The life paika is at the base of your neck."

"Where are the other ones?"

"Fire 's in the heart, air 's in the throat, an' water 's in the right eye."

"Why are the paikas there?"

"I 'm not sure. Now, get t' it."

"Sir, yes, sir," she responded, giving a sarcastic salute. She closed her eyes, and after a moment, commented, "It's purple, like an amethyst."

Reven chuckled, "Now that you 've found it, heal me."

She placed her hands over the bruise on his arm.

Jared put the book down and found himself leaning forward expectantly, even craning his neck. When she removed her hands, there was no sign a bruise had ever existed.

"It looks like we need t' get you more injuries t' heal," Reven said.

"Yeah," she agreed enthusiastically.

Jared immediately noticed Reven tensing.

Keegan too saw the change in his demeanor. "Wait, no."

176

"What do you want?" Kade said from the doorway.

Slowly, Reven got to his feet, "I need you t' hit me."

Keegan started to protest.

Without so much as blinking an eye, Kade punched Reven in the face.

Keegan grimaced sympathetically and began to chastise Kade. She was ignored.

"Again." Reven staggered back slightly but retook his place in front of Kade. "Once more."

Even Jared grimaced that time; Kade took a cheap shot and punched him in the stomach.

Reven hunched over, catching his breath. "Thank you."

"My pleasure," Kade responded, walking back into the shop.

"Why did you do that?" Keegan questioned angrily, making Reven sit.

"You needed somethin' t' practice with."

She gave him an annoyed look and set to work. It took her a while, but she eventually managed it. Once done, she reprimanded, "Don't do that again, or I'll be the one beating you."

"Yes, ma'am."

"Kade's already on his way, isn't he?"

"Unfortunately."

‡‡‡

One more day, Keegan told herself, trudging down the wooden stairs. Soon, they'd finally leave Suttan. While she wasn't looking forward to meager meals and sleeping on the ground again, being stuck inside with Kade made it seem all the better.

Downstairs, Reven was waiting for her, a knife on the table beside him.

"Where's Jared?" she asked, "He usually hangs in here."

"He went t' market with Kade."

As much as she wanted to protest the injustice, there was nothing to do about it now. "What've you got me doing today?"

Reven took the knife, placing the blade against his palm, and pulled it along. A line of red spilled forth and pooled in the concave of his hand. "Cuts," he answered, as if it wasn't obvious enough.

"Dumbass," she exclaimed, snatching the knife from him. "Where do you keep ban—oh… never mind."

177

"Cuts get a little trickier. You 'll need t' make sure that the muscles, skin, and nerves all reconnect correctly. Work from the inside out. That way, if you make a mistake, we do n't have t' reopen the wound."

She didn't respond and dove in. The life paika was a fragile thing that she simply had to touch to gain access to the magic. Purple light filled her vision and energy flowed through her into Reven. Though she couldn't see things on a microscopic level, she could feel the cells moving and shifting at her will. In what felt like no time, all that remained of the rift was a thin scar.

Reven examined his hand. "Impressive. People tend to' have difficulties with this. They find reconstructing tissue challenging." He closed his fist and when he reopened it, the scar was gone. He began rolling up his sleeve.

"It's like putting paste in a crack. You've got the base and you're just filling it in."

Reven nodded, picking up the knife again. "Let 's see how you do with somethin' deeper." He hesitated, readjusting his grip on the handle before cutting along the middle of his forearm. Blood started flowing heavily.

Keegan grabbed his arm, "I really hope you didn't cut one of your arteries."

While he hadn't entirely severed it, the blade had gone about halfway through the radial artery. She worked quickly to regenerate the wall of the blood vessel and proceeded outwards until there was hardly a trace of the damage. "Don't do that again," she yelled.

"I 'm fine, 'm I not?"

"That's not the point. If I hadn't been able to fix it, you might not've been doing so hot; you nicked your radial artery."

"How d' you know it was the radial artery?" he questioned sardonically.

"I'm a biology/marine biology double major; I took human anatomy last semester. So, I repeat, *don't* do that again."

"I 'm teaching you. I could 'ave fixed myself."

"Still. You've bled and been hit enough to give me something to practice with; no sense in doing more than necessary."

"I find it completely necessary, otherwise I would n't be doing it."

CHAPTER 23

It was late when Kade and Jared returned laden with supplies. Though they weren't leaving for another day, Kade had needed to do something besides sit in the bookshop. He'd bought Keegan and Jared proper packs, a sword belt for Jared, flint, and other nonperishable items. Thankfully, they'd also managed to trade Jared's Estoc for a claymore—even if it was a well-used sword.

They passed Thaddeus amidst the shelves and gave him a brief, "Hello."

Entering the back room, Kade dropped his bag. A pool of blood covered the floorboards. Behind the table, Reven lay on the floor, Keegan crouched beside him.

"Thaddeus," he yelled into the shop. "What happened?" he questioned, rushing over and to Jared, said, "Get some bandages."

Shakily, Keegan answered, "We were practicing, and he kept cutting his artery. I got it together the other times, but something went wrong this time; I-I can't do it." Her eyes were wide as she took deep breaths. "I-I tried fixing it once he passed out, but…. The only thing I could think of was to apply pressure and hope the bleeding stopped."

Thaddeus joined them and calmly instructed, "Keegan, step away, we will take care of this." When she didn't move, he pried her hands off the wound. "He's going to be just fine; I promise."

Jared pulled her away, giving Thaddeus access.

Thaddeus took one of the bandages and wadding it up, placed it over the wound. "I need your belt."

Hastily, Kade pulled it off.

"Wrap it around his bicep and cinch it as tight as you can." Looking to Keegan, Thaddeus asked, "How long has he been in this condition?"

"I don't know," Keegan said quietly.

"How many times did he cut?"

"I don't remember."

From the way she spoke, she was on the verge of breaking down.

Kade told Thaddeus quietly, "We need a healer. Now."

"None will make it here in time," Thaddeus answered, glancing at Keegan before looking back to Kade. "It is our only option."

"Do you think she can do it?"

"We do not have a choice." Thaddeus motioned for Keegan come go forward.

She gave him a dumbfounded look before kneeling between them.

"I need you to heal Reven."

"I-I tried," she choked.

"Keegan," Thaddeus said, making her look at him, "you can do this. Take a deep breath. Try again."

"But if I can't..."

"If you don't try, he *will* die," Kade told her.

Thaddeus took her hands and placed them over the wound.

She sat there, frozen.

Kade glanced at Thaddeus. "It's going to be all right, just do your best."

She still didn't move.

Steeling himself, Kade dove into her mind, prepared to implant the idea that she should begin healing, but found it was unnecessary. Trying to remove himself, he found he couldn't. There was no wall keeping him in, but an unknown force kept his consciousness frozen in place. A purple light overtook his vision and a sense of tranquility sang in his ears. Through Keegan, he felt Reven's artery rejoining, the muscle reconnecting, the nerves rewiring, and the skin becoming seamless.

The light faded and he was no longer held in place, but he stayed motionless in awe. He'd never been in another's mind as they performed magic and his magic had never affected him like that. The only thing he ever saw was the red paika, and the only sounds came from his internal thoughts. He finally pulled himself from her mind.

Thaddeus placed a hand on Keegan's arm, leaving a bloody print on her skin. "Jared, take her outside and get her cleaned up. You can fill the tub using the spigot."

Jared propelled her outside and Kade returned his attention to Reven, who white as a sheet.

"Help me get him upstairs," Thaddeus requested.

Kade slung one of Reven's arms across his shoulders and together they carefully maneuvered him up the stairs and into a bed.

Placing a hand on his shoulder, Thaddeus thanked him.

Kade nodded and headed downstairs; no doubt Keegan needed consoling.

‡‡‡

The wooden tub filled quickly. Jared had built a small fire to heat the bath and give them a light.

Keegan stood silently beside him, arms pulled close across her chest, dark blood staining her clothes and skin.

He closed the spigot, the water near the top of the tub, and waited for her to enter.

She stood frozen, glazed-over eyes staring at the flames of the small fire.

He gently nudged her.

"Turn around," she told him.

He faced the wall and waited until he heard the water settle. It went up to her collarbone and was already beginning to turn a pale red. He handed her a bar of soap.

"He's going to be fine," Kade said behind them.

Relief crossed Keegan's face and she began to rub the soap gently on her skin.

"I would wash your clothes, too," Kade told her.

She nodded and he went back inside.

"Can you hand them to me?" she asked, reaching towards the pile of clothing.

Jared scooped them up and gave them to her and she dropped them in the water, letting them soak.

He sat beside the tub, resting his back against it. "What happened? I've never seen you react like that."

"I panicked."

There was a deep grumbling and Jared looked over the edge of the tub at her. "What was that?"

"My stomach," she answered, sinking lower into the water. "Saving lives is tiring."

"Hurry up and I'm sure we can get some food."

She requested a towel and he obliged. She stared at him, as if waiting for something.

"Right," he said blushing and turning his back. After a few moments, he faced her again.

She stood wrapped in the towel, water dripping down her legs and arms. "I need dry clothes."

"Uh... Let me get some from Kade."

She gave him an unamused look and walked past into the shop.

Inside, Kade and Thaddeus were scrubbing the floor. So far, it looked like they'd diluted the blood and spread it around more than anything.

"Do we have any clean clothes for me?" Keegan asked.

"Oh, goodness," Thaddeus said, standing, quite at ease regardless of her state of undress. "I knew I was forgetting something. Just a moment."

Keegan stood awkwardly, waiting.

Thaddeus soon returned with a set of pants and a shirt.

After thanking him, she went upstairs to change. Dressed, she returned, the towel wrapped around her head. The pants were too long, completely covering her feet with a few inches to spare.

"Why have you done that with the towel?" Jared questioned.

"To keep my hair from dripping on my shirt," she told him, her stomach emitting another rumble. "Can I get something to eat?"

"I do not have anything prepared yet," Thaddeus said. "Will bread suffice for now?"

"Absolutely." She went to sit at the table and tripped over the long pant legs. "Screw this," she muttered, making her way carefully back upstairs. When she returned, she was wearing her jeans.

Kade looked at her questioningly.

"Not a word," she said.

‡‡‡

Thaddeus gave Keegan a loaf of bread to calm her hunger while he prepared a simple soup. Done, he retreated upstairs. Keegan informed him that Reven should drink lots of water. When Thaddeus asked why, she explained that blood was mostly water.

Kade wasn't sure he believed her and after watching her devour several servings of soup, made sure to save portions for Thaddeus and Reven, then left her and Jared to clean the dishes.

"How's he doing?" Kade asked from the doorway.

"Fine, the moment of danger has passed."

"Go eat."

"I am fine for now. For a life elemental, Reven is something of an exception. His natural gifts imply he would know much about the body, but days like this prove otherwise."

Kade laughed lightly. "He's always been more likely to rely on his brawn than his wits."

"I find that quite offensive," Reven said weakly.

"Good," Kade said, squatting beside the bed. "How are you feeling?"

"A bit drowsy. What happened?"

"You went unconscious from blood loss," Thaddeus said. "Gave us all quite a scare."

"I 'pologize, Grandfather."

"I am just glad you are all right. If you can manage, let us put some food in you."

Reven gave him a small smile.

Thaddeus stood and went to get a bowl of soup.

Kade took the chair and turned to his friend. "Sometimes I wonder if you have a brain at all. You, of all people, should've known better. It's almost as if you intended to pull something like that."

"I knew what I was doing," Reven claimed. "And she coped."

"She almost wasn't able to. When you became unconscious, she panicked. We don't know how long you were bleeding before we managed to calm her down and she was able to heal you."

Reven seemed surprised.

Quietly, Kade added, "I thought you were past this."

"I am, but I still 'ave bad days."

"You should tell Thaddeus. He can help you."

"No," Reven said forcefully. "He 'as enough t' worry 'bout without adding a depressed grandson."

"You're not depressed. You moved past that years ago."

"Like I said, I still 'ave bad days."

"We all do," Kade said, placing a hand on his friend's shoulder. "No more hurting yourself. To give Keegan something to practice with or otherwise."

"For now, at least."

"Reven," Kade snapped angrily, the usage of his friend's actual name signifying how serious he was.

"Oh, do n't get your britches in a bunch. I can work with 'er on manipulation."

"That'll suffice," Kade agreed as Thaddeus returned with a bowl of soup and a pitcher of water.

Setting both on the bedside table, Thaddeus said, "Eat up. Then you need to rest."

‡‡‡

Reven sat in bed, propped up against several pillows. While appearing fine, Thaddeus insisted he remain in bed for the day; Keegan agreed.

"So, what're we doing today?" she asked. If it required him hurting himself, she was going to have some strong words.

"Manipulation."

She breathed a sigh of relief. "Okay. How does that work?"

"Like this."

She felt a force present itself throughout her mind. It was similar as to when Kade got inside her head, but this was on a whole other level. She might as well have become a marionette. "That was awful."

"I 'm glad you feel that way. Manipulation should only be used when absolutely necessary. It 's more than just controlling someone's isolated muscles, you take control o' their entire body, which is done through the brain."

"Sounds a lot like mind control."

"No. Mind control takes over the thoughts and implants ideas, but they still retain control o' their body. I could tell you t' stand on one leg forever, but, at some point, you simply will n't be able to' any longer. Someone could force your leg down, or the implanted idea could be broken, freeing you. With manipulation, I take control of the function in the brain that tells the muscles in your leg t' rise and stay there. The only way t' break free from that is t' kill me, or if I decide t' release you. However, the downfall t' manipulation 's that you must actively retain control. Do you understand the difference?"

"I think so. Mind control's psychological, manipulation's physiological."

"Yes... I think. So, now t' begin. I want you to' start by imposing your conscious on mine. Once you 've done that, impose your will, which, if you can manage, I want you to make me stand."

Keegan closed her eyes. She was easily able to encompass his brain with her consciousness but enforcing her will was a harder task. She found that once she gave the command to stand, the impulse was swept away and diffused so that Reven remained sitting in bed. Frustrated, she pulled away. "I can't get it."

"You can; it 's just going to take practice," he corrected. "I 'm going to manipulate you again. Pay attention."

She felt him encompass her brain and he worked slowly to give her a better context of the process. She noticed he wasn't cordoning her entire brain, just the portion above her vertebrae.

Man, I should've paid more attention to parts of the brain and their functions when I took psychology.

"Did that help?" Reven asked.

"Maybe. I think it's that you're not taking control over my entire brain, just the portion that controls movement."

"How 's that helpful?"

"Well, I can focus on the part that matters."

"Give it a go."

Keegan closed her eyes and made her way into Reven's mind. Once she'd blanketed herself over the small portion at the top of his vertebrae, she started trying to make him stand.

There was a crunch and grunt.

Opening her eyes, she saw him rubbing his jaw. "What happened?"

"You made me knee myself in the face."

Grimacing, Keegan apologized profusely.

"At least it 's a step in the right direction."

CHAPTER 24

Everyone stood in the backroom. Three packs sat on the table, stuffed with provisions. Keegan had reluctantly donned the dress once more, though still insisted upon wearing trousers underneath. Thaddeus wore a somber expression and Reven had been sent to fetch the horses.

"We should head outside," Thaddeus said.

Kade nodded, shouldered his pack, and started through the shop. Behind him, Keegan grumbled about the early departure time. Once on the street, he stopped, breathing in the fresh morning air. The sun had yet to rise, but the predawn light was enough to see by.

Keegan dumped her pack on the ground and sat next to it, resting her head on it. "Why do we have to leave so early?"

"To put distance behind us," Kade said.

The clop of horses' hooves echoed off the cobblestones and Reven rounded the corner. From the other end of the street rode Taite, with him, another rider.

"It's not too late for us to make our own way," Kade said.

"No," Thaddeus said definitively.

He crossed his arms and turned to Keegan, "Stand up, you're not a child." She didn't respond and he realized she'd fallen asleep. He prodded her with his boot and her head popped up with a dazed expression. "Get up."

She ignored him and placed her head down again.

"Get up!"

"No need to be cranky," she griped, stretching and releasing a wide-mouthed yawn as he took Arso's reins from Reven.

"Taite," Thaddeus said as there was the sound of a creaking saddle.

"Is everyone ready to go?" Taite questioned.

"Almost," Kade said.

"Be quick about it, boy." He could hear the scorn in Taite's voice.

Gritting his teeth, he picked up his pack and began securing it to Arso's saddle. Jared and Keegan did the same.

I don't like him, Keegan announced, agreeing with Kade's stance.

"I did not know you were taking another person," Thaddeus commented.

"Ah, yes," responded Taite, "it was a last-minute decision."

"Of what element?"

"Air."

"Not too many of those in the city."

After that, Kade paid little attention to the conversation. He finished tying his pack down and went to help Keegan, who had yet to even get hers onto Bastille. "Can you do anything yourself?"

"It's not like I didn't try," she answered. "I'm just short... and weakish."

Jared snickered at her response.

Even Kade couldn't help but smile as he lifted the pack onto Bastille's back. "Can you get it from here?"

"Yeah."

Thaddeus beckoned him away from the group and said in a low voice, "Look after them; especially Keegan, she is the only family you have. And be careful; no doubt Caius has men everywhere."

"Yes, sir," he said in a serious tone.

Thaddeus pulled him into an embrace. "I just got you back, I am not ready to say goodbye again."

"At least there is a goodbye this time." Kade wrapped his arms around the man who had become a father to him.

As he pulled away, Thaddeus slipped something into his tunic pocket and whispered, "Open that only in imminent danger. Destroy it once you have read it or reached the Lazado. I pray it will be the latter. Let *no one* know you have it."

"We need to leave before the guards are overly aware," Taite said.

Kade looked into Thaddeus's eyes; the corners glistened with tears and shone with pride.

"You have become a man any father would be proud of. I am blessed to have been able to call you my own, even if only for a short time. Now, go, shape the world, and take my blessing."

"Thank you," he said, for the first time in a long while feeling a pull on his heartstrings. About to pull himself into the saddle, Reven stopped him.

"You 're forgetting someone."

"Am I?" Kade asked with a grin, turning back to embrace his friend. "Look after the old man."

"What else 'm I goin' t' do? Go on, get out o' here. I 'ill see you again."

‡‡‡

Jared was surprised another elemental was going along, but supposed she had as much right to leave as they. She hadn't said a word and Jared responded in kind. Keegan eyed her questioningly but remained silent;

187

he'd learned it took some time of being awake before she became talkative—and coherent.

Their new companion was stunningly beautiful, having lustrous black locks that reached the small of her back in loose spirals. Her eyes were a deep blue that seemed to become rich violet in most lights. She sat atop her appaloosa with an air of elegance, her skin as soft as honeyed milk.

By the time they reached the east gate, the sun was halfway above the horizon and the people of Suttan were beginning to rouse. At the gates, there were many people milling about, most looking like travelers trying to leave. Ahead, the gates were open, but no one seemed to be passing through.

"What's going on?" Jared asked.

"Wait here," Taite instructed, riding forward.

They waited tentatively, glancing awkwardly at each other.

It was then Kade noticed their new companion with a spark in his hazel eyes.

Jared glanced at Keegan; she'd seen his reaction, too. A slight scowl crossed Kade's face and Jared had no doubt Keegan had made some jibbing comment.

Kade maneuvered his horse over to the girl. "I'm Kade Tavin."

She brushed her hair behind an ear nervously. "Cassidy Wungim." There was a hint of fear in her eyes; clearly she was acquainted with his name.

Kade smiled and she looked away.

Taite returned. "Leave her be. The guards are questioning everyone who's coming or going."

An annoyed look crossed Keegan's face. "How're we dealing with this?"

Taite made a point to ignore her, but his response answered her question regardless. "We're going to split into two groups: Cassidy, Jared, and myself, and Kade and Keegan. My group will go first. Keegan say nothing; Kade, I trust you can handle this. We'll wait for you a mile down the road."

Kade nodded and Taite wheeled his horse around, Cassidy and Jared following him.

At the gate, uninterested and weary guards stopped them.

"Where are you going?" one asked.

"I'm taking my niece and nephew to Whendell to see their grandparents," Taite answered.

They were motioned through the gate and they casually made their way along the east road. As they neared the rendezvous point, a horn blew.

Jared spun around. From the gate, he could see two blurry figures racing towards them. *Keegan, what did you do?*

‡‡‡

She watched Jared, Taite, and Cassidy make their way through the gate. They talked to the guards for scarcely a moment before being waved through. Hopefully, she and Kade would have the same luck.

"Can we go now?" Keegan asked.

"Give it a bit," Kade responded.

She shifted uncomfortably in her saddle. "Now?"

"Now," Kade echoed.

As expected, the guards stopped them. "Where are you going?"

"Móverth," Kade told them.

"For what purpose?"

"To, uh, visit our parents' graves."

"Be on your—"

The second guard interrupted, "Do I know you, girl?"

Keegan shook her head.

"Can you speak?"

She nodded.

"Can you speak?" the guard snarled.

"Yeah, I can speak," she snapped.

"Then answer when we ask you a question."

"Didn't I just do that?"

"You will show us some respect," the first man said angrily.

Keegan rolled her eyes but kept her mouth shut.

Kade made to placate them, "Forgive my sister's crass behavior."

"After she apologizes."

Keegan bit the inside of her cheek and glared at Kade.

"Do it," he commanded with a stern look.

"Sorry," she said, glaring at them.

The first guard nodded for them to be on their way, but the second stopped them again. His eyes scrunched together, scrutinizing Keegan. "I do know you."

"I've never seen you." She could see the gears turning as he made his way to a bulletin board covered in posters.

He stared at them and pulled one off.

189

She could just make it out from atop her horse; it was a wanted poster in her liking. "Shit," she muttered, looking to Kade and jabbing her heels into Bastille.

Kade chased after her with the guards calling after them to stop.

Why'd you take off?

That was a wanted poster of me, she explained.

Behind them a horn blared.

‡‡‡

Jared shifted agitatedly, urging Kade and Keegan to reach them faster. Behind them, blurs of browns and blacks shadowed by a cloud of dust chased them.

As Keegan and Kade neared, Taite yelled, "What the royik happened?"

"They made us," Keegan told him, reining Bastille in.

Taite looked at her blankly.

"They recognized her," Kade clarified.

"Where did you tell them, you were going?" Taite demanded.

"Móverth. But if they're not as dull as they appear, or tell the Vosjnik, they'll know that was a lie."

Taite looked as though he wanted to say many harsh words. "Follow me." He steered his horse into the woods.

Cassidy was the first to follow with Kade coming last and looking like he would've preferred to stay and fight.

They rode at a near breakneck speed, low lying branches threatening to unseat them. After almost an hour, Taite had them slow down.

"Why are we stopping?" Keegan asked.

Taite ignored her.

"Okay, I'm getting real tired of your bullshit. Answer the flippin' question!"

"I don't take commands from you," was Taite's calm response.

Jared could see Keegan was seething.

She went to retort, but Kade responded before she could. "She may be rude and annoying and stubborn," he started.

"Thanks for the support, bro," Keegan said indignantly.

"But you have no right to ignore her; she poses a relevant question. Now, I suggest you answer her."

"And if I don't?" Taite sneered.

"You don't want to know."

190

They were immersed in an unsettling silence as Taite and Kade stared each other down.

Slowly, Taite returned his attention to Keegan. "We're not stopping; we're slowing down."

"Why?"

"It wouldn't look good to go flying past the South Gate."

Jared asked, "Wouldn't it have made more sense to continue east?"

"That's exactly what they expect us to do," Kade countered.

Taite began to explain further, "By going south through Aylentowne, rather than east through Bouyne—"

"They lose our trail," Jared finished.

Taite nodded and urged his horse through the undergrowth.

They emerged back onto the road, Suttan's South Gate behind them, where a few people walked along, while most were gathered outside the gate waiting to enter.

Taite led the way from the city casually.

‡‡‡

Nico stared at the ceiling, his eyes tracing the maze-like edges of the stones from one side to the other. There was the sound of scurrying and he flinched. He'd come to fear the rats. More than once, he'd awoken to them nibbling on his fingers or to see them staring at his face with their beady eyes.

He pushed himself upright on the pile of hay that served as his bed. In the din, he couldn't see the rat, but knew it was there. He pulled his knees to his chest and leaned against the wall. The stone was cold and raised gooseflesh across his arms.

From the hallway came the jangling of keys and the scraping of cell doors against the floor. The guards were coming to collect the plates and water pitchers from the morning meal, though it barely qualified as such. It was no more than a piece of stale bread and a pitcher of water. Dinner was little more than that—bread with vegetable stew. All food and drink had been infused with ether—thankfully, he couldn't taste it that way.

Nico turned away to avoid being blinded as the guards opened the door with a grating scrape.

"On your feet, boy," came a gruff voice.

Nico turned his head, squinting; it was Dax.

"On your feet."

Slowly, Nico responded, keeping himself in the back corner.

Dax strode across and grabbing his arm, pulled him into the corridor.

191

As futile as his attempt was, he resisted, but stopped after receiving a backhand to the side of the head, making his ear ring as they walked through the dungeon to the upper levels of the castle. In the courtyard, the Vosjnik waited.

Again, he was forced to mount, and his hands were bound to the saddle horn; the reins were tied to Dax's steed.

Connery led the way through the portcullis and a sinking feeling hit Nico's stomach. The Vosjnik appeared to be in high spirits—especially Vitia, whose wide smile revealed her pointed canines; they were on the hunt again. He had no idea if his brother would be able to stay ahead again, but he prayed to Sola and Lunos that he did.

CHAPTER 25

"Come on, boy, put some back into it," Waylan barked.

Lucas pushed on the bellow, sending a puff of air into the flames. The metal in the embers glowed bright red.

After another burst of air from the bellow, Waylan pulled the metal from the fire and sat it on the anvil. "Quickly. I don't want to have to reheat this. *Again.*"

His words died as the hammer in Lucas's hands came down. Waylan pulled the rod back slowly, allowing Lucas to flatten it along its entire length. Once the whole piece was flat, it was placed back into the fire until it glowed. This time, the metal was rounded until it made a perfect circle; a band for a small wine barrel. It was then dropped into a vat of water, steam rising in a quickly dissipating cloud.

Lucas wiped the sweat from his forehead.

"Good work, boy," Waylan told him. "You're done for the day."

Lucas gave a curt nod and made his way from the shop. While Waylan had finally started having him work in the forge, they were limited to simple jobs because of his inexperience. Waylan sent him home early so he could complete the more difficult pieces without having to yell instructions. Lucas wasn't about to complain.

The Fulpes' house soon came into view. From the foyer, he could hear Alivia and Laiyla talking, but he wasn't greeted. After rejecting Alivia, she had passionately been giving him the cold shoulder. Little good it did her, he preferred it anyway. No longer did he have to pretend to be cordial to spare her feelings.

He made his way upstairs quietly, just in case Alivia changed her mind. In his room, he found it was peacefully quiet after the din of the blacksmith shop. He changed from his sweaty clothes into something more comfortable and rested until dinner.

‡‡‡

His heart was heavy with loss, but Thaddeus knew he could no more keep Kade there now than he could have five years before. Kade was destined to walk a dangerous path that he seemed to go searching for. And although he was on a troublesome track, he also had the mettle to make it through. He pushed the thoughts away.

There was another pang in his chest, but this one was not from sadness. This was his Calling. He belonged with the Blind Prophet, yet he had denied that fate, but its call was becoming harder to ignore.

A cough pulled him from his thoughts, and he looked up to see several soldiers emerging from between the bookshelves.

"Can I help you gentlemen?" he asked, an unsettled feeling replacing the Calling.

"You can come with us quietly," one man said.

"Why would I do that?" Thaddeus asked, glad Reven was not present.

"For questioning about several elementals who were, until today, refuging here."

"I would like to say that I have no clue as to what you are talking about."

"Are you telling me you had no knowledge of elementals staying here?"

"No, I was fully aware of them." He stepped forward and the soldiers reached for their weapons. "I am not going to fight, do as you must."

The soldiers relaxed, circling around him, and allowed him to calmly walk with them out of the shop.

Outside, it did not take long for people to notice what was happening.

Thaddeus spied Reven out of the corner of his eye across the street and gave him a subtle shake of the head in warning to stay away. "Might I enquire who informed you about the elementals?" he asked.

"No."

Reven followed along at the edge of the crowd.

Get away from here, you fool, Thaddeus thought, wishing, not for the first time, that Reven was a telepath.

"Your grandson's a fool," the man next to him said. "He should've run when he 'ad the chance."

Realizing more soldiers were headed to apprehend his grandson, he yelled, "Run!"

Their eyes locked. Thaddeus saw the spark in Reven's eyes and shook his head, knowing what he wanted to do. Little good it did though as the soldiers around him toppled to the ground, their glassy eyes staring lifelessly.

Someone screamed, others joining the hysterical call, and Thaddeus watched as people began to flee in the face of an unknown assailant. It took him a moment to register what Reven was saying.

"We 'ave t' go!" Reven pulled him down the street and towards the stables. By luck, two horses were picketed outside and Reven did not hesitate as he pulled their reins free and swung up.

Thaddeus paused; he could not explain it, but his Calling was encouraging him to flee.

"Grandfather," Reven said frantically.

He was probably sensing more soldiers and swung into the saddle with more agility than he thought he possessed.

Reven spurred his horse and began their frantic dash towards the gates.

With each footfall, his Calling sang; he was headed to where he was needed—somehow. Ahead, he could see the wide-open gates.

People rushed to get out of the way and soon they were through the gates. His horse gave a shrill cry and the world tumbled around him. In the fall, he felt his wrist bend and break. His head struck the ground and for a moment everything was silent.

As his woes flooded back, a stirring he had not felt in years—not since Rosh's death—reappeared. His magic was rearing its head.

Reven pulled his horse around to go to his rescue.

"This is not your path," Thaddeus mumbled, reaching within himself to call upon his magic and release a shockwave. Reven slowed and he knew the message had been heard. But he also knew how stubborn his grandson was—a trait that ran in the family. "Caxone proytyct," he muttered.

It took Reven a moment to understand that Thaddeus had erected a barrier between the soldiers and him.

Knowing he could only maintain the barrier for so long, Thaddeus instructed, "Go. I promise this is not where I meet death."

"I wouldn't be so sure about that, old man," a soldier said, pulling him to his feet.

Thaddeus gave him a small smile. "You would be surprised what I know." Looking over his shoulder, he was heartened to see Reven was already a small figure in the distance.

‡‡‡

Jared often checked over his shoulder to see if soldiers rode towards them from the distance. None did and by early afternoon his nerves calmed. Mostly, they rode in silence.

They stopped in the afternoon for a quick lunch of bread and cheese. After that, they continued until the sun was touching the treetops. Camp was set up in a clearing not far off the road.

Cassidy appeared to be highly unaccustomed to the forest and simply sat and watched the rest of them work. Keegan wanted to protest but was sensible enough to keep her mouth shut. Camp was made quickly and Taite set to cooking meat on a flat stone in the fire while they sat around in an awkward silence.

Finally, Keegan broke the tension. "Cassidy, tell us about yourself."

Cassidy threw Taite a quick glance for reassurance. "What would you like to know?" Her voice came softly, giving gentle kisses on the ear.

Keegan shrugged, "I dunno; it's whatever you want to tell us."

Cassidy looked at her with searching eyes.

"How old are you?" Keegan encouraged, knowing the girl wouldn't offer much freely.

"Sixteen," Cassidy answered.

"I presume you are an elemental," Jared stated.

She nodded.

"What element?"

The word came like a whisper in the wind, "Air."

"Cool," Keegan said. "We'll have to spar some time."

An overwhelmed expression crossed Cassidy's countenance as her eyes darted between them all, questioning whether she was serious. "I… uh…"

"It's okay if you don't want to."

Cassidy said nothing, but it was clear she relaxed.

Taite handed out meat on tin plates. All readily accepted their portion and dug in. Once done, they washed the plates and cutlery with water from their skins.

When everything had been put away, Taite said, "Everyone to sleep."

Keegan raised an eyebrow. "It's not even late."

"Everyone to sleep," reiterated Taite.

Jared heard the words, but it seemed as if remnants lingered in his mind.

Keegan started to lie down then shook her head. Her eyes narrowed and she looked as if trying to solve some conundrum. She began to speak, but closed her mouth, unsure of what to say. "What did you just do?" she questioned, finally managing to put her thoughts together.

Taite looked at her, aggravated, "Nothing."

"That wasn't—"

"Leave it," Kade cut her off. "Go to sleep."

Keegan crossed her arms but complied.

Jared and Cassidy followed suit, getting comfortable in their bedrolls.

As Jared lay watching the smoke from the campfire drift up into the treetops, he heard Kade, *Careful, Taite's a telepath.*

Easy enough, was Keegan's response. *We'll just keep a wall up.*

Easier said than done, Jared came. *I still have to concentrate hard to even form a weak wall, let alone keep it standing.*

While that is a concern, Kade told them, *we don't need to be troubled about keeping walls up. What we need to worry about is that Taite's very good at planting thoughts.*

That's what happened! Keegan exclaimed. *Also, side note, that's a totally cool ability.*

How do we counteract it? Jared asked.

Keeping a wall up's the best way, Kade explained. *But, since neither of you is particularly good at it, just be aware of when he's doing it and keep your resolve to do the opposite strong.*

Sounds good, Keegan said, turning her back to the fire. *Lord knows I'm stubborn enough for that to work. Nighty night, see ya in the morning.*

✢✢✢

The pain ripping through his chest was iron hot and a voice yelled at him, "Betrayer! Marmarda! Soucer!"

"Az ryla sarig. Plazde, haxnug!" Braxton shouted.

Slowly, pain made him fade into darkness and he was sure this was death. Voices he had heard before began to rise from the depths and the same three men came forward: Kade, Aron, and the stranger. They stepped aside, letting Keegan through, fire flickering openly in her hair. She gave him a sly grin before Aron began to speak.

He blinked and found himself in the throne room, six people kneeling before him, all with heads bowed.

Someone behind him said, "Woth eya sesuna eyar kunyi?"

He tried to turn to see who had spoken but discovered he could only observe those in front of him. He studied their features, seeing if he recognized any of them, but the more he focused the fuzzier the details became.

"Naya," the first man responded. There was a metallic flash and the man disappeared.

A wailing filled the air and he pressed his palms against his ears, the action doing little to block the sound.

The question was repeated to the next person. This time the answer was, "Avu." Four more times that answer was given.

When the voice questioned the last man, no answer came. The question was repeated impatiently. Though the man looked at the floor, Braxton could tell he was smiling.

Slowly, the man lifted his head, his brown eyes holding a twinge of contempt. "Naya." Again, there was a flash, above his head. "Astæm az woth sesuna ayþ—"

Something tore across his chest, he awoke violently, and tumbled over the side of his bed. He groaned; the stone floor cold beneath his body. Slowly, he picked himself up, running a hand over his chest. He knew he had been dreaming but it all felt too real.

CHAPTER 26

They rose just after sunrise, had a modest breakfast of bread, and when the sun was barely above the treetops, set out. They proceeded in pairs— Jared and Keegan, Kade and Cassidy—with Taite leading the way.

Kade found himself staring at Cassidy constantly, her beauty truly captivating. She looked straight ahead, her raven curls swinging gently with the footfalls of her horse. He hoped she didn't notice his gawking.

"Uh…" Kade began, trying to strike up a conversation.

"You were one of the Vosjnik," she said softly.

He was surprised by her candor. "Yes."

"Why?"

"Why what?"

"Why would you join them, then turn against them years later?"

"Revenge."

Keegan twisted in her saddle, "Ooh, are we finally gonna get your backstory?"

"I suppose," Kade said, feeling uncharacteristically self-conscious.

"Yes," nodded Keegan, a strange gleam in her eyes.

"Both of my parents were elementals," Kade began. "My father, Kagen, was an earth elemental, and my mother, Korissa, was a water elemental. Both were Lazado agents, but their roles were primarily to keep a watch on the elementals in the city and soldiers' movements. When I was ten, the city guards did a round up and the Vosjnik were with them. My parents got caught up in it and resisted. I'd been out playing with Raven, and Thaddeus was taking me home. We arrived just as the soldiers were swinging their swords. I'll never forget the faces of the men who killed my parents; they belonged to Connery Sray and the previous earth elemental, Noriss Ett, whom I killed.

"I don't recall much of what happened after that. Next thing I knew, I was back at the bookshop. At the time, I didn't know what I was going to do, but Thaddeus took me in and treated me like his own. I vowed to kill the men who'd murdered my parents, but as a child, there was little I could do. A couple of years passed but I never forgot. Raven and I found ourselves in the underground world one night, we watched a fight, and a man approached us with the offer to join, which we accepted. Neither of us was very good at the start, but our capabilities grew and soon no one dared fight me. I was fifteen then. Knowing I had a chance, I slipped away one night, made my way to Agrielha, and sought an audience with Caius. When I requested a place in the Vosjnik, he laughed in my face and said he couldn't award that position, I had to earn it."

"Is this where you killed that dude?" Keegan said.

"Yes. I killed Noriss and joined the Vosjnik. During the next five years, I grew close to Connery and Caius. When I first set out, I'd planned to kill Caius as well but quickly realized I had no hope of doing so. That is, until you appeared, Keegan; I knew I could use you to achieve my goal. From there it was a matter of finding a way of getting hold of you and taking you to the Lazado. You haven't made my job easy. And here we are."

"Damn…" Keegan said. "I honestly don't know if I should hug you or slap you."

This elicited a chuckle from Taite.

While Cassidy was still quiet for the most part, she began talking to Kade. They discussed families, this and that. He learned her parents were some of the wealthiest merchants in Suttan, keeping her safe by concealing her existence from those but a few family friends and paying off the city guards whenever they did round ups. With rumors of Caius madly searching for a powerful entity, they'd finally decided to send her to the Lazado. In the winter, they planned to follow.

Once more, they stopped around sunset with a magnificent view of the Westerlies glowing blue in the darkening sky. Dinner consisted of bird stew, thanks to Kade.

"Hey, Kade," Keegan began.

He groaned; this could lead to nothing good.

"Wanna teach me how to use a sword?"

Taite, who was drinking from his water-skin, nearly choked. "Women do not use swords!"

Keegan looked at him, a mischievous gleam in her eyes. "Screw the system. Kade?"

Taite's disapproval made Kade want to train her just to spite him. He looked to Jared and shrugged. "It can't hurt to teach you. Both of you."

Keegan's lips pulled back into a smile and she held an open hand out towards Kade.

He looked at her, confused.

She sighed and grabbed his hand, making it meet hers. "We're gonna have to teach y'all how to high five."

"Jared, get your sword," Kade requested.

She had an impish grin and was drumming her fingers together deviously when he returned and handed it to Kade, "Should we be worried?"

"Not sure."

"Nah," was Keegan's response with a wave of the hand. "I'm just excited."

"This isn't a toy."

"I know."

Kade offered her the hilt.

She pulled the sword from its sheath, her arm dropping instantly. "Damn, this is a lot heavier than I thought it'd be."

Kade raised his weapon.

She looked at him startled, "Dude, you're gonna cut me to pieces!"

"Not if you block."

"Nuh-uh, I ain't playing this game. Block the edge, or use a stick, or somethin'."

He let the tip of his sword touch the ground. Earth rose and covered the edge. "Happy?"

"Yes," she said with a sharp nod.

Kade did the same to hers and they began.

She struggled with the weight and needed both hands to keep the blade elevated. In the long term, if he was going to train her, she would probably need to use his arming sword over Jared's claymore, which was long and awkward for her short stature. But tonight, it would suffice as the point wasn't to teach her technique.

He lunged and slashed at her shoulders. She jumped away, managing to block his attack. His next strike came down; she was slow to react, and it made heavy contact with her.

She yelped, the sword dropping from her hands. "Son of a..." she grumbled, rubbing her shoulder.

On the sidelines, Taite chuckled.

She scowled and picked up the sword, her stubborn nature presenting itself.

"Ready?"

She nodded and he attacked again, this time with a slash to the hip. She stepped back, avoiding his hit and tried to counterattack with a jab, but over-extended. Kade grabbed her wrist and pulled her forward, sending her tumbling to the ground as he placed the sword against her neck.

She stood up, grabbing the sword again. This continued for a while, but before long she was moving slower.

Keegan sat on her backside this time; bruises would form by sunrise. "Okay, I'm done." Getting to her feet, she handed the sword back to Jared, then made her way over to her bedroll. After nestling into it, she promptly fell asleep.

"We should follow her example," Jared said.

Kade returned his sword to its sheath and placed it beside his bedroll. With the fire dying, he lay down and stared across the campsite at Cassidy until he fell asleep.

‡‡‡

Keegan awoke to the sound of flint on knife. Groggily, she opened her eyes and saw Taite kneeling beside a now flaming handful of leaves. She rolled onto her side, facing away from the fire, her body protesting and forcing her to stifle a groan.

"Up," Taite instructed.

She looked over her shoulder and saw him rousing Kade.

"Wake everyone else."

Kade sat up, blinking the sleep from his eyes.

She let out a breath, pushed herself upright, and watched as Kade woke Cassidy with a gentle shake of the shoulder and a few soft words.

Noticing she was up, he told her, "Wake Jared."

She looked over to where Jared lay. From where she sat, it looked *so* far away. Glancing around, she found a stick and tried to jab him, but it fell short. She pursed her lips, about to get up. *Yo, get up,* she said, grinning at her ingenuity.

He turned over and mumbled something but remained steadfast in sleep's grip.

Come on, up and at 'em.

Jared turned onto his side.

Up, she said forcefully.

He bolted upright, letting out a yelp of surprise. He looked at her blearily and confused.

"Mornin'."

Behind her, Kade chuckled.

"*Never* do that again," Jared growled.

"That was kinda funny."

"Are you really that lazy?"

"Yeah," she answered feebly. She'd sooner let them think she was lazy before they knew how sore and bruised she was.

"Liar," Kade butted in. "You're sore from last night."

She realized he'd been in her mind and fortified her wall, giving him a mental finger.

"Didn't Reven teach you how to heal?" Jared asked, getting up.

"Ye–" Keegan cut herself off at the sound of sizzling, "–ah."

202

In a small frying pan, Taite was cooking bacon.

She looked at it longingly. "Extra crispy, please."

Taite looked up at her. "Pardon?"

"I like mine cooked extra crispy."

"How well done is that?"

"A bit more than crispy, but not quite burnt," she said before returning her attention to Jared who now stood before her. "Yeah, he totally taught me how to heal! But I've never tried it on myself." She stared at her forearm, found a bruise, and reached for her life magic. It flowed forth and she felt her skin tingle. After a few seconds, she pulled away. The bruise was only half-gone, which surprised her, as it would've been completely healed on Reven. "Why didn't it work?"

"It's hardest to perform magic on yourself. Something about the energy being in a loop," Kade told her.

She sighed. "I think you're talking about the first law of thermodynamics, but at least I'll get plenty of practice."

Each received a few pieces of bacon, and mostly were content to keep their sleepy thoughts to themselves. Breakfast eaten, the bacon grease was buried, the fire was put out, and they left the campsite at an amiable walk.

The day was long and Keegan spent the ride flitting between letting her mind wander and trying to heal herself. By the time they stopped, her bruises barely looked better. While not looking forward to having bruises, she treated them as battle scars and lessons learned.

Dinner consisted of bread and a rabbit, kindly provided by Jared. Afterwards, she waited anxiously for Kade to begin the night's training.

Kade grabbed two sticks and tossed one to Jared. "Ready?"

"For what?" was Jared's response.

"To train."

"Why are we doing it with sticks?"

"Do you want to end up like Keegan?"

Jared looked over at her and shook his head.

Keegan frowned, "You couldn't've done that last night?"

"No," Kade said.

Jared mirrored Kade and raised his weapon. He had one foot back, but it looked like he was trying to balance on a tightrope.

"Put your feet shoulder-width apart," Keegan commented. "You'll have better balance and movement."

Jared looked to Kade, unsure if he should listen.

Kade nodded. "That's correct. I'm surprised you know that."

"I've actually done something similar to sword fighting; I'm not *entirely* incompetent."

"If that's so, then why are you covered in bruises?"

"Cause that sword weights a crap ton. I'm used to a short, like two-pound, padded stick," she answered, using her hands to give an idea of the length of the weapon.

"That so?"

"Yeah."

"When I'm done here, you can prove it."

"Gladly."

Returning his attention to Jared, Kade said, "Keep the weapon in front of your body. You need to be able to block and attack." He held his stick out and Jared did the same, making an "x". Taking a step out with his front leg, Kade cut at Jared's side. Jared brought his stick down, attempting to block, but just caused the attack to hit him on the upper thigh.

"Don't block down," Keegan said, "unless you're moving back at the same time or it's an uppercut. Otherwise, the hit's still going to land, it just might not be on target."

Jared nodded, keeping his eyes on Kade, who had taken a step back and started to move around. He followed Kade's movements with his eyes, feet remaining rooted in place.

"Move with me," Kade said calmly. "Never give your back to an opponent."

Jared nodded and moved his back foot, crossing it behind his other leg, to turn and match Kade.

"Don't cross your legs," Keegan said. "It'll put you off balance. In this case, lead with your front leg."

Jared stopped and let his arm fall, the stick slapping his leg. "Can you just let me fight without critiquing?"

"I'm not critiquing, I'm helping. Well... both."

"How is this helping me?"

Keegan got to her feet. "Stand like you were before." Jared did so and she pushed his shoulder, sending him stumbling back. "Stand like I told you to." He did and when she pushed him again, he didn't give. "Get it now?"

She retook her seat and Kade continued the lesson. Jared struggled to fend off the attacks, but that was expected. Every so often, she or Kade gave some advice or correction. When they were through, red welts marked where bruises would form.

Jared handed the stick to Keegan and she animatedly took his spot across from Kade. Compared to him, and in the eyes of an untried swordsman, she looked inexperienced. While Kade held the stick with both hands, she held it with her right, the left free and held in such a way that guarded her head and torso.

"Ready?" Kade asked as they crossed their makeshift weapons.

She nodded and quickly pulled back to give room for movement.

Kade began circling and she followed his movements nimbly. As he lunged, she stepped off to the side and brought the stick down on his knuckles, catching him off guard. Taking advantage of this, she brought the stick up to whop him across the ear and side of the face.

Taite laughed loudly and Keegan gave a waggish smile. It faded quickly as she saw the storm brewing in Kade's eyes, and a sense of humiliation washed over her. The next set of attacks came in a furious flurry. A blocked slash across the chest, a whack to the leg, a dodged sweeping strike at the neck, a jab to the shoulder, and finally a down strike that she caught on her own weapon, the force splintering and snapping the stick.

Her eyes widened and she did the only thing that came to mind, throwing the smaller piece, hitting Kade in the face. It was enough to make his next attack falter. She rushed in, placed both hands along the length of the weapon, and wrenched it from his grasp. Reversing the orientation, she brought it across his face, then delivered a kick to his stomach.

He bent slightly and she brought the stick down across his back from hip to shoulder. He grabbed her leg and pulled it out from under her, sending her tumbling to the ground. He then lunged at her but was restrained by Taite and Jared and struggled as they pulled him across the campsite.

Keegan scrambled back, suddenly finding Cassidy beside her, saying something that was drowned out by the blood pounding through her ears.

Kade shoved Jared off and made to punch at Taite.

"Kade!" Cassidy yelled, panic in her voice.

He froze.

"Stop."

Slowly, he relaxed and Taite and Jared stopped trying to restrain him.

Jared went to Keegan, "Are you all right?"

"Yeah," she brushed him off. Getting to her feet, she yelled at Kade, "What the hell is wrong with you?"

He turned and stormed away.

Cassidy glanced back at Jared and Keegan, before chasing after him.

‡‡‡

Kade pushed through the undergrowth, anger leading him.

"Wait," she called after him. "Kade, wait!"

He ignored her.

She ran to catch up and when close enough, she reached out and grabbed his arm.

"What?" he snarled.

She shrank back. "What happened back there?"

He started to walk again. "Nothing."

"That was not nothing. You… seemed so full of hatred."

"I was."

She was shocked by his answer. "Why?"

"It's nothing I can discuss with you."

"I am sure you can if you try."

He turned to her, eyes steely, "No."

Cassidy found a moss-covered log and sat down.

Reluctantly, he sat beside her and listened to the music of the night for what seemed half a lifetime. "It just made me so angry," he began.

"What did?"

"Keegan. She…" he paused to think. "She can fight."

"I cannot see why that would anger you."

"It wasn't that. It's the fact that she was able to strike me."

"So, she wounded your pride."

He stared into the dark forest.

Noticing the scrape along his cheek, where blood sat in droplets, she placed a hand on his face, and ran a thumb along his skin. "Does it hurt?"

"Does what hurt?" He ran a hand across his face and seemed mildly surprised to see blood. "Only now that you mention it. Is it bad?"

"No, barely a scratch."

"Maybe you should kiss it."

"Maybe." She hesitated before leaning forward and gently kissing his cheek. Pulling away, she stared into his eyes, becoming mesmerized as greens and browns danced around his pupils. He began to lean forward, and she reciprocated the movement. They were close, so close she could feel his breath on her lips.

Kade jerked back and she turned away, blushing.

"We should head back," he said, avoiding looking at her.

She nodded and stood, brushing the moss from the seat of her dress.

The walk back to camp was a silent one and when they returned, they found Jared and Keegan asleep.

Taite was not one to talk, at least not to them, and settled for giving Kade a hard glare.

Kade and Cassidy separated, each going to their own bedrolls on opposite sides of the fire. She had just gotten inside hers when she found Kade beside her; she fell asleep smiling that night.

CHAPTER 27

Waking up, Jared noticed Kade wasn't where he was supposed to be, but across the campsite with Cassidy. He had nothing against the girl, but the two together didn't seem right. He woke Keegan and had no doubt she was still upset.

Taite soon had breakfast cooked and everyone sat around the fire eating quietly. Keegan stole subtle glances at Kade, while he looked apathetically at the food before him. Neither said a word, maintaining an icy silence.

Just before they left, Jared overheard Kade half-heartedly apologizing and was impressed he'd swallowed his pride. Keegan readily accepted the apology but couldn't resist making a less-than-witty comment.

The day of travel yielded nothing of excitement, though Kade might not have agreed; he and Cassidy chatted in earnest.

Keegan spent the ride trying to heal the remnants of her bruises, having little success, and conceded to bearing them.

They stopped once more just before nightfall and repeated the process of pitching camp and eating. They sat silently for a while, stealing awkward glances at each other or staring at the fire.

Finally, Kade began the night's events.

Jared looked to Keegan for a cue as to whether or not he should spar. She gave him a blank stare and decided to take his chances.

They squared up and began. Kade's movements were slow and his blows, light, though that didn't mean they wouldn't cause injury. He was holding back and Jared presumed it was in light of last night. He didn't complain; he had no wish to feel that kind of anger.

When they finished, he made to hand the match over to Keegan. She looked at him inquisitively and when she made no motion to take the stick, he tossed it into the woods and sat next to her.

Kade gave her a blank stare, before dropping his stick into the fire and sitting beside Cassidy. They began to talk and laugh.

Jared nudged Keegan; she'd been uncharacteristically quiet all day. "Are you all right?"

"Yeah."

"You don't seem to be."

"What makes you say that?"

"You've been quiet."

"Is that a crime?"

"Well... no. It's just unusual for you."

"I'm an unusual person."

✝✝✝

The days were long and hard and the nights short. A week ago, the Vosjnik had left Suttan at a breakneck pace, dragging Nico along. The guards at the gate swore they saw Keegan and Kade heading east towards Bouyne. There was no mention of Jared and Nico felt a pang as he wondered at the fate of his brother.

Everyone's fuses had worn down—sleep was a sought-after commodity and anger was the currency of exchanges. Though they were sure they were close behind Kade and company, they'd seen no signs of them.

They'd stopped securing him to a tree at night, but still bound his hands. Nico often contemplated making another bid for freedom, but Vitia's glares chilled him to the core. He hoped to never see her wrath, for, on a good day, she was prickly.

Midday was drawing to a close and in the distance, Bouyne appeared. The river city was a brown mole on the horizon, the Tatat River winding behind it like a wound on the earth. The mud walls around the city were painted in faded murals that depicted the rise and fall of the Dragon King. Though Nico could only see the beginning and end of the story, every man, woman, and child knew the tale.

Centuries ago, a warrior had come from a far, foreign land. He'd had a name once, but it'd long been forgotten and a new one, the Dragon King, was given to him. When the Dragon King arrived, humans were slaves. Wanting peace rather than war, the Dragon King held council with the other races and implored them to release the humans. Slavery had been on its deathbed for near a century, but only the dragons were willing to grant humans freedom. The only reason they sided with him was due to his being bonded to a beast of flame. After much time, the other races agreed to free their slaves, under the stipulation that homage was paid to them. The deal struck, humans were granted the lands west of the Yarav Forest to plant crops and a third of whatever they grew was to be given as tribute each year.

The newly freed humans spread across Arciol in a state of disarray, fighting amongst themselves. The Dragon King hoped to let humans rule themselves, but soon realized it was an impossible dream. With a sword red as blood and his dragon of the same color, he conquered the lands given to humans and united the peoples. He raised great cities and made sure peace ensued. As his reign neared a century, people began to question his long life. He shared a bond with his dragon, which allowed his life to be prolonged for as long as the beast lived. A few tried to kill the creature, but failed, for no one could withstand the fire from a dragon's maw.

As he continued to rule, humans lost their boorish ways, beginning to see the amazing contributions of their benefactor. He'd brought learning, religion, culture, and crafts that benefited all. Never had he killed without a reason and the Dragon King did his best to help all in any way he could, regardless of how small the act.

With no rebellions to take care of, the Dragon King set to building the home from which he would rule. It wasn't long before the castle of Agrielha was raised on the plains between two rivers. A city thrived nearby, but the castle was away from it to give room for his ever-growing dragon.

It was near the end of his fifth century of rule that he took a wife, a maiden from the southern city of Móverth by the name of Suki Vælar. Together, they ruled Arciol with kindness and the world prospered. Years passed and the Queen suddenly grew sick. The Dragon King took her south, into lands unknown to the people of Arciol. When they returned, the queen was in radiant health and came bearing a child and an emerald dragon. She too had become bonded with a beast of flame.

Soon, it was not only that child's tiny feet that pitter-pattered in the halls of the castle; the king and queen were blessed with eight beautiful children: Seleena, Fraisher, Ocea, Uri, Caldon, Bevel, Esen, and Aræhgan. They grew quickly and followed in their parents' footsteps as defenders of peace, which lasted for a number of years before rebellion sparked.

Some had grown tired of the Dragon King in his long rule. To placate them and avoid war, he granted them Suttan as a free city, but soon they came back demanding more. He acquiesced, but when even this didn't result in peace, he was forced to take up his bloody sword once more.

Many humans stood with the king, as did the dragons, Merfolk, Torrpeki, Buluo, and Alvor. In the final battle of the rebellion, the Queen's dragon took a poisoned arrow to the eye. The emerald beast died in screams of agony, but somehow, the Queen lived. She wasn't the same though; her mind was lost and she begged for death. The Dragon King, with sad eyes, granted her wish and the red of her blood mixed with the red of his sword.

In his sorrow and grief, he and his dragon bathed the battlefield in fire and the rebellion was no more. The realm wept along with him at the

210

outcome. While others were sad for a time, the seasons turned and they forgot their sorrows, but not the Dragon King. As time went on, nothing lessened his grief.

Finally, he decided his rule would end after nearly six and a half centuries. No dangers threatened the realm, and it was time he grieved for his beloved in earnest. He gave the throne to his eldest, Seleena. To ensure that no such hardships as he'd faced would befall her, he created the Blind Prophet. While someone of Seleena's immediate blood line should rule, the Prophet would remain. As a final parting gift to all of his children, he endowed them with long lives. He then mounted his dragon and became nothing more than a part of the red sunset.

Now that they were closer to the wall, Nico could see the finer details of the pictorial. Given the chance, he would've marveled at it all day. The Vosjnik rode through the earthen wall, the guards letting them through without so much as a word. Once again, they made their way to the city's castle. Words were exchanged with the lord of the city and Nico was escorted to the dungeon.

✝✝✝

The door to the cell swung open.

When the guard entered, Thaddeus was waiting patiently for him. "Make no trouble, old man."

"Never," Thaddeus said, pushing off the wall. "I take it my journey to Agrielha is about to begin."

"How d' you know that?" the man asked, a frown marking his suspicion.

Thaddeus held his arms out to be shackled. "Lucky guess."

The guard eyed him before slowly doing so.

Thaddeus could not help but smile; this unsettled the guard even more.

He was brusquely pushed from the cell and from the man's tense nature, Thaddeus knew he expected the worst. He might be well-numbered in years, but the fight had yet to leave him and with the reawakening of his spell-casting abilities, there was much he could do to escape the current and impending situations. But he had no such intentions. His Calling, for the first time in years, was calm, as if it knew he was headed in the right direction.

When they emerged under the sun's rays, Thaddeus shielded his eyes, the daylight blinding after a week of gloom.

211

A wagon waited in the courtyard, the faint sounds of sobbing coming from within. The door was yanked open, causing the inhabitants to hiccup and shy away. Thaddeus climbed into the cart and allowed himself to be chained to its wall. The door was shut, a padlock clipped into place. He heard orders being called to the guards outside and they lurched forward.

A woman beside him buried her face in her hands, tears rolling down her cheeks. He wished he could offer words of comfort, but they all knew where they were headed. No words but one would save them.

CHAPTER 28

The next few days found Keegan abnormally quiet. Kade and Cassidy were too enraptured in each other to notice and Taite preferred her silence. Jared was the only one concerned, even if she found no reason for it.

Kade had apologized the morning after their scuffle and was forgiven, but she remained wary of him when sparring. His movements were slow and deliberate but when she landed an attack, he struggled furiously to swallow his pride.

The days of riding were long and after eight of them, they reached the next large city, Aylentowne. Being the last to enter at dusk, the gates were shut for the night.

The travelers' inn they stayed at, Magnenpie, wasn't her first choice in accommodation; the folk in the tavern eyed her with taciturn eyes that she shied away from. Cassidy felt her sentiments, though she had Kade to 'protect' her; he linked his arm with hers when he saw her discomfort. Over the last week, she'd watched the two become close and was skeptical of Kade's intentions.

Taite led the way to their room in the middle of the hall on the second floor; it reminded her of Gydrick's. There were two beds pushed against the walls this time though.

"How long are we staying?" she asked.

"Couple of days," Taite answered.

"Why so long?" Kade questioned, sitting on a bed.

"We're in no particular rush," Taite continued. "We can afford to spend a few days recuperating and resupplying."

Keegan exchanged a glance with Kade and shrugged. "Who gets the beds?"

"I get one. The rest of you can fight for the other," Taite said.

"And they say chivalry's dead." She turned to Cassidy, "You want it?"

Cassidy's blue-violet eyes exuded relief. "Yes, please."

"Take it. I just want a pillow."

"Oh, take both."

Keegan grabbed the corner of the nearest pillow and tossed it on top of her pack. "One's fine."

"Shall we eat?" Jared suggested.

Taite answered by pulling the door open.

‡‡‡

The tavern was as packed as before, only now the men were more content with harassing the barmaids. Taite got them food and they attempted to find seats together, giving up when a barmaid approached with their drinks. They split into a group of two and three, Kade and Cassidy, and Jared, Keegan, and Taite.

As Jared brought his tankard to his lips, Keegan said, "That'd better be water."

He pulled the bitter liquid away. "Pardon?"

"That'd better be water."

"Who are you to stop a man from drinking?" Taite griped. To make a point, he downed his pint, which was quickly replaced with a full one.

"The person who looked after his drunk ass last time," she said coolly.

Jared felt his cheeks flush.

Taite muttered something under his breath.

"It's not shameful," Keegan defended. "It happens; lord knows I've spent a night or two bent over a toilet."

Taite took a few gulps of ale.

"Why would you be bent over that?" Jared questioned.

Keegan gave him a funny look. "Oh. My toilet and your toilet probably don't mean the same thing. Mine's a big porcelain bowl that you piss and shit in."

"That's a chamber pot," Taite said, finishing his drink. Again, as soon as he set the tankard down, it was picked up and replaced.

"No, it's bigger and it's got plumbing."

"Plumbing?" Taite questioned, taking a swig from the fresh tankard.

"Uhh… drainage pipes."

Taite looked at her incredulously. "What a strange place you talk of."

"It's less strange than this world."

"How so?"

"In every way."

"That doesn't prove anything," Jared told her with an amused look.

Keegan gave him an annoyed glance. "Well, I can't really prove it. Plus, the things I consider normal would be like magic to y'all."

"I'm not understanding the analogy."

"What I consider normal would make you react the same way I did when I found out magic was real."

Taking a drink, Jared said, "Out of curiosity, what kinds of things are you referring to?"

"It's not like you'd believe me."

"Try me," goaded Taite.

"Okay, fine," she said with a smug air. "Magic isn't real. We have these metal contraptions that go faster than a horse, and some can fly, and some can let people survive underwater."

Taite looked at her unfazed, though disbelief pulled at the corners of his expression.

"We've been on the moon."

"Impossible," Taite balked.

"Nope, they're all true and that's barely scraping the surface. We have these little rectangles that let us talk to anyone on the planet, give us access to just about any piece of information, no matter how mundane or obscure, and you know what we use them for? To watch videos of cats and porn."

Plates of food were set before them. The barmaid went to refill Taite's cup, but he waved her off. "That's not a normal world."

Keegan took a bite, and retracted her previous argument, "Normal is relative."

"I'll agree to that."

She commented, "Wow, a first."

"And a last."

After that, they were content to eat their meal in silence. Keegan kept stealing glances down the table towards Kade and Cassidy, her eyes always returning to her plate with a roll.

Jared followed her gaze, and while he understood Kade's romanticisms, he also took Keegan's attitude that this was neither the time nor place.

Her plate cleared; she stifled a yawn. "I'm headin' to bed."

"I'll join you," Jared said, standing alongside her.

She snickered, "Not in the same bed."

Taite, who was taking a drink, nearly choked, "You should never make jokes about that. You're a lady; act like it!"

Keegan looked at him blankly and snorted. "I'm not a lady and good luck making me act like one." She made her way along the tables and coming across Kade and Cassidy, stopped to talk to them.

"You need to control that girl," Taite said.

Jared smiled. "Kade's tried, and I like her the way she is."

‡‡‡

All Kade could focus on was Cassidy: her radiant smile, the richness of her blue eyes, the way the corners of her mouth wrinkled, the slight reddening of her cheeks.

"Yo," Keegan said.

He saw no need to respond and she took this as an invitation to sit.

"Tell me more of your adventures," Cassidy said, leaning forward, cupping her chin in her hands.

"I'm su—" he began, only to be cut off.

"I thought you were headed to bed?" Taite said gruffly to Keegan.

"I'll get there eventually."

"Stay no more than twenty minutes."

"We're not children."

Taite leaned down and snarled into her ear, "Mind your tongue."

Kade could see Taite becoming angry—probably enhanced by the alcohol—and to placate him said, "We'll be up shortly."

"Humph," was Taite's response as he began stumbling towards the stairs.

"I am shocked by your audacity," Cassidy told Keegan.

Her eyebrows creased. "Why?"

"Men are our protectors. It is our duty to listen to them."

Keegan let out a snort. "Men are no more our protectors than we are theirs. You listen to them 'cause society's told you ya have to. You're just as capable as men are—if not more so."

Cassidy stared at her with a look of shock. "How can you even say that after all Kade has done for you?"

Keegan blinked a few times. "After all *Kade* has done for me? We're talking about the same person, right?"

Cassidy remained silent.

"I'll admit he's saved my hide a few times, but he takes too much credit."

Kade scoffed, "You'd be back in a cell if it weren't for me."

"I did say you saved my butt a few times."

"Is every woman from your home like this?" Cassidy asked.

"No. There are still many countries where women are considered subservient. But where I'm from, men and women are treated pretty equally. I mean, some things are still off, but it's *way* better than here."

"How so?"

"Well, women can do anything a man can. We can own property and businesses, and women rule some countries."

"And this has always been?"

"No, we've been clawing our way out of hell for centuries and in the past hundred-ish years we've made leaps and bounds."

"And how did you manage that?" Kade dismissed.

"We stopped taking your bullshit," Keegan sneered.

"Our vito?" Kade said, a hint of anger in his voice. "We do nothing but protect you."

"Protect us?"

"You need us; women are weak."

"*I'm weak*? Wanna run that by me again? 'Cause I can hold my own, and you know it."

"St-stop," Cassidy interjected. "Please. Let us go to bed."

Keegan glared at Kade as she stood. "I put up with a helluva a lot of shit. Until men can do everything a woman can without bitching and moaning, you will *never* be better than us. And even then, we should be equal."

Kade turned back to Cassidy. Hints of worry blemished her features, but there was something else, too—hope.

✝✝✝

Aron watched the castle gate from his room. A few straggling carts were pulled through the portcullis before it closed for the night. He had considered bribing one of the merchants to give him and Shiloh passage out, but with her being wary of Braxton, he knew they had to carry themselves out on their own two feet.

They needed some diversion, but what would be enough to let them go unnoticed? Aron pushed himself away from the window and started making his way to Alyck, but halfway there, turned around. He was not ready to say goodbye to Shiloh, and until such time, Alyck would refuse him.

Walking back through the halls, he became lost in his own thoughts and found himself where the hidden passage was. He pressed the stone and stepped into the darkness. At the end of the corridor, a crescent moon illuminated the gable. He sat in the middle of the rooftop and looked up at the stars.

A fire might be a good distraction. No, there was no way to create a large enough fire, and they rarely spread because almost everything in the castle was stone.

He toyed with other ideas, ranging from ridiculous ones like killing Kolt, to potential ones, like killing a guard to insinuate an attack. None would work though, and he still had no plan as the moon neared its peak.

From the plains surrounding the castle came a deep screech. He strained his eyes, but for all his worth could not spot the night eagle. The bird called again, and it reminded him of another sound he was familiar with. He smiled as the night eagle flew overhead, soaring on a light wind.

‡‡‡

His hair whipped around his face and his clothes pulled against his body. A shrieking was added to the wind. Braxton looked at the sword in his hand, which was covered in purple blood.

"Betrayer! Marmarda! Soucer!" a voice screamed.

"Az ryla sarig," Braxton cried. "Plazde, haxnug!"

"Betrayer! Marmarda! Soucer!"

His chest was ripped open, forcing a wild yell from his throat. Darkness surrounded him and whispers danced in the air.

His chest seamlessly repaired, and he saw four figures across the void from him.

He already knew what they were going to say and one at a time, all repeated the lines he had heard so many times before. Then together they said, "Psodæ woth yarv." Slowly, their voices jumbled and faded to whispers as their forms melted into the darkness.

He repeated their words, hoping he would be able to recall them when he awoke.

The world began to brighten, and he stood in the throne room, six individuals kneeling before him.

A voice asked, "Woth eya sesuna eyar kunyi?"

"Naya," the first man responded. There was a flash and his body fell forward, truncated.

Sobs filled the air as the same question was repeated to the five-remaining people. Four responded "Avu."

When it came to the sixth man, he raised his head and smiled. "Naya." A streak of gray appeared over his body. "Astæm az woth sesuna ayþ bindiar darvesen."

Momentarily confused, he realized he was awake and staring at the ceiling. He sat up, relieved to not be in pain. Outside his window, the sun shone brightly—he had slept through the night.

Throwing back the covers, he went to his desk and began trying to recall the prophecy as it had been told in his dream. Only one fragment seemed to have stuck in his memory: psodæ woth yarv.

218

CHAPTER 29

Cassidy was the first to greet the day. She rolled onto her side, studying her companions on the floor. Keegan slept diagonally between Jared, who had his back to her, and Kade, was within arms' length.

She reached over and ran her fingers through the auburn hair. A small smile formed on his lips, making her grin.

His eyes opened. *Good morning.*

It still felt strange to communicate telepathically, but she responded in kind, *Good morning. How did you sleep?*

Well. When Keegan wasn't kicking me, that is.

Cassidy gave a light laugh and he looked up at her unamused.

It was not long after that the others roused as well. They breakfasted in the tavern, eating a few pieces of freshly baked bread, and once satiated, returned to the room.

"So, what's on the agenda?" Keegan questioned.

Tying a purse to his belt, Taite answered, "I need to go to the market."

"Okay. What're the rest of us supposed to do?"

"Stay here."

"Ugh, that's so boring," Keegan said dramatically.

"That's not my—"

"I could go for a bathe," Cassidy commented.

"Abs—" Taite started.

Keegan cut him off. "I like the sound of that."

Pinching the bridge of his nose, Taite growled, "Fine." He dug through his purse and pulled out a few bronze coins, which he handed to Kade. "For the bathhouse."

Kade passed the coins along to Jared. "I'm going with you. I don't trust you."

Realizing Kade was not going to have it any other way, Taite snarled, "Suit yourself."

"So..." Keegan began as soon as they had left, "how does this work exactly?"

"We need to find a bathhouse," Cassidy said.

"I'd be inclined to believe one of the innkeepers would know," Jared said.

Downstairs, the tavern was mostly empty, a few people still eating, and one man hunched over a table, drool pooled on the side of his face.

Keegan stopped and pushed Jared towards the bar. "You ask."

He was brief talking to the inn keeper. "He said there's one not too far from here."

"Cool. Did he perchance tell you how to get there?" Keegan asked.

Jared refrained from rolling his eyes as he led the way out.

The streets had people going about their daily lives. Women carried empty baskets to market and others carried them piled high with fruits and vegetables as they made their way home. Children with wooden swords ran past them, reveling in the mockery of battle.

The buildings of Aylentowne were mostly made of a mixture of stone foundations with plaster uppers imbedded with wooden timbers for support. Windowpanes were crisscrossed with veins of dull gray metal and the streets were cobbled with worn stones cemented together with dirt.

Jared stopped. The building they stood outside of was wide, taking up what should have been several house fronts. It was built from a pale stone and there appeared to be few seams in the rock. Walking through the doorway, Cassidy instantly felt the difference in humidity weighing down on her.

A fat woman sat behind a table. "Three coppers," she said lazily.

Jared fished the money from his pocket and handed it to her.

In return, she gave them three folded linens to serve as towels. "Will you be needing an attendant?"

Jared looked to Cassidy. She gave him a slight nod and he answered, "Yes."

"Phinne," she yelled.

A young man came forward. He was handsome, but Cassidy could immediately tell why he had such a lowly job—a rich fire-mark starting under his right eye that made its way across his nose and down the side of his face.

"If the gentleman and ladies will please follow," Phinne said, starting through a doorway.

They were hit with a wall of steam, and pushing through, came into a wide, open area. There was a large pool in the center with tubs of varying sizes surrounding it. Small groups of people sat in larger tubs, letting attendants wash their hair or rub soap across their backs. In the pool, people lounged, happily talking to one another or swimming across the clear water.

As they walked across the room, Cassidy noticed Keegan's discomfort.

Phinne led them around the room to a large tub. "If you will disrobe."

Jared seemed had few qualms. Keegan, on the other hand, was less enthusiastic and stood awkwardly.

"Would you undo the lacing?" Cassidy asked, turning her back to Keegan.

With nimble fingers, she pulled away the ties.

"Thank you," Cassidy said, facing her. "Why have you not begun to disrobe?"

"This isn't how I imagined a bathhouse would be. I thought it'd be more... private."

Cassidy let her dress fall to the floor and, stepping into the water, told her, "It is not so bad, especially once you are in the water."

Gritting her teeth, Keegan began to undress, and as the last piece of clothing fell away, quickly got into the tub in an attempt to hide. She pulled her knees up and folded her arms across her chest; it concealed little as her bosom was more than ample.

"Relax, sweetheart," Phinne said. "Here, we're all as Sola and Lunos made us."

She eyed him for a moment before saying to Jared, "This is the first time I've heard any mention of religion."

"Really? How strange," commented Phinne, pouring water from a pitcher over Jared's head. "If you don't pray to Sola and Lunos, then who do you pray to?"

"No one really."

Phinne began to lather Jared's hair with a pale balm. "Who do you look to when seeking guidance or help?"

"People and science. Honestly, I feel the existence of gods can neither be proven nor disproven and until such time, I choose to remain neutral on the matter. Though, I do tend to gravitate towards science."

"Are all people like this where you're from?"

"Nope. There are a lot of religions and just as many gods to go with 'em."

"Impossibly impressive; I do wonder how you all live in harmony," Phinne said incredulously.

Keegan gave a snort of laughter as Phinne moved over to Cassidy. "We don't, not by a long shot."

"A strange place to live in."

"You don't know the half of it," she muttered under her breath.

"Where was it you said you're from again?"

"I didn't."

Phinne had the sense to not press further. The water he poured over Cassidy's head was warm and had a faint smell of violets as his fingers worked gently through the knots in her dark hair. Once he had washed Keegan's hair, he told them, "Feel free to lounge in the central pool for as long as you like."

"Thank you," Cassidy said. "You may excuse yourself until further notice."

"As you wish," Phinne said, bowing his head and walking away to sit on a stool along the wall of the bathhouse.

Keegan was not keen on moving to the large pool but followed after some cajoling.

The water was much cooler and clear as crystal. Benches were built into the wall to allow bathers to sit. People took little notice of them, though the occasional man ogled for a moment before remembering to look at their faces.

When they clambered from the water, Phinne offered them towels. They dressed quickly and made their way back to the inn. Kade and Taite had yet to return and they satisfied themselves by lounging and, in Keegan's case, napping.

‡‡‡

"Hurry up with that barrel band," Waylan chided.

Lucas brought the hammer down on the metal a few more times before stepping away from the anvil to allow Waylan to inspect his work.

He'd been working under Waylan for the better part of a month now. While his skills still needed honing, they were well on their way, and today the master decided it was time for a test. As soon as Lucas had arrived that morning, he was tasked with making a barrel band on his own.

As he looked over the band, Waylan gave a few grunts. "Not half bad. May make a smith out of you yet."

Lucas felt the corners of his lips begin to pull up.

"I need nine more. I trust you can manage by yourself."

"Yes, sir," Lucas said.

"Hop to it."

Lucas gave the fire a few puffs from the bellow before sticking nine rods of steel into the flames. Once they glowed red, he removed one and set to forming it, the hammer in his hand setting a steady rhythm. In the background, he could hear Waylan working on a project of his own.

Slowly, he made his way through the steel rods. When he reached number seven, he heard Waylan curse. He turned to see what had made the usually austere man react. In his hands, Waylan held the pieces of a cold chisel. Lucas returned to his work as Waylan began searching for another.

Not long after, Waylan cursed again. "Finish those bands and watch the shop," he instructed, walking by. "If a customer comes in, tell 'em I'm out and they'll need to come back tomorrow."

Lucas called after him, "Where are you going?"

"To Arkav's to see if he'll lend me a chisel."

"Just make a new one."

"That crest goes out tomorrow, I don't have time."

Satisfied with the answer, Lucas returned to the bands. He finished quickly and as he was cleaning up, heard the bell on the front door chime. Peeking into the front room, he saw four soldiers, all roughly his age. "The smith's not here, you'll need to come back tomorrow," he told them.

"Who are you then, boy?" one asked. The man had long, greasy brown hair and wide-set eyes, giving him a dull appearance. He appeared to be the leader of the group.

"His apprentice."

"Then you'll take my order; I, Maryn Arst, squad three of the inner quarter's corps newest second lieutenant, need a helmet in the form of a dragon's head."

The ego on this fool. "No. Orders will be received tomorrow when the smith returns."

"You'll take it now."

"I've been instructed not to and for an order like that, measurements and preferences will need to be taken."

"Boy, we are soldiers! You will do as we say!"

Lucas laughed. "Unless you'd like to craft it yourself, you'll have to wait until the morrow."

"You dare deny us?" one of the other soldiers spoke up, his voice high-pitched.

"Quiet, Elza," Maryn snapped.

"I'm not refusing you," Lucas bit. "The smith has just asked that you return tomorrow to place the order when he's here."

"Piece of vite. How dare you refuse me, squad three of the—"

"No one cares," Lucas cut him off and with a wave of the hand, told them, "Now leave, I have no time for dumb animals."

As he turned, a force struck him in the back of the head, sending him careening into one of the posts that bore the upper level. His head struck the corner of the wood and his vision blacked momentarily. He could feel blood trickling down his forehead.

"Graw, Hynde, grab his arms," Maryn ordered.

Still dazed, he was unable to react before they latched onto his arms and Maryn punched him in the face. "Son of an bw—" he began as he was struck in the stomach and hunched over coughing.

"Be quie—" Maryn ordered.

"Is that all you've got? I know women who hit harder."

Flying into a rage, Maryn continued to strike. Not being one to back down, Lucas took each hit and returned it with an insult. Each one infuriated Maryn more, which only made each insult truer.

Seeing that hitting him wasn't having the desired effect, Maryn paused, breathing heavily. After a moment, he asked, "What do we do to dogs that enjoy being hit?"

"We brand them," Elza answered, taking a handful of Lucas's hair.

With a nasty smile, Maryn took a rod of metal and shoved it into the fire.

Lucas began to tug against Graw and Hynde in earnest.

"Oh look, the dog fears fire," Elza sneered.

When the rod was cherry red, Maryn pulled it from the flames and neared Lucas' bare neck. "Hold him still."

Lucas could feel the driving heat when the soldier was yanked away.

"What the fuck do you think you're doing?" roared Waylan. He grabbed Graw and threw him on top of Maryn. "Get out of my shop, you bastards of swine!"

Hynde released Lucas and tried to draw his sword. Waylan placed an open hand over his face and shoved him backwards. His head struck Elza's, who had been coming to his aid, and the two fell to the floor, dazed.

"My commander will hear about this," Maryn threatened.

"And he'll beat your ass for it," Waylan yelled. "Every commander knows who I am, knows the value of my work. Get the fuck out of my shop. And don't come back."

The men scrambled out, holding their injuries.

Lucas lay on the floor, thankful for Waylan's impeccable timing.

The smith offered him a hand. "What were you thinking egging them on?"

"They wouldn't leave when asked nicely."

Waylan shook his head. "Clean yourself up and go home." He walked away muttering under his breath, though Lucas did hear one thing, "Idiot."

‡‡‡

Caius stood before the Looking Glass. "Where is Connery?" he questioned.

Braxton was surprised he was the only one whose presence Caius had requested.

"He's... preoccupied," Vitia answered slyly.

Something about the way she said it did not sit right with Braxton.

"Have you found the girl?"

"No, sir," Vitia answered with a hint of shame.

"And why is that?"

"Uh... we..."

"Out with it."

"They seem to have vanished. We thought they were headed to Bouyne, bu—"

"You thought?" Caius cut her off.

Vitia declined to respond.

Caius stormed towards the door, "You imbeciles!"

"What about the boy?" Braxton asked.

His father paused.

"What boy?" Vitia asked, feigning ignorance.

"Yes, the boy?" Caius said, returning. "Do you still have him?"

Vitia was slow in answering. "Yes."

"What was his name again?"

"Nico Sieme," Vitia answered. Clearly, she was not making the connections his father was.

"I want him brought here. Unharmed."

"But he's just a stup—" Vitia started.

"Unharmed."

Finding she had no other choice, Vitia responded, "Yes, sir," with a bow before walking away.

A shrewd smile played across Caius' lips as he left the room.

Braxton chased after him. "Why did you only ask for me today?"

"As much as I prefer Kolt," Caius answered, "you are the one poised to take the throne. There is no need to involve Kolt in such mundane things, but you must learn to handle any situation. And, unfortunately, I must thank you for reminding me of the boy."

"Why the sudden interest in him?"

Caius walked away. "He will be of use."

‡‡‡

Kade crossed his arms and followed Taite through the market; they were finally on the last item on the list. He leaned against the pole of the stall and let Taite talk to the merchant. The transaction finished, they headed back to the inn and he was more than happy to let Taite struggle to carry the purchases.

Back in the room, they found Jared and Cassidy lounging and Keegan asleep on the floor.

Taite grunted in greeting, then mumbled something about going to the bar.

Kade sat on the bed next to Cassidy and wrapped an arm around her. "I presume your day was better than mine."

"I would hope so," Cassidy said with a smile. "Spending that much time alone with Taite cannot be enjoyable."

She had held Taite in high regard in the beginning, as one would a Kojote. But as they traveled, she too began to dislike him, finally noticing he never had a kind word and how he treated them with disdain.

Kade let out a sigh and pulled her closer.

Opening her eyes, Keegan mocked, "Daw, look at the lovebirds."

Kade quickly retracted his arm and Cassidy looked away, her cheeks coloring.

Must you always do that, Kade snapped.

Yeah, she said with a small snigger. *It's hella funny. Plus, you don't need to be hooking up with Cassidy.*

Hooking up?

Doing anything sexual. It's not the time or place, and Cassidy doesn't need to be hurt by your lack of restraint.

Kade stared at her angrily.

"I really dislike it when you two do that," Jared commented.

"Do what?" Keegan asked.

"Have your own private conversations."

"I can understand wanting to hear me chew Kade out, but it's best not to air one's dirty laundry."

"Air dirty laundry?"

"Make yourself look like an ass."

"You do that just fine already," Kade said, pushing off the bed and storming across the room, making sure to slam the door behind him. He stomped down the stairs and made his way to the bar. "Give me a pint."

The man looked at him doubtfully. "Bronze coin."

Kade pulled a coin from his pocket and slammed it onto the counter.

"That didn't take long," Taite said beside him.

Kade gritted his teeth and turned to see the Kojote nursing a pint. The barman placed a tankard before him, which he took and downed. "Another," he snapped, throwing a second coin onto the counter.

"She put you in a state," Taite commented.

He returned, "She's put you into plenty of states, too."

"That she has."

Kade felt a gentle tap on his shoulder. Turning around, he barked, "What?"

Cassidy pulled away at his aggressive response.

"I'm sorry; I thought you were Keegan."

"May I talk to you?" she said softly.

"Of course."

She took his hand and led him across the bar, out the back door, and into the stables.

"Couldn't we have talked inside?"

"I didn't want Taite overhearing us. Keegan told me what she said."

Kade gritted his teeth and started to speak.

"I think she is wrong."

"In what way?"

"You do not sully me. I find that you bring out parts of me that even I have not yet discovered." Her dazzling eyes looked up at him. "Like the parts of me that are not afraid of the world. The part that is not afraid of my magic, the part that has learned to trust another."

He was drawn by her gaze, the sincerity in her irises mesmerizing. Suddenly, their lips were touching, hers soft and gentle against his. He broke away. "We shouldn't."

"Why?" Cassidy questioned gently.

"I don't want to hurt you. You know my reputation. And looking after the opida needs to be my priority."

Cassidy placed a warm hand on his cheek, "I don't believe you will hurt me."

"I wish that were true, but I'm a killer and have little capacity to change."

"Everyone is possible of change, even you."

"Doubtful," Kade said, holding her hand against his face.

"No," Cassidy said definitively, kissing him again. "I have seen it. You can be kind and gentle when you want."

Giving into his temptation, he told her, "With you, I want to. But I'm not sure that's enough."

‡‡‡

227

Bouyne's dungeon was hardly better than Suttan's. Instead of a pile of hay for a bed, Bouyne had platforms bracketed to the walls. While the board was hard, Nico found it preferable to being on the floor with the rats.

It was tricky keeping track of how much time had passed in a place where light shone through a tiny hole for only a few hours a day. The food was often gruel with a slice of bread and water—never enough to satisfy his hunger.

Mostly, he slept. There was little else to do and it was the only time he wasn't hungry. Sometimes, he *almost* wished the Vosjnik would catch their quarry so he wouldn't be alone.

It seemed like months before Dax came to collect him, but he knew it'd only been a few days. When he went outside, the sky was dark, clouds obscuring the moon and stars. Six horses stood saddled in the courtyard; only four had riders. In the gloom, it was hard to make out who was missing.

"Where's Connery?" Nico asked, dread in his heart at the realization of who was missing.

"Dead," Vitia answered, smiling cruelly. "He tried to flee."

"More like gutted in his sleep," Dax muttered under his breath.

"He was a dead man," Vitia sneered. "He was charged with capturing Keegan and failed. He knew if he rode to Agrielha, it was to his death. So, like a coward, he tried to flee, but didn't get far before I drove my sword through his belly."

"Didn't get anywhere at all, sleeping men don't run."

Nico felt his heart pounding away in his chest; Connery had been the only one keeping him alive.

"Don't fret," Dax said, helping him onto a horse, "the king's commanded that you be brought to him unharmed."

Nico cursed to himself; it'd be better to die now than face the torments of the king.

CHAPTER 30

Aron rounded the corner in the dark passageway, the pit in his stomach weighing heavily. That morning, he had found a note from Shiloh requesting they meet on the rooftop at midday. While they had used notes to set up a rendezvous in the past, it had only been in dire emergencies. And to be meeting in the middle of the day was unusual.

He reached the second doorway and stopped, his heart beating a little faster. Opening the door, he stepped out onto the gable. The sun was blinding, and he shielded his eyes.

His sight adjusted and across the way, he saw Shiloh, tears streaming down her face.

Kolt held her arm.

Aron's stomach dropped like a stone and he rushed forward, barely making it a few feet before two guards grabbed his arms. "Kolt!" he bellowed, straining against the men.

Pleasantly, Kolt said, "Why, hello."

"Let her go!"

"Oh, come. I am offended you have not introduced me to Shiloh."

Aron stopped pulling against the guards, his body refusing to move.

"She is quite beautiful," Kolt continued, reaching towards her face.

Shiloh pulled away, giving an anxious hiccup.

Kolt jerked on her arm, forcing her closer to him and ran his hand along her cheek, brushing away the tears.

"Please, let her go," Aron said. "I will give you whatever you want."

Kolt laughed, "You cannot give me what I want; no one can." He drew his knife and watched the sunlight catch its edge.

"Your quarrel is with me. *Please*, let her go."

"That is true. However, the issue is, Shiloh makes you happy and that makes me very *un*happy. See the dilemma?"

"No!"

"You took someone I loved away from me."

"It was not my fault," he said, finally understanding.

Kolt's calm and cool demeanor disappeared to be replaced by one of pure hatred. "You killed her, you killed Mother!" Taking a deep breath, he collected himself. "And now I am going to kill her."

"No!" But it was too late. Helplessly, he watched Kolt jam the knife into Shiloh's stomach. A sickening crimson instantly stained the cloth around the wound.

Shiloh touched her stomach, her fingers becoming coated in slick blood.

The guards released him, he started towards her.

Kolt scoffed, "You think I would allow you any chance to save her?" With that, he pushed Shiloh back and over the wall.

Aron knew he was screaming but could not hear himself.

Kolt pulled him back from the edge. "Cannot have you following her, *dear* brother. Father would have my head. But do look."

Far below he could see the mark that was once Shiloh.

"Take him to his chambers," Kolt said, passing him off to the guards.

The guards propelled him along, his body uncooperative, and he took no comfort in knowing they were injured at every pitfall. His mind entered a blank state and his body went numb.

Suddenly, he found himself sitting on his bed. No one was around, the sky was dark, and a single candle by the door lit the room. Exhaustion hit him like a brick, and he knew he should blow it out, but his body refused to respond.

At some point, he fell back onto the mattress and his eyelids closed, sending him into yet another nightmare.

There will be no happy ending.

‡‡‡

Kade and Cassidy explored the streets of Aylentowne, or so they claimed, and didn't return until well after he and Keegan had finished dinner.

Jared glanced at her; something was weighing on her.

Again, Cassidy slept in the bed while the rest of them slumbered on the floor. Taite came barreling into the room during the middle of the night and in the morning, his brown hair stuck up in some places and was plastered to his head in others. His eyes were bloodshot, and he was even less amiable than usual.

They quickly breakfasted before leaving the inn, and exiting the city wasn't as much of a trial as leaving Suttan. Kade and Cassidy stayed near each other throughout the day, communicating telepathically—Jared had a fairly good idea why. Taite's bad mood transferred to Keegan, making her touchy.

The evening passed in verbal silence, but often a smile played on Kade or Cassidy's lips, eliciting rolled eyes from Keegan.

The night's training started, and as always, Kade made his movements seem easy and fluid. Jared wasn't as graceful and found his hands and feet stopping as his brain struggled to direct them. Keegan often yelled at him for telegraphing, though he had no idea what that was. While there was still no contest, he was getting better.

Soon enough, Kade ended another bout and let Jared rest. Keegan took his spot with none of her usual energy. They began, she with her one-handed grip and Kade with his two-handed one.

"Why do you fight like that?" Cassidy asked.

"Like what?" Keegan said, keeping her attention on Kade.

"With a singled-handed grip."

"It's how I was trained."

"You should learn to use both hands," Kade told her.

"I'll do that when this stop working."

They began edging around each other; it would be a battle of wits as well as strength. Keegan lifted her front foot and stomped it down, faking an intention to lunge forward. Instinctively, Kade's arm twitched. Jared watched, knowing that soon Keegan would actually attack; she often did things like this to test Kade's reactions. When still unaccustomed to the other's fighting style, her tricks had worked and she had easily landed an attack; now that Kade had learned the praxes, it took a bit more before she was successful.

Kade made the first attack with a slash.

She parried and retaliated by rolling in against his arms, making her way to his back. Before he could launch another attack, she had her weapon against his neck. "I win."

Without warning, Kade spun, swinging his weapon.

She dropped and brought her stick across his shins, then jabbed it up into his ribcage. "Step it up."

"Remember, you asked f—" Kade started as she kicked the side of his knee.

Jared saw Kade's leg buckle and knew she'd hit the nerves. Kade stayed on his feet but struggled to put weight on the leg. He swung at her, but both knew it would do no good.

She easily evaded the strike and placed the end of the stick against his chest. "You're losing it."

"No," Kade said, tossing his stick aside, "I just don't want to hurt you."

"Letting me win teaches me nothing."

"Let's be honest, it's not because I'm going easy that you're mad."

Keegan threw her stick into the fire. "Not entirely, but it isn't helping."

"What have I done to anger you?"

"Nothing."

231

"Then what's upsetting you?"

"Nothing," she answered, making her way to her bedroll.

"Bulla vite." Her declining to respond only angered him more. "I'm getting really ti—" He cut himself off and glanced at Cassidy.

Damn telepathy, Jared thought.

Kade shot Keegan a glare, then sat beside Cassidy. Taite was leaned up against a tree, arms across his chest, and a smirk on his face, no doubt enjoying this.

Jared gave him a scowl before looking at Keegan. She lay on her bedroll, her back to them. Now that she faced away from everyone, her anger dissipated to be replaced by gloom. He couldn't explain how he knew how she felt. The air in the camp was awkward and with nothing better to do, he followed her example and went to sleep.

‡‡‡

Keegan awoke to the sounds of birds chirping gaily. From the stillness in the camp, she was the first awake. Rolling onto her side, she stared into the forest, her eyes glazing over. She wandered about her own mind, clenching her jaw to keep emotions from tumbling forth. Today was going to be a day in proverbial hell; homesickness had hit like a brick.

Drawing her knees up, she pulled the bedroll over her head. Behind her, someone got up and trudged into the underbrush. Then came the sound of falling water. She was glad she was enveloped in the bedroll, saving her from embarrassing whoever it was.

After that there was the sound of a knife against steel and the crackling that accompanied burning foliage. Rolling over, she peeked out from the bedroll, finding Kade adding kindling to a newborn fire.

He looked at her for a moment, then returned to tending the fire.

"I'm sorry," she said quietly.

He looked up. "For what?"

"For last night; I was being a bitch."

He gave a silent snort of laughter. "I've grown used to it."

"You shouldn't've had to."

He glanced around, making sure the others were still asleep. "When my parents died, I took it hard, and was awful to Thaddeus. Sadly, it was also what fueled me."

She wasn't sure where he was going.

"I can't understand what you're going through in its entirety, but to a degree, you're entitled to be a bit of a bwint, just make sure it doesn't become a defining trait."

"Like you?"

"This is what I'm talking about."

Keegan bit her cheek.

"But I also think this is how you show affection."

She raised an eyebrow, watched his lips pull back into a small smile, and admitted, "Just a bit."

He shook his head and began cooking breakfast.

When he looked away, the moment of happiness faded, and melancholy returned. Sighing, she turned onto her stomach, resting her head on her arms.

The others awoke shortly thereafter and sat around the fire, waiting for breakfast. Once done, Kade handed out the food. She kept herself in the warmth of the bedroll.

The others had started eating when Kade noticed she hadn't come to receive her portion. "Come eat."

Her stomach grumbled quietly but food seemed physically unappetizing. "I'm not hungry."

Jared gave Kade a concerned look and asked, "You sure?"

She nodded.

Kade shrugged and began eating.

‡‡‡

The day was spent in an unusual hush. Keegan said little, whereas Kade and Cassidy were enraptured in each other. Taite couldn't have cared less about what they did as he rarely talked to them anyway. While Keegan, like everyone, had days when she was more introspective, Jared was beginning to worry, as she seemed downcast and fragile. He also knew that if he continually asked if she was all right she'd eventually snap.

That night, when they stopped, he pulled Kade aside. "I think something's bothering Keegan."

"She seemed fine when I talked to her this morning," Kade said, stealing a glance at her.

"When did you talk to her?"

"Before the rest of you were awake."

Jared crossed his arms. "What did you talk about?"

"She apologized for being a bwint last night."

"She *apologized*?"

"Yes. I was just as surprised as you."

"That's very out of character for her," Jared said.

"Oh no, something may actually be wrong with her," Kade said sarcastically. He was quiet for a moment. "She didn't eat breakfast and barely touched lunch."

"I wouldn't have said anything if I didn't think there was a problem."

"I'll talk to her."

Jared stopped him, "Are you sure that's the best idea? You'll just end up fighting."

"Fine," Kade snapped, "you talk to her."

Jared nodded and turned around. Both Keegan and Cassidy were gone. "Where are they?"

"How should I know! I was talking to you."

"Where are Keegan and Cassidy?" Jared questioned Taite, who was tending the fire.

"Wandered off," Taite answered apathetically.

"Did you not think to ask where they were going?" Kade said angrily.

"No. They can only get so far."

Kade clenched his fist to stop himself from lashing out. "We'll split up and look for them," he told Jared.

CHAPTER 31

The wagon jolted to a stop and an air of fear arose. Thaddeus remained calm, knowing the guards would not be excessive without cause. Only one man insisted on giving them trouble and he bore the evidence of it.

The door was pulled open and the other occupants shied away, but Thaddeus greeted the guard, "Good evening, Laydeon. I take it we are stopping for the night."

Laydeon gave him a nod. "You know the drill."

One by one, they were taken out and allowed to relieve themselves. As they were made to re-enter the wagon, a small loaf of bread and a cup of water were jammed into their hands.

Night fell quickly in the wagon, sending them into darkness well before the sun disappeared. The young ones huddled against each other, quickly falling into a fitful sleep. On the first few nights, the children had shed tears. Now, there were hardly any left to wet the eyes.

Through the small bars, Thaddeus could hear the soldiers laughing around a campfire. It was chilly in the cart and he would give much to have the warmth of the flames. He shifted, wincing as the manacles pulled at open sores. He muttered, "Hamoomph," and watched his skin heal. Once the others were asleep, he would attempt to heal them, too.

While his magic had returned, he was still testing his limits. Before Rosh died, he had been a force to reckon with; now, even small acts of magic left him exhausted. There was much to do before he returned to his former strength—if he could ever regain it.

Letting his mind drift, his thoughts turned to Reven, recalling the message of sorts he had been able to send, telling him how to reach the Lazado, and imploring him to flee. Whether he heeded the request was another matter.

A snore from the man beside him jolted him back. He glanced around, making sure everyone was asleep and began healing their wounded wrists, starting with the children. They shifted in their sleep as his magic worked but they did not awaken.

The others did not stir when healed, though sighs of relief were emitted. When he came to the man who insisted on resisting, his attempt at healing the many injuries hardly got past a few bruises before exhaustion overtook him. He had mended too few for the man to even notice.

Quietly, he made his way back to his place and leaned against the side of the wagon, his eyes quickly closing.

‡‡‡

As soon as they stopped and set up camp, Jared pulled Kade aside and spoke to him in hushed tones.

Cassidy, presuming it had something to do with Keegan, approached her. "Would you come get firewood with me?"

"Doesn't Kade usually go with you?" she said, unfurling her bedroll.

"Yes, but he is preoccupied."

Keegan looked up. "Uh... fine."

Cassidy gave her a quick smile as they started into the forest.

Keegan automatically began to pick up sticks at the tree line.

"Not those."

"Why?"

"Just not those," Cassidy insisted, continuing to walk.

Keegan hesitated but followed, dropping the sticks.

They walked silently for several more minutes before Cassidy stopped. "This should be far enough."

Quietly, Keegan started collecting sticks again.

Cassidy placed a hand on her arm. "Leave those, I want to talk to you."

Keegan questioned defensively, "About what?"

"Something is weighing on you; do you want to talk?"

She pulled away, crossing her arms, "Not really. Even if I did, why would I talk to you?"

"I just figured you would be more open with me—considering how you are around the boys."

"And how is that?"

"You try to act like them and make it appear as if nothing bothers you."

"That's not acting."

Softly, Cassidy said, "You and I both know that is not true."

Keegan declined to respond.

Cassidy sensed the emotions radiating from her and recalled how Kade had explained that when telepaths experienced strong emotions, they inadvertently broadcasted them. Waves of anger and misery emanated from Keegan and it was then she realized what she needed. Gently, she wrapped her arms around her. "It is going to be... okay."

Keegan remained still for a moment, surprised, then slowly reciprocated.

Cassidy could feel hot tears on her shoulder.

236

"I can't do this," Keegan broke, pulling away to sit against a tree, tears flowing freely.

Cassidy knelt beside her. "What can you not do?"

"Anything," Keegan cried. "I can't save y'all; I can't even save myself. I can't be this person that everyone wants me to be. All I want is to go home."

Cassidy made to respond, but Keegan buried her face in her hands, beginning to cry in earnest with sobs that shook her body.

Jared materialized from the woods like a spirit and knelt beside her, placing a hand on her shoulder. Keegan's head jerked up and he pulled her close, letting her cry as he held her.

As the sobs subsided, she pulled away, sniffed, and gave a broken laugh. "God, I'm such a mess."

Jared wiped away her tears, "No more than the rest of us. Do you want to talk?"

"There's not much to talk about; I'm just really homesick. Yesterday was my birthday, and it's the first time since I was adopted that I haven't spent it with my family."

Jared took her hand, "We are *always* here for you."

Keegan smiled. "I know, thank you."

‡‡‡

"Keegan! Cassidy!" Kade yelled as he tramped through the forest. He'd been searching for what felt like hours. In frustration, he gave up and stormed back to camp, finding everyone sitting around the fire. "Where have you been?" he asked furiously.

"Around," was Keegan's answer.

He made to retort but stopped; she'd answered in a way that didn't convey anger or attitude and seemed calm—which was a welcome change. He took a seat next to Cassidy. *What happened?*

She is not as strong as the façade she puts up.

What's that supposed to mean?

Cassidy smiled sweetly, *I have faith you will understand in time.*

Jared handed him half of a grouse; the others had already eaten.

"We practicing tonight?" Keegan asked quietly.

"No," Kade answered. On a normal night, he would've made them, but there was something brittle about Keegan.

They were silent, the only sounds coming from the forest and the fire. Keegan wiped her eyes with the back of her hand and moved closer

237

to Jared. At first, he didn't seem to notice, but when he did, he wrapped his arm around her shoulders and let her rest her head on his chest.

Taite raised an eyebrow but didn't care enough to comment.

Taking note, Kade questioned, *Did I miss something?*

Oh yes, Cassidy responded, *but it is not what you think.*

Are you ever going to tell me what happened?

It is not my place.

Kade got to his feet and offered Cassidy a hand. *Walk with me.*

"Where are you going?" Taite questioned.

"To get firewood," Kade lied.

A laugh came from Cassidy, *We used that excuse earlier.*

Taite glared at him. "Don't lie to me, boy."

For a moment Kade worried Taite had gotten through his wall, then realized he was bluffing. "Prove it," he said, pulling Cassidy from the campsite.

Once out of earshot, she asked, "Where are we going?"

"A place I found earlier."

She let him lead her along and after a time, they emerged from the forest at the base of a small hill. They climbed to its crest, a breeze pulling at them gently.

"What is so special?" Cassidy questioned, looping her arm through his.

"You can see the sky here."

She glanced up. "They are just stars."

"I know, but that's not what made me want to bring you here."

"Then what?"

"Tell me, what do you see that's different from what you saw in Suttan?"

"I have never studied astronomy."

"You don't have to have studied the stars before."

Scrutinizing the sky, she said, "I cannot discern a difference."

"Exactly."

"What is your point?"

"No matter where you are, we all see the same sky. The only thing that changes is time."

"How do you know that?" Cassidy asked, looking back up.

"I've traveled across Arciol," he said. "Over all that time, the sky was the only constant. It's what made it a little easier to let my old life go."

Cassidy leaned against him. "Do you ever miss it?"

He enveloped her in his arms and kissed the top of her raven curls. "Every day. But I've learned the past is said and done. The only thing to do is move forward."

‡‡‡

"Tomorrow?" Virgil exclaimed.

A few people in the tavern turned to look at his outburst.

"That gives me no time to put my affairs in order."

"That's when I leave," Jehrick said. The man had his hood pulled down, making it hard to discern his features. His voice was low and gruff, which only added to the mystery of his persona.

"When will your next trip be?" Virgil pressed the Kojote.

"This is my last one. The state's become increasingly dangerous for elementals and the like."

"We can always talk to another Kojote," Jude said quietly to Virgil.

"No," Virgil responded, "Jehrick is the only one I trust."

"Then there's no other choice."

"When do you leave?" Virgil asked Jehrick.

"Dawn. Meet me at the north gate." The Kojote stood and made his way from the tavern without looking back.

"Why did you need us here?" Carter asked.

"Safety in numbers, my boy," Virgil answered. "The country is uneasy, and soldiers have become quick to draw their swords."

"We should return home. I'm sure Laiyla and Alivia have much to prepare for," Jude pointed out.

They quietly made their way from the tavern and into the humid night air. Across the street, the door to another tavern opened, spilling light and four stumbling soldiers.

The soldiers were making their way behind them and after some time, Lucas stole a glance back. It was Maryn and his crew of idiots. He turned around quickly, hoping he hadn't been recognized.

"Boy!" Maryn called out drunkenly.

"Keep walking," Lucas hissed.

"Boy, I um talkin' to ya," Maryn yelled.

A hand grabbed his arm. "'Id yu not hear 'im?" Graw asked.

"Leave him alone," Carter said.

Elza pushed Carter, "Mind ye own business."

Carter stumbled into Jude, who had to stop him from rushing forward.

239

"Gentlemen, what is the problem here?" Virgil questioned, stepping in.

"'oy here insulted meh," Maryn said, punching at Lucas.

He was too far away to bother reacting defensively. Recalling the heat from the iron, he lunged at Maryn.

Virgil stepped between them. "Let us be civil."

"I um always 'ivil," Maryn said, puffing out his chest, "but dogs j'st d' n't know h' to do wha—"

His words were cut out as Lucas pushed past Virgil and shoved Maryn to the ground. The other soldiers stared and unsteadily drew their swords.

"N', this 's ma fight," Maryn yelled at them.

Lucas glanced down to see he'd drawn a dagger, which he threw. It went wide and sailed past him safely. "Fool." But there came a gasp from behind him and when he turned, he saw the knife protruding from his father's chest.

Jude gagged, staggered, and fell to his knees.

Fury rose in Lucas and he began to strike Maryn. The drunken man didn't fight back, and his head smashed into the ground with each punch. Soon, his face was distorted, and life had left him.

Virgil pulled at him. "Lucas!" he roared, finally getting his attention. "We need to leave."

He stared at the other soldiers, who seemed dazed, as if waking from a dream, and begrudgingly followed Virgil, Jude stumbling along as Carter supported him.

After a few minutes, Jude forced them to stop. "I can't," he said, leaning against a wall and coughing, droplets of blood coating his lips.

"No, we can't lose you, too," pleaded Carter.

"Lucas, look after your bother. Find Jared and Nico," Jude instructed. "Go with Virgil and *listen* to him. Don't be a fool."

"You're coming with us," Carter protested.

Jude coughed again, spurting red onto his son. "Carter, keep Lucas levelheaded. I love you boys. Pass it along." He gave a final wheeze before his eyes glazed over.

Tears began to fall down Carter's cheeks and Lucas knew his brother would've remained there had Virgil not pulled them along.

"Nothing we could do," Virgil said in a pathetic attempt to console them. Once inside the house, he began scrambling to prepare Laiyla and Alivia to flee.

Lucas and Carter sat on the steps, their lives crumbling about them again.

"Pack, boys," Virgil said, passing by.

"No, we're staying," Lucas said.

"Your fath—"

"I know what he said, and we're staying here!"

"I know you are upset," Virgil said softly, "but trust me, it is in your best interest to come with us."

"We're staying."

Seeing there was no use in arguing, Virgil shook his head. "You are grown men and I cannot force you to do anything. Just know that you will not be able to stay here much longer."

"I don't care. I don't care about anything but revenge!"

"We should go with them," Carter said feebly.

"No, we're going to stay here and kill the men who murdered our father. Then, we're going to kill the Vosjnik."

CHAPTER 32

With no one to chase after, travel slowed to a comfortable pace, but each passing day filled Nico with dread and Vitia reveled in the knowledge. When they came across Lake Romann, they were waylaid a day by a passing storm. In the morn, they boarded a boat with the horses and crossed. Nico spent the whole time hunched over the railing divulging the contents of his stomach. Strangely, Dax was beside him, his face green.

Since morning, the castle of Agrielha, sitting on its lonely hill and the city itself, up against the winding river, had been visible. When the castle was no more than a few miles before them, the brickwork turned to a dark color that contrasted against the lush green of the grass around it. By afternoon, they were in its shadow.

Vitia took them to a low-lying building where the horses were handed over to stable boys.

Dax pulled Nico back outside. Since Connery's death, Vitia had stepped into command and Dax had become her lieutenant.

Hauled towards the castle, he desperately thought of escape. To run meant death, and to be taken to Caius meant death. Since the Vosjnik had captured him, it was simply a matter of when. *June 18th,* he thought, *the day my name is forgotten.*

The inside of the castle was cool and dark but Vitia and Dax barely slowed, and Nico stumbled as his eyes adjusted to the dimness. They marched up flights of stairs and by the time they reached the upper levels, his heart was pounding.

They came upon black oak doors with rearing griffins carved into each side. Guards pulled them open and Nico was pushed through. The room was cavernous, their steps echoing off the walls. Ash sat between the stones like gray blood and a throne inlaid with copious amounts of gold sat against the far wall. The man sitting on it bore a deep scowl that was only heightened by the scruff on his jaw. Two young men stood to either side of him.

Just before they reached the steps leading up to the throne, Vitia stopped. "Kneel before your king." When Nico remained still, she pushed him forward. "I said kneel!"

Vitia went to smack him, but the king stopped her. "Where is Connery?"

Hand still raised, Vitia answered, "Dead."

"By whose hand?"

Pulling away, she looked the king in the eye and said, "Mine, sir."

242

"Why?"

"Coward tried to run."

Dax's jaw tightened as he restrained himself.

Satisfied, Caius told her, "You are the new Commander of the Vosjnik. I take it you have chosen Dax as your lieutenant."

"Yes, sir."

"Good. Go replace the members you lost, then report back to me."

Vitia turned on her heels and made her way from the room, Dax following.

Nico could feel his body shaking. Gritting his teeth, he looked up at the king.

The man simply studied him, his brown eyes boring into him.

Nico lowered his gaze.

"Nico," Caius began, "you will enter under the tutelage of Braxton."

His head snapped up in surprise.

"Now, there are a few ways in which we can proceed; you can do as you are told, or you can resist, and he will break you."

"I w—" Braxton started to butt in.

"Silence," the king snapped and returned his attention to the boy, "Which shall it be?"

"I will never serve you," Nico said, mustering all his courage.

The other man standing beside Caius let out a laugh.

"Never."

The king waved his hand and two guards led Nico from the throne room. "Never say never, boy."

✝✝✝

"I will not—" Braxton started as he chased after his father.

Caius cut him off nonchalantly, "You can, and you will."

"He is just a child."

"That means nothing."

Braxton stood before him, blocking his path. "I will not do it." Blackness overcame his vision. "Betrayer! Marmarda! Soucer!" a voice called. He could feel something sharp ripping across his chest. The world came to light again.

A sneer crossed Caius' face. "You do it, or I will. Which would you prefer?"

Braxton stared angrily.

Thinking he had won, Caius pushed past him.

"I *will not* do it."

243

"Fine, be stubborn. I will start the process. Just let me know when you wish to take over."

Voices whispered words in his ear that he had heard in dreams. He shook his head and returned to the present then berated himself; he had just condemned the poor boy. Few grown men lasted long under his father's thumb—a child would fall even quicker. He turned to walk in the other direction and knocked into Kolt.

"Watch where you are going," Kolt growled, shoving him.

Angry at the cards life had dealt him, Braxton pushed Kolt back, sending him into the wall. "You may be father's favorite, but do not forget who I am," he snarled, clutching his brother's shirt to keep him in place.

Six people knelt before him, and a question was asked. A man disappeared. The question was repeated, and the answer changed.

"And who would that be?" Kolt tested with a sneer.

He cleared his thoughts before answering, "The heir." Then tightening his grip on Kolt's shirt, he snarled, "I should rid myself of you now, little monster. The only thing you do is take up space."

"But you will not," Kolt said dismissively, loosening Braxton's grip and walking away. "Run along now, we all know you will never lay a hand on me. Oh, you might want to check on the youngest." With a laugh he added, "Something seems to be upsetting the poor bastard. I wonder what it could be."

He immediately started making his way towards Aron's room, but before he did, went past his own. As soon as his altercation with Kolt diffused, he had begun repeating what he had heard. But with each reiteration, he recalled less and less. Now that he was in his room, he could only recall 'psodæ woth yarv'.

✚✚✚

Aron lay beneath the covers, staring at the opposite wall—the same one he had been staring at for so many days he had lost count. On the bedside table sat a tray of untouched food. His stomach gave a soft gurgle but he ignored it, knowing he would not be able to keep it down.

He closed his eyes and saw Shiloh's face, the look of terror as she fell over the edge, deepening his own darkness. He opened his eyes, unable to stand her frightened face anymore. Sadness welled and he buried his face into the pillow.

There was a knock at the door, but he made no motion to answer it. The knock came again. He hoped they went away—wanting nothing

244

more than to be left to wallow in his misery. In time, he would fade from memory and this world.

The knock was more persistence. "Aron, open up," Braxton called. "I know you are in there."

Aron wanted to yell, tell him to leave, but could not muster the energy.

"Open the noxþox door," Braxton shouted. Finally, in frustration, he barged in. His face was hard and angry, but when he saw Aron, it softened. He poked his head out of the doorway and instructed a servant to draw a bath. "You cannot hide in here forever," he said, approaching the bed.

Aron kept silent.

"Kolt has done some vicious things to torment you over the years, but I have never seen you act like this; what did he do?"

Aron looked at his brother, pain reflecting in his eyes. "He killed her."

Braxton paused, "Who?"

Aron choked on her name, "Shiloh."

"The girl who fell off the roof last week?"

"She did not fall, she was pushed."

Braxton sighed, "By Kolt."

"After he stuck a knife in her."

There was a knock and a servant entered carrying a tub. Others followed with buckets to fill it. Once the tub was full, a fire elemental heated it until a light steam rose off the surface.

"You stink," Braxton told him.

Aron looked away.

Braxton took this to be his argument against bathing and pulled back the covers. "You cannot sit in your own filth forever. People die, it happens. Celebrate the life they had instead of mourning their death."

"I loved her," Aron said, reaching for the blanket.

Braxton grabbed his arm and pulled him upright. "And that is why Kolt killed her. If you want to get back at him, do not let him know it hurts you this badly."

"Easier said."

Getting him to his feet, Braxton started pulling him towards the tub. "At least try. Undress." When Aron did not, he continued, "*Please* do not make me do that for you."

Aron gave his brother a hard stare before slowly disrobing and climbing in. The water was warm and soothing, and he slipped to where his nose was just above the waterline.

245

Braxton dumped a pitcher over his head, making his hair plaster over his eyes, and handed him a bar of soap. Getting a blank stare, he stated. "Wash."

As Aron scrubbed, he wished he could wash away the sorrow.

"Father requested your presence earlier."

"What for?"

Braxton gritted his teeth and looked away, "The Vosjnik returned."

His stomach sank. "Did they have the girl?"

"No, worse. They have an elemental that father has given to me to train."

"How is that so bad?"

"He is still resilient," Braxton said, standing and making his way to the window. "Father wants me to break him."

Aron pulled himself from the water and wrapped a towel around his waist. "What are you going to do?"

"I do not know." Braxton turned back to face him and for the first time, Aron could see the toll life had taken on his brother. His face was covered in small scars and he was perpetually tense. There was no happiness in any of his mannerisms—never had been. Staring out the window, he reiterated, "I do not know."

‡‡‡

The house was eerily quiet. The Fulpes had left a week ago, Alivia pleading for Carter to go with them, but he'd chosen to remain with Lucas.

Lucas had considered making Carter go, but he had as much right to revenge as he did. He also considered continuing working with Waylan but couldn't be bothered. Carter still worked at the carpenter's though, and each night came back with a loaf of bread, cheese, a small portion of meat, and a few coins.

Vengeance kept them in the city, though Lucas had no idea whom to exact it upon. He considered going after the men who had been with Maryn but knew it would be hard to find a few rats in a city full of them. The other path was to go after the Vosjnik, which would require time and funding.

Waiting for Carter to return, a knock came from the front door. He thought nothing of it until he realized Carter wouldn't knock. He pulled the knife from his boot and made his way through the foyer. Holding the knife against his leg, he opened the door. "You," he snarled. Anger welling, he raised the knife to drive it into Elza's chest.

246

"I came to apologize," Elza said quickly.

He paused.

"I need to apologize for what happened. It wasn't my fault."

"You did the deeds; how can they *not* be your fault?"

"Maryn is—was a life elemental. He forced us to do those things. May I come in?"

"No. How did you find us?"

"I followed your friend home yesterday. There's something I want to do... it's hard to explain without going into the entirety of it."

"I don't trust you."

Elza unbuckled his belt and handed Lucas his sword. "Do you trust me now?"

"No." Nevertheless, he opened the door and let the soldier in.

Carter was just reaching the bottom of the steps. "What—"

"Just go with it," Lucas told him.

Carter gave a nervous look but followed Lucas' lead as he led them to the kitchen.

Elza took a seat at the table and looked at them tentatively.

"Speak," Lucas barked.

"All right, here's the thing," Elza began, "I'm not happy. When I told the higher-ups what Maryn did, they laughed and said they would've done the same."

"How's that our problem?" Carter asked.

"I want to get back at them," Elza said with a sly grin. "I want to start doing right."

"Why should we help you?" Lucas growled.

"Well, you'll get to knock a few heads together, create some chaos."

Lucas considered the offer. As much as he'd like to, it would unnecessarily endanger Carter, and he wasn't willing to risk his life for Elza's petty payback; either he attacked the head or none at all. If Elza had offered retribution towards the Vosjnik or his commanders, it might have been a different story.

"We accept," Carter said in a low tone.

Lucas turned to him, surprised. "No."

"Look around you," Carter said angrily. "The world has taken a giant vite on us. It's time we gave some of it back."

"It's not worth it." Lucas paused; it was unusual for him to be the levelheaded one. "Why attack lowly peons?"

Elza chimed in, "You have to make enough of a nuisance before anyone of worth will look at you."

"Why do you even want to get back at them?" Lucas snapped. "You call those bastards comrades."

"I became a soldier to protect the people of this city," Elza said, standing. "Instead, I've been told I'm of no importance and it seems I've been protecting political standing more than anything. You don't have to help me, I just thought you might like the opportunity." He began to walk away, "But seeing that you'd rather wallow in filth, I'll show myself out."

"Wait. What *exactly* do you have in mind?"

"How big of a risk are you willing to take?"

‡‡‡

In the last week, Keegan seemed to have changed. She was no longer hostile towards everyone and had begun to genuinely laugh more. Kade also noticed that she and Jared were becoming increasingly familiar with one another. Often, he wondered if it was more than platonic, but that was none of his concern—he had Cassidy to worry about.

They'd openly become close and it still elicited commentary from Keegan. Some nights they slipped away for a quiet walk—this was one of those times.

He looked over his shoulder to make sure they were far enough from camp and gently pushed Cassidy against a tree. She stared at him with her indigo eyes and wrapped her arms around his neck, pulling him close. As their lips met, he let himself fall into the moment. The rush was euphoric—nothing compared to anything he'd felt before. Each touch warmed his body and sent shivers down his spine.

Cassidy began fumbling with his belt buckle.

He pulled away. "You don't have to do that; I'll never force you to."

"I know," she said. "I want to."

Kade smiled and kissed her again. The buckle came undone and his pants worked their way down his legs. Placing his hands on the small of her back, he pulled her away from the tree.

Your ass is showing.

Startled, his teeth knocked into Cassidy's. He pulled away and spun around, expecting to find Keegan behind him. *Where are you?* he asked angrily.

Camp.

How do you know my ass is showing then?

Cause your wall came a-tumblin' down. Taite and I know exactly what hanky-panky shit y'all're doing.

248

Kade grimaced, knowing he'd never hear the end of it.

"What happened?" Cassidy asked.

He turned to face her, and she stifled a giggle.

Looking down, he realized his pants were still around his ankles. He fumbled to pull them up, muttering, "My royiken sister, that's what happened." He'd been working on accepting Keegan as his twin, but until that moment, had been failing miserably.

A hush fell over them.

"Your sister?"

He took a deep breath. "Yes, Keegan's my sister. Twin to be precise."

"Oh... my..."

"You can't tell her."

"She does not know?"

"No... and I only just found out myself." He told her about the letter.

"I cannot believe it," Cassidy said once he'd finished. "That is all so inconceivable. Is she really the Child of Prophecy?"

"Yes."

"And is she really from another..." she trailed off as he nodded. "I knew she was not from around here, but to be from another world entirely... It makes it much more understandable for her to be so homesick."

"Homesick?"

"Yes," Cassidy said sheepishly. "That is why she was upset last week, but you are not supposed to know that."

"Hmm..." Kade said, giving her a quick peck on the lips, "I won't tell if you won't."

Cassidy pulled him close. "It is a deal."

‡‡‡

Keegan had her head in Jared's lap, and he ran his fingers through her hair. With a devilish grin, she asked, "So, if you had to guess, what'do you think they're up to?"

Jared looked at her. "I really don't want to know."

"You're the lucky one."

"How so?" His fingers got stuck in a knot, making her wince.

"Kade's wall faltered and let's just say he and Cassidy are having a bit of fun."

"That's what you were laughing at earlier?"

She nodded.

249

Kade and Cassidy decided to walk back into camp at that moment.

"Speak of the devil," she said, sitting up.

Kade shot her a glare. "I don't know what you find so funny."

"Dude, your dumb ass got caught with your pants around your ankles and it's your fault. Everything in and of that's hilarious."

"How would you like it if you were I?"

"I wouldn't be in your situation cause I'm not dumb enough to do that in the woods. And I really hope y'all don't have splinters in your asses."

"You are never going to let that one go, are you?" Cassidy stated.

"Nope," Keegan said. "And if I do anything as stupid, I'd expect nothing less from y'all."

To change the subject, Jared asked, "When will we reach the next city?"

"Early tomorrow," Taite answered.

"Are we going to stay in the city again?" Cassidy asked hopefully.

"Most likely."

"I don't see why we should," Kade argued. "We'll have all day to get supplies and it'll save money."

"Come on," Keegan groaned, "don't you want to sleep in a bed?"

"I won't get to either way," Kade pointed out. "And, as much as I want to, the sooner we get you to the Lazado, the better."

Keegan rolled her eyes. "One night won't kill us."

"I don't know why you're trying to convince him," Taite said, "He has no power here."

"Oh, yeah, I keep forgetting he's not in charge," Keegan said.

"Are we staying in the city or not?" Cassidy asked.

Simultaneously, Kade answered, "No," while Taite said, "Yes."

"Okay, since you two will never agree, let's take a vote," Keegan suggested. "I vote we stay in the city. Cassidy?"

She remained quiet for a moment, "I agree with Kade."

Keegan sighed. "Jared?"

"I agree with Kade, too."

Keegan looked to Taite disappointed. "Sorry, it seems we'll be camping again."

Taite looked like he wanted to argue but knew no one was willing to budge. "Get some sleep. *Apparently,* we have a long day ahead."

‡‡‡

Nico awoke to what felt like twilight. He stretched out on the cot; after sleeping on the ground for weeks, it was a welcome change. He bolted up as the door scraped open.

Caius entered and Braxton followed with a tray of food, avoided his gaze, and stood behind the king sullenly.

"Will you serve me?" Caius asked.

"No," Nico spat.

Lazily, Caius said, "Fine. Braxton."

Braxton handed him the tray with an anxious look.

He looked at the tray warily.

"Go ahead, eat," Caius said with a wiry smile.

Braxton gave a minute shake of the head.

Cautiously, Nico picked up the chicken leg, turning it over. Finding nothing visibly wrong, he decided to take his chances. The meat was dry, but he wasn't about to complain.

Caius' grin grew. "Tell me, boy, where are you from?"

"Don't you know that already?" Nico snapped.

"Ah, yes, Suilenroc. I am aware the Vosjnik killed your mother, but I presume you have other family still living."

Nico looked at him blankly and took another large bite.

"Of course; three brothers and your father. I need to have a word with Vitia about her thoroughness."

Nico froze; there was no way he could have known that.

"And now you are curious as to how I knew that."

His eyebrows furrowed in confusion.

"Serve me and I shall tell you."

"No."

"Tell me about your brothers. How many of them are elementals?" Before Nico could even formulate his thoughts, Caius said, "Ah, just the one, Jared."

What is going on? Nico wondered.

"Keep eating. We cannot have you starving."

Something seemed off, but he continued anyway.

"Tell me about Jared."

"Why—"

"Another earth elemental. They, in particular, seem to be causing a bit of bother lately; I will have to do something about that."

"How are you doing that?" Nico questioned, aggravated that he could keep nothing from this man.

"Serve me and I will tell you, but your answer is still no."

251

Nico looked to Braxton, who avoided his gaze—he was ashamed, that much he could tell.

Caius continued, "Jared befriended that lovely girl, Keegan. He will be an easy convert; I have the perfect weapon against him. You."

As anger welled, Nico threw down the tray and jumped to his feet. Something in his stomach dropped and a shooting pain spread fast. He clutched at his abdomen, sucking in a ragged breath.

"I see it has taken effect," Caius said, motioning for Braxton to collect the tray.

Nico grimaced as another bolt of pain ran through his stomach. "What are you talking about?"

"Will you serve me?"

"No," he snarled.

Caius walked away. "Then there is nothing to tell."

Braxton followed.

As they neared the door, Nico called out, sinking to his knees, the pain burgeoning as if thousands of knives were driving into him. "What did he do?"

He was met with silence and the feeling continued to grow. Soon the only thing he could do was lie on the cold, stone floor and pray it would end.

CHAPTER 33

Ohvenail was nothing like Suttan or Aylentowne. There was no castle, no large buildings, no wall for protection. The city was built on both banks of the Tatat River, with a few homes even floating on the slow waters. Buildings were mostly made of mud bricks and clay mortar with grasses and reeds pressed into the roofs and sides. The tallest building only looked about three stories high.

The roads leading to the city were dirt that slowly became littered with cobbled stones. People milled about as Taite led them to a stable and the residents seemed lively compared to those in the other places they'd been.

"So, what're we doing while you shop?" Keegan questioned.

"Staying here," Taite said.

"That doesn't make a lot of sense," Jared commented. "Why don't we split up and each buy a few things?"

"I don't trust any of you to not get into trouble," Taite countered.

"We did just fine in Aylentowne," Keegan remarked.

"No."

"Keegan, you and Jared go with Taite," Kade said.

"What did I just say?" Taite snapped.

"It'll save time and I don't trust them or *you* wandering off alone," Kade explained.

"That's not what we're doing!"

"It is now." Kade took Cassidy's hand and walked away before Taite could get another word in.

"Stay here," Taite instructed.

"Uh, no," Keegan said blatantly.

"That wasn't a request!"

Keegan shrugged.

"Stay here."

"Try and stop me."

Taite's face was red with fury and with clenched fists, he stormed from the stable.

Keegan gave Jared a small smirk before ambling after him.

The market was a hectic place. Vendors sold immense amounts of items, ranging from food to jewels, and Jared was surprised to find a section dedicated to spices; a pungent smell emanated from them that Keegan seemed to enjoy. Once they entered the bustle, they fell away from Taite, while being mindful to kept him in sight.

Keegan walked from stall to stall, taking it all in, gravitating towards stands selling small trinket. When vendors asked if she wanted to buy anything, she'd give a small, sad smile and walk away. Although she kept to herself, Jared could tell she was savoring the experience. He, on the other hand, disliked being surrounded by so many people; it reminded him too much of Tratoleck.

"What's Taite doing?" Keegan asked, not bothering to look for him as she was too short to see over the crowd.

Jared searched the throng. "I don't know."

She caught the uncertainty in his voice. "What's happening?"

"He's talking to a soldier."

"Why?"

"How should I know?" Jared bit, eyeing the exchange.

Taite and the soldier talked for only a few minutes before going their separate ways.

"He's coming over."

"We have everything. Time to go," Taite told them.

"Okay," Keegan responded nonchalantly. "Why were you talking to that soldier?"

"We grew up together; he was just saying hello."

"Oh." She let Taite lead the way from the market, then leaned over to Jared and whispered, "Do you think he's telling the truth?"

"No idea." Jared was inclined to disbelieve him, but it was possible; rarely did people travel too far from their hometowns—unless they were elementals, Kojotes, or forced to become soldiers for the king.

‡‡‡

Cassidy and Kade strolled through the market, while vendors called them over to look at wares. They were ignored. She hugged Kade's arm; it felt right being by his side. A table of trinkets caught her attention and she dragged him over.

"Ho' are 'he lady and 'he gentleman?" the vendor asked in a thick Northron accent.

"Wonderful," Cassidy answered.

"Wha' a beautiful voice tha' sends sweet 'isses t' 'he ear," the man commented flirtatiously. "Befitting o' such a stunning lady."

Cassidy giggled, color rushing to her cheeks.

Kade wrapped an arm around her waist.

The vendor gave a hearty laugh. "No need t' worry, son, ol' Dunkan Yaw 's not on 'he market."

254

Kade did not move his arm.

"D' you see anything you like, m' dear?"

"They are all so beautiful," Cassidy commented, eyeing the necklaces displayed.

"Sha' I surprise you 'hen?"

She looked to Kade and he gave a small nod.

"Lo'ely." Dunkan surveyed his wares and after a moment, reached forward and picked up a simple piece. The stone was a pale blue larimar encased in an intricate wire setting with a thin silver chain. He offered it to Cassidy.

She marveled at it. "Oh, it is gorgeous."

Kade pulled his hand from around her waist. "How much?"

"For you, ah silver coin," Dunkan said with a charming grin.

Kade fished a coin from his purse and handed it over.

"Help me put it on?" Cassidy asked.

Taking the necklace, he set the pendant on her chest and did the clasp.

She turned to face him and standing on her toes, kissed his cheek.

A perturbed look crossed his face.

"What's wrong?"

"Taite," Kade answered. "It's time to leave."

"Then we should go meet him."

"Do we have to?"

Cassidy gave a little laugh. "Unfortunately."

Kade allowed her to pull him along to the stables, where the others were waiting.

"Where to next?" Cassidy questioned.

"Revod," Taite answered impatiently.

✇✇✇

A knock came at Aron's door, followed by, "The king demands your presence in the Glass Chamber."

He had no desire to get up but decided to take Braxton's advice. Kolt was aware of how he felt, so even just seeing him out of his room would put a damper on his smugness.

He placed a hand on the doorknob then turned and went to his bedside table, placing the only key he possessed in his pocket.

Contrary to popular belief, the Glass Chamber was not made of glass—it simply housed the Looking Glass. The walk there seemed gloomy despite the warm sunshine illuminating the hallways. His father and brothers were already inside.

Seeing him, Kolt sneered, "Aron, how—"

"Be quiet," Braxton snapped.

Kolt was about to retort when the surface of the mirror rippled, and a man's image appeared.

"Sir," the man said, bowing.

"What is so pressing it could not wait for your monthly report, Captain?" questioned Caius.

The man stepped aside and was replaced by a low-ranking soldier. "Sir," he said nervously.

"Out with it, I do not have all day."

"The girl you've been looking for, Keegan Digore, will be in Revod in a week."

"How do you know this?"

"A Kojote approached me and said he has this girl, as well as three other elementals."

"What is the name of this Kojote?"

"Taite Ault."

"He usually delivers elementals in Bouyne. Why the change of location?"

"He was apparently forced to take them along a southern route to dispel suspicion. One of the Vosjnik, Kade Tavin, is with him and doesn't trust him. He had enough of a hard time telling me this without them being any the wiser."

"Dismissed." Caius waved a hand over the surface of the mirror and the image went blank. With another wave, the Glass Chamber in Revod appeared. "Get your Captain," he ordered the timid-looking guard who sat in the room.

The man rushed away, time slipping by slowly before he returned. Breathlessly, he informed them the Captain was on his way and gave a bow before being replaced.

"I want every guard on high alert." Caius announced.

"May I enquire why, sir?"

"The girl I have been looking for, as well as three others, will reportedly be passing through Revod in a week. Your guards should engage only if absolutely necessary, otherwise, leave them to the Vosjnik."

The Captain bowed. "Yes, sir."

As the Captain turned to walk away, Caius added, "They are to be taken alive and I want the girl unharmed."

"Of course."

The mirror's surface rippled and Caius' reflection stared back. "Get the Vosjnik," he told Milo, walking from the room with and unsettling grin.

They waited until Caius had left before taking their leave, Kolt and Braxton heading towards the throne room while Aron stood in the hallway, unsure of where he should go.

As Braxton turned to look at him, he took off running in the opposite direction.

✛✛✛

Lying on the cold stone floor, Nico had no idea how long it'd been. His clothes were damp with sweat and his hair was plastered to his face. As he tried to move onto the cot, a jolt lanced through his stomach and he fell back, crying out. The pain waned slowly, and he struggled to pull himself up before the next jar came.

Shadowed light came from the window. *Has it really been only a day?*

Mercifully, the ache subsided completely, and he began to relax. His eyelids were heavy, he knew it wouldn't be long before he drifted off. The door scraped open and he turned to see his visitor.

Instead of Caius, a dark man entered, followed by a servant carrying a tray. They stood across from where he lay on the cot and he had trouble focusing on them.

"Will you serve your king?" the dark man asked.

"No," Nico managed.

"Give the boy his dinner."

"No."

The dark man grinned.

The servant approached and he desperately slapped the tray from his hand, sending its contents tumbling.

"Hold him."

Nico struggled under the weight of the servant but couldn't get free.

The dark man pulled a bottle from his pocket, removed the stopper, and poured a few drops into Nico's mouth. After instructing the servant to clean up the food, he walked away.

Thankfully, there was no pain and he eyed the servant warily as he went about his duty. After he left, Nico relaxed and closed his eyes, exhaustion overcoming him. He bolted up; he'd just seen his mother's final minutes.

257

After taking a deep breath, he lay down again, warily closing his eyes. The moment he entered darkness, the vision replayed, and his eyes snapped open. In the light, he watched it happen again. As soon as his mother died, the scene began anew.

He let out an anguished scream at the image of Connery pulling the knife across her throat. He raced forward to try stop him, but simply passed through the mirage. Confused, he looked about the cell, only to watch it all over again.

He sank onto the floor, tears rolling down his face. His nightmare had come to haunt him during his waking hours.

‡‡‡

The Vosjnik filed into the throne room, Vitia leading the way arrogantly.

Braxton was surprised to see she had managed to fill all three of the open positions in the day they had been back. While she had found substitutes, he was sure none would stand long.

Mara Foxire, the new telepath, was a mousy girl of fifteen—barely more than a child really. It had taken Caius over a year to break her, proving her strength and mettle. He was also surprised to see his own tutor, Evard Poukyn, had filled the earth elemental position. The man was brutish and had often intentionally inflicted pain; he could not say he was unhappy the man had made himself a target for death. The fire elemental, Nicandro Quolt, was much older than the other members, being at least sixty. What little hair he had was stark white and he stood with a slightly hunched back.

"I see you had no trouble finding replacements," Caius said with a pleased grin.

"Would you like to test them to see if they are fit?" she asked.

"I would, but a more pressing matter has arisen. In a week, the girl Connery failed to capture will be in Revod."

A vicious smile crossed Vitia's face. "We'll depart immediately."

"I want the girl brought back alive *and* unharmed."

Vitia made to leave.

Caius stayed her, continuing, "I have been informed three other elementals are traveling with her. I take two of these to be Kade and Nico's brother. I want them brought back alive and in decent health. As for the fourth one, deal with it as you see fit."

He could see she was displeased at the prospect of having to leave Kade alive.

Nonetheless, she bowed, answering, "Yes, sir."

258

‡‡‡

Aron made his way through the castle, the path ahead lit sparsely, and his heavy footfalls echoing off the stones. He came to a stop outside the door, took the key from his pocket, and rammed it into the lock.

Inside, Alyck sat in his usual chair, a look of sadness upon his face. "I am sorry for your loss, Little King; I did try to warn you."

A wave of guilt washed over Aron.

"But that is not why you are here though."

"Father knows where Keegan is going to be. What should I do?"

"What you were going to do originally." Alyck leaned forward and whispered, "Run." When Aron made no motion, he repeated, "Run, boy. You do not have much time."

He backed slowly towards the door, his eyes still on Alyck as he pushed it open.

Alyck rose to his feet. "Go!"

Aron turned and ran, making his way back through the castle quickly, only stopping when he came to the hidden door. He hesitated, then pressed the stone, and easily made his way through the dark passage.

On the rooftop, the air was warm and the sky a clear blue, tinged with orange as the sun set. A light northward wind gently pulled at him and something about it felt familiar. To the south, a line of horses galloped away, and he figured they must be the Vosjnik going to retrieve the Child of Prophecy. And here was his choice; run towards nothing and save himself or follow the Vosjnik and save Keegan.

There was a shift in the wind, and it began to blow in a southerly direction.

Aloud, he said, "It seems you have made the decision for me. I know I could not save you, but I will save her. It does not make up for my failure, but it is what you would have wanted me to do—the right thing."

259

CHAPTER 34

Aron peered around the corner; a single torch at the end of the corridor lit the way. Two men guarded the door. Taking a breath and gripping his bow tighter, he stepped into the middle of the hall. As the men spotted him, he released two arrows, both piercing leather armor and flesh with ease.

Taking the keys from the belt of one, he opened the door. Inside was dark and he returned to the hall for a torch; the griffins shied away from the sudden brightness. Legends spoke of noble creatures to be reckoned with, but the griffin he beheld were forlorn and dejected.

He cautiously approached one with pale bronze feathers. "I know how you feel," he whispered.

It stared back at him with glossy black eyes.

Reaching forward, he unlocked the bond around its neck. As soon as the iron was removed, it pounced, sending him sprawling, the bow clattering away, and the torch landing out of reach.

The beast stood atop his chest, pinning him. It lowered its head, its beak coming within inches of his exposed throat. It sent a puff of warm breath over his face and turned its head to look at him. Then, it took off, leaving him unharmed, and approached its brethren. With mighty swings of its taloned paw, it broke the chains holding them.

Frozen, Aron watched as the eleven other griffins were released. Where he assumed a wall existed, they ran through, dropping into the night, leaving a lingering thought that filled him with a sense of freedom and thanks.

Shakily, he got to his feet, retrieved the torch, and made his way to the opening. Looking out, he watched as twelve shadows began ambushing the men along the battlements. He watched for a moment, then raced back to the door, retrieving his bow along the way.

Now, he needed to get to the stables without being seen by guards or attacked by a griffin. Inconspicuously, he made his way to the door that led to the plains. While he could not see the griffins above, he could hear them and the cries of the men they assailed.

Inhaling deeply, he sprinted across the grass. Inside the stables, he saddled Kolt's sabino palfrey. He could take any horse he wanted, but this was meant to be the final affront. The horse gave a few snorts of protest, but otherwise was well-tempered.

He turned back to look at the castle, screams of men and griffins breaking the night. Looking into the darkness, he spurred the horse away with a smile.

‡‡‡

Braxton slashed at a griffin as it dove at him, feeling his blade dig into flesh and hearing a scream; he was not sure which one it was. As the griffin pulled away, it left his sword bathed in dark purple blood. There was a lull in the attacks, giving him time to think. "Grab those chains," he yelled at the men nearby. "Hurry, we do not have much time!"

Kolt walked up to him, clutching a wound on his arm. "What are you planning?"

"We can throw the chains at them. They will wrap around their wings and ground them."

"That is a stupid idea."

Braxton turned to him. "I do not see you coming up with anything better. So, until such time, shut the royik up and do as I say!" To the men on the wall he yelled, "Here they come!"

The griffins dropped out of the night and once more yells surrounded him. He heard chains clinking together, a loud *thunk,* and the cry of a griffin.

He rushed over. "Keep it down!"

It was Myrish, his wings and legs entangled in the chains.

Please, stop! he begged, struggling to make his thoughts heard.

Betrayer! Myrish screamed, thrashing.

Myrish, I do not want to kill you. Please do not make me.

Murderer! Finding he could not stand, Myrish began to thrust out his large head to snap at the men, seizing one by the leg and pulling him to the ground.

His companions grabbed hold of his arms; there was a sickening snap and a blood-curdling scream as his leg was severed.

Braxton looked around. Finding a long, leather cord, he jumped onto Myrish's back, and quickly wound it around his beak. As he worked, he yelled, "I need a life elemental."

A soldier stepped forward. "What do you need?"

"Take his energy."

"We tried that before; there's too much."

"Distribute it amongst us," Braxton said as Myrish struggled under him. "Quickly!"

The man held his hand out toward the griffin and began to concentrate.

After a moment, Braxton felt his fatigue melting away and the beast beneath him settle. Soon, Myrish could do little more than breathe. *I am*

261

sorry, he told the griffin then turned to the man, "Good work. Come with me, we are going to need you." To the others, he ordered, "Two of you take that man to the hospital; the rest of you, get the griffin back to the stable."

"Yes, sir."

A screech came from the sky and he looked up. Time stood still and he recognized the scene of chaos from his nightmares.

Betrayer! Murderer! Coward! the descending griffin shrieked.

Talons reached for his chest and pierced his skin, burning as they cut through him. He was thrown sideways as the beast landed atop him and he could just make out the spear protruding from its neck.

Betrayer, murderer, coward.

Stay with me, Braxton murmured.

Betrayer, murderer, coward.

Iwin, do not go dying on me. Please, the others need you.

His words were scarcely more than a whisper, *Betrayer, murderer, coward. Hero.*

As life left the old beast, Braxton's world sank into darkness, leaving him feeling as if he was tumbling through space.

"Jyken eya meki lunviyda zæ psodæ ri ayþ drackyn, æay woth viæn nuþ qalx ayþ æyscs fayo eyar oywn þen," Aron said harshly, suddenly materializing and placing a hand over his ravaged chest.

"Nackh jyken eya casne, fackyon ictotm, iruh du woth unla ryo iruh ayþ adæmno," Kade added, putting a hand on his forehead.

Heat began to sear across his body and he tried to call out.

Kade and Aron smiled cruelly before continuing, "Psodæ woth yarv rhæpn casne jappec eya."

A third man behind Braxton said, "Qalx ayþ buna, qalx ayþ waysne, qalx okæpyio, qalx ayþ payn ri luxyen, zæ psodæ woth viæn," placing his hands on his shoulders, pushing him down.

Keegan appeared before him and paused before speaking. "Astæm egreþer du woth ryo eyar oywn foylisha ghæ woth solcan eyar hayclen oh kævoka kunyi." She leaned over and gently kissed him, sucking the breath from his lungs as a pressure squeezed his body, then told him, "Eya wye rimbor."

His eyes snapped open and found his father crouched over him.

"Calm," Caius said. "You are not fully healed yet."

He had a moment to take in the people holding him down before he was sent back into darkness.

‡‡‡

Exhausted, Braxton trudged up to the stable. He placed a hand against his chest, feeling the tattered remains of his shirt. Underneath, his skin was unmarked. He had woken with the rising sun to find his father still healing him. He stood outside the door a moment, knowing many of the griffins had been slain. Steeling himself, he entered. Inside, stood only five: Myrish, Niyth, Crowlin, Phynex, and Oxren. His heart grieved for the other seven.

The griffins pulled against their chains and emitted low growls.

Jyken eya meki lunviyda zœ psodœ ri ayþ drackyn, œay woth viœn nuþ qalx ayþ œyscs fayo eyar oywn þen, he repeated to himself then asked the stable master, "How did they get loose?"

"Someone released them."

"Why would anyone do that?"

"To create confusion."

Braxton sighed, "Attend to their injuries." He slowly began making his way from the stable, doing his best to keep tears from sliding down his cheeks.

Nackh jyken eya casne, fackyon ictotm, ıruh du woth unla ryo iruh ayþ adœmno.

His body felt heavy and his clothes were soaked in blood. Some was his, but most belonged to the griffins. Nearing his chambers, he saw Milo Sewth.

"Your father requests your presence."

"Can it wait?"

"I would say so, but you know your father."

Exhaling, Braxton made his way to the throne room. It was strange to be standing before his father.

Psodœ woth yarv rhœpn casne jappec eya.

"How many griffins still live?" Caius asked.

"Five," he answered.

"I suppose you saved as many as you could."

Tiredly, he nodded, "Yes, and we still have the hatchlings. Whoever released the griffins did not know about them."

"Someone freed the griffins?"

Qalx ayþ buna, qalx ayþ waysne, qalx okœpyio, qalx ayþ payn ri luxyen, zœ psodœ woth viœn. "It appears so."

"While I am not pleased with the outcome," Caius began, "you fought well. Go rest. And once you have, find the culprit."

Braxton bowed and made his exit.

Milo walked with him. "I am surprised Caius was not livid with you."

"I hold your sentiments. But Father can be fickle. Do me a favor and begin the investigation."

"Of course," Milo said, turning down a different hallway.

Astæm egreþer du woth ryo eyar oywn foylisha ghæ woth solcan eyar hayclen oh kævoka kunyi.

It took an eternity to reach his chambers and once there, he locked the door, not wanting anyone to disturb him. He stripped his soiled clothes and left them scattered about the floor. Taking a wet rag, he wiped away the blood from his hands and face. What he could not wipe away was the contrition.

Tears began to slide down his face and he did nothing to stop them. He went to his desk and pulled out a fresh sheet of parchment. Slowly, he transcribed the prophecy. Something had changed after Iwin died; he could remember every detail now. Once complete, he stored the paper in a drawer and crawled into bed.

‡‡‡

Over and over Nico watched his mother's death. At first, a flurry of emotions had raged inside, now, as the image blurred and faded, he could barely feel anything—except exhaustion.

With the mirage finally gone, he lay on the cot, letting his weary eyes close. As soon as they did, the cell door opened. Groaning, he opened one eye to find Caius standing opposite him.

"How are you today?" the king questioned.

Nico glared at him.

Caius pulled a small vial from his pocket. "Will you serve me?"

Naturally, there was some form of torment inside. He couldn't keep doing this.

"Excellent," Caius said, putting it back in his pocket. "I was almost hoping you would be more tenacious. Oh, you are going to *love* this; in a week, I will have possession of your brother, Jared."

Jared. There was no way he would've given in already.

"It will be brilliant watching you break him."

His attention snapped to Caius. Furiously, he yelled, "I will never hurt my brother, and I will never serve you!"

"H-ho," Caius said grinning, "there is still some fight in you yet." He took the vial out again and made his way over.

264

He wanted to fight, but some unseen force prevented him from doing so.

Caius forced a few drops into his mouth and walked away.

Nico sat on the edge of the cot, wondering what distress this new poison would bring. A fly buzzed by his ear and he swatted it away. It soon returned and refused to leave him alone. He gritted his teeth and did his best to ignore it. He could feel something crawling on his leg and, looking down, saw ants scuttling up.

He jumped to his feet, frantically brushing them off. The fly was back, buzzing loudly, but now it was more than one. Bugs were everywhere, crawling, buzzing, biting... No matter how many he brushed away, more always came.

‡‡‡

The day passed in its usual boredom. Cassidy and Kade had things to talk about, but they were beginning to find it difficult—spending so much time in close proximity the past few weeks felt like a lifetime.

As customary, they stopped before dusk. Taite cooked dinner and once the stars appeared, Kade began the night's activities. Keegan went first.

They were using swords now and her movements were slow and the strikes not as powerful. Which was understandable; her arms tired from the weight quickly, and it was all she could do to block. After a particularly heavy hit on the leg, she said enough and handed the sword over to Jared.

Compared to when he had started, he had made significant progress. He could now easily dodge and counter—and with power to match. Kade still bested him, but it was more of a contest. They sparred for a while and when they stopped, both were sweaty and out of breath—something unusual for Kade.

The camp was peacefully quiet as Kade took a seat beside Cassidy.

"Why don't we ever practice magic?" Keegan questioned.

Kade shrugged. "Teaching you sword fighting has been the primary concern and it usually wears you down. Do you want to practice?"

"Kinda. I feel like I'm getting rusty on what little skills I had."

"Fine." Kade turned to Jared, "Do you want the honors?"

Jared rubbed a welt, "I'll let you take it."

They met in the middle of the camp and Kade invited, "Whenever you're ready."

With a devious smile and a quick movement of her hands, she encased his feet. He immediately caused blocks of earth to rise and wrap around her arms. She pulled against them, but they held.

Kade crossed his arms. "That was pathetically easy."

"We're not done yet."

"Oh, really?"

"Really." Her brows knit together.

His face took on an expression of distress.

Cassidy watched with a feeling of uncertainty as he slowly released one of Keegan's arms.

With her free hand, Keegan made him sink into the ground up to his chest.

He shook his head—as if trying to clear it of a foreign entity—while she removed the earth from around her other arm. "Did you just... manipulate me?"

"Uh-huh," she said proudly.

"I a—"

"Hold on," Cassidy stopped him, "How could she manipulate you if she is an earth elemental?"

"She's a life elemental, too," Kade stated.

Cassidy shook her head. "That is not possible."

"I take it Taite didn't tell you," Keegan said.

"Did not tell me what?" Cassidy pressed.

"I have all five elements."

Taite let out a laugh, "Thaddeus told me you possessed all five, but that's impossible. Don't make such outrageous claims."

She made her way over to him and exposed the underside of her wrist. "Am I lying?"

Taite stared in shock, then grabbed her arm and began trying to wipe away the marks.

Keegan pulled her hand away. "Ow."

"That... can't be," he sputtered.

Giving a small shrug, Keegan said, "Everyone keeps telling me that."

"Why wasn't this brought to my attention sooner?"

"You were told," Kade reminded him. "It's not our fault you didn't listen."

Running a hand through his hair, Taite muttered, "This changes everything."

Watching him, Cassidy saw a devious smile play upon his lips.

‡‡‡

Aron had not gone far before he needed to stop. He awoke when the sun was high in the sky and instantly his body protested rising and pressing on, but mounting the palfrey, he spurred it away from the wooded area.

In the daylight and out on the grasslands, he felt exposed. He scanned the skies and horizon for any evidence of pursuers; none materialized, no matter how much he strained his eyes.

With any luck, it would be several days before anyone noticed his absence. He wondered who would discover it. While Kolt enjoyed tormenting him, he usually did not go out of his way to do so. His father would call upon him, and while he customarily made an appearance, he was free to decline without consequence. He had barely seen any of the castle's servants—aside from Shiloh. That left Braxton, who, when permitted, chose to spend time with him.

He hoped that releasing the griffins would prevent Braxton from doing so for quite some time. A feeling of guilt struck him as he realized he had abandoned the one person who might care about him. He pushed the thought aside; there was no going back now.

CHAPTER 35

Braxton opened his eyes groggily and groaned, his muscles tense and sore. As he pushed himself into a sitting position, a servant shuffled in with a tray of food. She placed it before him, then stood against the wall passively.

The food released an appealing aroma and he needed no goading to dig in. As he ate, a thought struck him. "I take it you needed an elemental to open the door."

"It wasn't locked, sir," she stated.

"If you did not unlock my door, then who did?"

"I don't know."

"Leave."

She bowed and exited.

Once the woman was gone, he rose from the bed, and dressed quickly in a fresh pair of pants and a rich, red silk shirt. He paused and traded it for dark green; the red reminded him too much of blood. As he buckled his sword around his waist, a slip of paper on his desk caught his attention.

It appears you have made progress. Do not leave it too long.

"Alyck."

He pulled out the pages with relevant information from his desk drawer but paused. Now was not the time to be doing this. Knowing he needed to be careful about where he left the information, he locked it away in the trunk, along with the *Evolution of Languages*. However, there was something he needed to discuss with Alyck.

As he walked through the halls, it was hard to miss the diminished number of guards; the griffins had dealt a heavy blow to the castle's security. When he stood outside the door, he paused, formulating his thoughts. He entered and found Alyck waiting—like always.

"I– I have been having these dreams… but now I do not think they are dreams," Braxton began.

"What do you think they are?" Alyck asked, genuine curiosity hiding in his words.

"I am not sure. That is why I came to see you."

"I wish I had answers for you."

Braxton creased his eyebrows. "How is it that you know nothing about this? You know everything."

Alyck sighed, "I know everything, except when it pertains to you. And I cannot answer why, as I do not know."

"Then how have you been able to tell me… things?"

"Through some very creative means. Since I cannot see your path, I look at how you affect the people and objects around you. From that, I can paint a picture."

"You must know what these dreams mean," Braxton said, almost pleading. "They are driving me mad. I wake up almost every night in a panic, feeling like someone has tried to kill me. I kept dreaming about talons ripping me apart and—" he broke off, the cobwebs beginning to fall away.

"You dreamt the future?"

He hesitated, "I think so."

‡‡‡

Lucas crept forward, using the shadows to hide. His foot struck a loose rock, sending it skittering. He cursed and froze, but the guards he was tailing didn't seem to hear. Behind him, Carter sighed. They gave it a few moments before slinking forward again.

The two soldiers stopped outside a house; inside lived a family of elementals. While Lucas didn't see the point in freeing them, Elza assured him it was part of the master plan.

The men traded words with a third at the door, then continued down the street. They would walk to the next alley, about face, and make their way back.

He made sure Carter was concealed behind some barrels before picking up a few stones and joining him. Every noise seemed incredibly loud, even his heartbeat. Soon, they heard the soldiers' footsteps. "Ready?"

"Yeah," Carter returned in a low tone.

As the soldiers passed the alleyway, Lucas threw a pebble.

They paused and one called, "Who's there?"

"Just a rat, you dastard," the other jibed. About to continue, Lucas threw another rock, hitting the first soldier on the head.

"Can a rat do that?" the man exclaimed, drawing his sword, and making his way towards them, searching the alley's gloom.

Using their daggers' hilts, Lucas and Carter struck them on the back of the heads. Lucas' victim fell forward like a tree while Carter's man stumbled but remained standing. He began to turn, and Lucas hit him on the temple.

"Hit harder next time," Lucas advised as they dragged the guards behind some crates and took their swords.

"Two down, one to go."

269

Lucas peered around the corner to look at the guard in the doorway, who was craning his neck to see where his counterparts had gone, shifting from foot to foot. Curiosity overpowered duty and he abandoned his post, looking over his shoulder to check that the street was desolate. Warily, he made his way towards the alley, but wasn't smart enough to draw his weapon.

As soon as he was within reach, Lucas jumped from behind the wall and punched him in the face. The soldier held his nose as tears welled in his eyes. Taking a handful of hair, Lucas rammed his head into the wall, and he slumped over.

They quickly made their way towards the house.

Carter grabbed the door handle; locked. He cursed. "They must have the key."

"I don't have time for this," Lucas said, kicking down the door.

It landed with a heavy boom and there were shrieks from the inhabitants within. Lucas entered and found a man standing protectively in front of his wife and two daughters. At first, the man looked alarmed, but soon relief crossed his face.

"Go, quickly," Lucas told them.

"Are you with the Lazado?" the man asked.

"No," Carter said.

"Then who are you?" the woman questioned.

"Doesn't matter," Lucas said. "You'd best leave before the soldiers wake up."

The man turned to his children, trying to soothe them, "No need to be afraid; everything's going to be just fine."

"Thank you," the woman said, harrying her family past them.

As the man walked past, Lucas stopped him and shoved the sword into his hand, "You might want this."

The family pushed out into the night and took off down the street, the girls hiccupping with uncertainty.

Carter crossed his arms, "That was easy."

"Humph," was Lucas's response. "Let's get out of here."

‡‡‡

In Nico's state of sleep deprivation, it was difficult to know how much time had passed, but the fact that Caius or one of his men visited once a day, helped him keep track. Each time, the same question was asked, and when he responded, "No", a poison was forced down his throat. So far, he'd been given four. Two caused pain, one hallucinations, and one both.

The previous day's fare was fading, and he lapsed into a blissful few seconds of unconsciousness, only opening his eyes when shaken awake. He had trouble focusing on Caius, finding his image blurry and constantly shifting. At times, he swore the man had two faces.

"Are you ready to serve me?"

Nico heard the words, but they refused to register. "Pardon?"

"Are you ready—"

"I don't understand."

"Will you s—"

"Will I what?"

"Serve me," Caius finished, his aggravation beginning to show.

Nico looked at him confused, "Serve you what?"

"You insolent boy!" Caius said, knocking him about the head. "You know what I mean."

"I really don't."

Caius leaned back against the wall. "Tell me, would you like to sleep?"

He nodded.

"Then join me."

"Join you where?"

Caius clenched his fist and stormed from the cell furiously.

He wondered what had upset the man but was too tired to truly care. There was a yell of rage and a clang. He considered getting up to see what had caused the ruckus but blinked and fell asleep.

✦✦✦

"Where is he?" Kolt yelled, crashing through the door.

"Wha—" Braxton started groggily.

"Where is he? Our royiken bastard of a brother!"

Braxton rubbed the sleep from his eyes. "How the royik should I know?"

"You—" Kolt stammered furiously, "You are the one who likes the bwint."

He got to his feet. "That does not mean I know where he is at all hours. Now, get out."

Anger contorted Kolt's face as he struck out.

Braxton stopped his fist mid-punch and wrenched his arm aside. "Do not take your anger out on me. What did he do anyway?"

"Stole my horse," Kolt grunted.

Braxton released Kolt's hand and snorted. "Why would he do that? He is not allowed to leave the castle grounds."

"That makes no difference. He stole my horse!"

"I find that hard to believe."

"I do not care what you believe, he stole it, hid it, whatever!"

Braxton crossed his arms. "What do you want me to do about it?"

"Fix it!"

"Get out."

Kolt gave him a final glare before storming out.

Braxton rubbed his eyes; it was always something with his brothers. He dressed and went to Aron's room.

Knocking on the door, he called, "Aron, we need to talk." There was no answer. He knocked again. "Aron?" Growing impatient, he pushed the door open.

The room was dark and eerily still, the bed appearing as if it had not been slept in for days. He cursed as he stormed off; it was *always* something.

‡‡‡

"Aron is to be brought back unharmed," Braxton told the assembled soldiers. "You will ride for a day; if you find no sign of him, return to the castle. Norm, Orville, Jai, and——"

"And I," Kolt cut him off, "will be leading the teams."

Braxton grabbed his arm. "What do you think you are doing?"

"Finding my bastard of a brother."

"No."

"Try and stop me. And you had better hope I do not find him; I cannot imagine he will be in great shape if I do." Turning to the men, Kolt barked, "Move out."

The soldiers formed groups and mounted their horses, each group choosing a direction. A dozen men remained to be split between Braxton and Kolt.

With a sneer, Braxton said, "Hammond, you are taking over Kolt's squad."

Kolt started, "What do you think—"

"You have no horse; how do you expect to ride along?" He did not give Kolt time to respond before yelling at the men to depart.

‡‡‡

272

Someone was shaking his shoulder and he awoke startled. The man looked familiar and Nico recalled seeing him with Caius on that first day in the throne room. He looked a few inches shorter than Braxton, his fine, ash blond hair was cut short, and dark brown eyes scowled at him.

"What's going on?" Nico questioned, blinking the sleep from his eyes.

The man pulled him to his feet.

He expected to be dragged away, but instead was thrown into the corner of the cell. "What are you doing?" Something was wrong.

"Teaching my brother a lesson," the man growled, punching him in the stomach.

Nico coughed, hunching over. The next strike landed on the side of his head, flinging him into the wall. Then a punch to the back of his head sent him to the floor. He brought his hands over to shield himself, which only seemed to anger the man more. He lost his breath as a boot connected with his chest.

It seemed an eternity before the man grew bored and left, leaving him on the floor, his body numb, throbbing, and beaten. Gingerly, Nico pushed himself up and stumbled back to the cot.

Blood came from his mouth and he choked on the iron taste. Already, one of his eyes was swelling, making it difficult to see. The ringing in his ears was beginning to fade, leaving him with a pounding headache.

Groaning, he lay on the cot. Hopefully, the next person to visit would take him to the infirmary, otherwise, he was in for an even more grueling ordeal if this was to become the norm.

‡‡‡

"Did you see the look on their faces?" Carter said, laughing excitedly.

Out of breath, Lucas slowed to a walk. "I did."

Over the last three days, they'd been causing disorder in the city. They'd knocked soldiers out and stripped them of their armor and weapons, freed elementals under house arrest, taken cartloads of food headed to the barracks, and even liberated some soldiers of tax money. No one had been seriously injured, but they were causing enough trouble that there were whispers about who was committing the deeds.

Lucas had already heard several theories. Most believed it was Lazado agents, others thought it was youngsters, and some thought it was rogue citizens. *If only they knew it was just two shepherds.*

They climbed the steps to the house and were joined by Elza.

"Seems you two have been keeping busy."

Carter led the way inside, "Can't say otherwise."

"What're you doing here?" Lucas asked. While he went along with Elza's plans, something was off-putting about the man and he didn't entirely trust him.

"It's time to step up our game," Elza said.

"There isn't much else we can do just the two of us," Carter pointed out.

"I'd say otherwise."

"What scheme do you have this time?" Lucas asked.

"I was thinking we could release everyone from the dungeon."

"Are you insane?" Lucas barked. "That's a great way to get us killed."

"It won't be that hard," Elza said, playing it off.

"Oh, really?"

"Yes. If you look like you belong there, no one will bother you. After that, it's pretty simple."

"How do you propose we look like we belong?"

"Well, there are two options—you look like a soldier, or you look like a prisoner."

"You're going to get us killed."

"I think it'll work," Carter contradicted.

"Then do it yourselves," Lucas told them. "Count me out."

"Really? After all you've done these past few days, you balk now?"

"To dress like a soldier is treason; it means our heads if we get caught. And I'll never allow myself to become a prisoner willingly."

"Elza, come back tomorrow. Give me some time to work on him," Carter said.

Giving a wave, Elza said, "Let your answer be the right one, Lucas."

✢✢✢

Night was settling all around as Aron sat next to his campfire, watching a rabbit cook. In the distance, he could see the smoke from another fire and was certain it belonged to the Vosjnik. He had managed to catch up and follow at a safe distance but had no idea how much longer it would take to reach Revod. He assumed they would arrive within three days, as any longer and they would miss Keegan.

He was both dreading and anxiously anticipating their arrival— eager to aid Keegan once more and to see the world outside the castle but fearing reaching Revod because he had yet to formulate a plan. If the

Vosjnik captured her, there was little he could do to free her. There was no good way to face facts and he had resigned himself to simply roll with the punches.

He lay back on his bedroll, pinching his shoulders together to alleviate the tension in his back. Sleeping on the ground did not agree with him after a lifetime of princely beds. But given the circumstances, he was doing remarkably well on his own.

CHAPTER 36

Angrily, Braxton slammed the door to the stable. Two days of searching and no one had found a trace of Aron. He had not expected much, but regardless, he was still frustrated.

He stormed across the grass and through the castle, on the lower levels running into Milo. "Do you have any news about who released the griffins?"

"No," Milo said. "Whoever it was covered their tracks well. The only things they left behind were the arrows in the guards."

"Anything unique about them?"

"No, standard issue from the armory."

"Keep looking."

Milo bowed as Braxton walked away. "Oh, your father requested you cater to the boy tonight."

Braxton gave him a lazy wave to show he had heard, muttering under his breath, "Of course he has me acting like a servant. Of course, he has me doing this the moment I'm back. Of course, of course, of course!"

Unhappily, he made his way to the kitchens. There, a small tray of food and a vial with a thick red liquid awaited him. He picked up the container and let light shine through it, wondering what unpleasantness it contained.

Taking the tray, he made his way through the halls. Kolt passed him at one point and gave an intentionally audible snigger. Heat rose in his ears and he had to refrain from bashing his head in with the tray.

Outside the cell, he paused. Nico lay on the cot, staring up at the ceiling. Having no desire to do this, he took a deep breath, opened the door, and entered.

Nico looked up at him, dark bruises covering his face, and sat up warily.

He set the tray down quickly, made his way over to the boy. Kneeling in front of the cot, he took Nico's head and turned it to the side. "Who did this?"

Nico avoided his gaze.

"Who did this?" he demanded.

"I don't know," Nico said submissively.

"What did he look like?"

Nico rubbed his jaw. "Average, had a big ring…"

Braxton turned Nico's head to look at the bruise again; it had an impression. The form was misshapen, but he would know that symbol anywhere. He removed the ring he wore on his right hand. "Did it look like this?"

"I think so."

Without another word, Braxton slipped his ring back on and stalked out. He was going to kill him; Kolt had no right… and how could he do that to a child? His anger grew as he stormed through the castle. His brother had gone too far. When he reached Kolt's room, he did not bother knocking and kicked the door in.

Two women were kneeling on the bed, enraptured in each other, both wearing nothing. Another, clothed in only a skirt, was leaning over Kolt, who sat in a chair, a smug smile on his vile face. The three women shrieked as he barged in and made pathetic attempts to cover themselves.

He rushed over and pulling Kolt out of the chair, punched him in the face. "Do not touch that boy ever again!"

Kolt tried to retaliate.

He knocked him to the floor. "Do you hear me?"

Kolt feigned ignorance. "What are you talking about?"

"NICO!" Braxton struck him again. "You beat the boy because I did not allow you on the search for Aron."

"What if I did?"

"You little vitot," Braxton bellowed, striking him in the mouth.

Kolt gave him a bloody grin. "What are you going to do about it?"

He punched him in the ribs. "What the nastor do you think?"

There was a satisfying crack and Kolt dropped to the floor, clutching his side.

"Do not touch the boy again."

"You are not his tutor; you have no say."

"I am now. Touch him again and I will leave you with little more than your life."

‡‡‡

"Hey, we've made pretty good time," Keegan commented as they emerged from the forest. "You said it'd take a week and we made it in six days."

"Yes," Taite said absentmindedly. There was something else he mumbled that she didn't catch.

"You gonna let us stay in the city tonight?" Keegan questioned Kade.

Kade started, "I don—"

"We'll see how we feel later," Taite interrupted.

Keegan turned her attention to the city before them. They were approaching from the southwest, the sun casting long shadows of the city's profile. Tall walls rose well into the sky and only a few roofs peaked their heads over the battlements. The stones constructing the ramparts were a dark, somber gray. Flags flew from the top of the wall, gently waving in the breeze. A mass of people milled about outside the gate.

"Why isn't anyone going in?" She asked.

"How should I know?" Taite snapped.

"Geez, someone's cranky."

A man beside them answered, "The portcullis is broken. They think they'll have it fixed around midday."

Taite gave the man a nod.

"What now?" Keegan probed.

"We could go to another gate," Cassidy offered.

"It'll take us longer to get there than it will to fix this one," Taite said. "We wait."

Time passed slowly and Keegan swore she could feel herself aging. This was one of the times she missed her phone. At first, without it, it'd felt like a piece of her was missing. Now that she was used to not relying on it, it wasn't so bad. But times like this brought back the yearning.

Once the gate was fixed, they had no problems getting in. Inside, Revod seemed as grim as the outside looked. The buildings were all made of dark stone and the inhabitants dressed in drab colors.

They stabled the horses and Taite released them on the city, knowing they would do what they wanted anyway. Kade and Cassidy eagerly went their own way but she and Jared, not knowing what to do, did as before, and followed Taite to the market.

"Ten bucks says Kade and Cassidy go to the closest inn," Keegan remarked.

"Ten bucks?" Jared questioned. "I'm impressed you can carry that many deer."

"Hey, you're picking up sarcasm!"

"I'm not sure that's a good thing."

Keegan waved her hand. "Psh. I didn't mean deer. 'Bucks' is another word for money. Here, I guess it'd be like betting ten coins."

"I see. And why would you bet they're going to an inn?"

"I wasn't literally betting money, it's kind of a figure of speech. And they would go to an inn to... well, to do the thing Kade really likes."

Jared gave her an unamused look. "I can't believe you say things like that."

278

Once they reached the market, they left Taite, but kept him in sight. They wandered around, looking at the wares and she pulled Jared over to a vendor.

"I thought you hated dresses."

She scrunched her nose. "To a degree, but sometimes it's fun to wear a dress—like when I wanna look cute and stuff. But here they're just meh and it's kinda hard to get on and off a horse in a dress without flashing someone."

"Flashing?"

"Uhh... showing your underwear."

He raised an eyebrow. "Cassidy seems to manage."

"Lord knows how."

She ran her hands over the fabrics; most felt coarse.

"Taite seems to know many people," Jared noted.

"Huh?"

Jared pointed through the crowd, "There."

The Kojote was deep in conversation with a soldier and it looked like he was trying to convince him of something.

"Something's off," Keegan muttered.

They watched the interaction fervently until Taite pointed in their direction and her heart began to beat faster as more soldiers gathered around. She locked eyes with him, and he started pointing furiously and yelling.

Frustrated, Taite started exuding his feelings and she felt the bottled-up emotions spilling forth. There was something else; excitement—no, anticipation and—it had something to do with them.

She began pushing Jared. "Run. The cunt sold us out."

Jared led the way as they shoved through the market, soldiers yelling at them to stop. He started pushing farther ahead of her and she called out to him, but her words were lost as the crowd swallowed him up.

Soldiers were getting closer and knowing there was nothing else to do, she took off. For once, she was glad to be small; it made getting through the multitude easier than for her bulky pursuers. She needed to warn Kade and Cassidy. *Kade,* she yelled, praying he hadn't set up an impenetrable wall.

What's wrong?

Taite sold us out.

Behind her, men yelled, "Seize her."

She started running down the street.

Get somewhere safe, Kade instructed.

And where would that be? she snapped.

Just get somewhere, I'll find you.

Okay. You'll need to find Jared, too.

There was anger in his next question. *Why isn't he with you?*

We got separated. She felt his frustration. *It's not his fault.*

Just get somewhere safe, he said before breaking contact.

Keegan stopped, a stitch forming in her side. Looking behind, she noticed a mass of men further up the street. "Goddamnit."

Within minutes, she had to stop again. Breathing heavily, she looked around for some place to duck into, but there was no time; the soldiers were within eyesight. Cursing, she took flight again.

She rounded a corner and nearly tripped over a few children huddled against the wall. Ready to move around them, a thought struck her and instead, she took a seat beside them. "Shh," she whispered, pressing a finger to her lips and pulling the smallest child onto her lap. None protested, though they did give her looks of wild confusion. As the soldiers rounded the corner and sprinted past, she kept her head down, heart still hammering as she waited for one to grab her. When she could no longer see them, she slid the child from her lap. "Thank you."

Please tell me you're close by, she said to Kade, walking away from the children.

I'd be closer if you'd stop moving.

Well, sorry, I'm being chased. What was I supposed to do?

Just stay where you are.

Spotting a side alley, she made her way in. *Hurry.* The lane came to a dead end and she stared at the wall for a moment.

Behind her, a man yelled, "Lex, over here."

She turned to see a soldier standing at the top of the alley, making his way towards her, and followed by another man.

"We found her, Reye," Lex exclaimed.

Both were overweight, their enlarged bellies hanging from under their leather armor. Lex was stout, with the beginnings of a waddle. Reye looked like he belonged on a football team he was so big.

"Shit," she grumbled. "Look, just let me go and... just let me go."

"Why would we do that?" Reye questioned.

She gave a nervous smile. "Please."

Neither responded and began inching towards her.

She looked around and seeing nothing to use as a weapon, reached for her magic. As Lex lunged at her, she sent a column of earth into his stomach, stopping him in his tracks.

Reye came at her with a punch, which she ducked under, and retaliated with an uppercut to his ribcage. Lex made to join the fray and she kept him at bay with a well-placed sidekick. With her distracted, Reye managed to land a hook punch to her jaw.

She stumbled, quickly regained her composure and realized her back foot was against the wall. The soldiers stood awkwardly in front of her, as if unsure how to proceed. She lunged at Reye then attacked Lex, punching him in the jaw and pulling him into Reye.

While the two men disentangled themselves, she ran up the alley, and was halfway to the street when Lex grabbed her hair, pulling her back.

She winced and swung an arm wildly.

Lex caught it and twisted it behind her back. "Quickly," he called to Reye.

Reye began pulling something from his pocket.

Not knowing what it was, and not wanting to find out, she strained against Lex.

He twisted his fist into her hair. "You're not going anywhere."

Reye pulled out a bottle of green liquid, which he soaked a rag in.

She kicked back at Lex, aiming for his knee. Her foot found its mark, and there was a crunch as the force broke his patella. Lex fell to the ground, screaming in pain, pulling her down with him. In the fall, he released her, and she scrambled to her feet.

Reye grabbed hold of her and slammed her into the wall, blurring her vision. Taking advantage of this, he punched her, making her head hit the wall again.

Her eyes watered, making it even harder to see straight.

He placed a hand over her throat to keep her in place while he endeavored to pull the rag back out of his pocket. With her vision beginning to clear, she struggled against him and he had difficulty holding her in place with one hand.

Just as the rag touched her face, someone pulled the soldier away. Whatever the rag was soaked in made her throat sting, making her cough and gag. There was the sickening crack and Reye fell to the ground, his neck broken.

She coughed violently as she stared at Kade, her mind fuzzy. "Bloody good timing you've got," she wheezed.

‡‡‡

"Where are we going?" Cassidy asked with a light laugh as Kade pulled her through the streets of Revod.

With a smile, he answered, "I don't know yet."

281

They walk around hand in hand and eventually found themselves on the outskirts of a main square. Street performers pranced about; some juggled, while a few danced to merry jigs, and others were telling stories with the aid of puppets.

Approaching the puppeteers, they watched the story unfold. From what Cassidy could tell, it was the fable of the cat and the dragon. Children sat on the ground, laughing at the ludicrous animations.

Kade was relaxed, something rare, and wrapped an arm around her. She smiled as they watched the show, gently leaning against him, wishing the moment would never end. Suddenly, she felt him tense and looked up to find a worrisome expression on his face. "Is everything okay?"

"No." He dragged her away from the crowd. "Taite betrayed us."

She covered her mouth in shock. "What are we going to do?"

"You're going to stay here while I look for Keegan and Jared."

"I want to go with you."

"No," he told her, placing a hand on her cheek. "I'll be faster on my own, and it'll be safer for you here."

"Fine, but hurry."

He gave her a quick peck on the cheek before starting away, not making it far before Jared ran headlong into him.

"Oh, thank Sola and Lunos. Taite—"

"I know."

"Good, but I lost Keegan."

"I know that too, I was just going to get her. Go get the horses and meet us at the north gate," Kade said, not giving them time to respond before he was gone.

Jared gave Cassidy an anxious look.

"Well, what are we doing just standing here?" Cassidy said, taking charge.

CHAPTER 37

Kade turned down a street and faced a dead-end. He cursed, having no idea how to reach Keegan—and to make matters harder, she was moving.

Please tell me you're close by, she said.

I'd be closer if you'd stop moving, he told her.

Well, sorry, I'm being chased. What was I supposed to do?

Just stay where you are.

There was a slight pause. *Hurry.*

He took another turn and found another dead-end. Backtracking, he thought, *If I can't even find Keegan, how are we going to find the Lazado?*

The Lazado... In the chaos, he'd forgotten they no longer had Taite to rely on. He cursed under his breath and stopped in an alley.

He ran a hand over his jaw, thinking, *Why couldn't Thaddeus just give us directions?* He then remembered the letter. This certainly qualified as an emergency. Pulling it out of his pocket, he ripped the envelope open.

Kade,

If you are reading this, then some calamity has happened. Or you just could not listen—which, if that is the case, shame on you.

The Lazado are in Edreba, as everyone knows. They do not keep themselves hidden for several reasons, the main one being that no man ordered by Caius can cross the boundary that separates our kingdom from the other races. However, they are still cautious about allowing outsiders in.

To gain entrance, you need to answer their questions correctly. You will be asked the following:

1. Who are you? Kade Tavin, son of Kagen Tavin, ward of Thaddeus Broyker, subject of none.

2. Where do you come from? A land of subjugation and hate.

3. Why should we admit you? War cannot be fought only in the minds of men. It must be fought on the field, with payment of blood, in the hopes that Sola and Lunos will see us through.

After you give these answers, there should be no problems and they will welcome you with open arms. Memorize these responses and destroy this letter. Be safe and look after your family.

Thaddeus

283

He reread the missive before tearing the paper to ribbons, throwing a handful in a puddle, and shoving the rest into his pocket to discard later. He reached out to find Keegan's consciousness shrouded by adrenaline-addled thoughts and could sense she was close; he just had to find her.

About to run past an alley, he saw her held against the wall by a man with a rag, which was no doubt soaked in ether.

He raced towards them and pulled the soldier away. Giving a sharp tug, he broke the man's neck.

Keegan bent over coughing. "Bloody good timing you've got."

"Come on."

"Where's Jared and Cassidy?"

"Waiting for us at the north gate."

She took the fallen soldier's sword and followed him. "What was on that rag?"

"Ether." He peered around the corner of the wall. There were a few people talking in the street.

"What does it do?"

"Inhibits magic."

"Should I be worried?"

"No, it'll fade in a bit. Follow me and do *exactly* as I say." He turned to her and pointed to the sword, "Hide that."

She fumbled to conceal the weapon in the folds of her dress as they left the cover of the alley.

They quickly made their way through the city, doing their best to not look questionable. It was slow going, but they eventually reached the north gate. Hiding behind some barrels, they looked for Jared and Cassidy.

"I don't see them," Keegan said worriedly.

Kade pointed across the way, "There they are."

‡‡‡

Cassidy and Jared had started down the street casually, or at least trying to appear that way. It seemed to take an eternity to reach the stable. The whole time she was sure soldiers would stop them.

Thankfully, their horses were handed over without questions and they led them towards the north gate, which was a challenge, as neither were familiar with the city. After a fashion, they found it and ducked into an alley to wait for Kade and Keegan as the sun neared the tops of the battlements.

284

An unpleasant feeling sat in Cassidy's stomach. "I think something is wrong. We should go look for them."

"No." Jared said calmly. "Kade can manage. And if we leave it could create complications."

"How long can we wait?"

"I see them," Jared said in a hushed voice, pointing across the square.

Spotting them, Cassidy was about to make her way over.

No. Stay there, Kade said.

But—

It'll look suspicious.

What're we doing? Keegan questioned, forcing herself into the exchange.

When I say, meet in the middle of the square, Kade instructed.

Cassidy looked towards the gate; they were wide open, and people bustled through like nothing was amiss. She watched a man approach one of the guards. After a moment, the guard called to the men on top of the gate. Knowing they were about to close the portcullis, she grabbed two of the horses and ran out into the square.

The others were caught off guard, but followed, realizing there was nothing else to do. As they ran, soldiers yelled at them to halt. The two groups converged in the middle, mounted, and raced towards the gates as they began to close. Cassidy rode through first, followed by Keegan and Kade. Jared was the last through, and only just made it.

✦✦✦

Keegan yelled to be heard, "We need to stop."

"Why?" Kade snapped, reining in his horse.

"We need to figure out where we're going."

"I know where we're going."

"Are you sure? We've been heading north."

"No, we haven't."

"What makes you think we're heading north?" Jared questioned.

"The moon's descending on our right," Keegan explained.

Kade countered, "It's cloudy and we've barely seen the moon."

"Stop for a minute and prove me wrong."

"Fine."

From the way he answered, she could tell he felt unsure.

They came upon a clearing and dismounted. Kade looked up at the dark sky, watching for a break in the voluminous, grey clouds. About to

285

give up, a cloud shifted, letting pale moonlight shine through. His countenance shifted from one of annoyance to one of concern and frustration. "We've been heading north," he mumbled.

"Glad I made us stop," Keegan said.

"Be quiet."

She was about to pull herself up into the saddle again when there was a sound from within the forest. "Did you hear that?"

"Hear what?" Kade questioned, placing a hand on the hilt of his sword. "Get on the horses now."

As soon as he said that, eight figures emerged from the trees. A man tried to grab Keegan and she swung her ill-begotten sword, catching him with a slash to the arm. He stepped away cursing. The figure closest to Cassidy seized her and pulled her away.

Keegan recognized a few of the attackers and backed into the middle of the clearing, as did Kade and Jared with their swords drawn.

"Let her go, Vitia," Kade snarled.

"Why would I do that?" Vitia asked with a smug look.

"I'll kill you."

Keegan had no doubt he'd live up to those words.

Vitia laughed. "I doubt that. Drop your weapons or the girl won't be doing so well."

Kade gritted his teeth but made no move to do as instructed.

Sighing theatrically, Vitia continued, "I'm not patient like Connery. I gave you a chance." She placed her hands on the sides of Cassidy's head and gave a quick jerk.

There was a sickening snap and Cassidy fell to the ground, her beautiful bright eyes no longer reflecting life and light.

Kade only remained rooted in place long enough for the blood to drain from his face before giving a ferocious yell and charging at Vitia.

Keegan could feel anger and anguish roiling from him and would've followed had Jared not held her back.

As Kade neared Vitia, he slowed, his face contorting in pain, and dropped to his knees, clutching his head.

Keegan watched as Vitia's malicious grin grew and Kade began to cry out in pain. Within a moment, he became silent and collapsed beside Cassidy's body. She gripped the sword tighter, preparing for the onslaught.

Vitia started towards them, clearly proud of what she'd done.

A piercing pain began in Keegan's head, the sensation increasing with each passing second. She scrunched her eyes together, dropped the sword, and clutched at her temples as it felt like shards of glass grinding into her skull. Automatically, she reached for her life magic, focusing its power on herself. It didn't completely alleviate the pain, but did make it more bearable; Jared wasn't as lucky, screaming helplessly. Dropping to her knees, she hunched over as he continued then became deathly still.

Hands wrapped around her arms and pulled her to her feet. It was only once she was standing, she realized how drained she felt; it was almost too much of an effort to stand. She looked up to see Vitia approaching, a deep scowl on her face.

"Now, how is that possible?" Vitia drawled, stepping over Jared. "You're just a little earth elemental."

Keegan pulled against the men; they didn't know.

Vitia took her arm and forced her wrist up. She stared at the marks with a look of disbelief. "That can't be." There was a pause. "How can this be? Get the ether!" she snapped at a girl Keegan didn't recognize.

The girl returned with a rag.

One of the men holding Keegan grabbed the back of her neck, anticipating resistance.

She wasn't completely prepared for the reaction the ether caused. Her throat burned and it felt as if someone were searing the inside of her lungs. The more she breathed, the fuzzier her mind became.

When Vitia pulled the rag away, she was left doing her best to simply breathe. She bent over and they let her fall. Slowly, she managed to stop coughing, containing it to a wheeze. As she attempted to stand, and a blinding pain radiated across the back of her head.

287

CHAPTER 38

Jared tasted dirt and his throat stung. He coughed and a wave of dizziness washed over him. Hands clutched his arms and pulled him up. Looking around, he became acutely aware of their predicament. He was dragged over to a tree and his hands were bound and forced above his head.

Vitia approached and he tensed, assuming she was going to cause him pain, but the only thing he felt was a gentle scrape against his inner forearms. Looking up, he saw she had made a branch grow from the tree behind him, which went between his arms, keeping them raised. He glanced at Keegan; she was still unconscious and dry blood stained her hair.

Vitia snapped her fingers to get his attention. "You're going to want to focus on me."

He glared at her.

She grabbed his chin. "Oh, come now; this is going to be fun."

He pulled away. "What do you want with us?"

"Absolutely nothing. However, the king wants something."

"What does *he* want?"

"You can ask him yourself when you see him."

Jared shifted uncomfortably as his arms began to tingle.

"Anyway, let's get to business. How do you get to the Lazado?"

"I don't know."

"Evard."

A pale-skinned man stepped forward and the scowl he bore sent a chill down Jared's spine. His trimmed dark brown hair was interrupted by a thick white scar on the left side of his head.

"Would you like the honors?" Vitia invited.

Evard's lips pulled into a malicious smile as he cracked his knuckles and rolled his shoulders before rushing forward, hitting Jared mid-abdomen. Had his hands not been restrained, he would've doubled over.

"Tell me how to reach the Lazado," Vitia demanded.

"I don't know."

"Tch, Kade must've told you."

"Kade doesn't know either. None of us do. The only person who knew was Taite."

"Ah, Taite Ault." Vitia reached over to the girl who stood in the circle around him and pulled her over. "Do you remember Taite, Mara?"

Jared studied the girl; dark red hair fell gently over her shoulders and she looked no older than fifteen. His gut wrenched as he was reminded of Nico.

288

Mara stood tensely beside Vitia, letting her hair conceal her face.

"I asked a question," Vitia growled.

"Yes, ma'am, I remember," Mara answered quietly, glancing at Jared with pain in her crystal blue eyes.

Vitia released Mara, and she backed away, lowering her eyes to the ground again.

"Tell me how to reach the Lazado."

"I don't know."

Evard delivered a blow to his side.

"T—" Vitia started again.

"I can't tell you something I don't know!"

"You have to know," Vitia growled, slowly approaching.

"He doesn't," Mara said quietly.

"What was that?" Vitia snapped.

"He-he doesn't know," she repeated, trembling.

Vitia pulled out a knife. "Hmm. Regardless, I still haven't had any fun yet."

Jared strained against his bonds, causing many of the Vosjnik to chuckle.

With a smile that revealed her pointed canines, Vitia placed the knife against his neck. "As much as I'd like to see you bleed," she whispered, "I've been instructed otherwise." She dropped the knife to the neckline of his shirt and ran it through the cloth, pulling apart the seam to reveal his naked chest. She gave a disappointed sigh, running her fingers down his stomach. "Not what I thought."

His skin burned where she touched and he grimaced, inadvertently giving a pained grunt. She let her palm rest on his collarbone, his skin sizzling. He began to shake, refusing to cry out.

Vitia pulled away, leaving him with a burn that would scar in the shape of her hand. "So docile. Nothing like Nico."

He felt a constriction in his chest and his heart felt as if it was clutched in a fiery grasp. "You opida."

"I see where he gets his mouth from though."

"Murderer! Roy—" He was cut off by a strike to the jaw.

"Murderer? I didn't kill him. Didn't Kade tell you?" she questioned with an air of arrogance. "Nico's alive and well. Maybe not well, but alive."

"He's alive?"

"Isn't that what I just said?"

Jared merely stared at her.

Vitia waved a hand, "Get him down, and take his shirt."

The branch between his arms receded and he groaned as needles shot through his limbs.

Two men led him to the middle of the clearing, stripped his shirt before rebinding his hands behind his back, and shoving him into the dirt.

He was left with his racing mind; *Nico's alive.*

‡‡‡

Kade felt someone gently running their fingers through his hair. Smiling, he opened his eyes and looked straight at Vitia. He scrambled away, quickly rising to his feet; it took him a moment to recall what had transpired. He threw himself at Vitia and was within inches when he was dragged away. "I'm going to kill you," he screamed. "I royiken swear it!"

Vitia gave a cold-hearted laugh. "I await the day so I can run you through."

He strained against those holding him, almost pulling free. Vitia caused his vision to blacken, and while he still fought, was no match blind. His hands were bound and forced against a tree. He could feel the rough bark of a branch between his arms.

Slowly, his vision returned. Around him stood the Vosjnik, staring murderously, the new members mimicking the others' looks. He was surprised to see Nicandro, who was well past his prime. Evard stood near Vitia and Kade had no doubt he'd quickly become a favorite. The man wasn't known for being kind and had been vying for Kade's position for years. "Your new recruits are an old man and a bwint," he goaded. "You must've been desperate."

Realizing the insult was directed at him, Evard stormed forward and punched him in the face.

Kade tasted blood and spat to alleviate the tang. "Losing your touch there."

Evard's face reddened and he brought back his fist.

"Leave it," Vitia barked.

Evard looked back at her furiously. She gave him an unwavering stare and he walked away.

"Who put you in charge?" Kade said in a belittling tone.

"Caius," Vitia answered coolly.

It was then he noticed the red out of the corner of his eye.

Mara noticed his gaze and guiltily looked away.

He'd heard the stories of when she had been handed over to Caius. She'd been a child, eight, and for one so young, had resisted the king longer than most adults, lasting over a year.

"It's all right," he told her. "Just do as she says."

Her cheeks reddened deeply, and the others laughed loudly.

As the laughter died down, Vitia said, "Formalities over, let's begin. Who's first?"

"I am," Thahan said. He took a few quick steps to reach Kade and violently brought his knee up between his legs.

Kade groaned then pain shot through his face as he was struck in the nose. His eyes watered and a large globule ran over his cheek. He could feel blood trickling out of his nostrils and tasted it on his lips.

Thahan delivered several heavy blows before Vitia called him away.

"I've barely begun to repay my debt," Thahan said, stepping back.

"Yours is piling up," Kade bit.

Dax pulled the stopper off a water-skin and jerked it towards Kade. It wasn't a lot of water, but it had the desired effect as it painfully forced its way through the nose and mouth.

Kade gasped, but all he got was more water entering his lungs, which stung as his body pleaded for air. Dax removed the water just long enough for him to take a breath before forcing it back, and so it went until he was left feeling dizzy and light-headed.

Nicandro went next, creating a ball of flames in both hands before holding them close to the exposed underside of Kade's arms. He shifted uncomfortably, clenching his jaw, but the pain became unbearable as his skin blistered, and he gave a deep yell.

Having achieved what he wanted, Nicandro pulled away.

Guthrie was content to send a biting stream of wind that caused his neck to snap painfully.

Evard shot rocks at his stomach and Kade was surprised he was so passive. It hurt to breathe, he was certain a few ribs had been cracked, but it should've been much worse.

Brennian chose to carve a griffin into his lower back and while the blade didn't cut deep, it was still agonizing, especially when he rubbed salt in the wound.

There was a lull after Brennian stepped away.

"Mara," Vitia snapped.

The girl shook her head.

Vitia rushed at her and Mara flinched. "Do it!"

"I can't," Mara mumbled, "he's done nothing to me."

Vitia struck her, sending the girl tumbling to the ground. "You will do as you're instructed!"

Mara's eyes took on a watery sheen.

"Just do it," Kade said. When she looked at him bewildered, he roared, "Do it!"

Mara picked herself up, approaching slowly, and entered his mind, gently pushing her way through his consciousness.

After a moment, he realized her ploy and scrunched up his face, playing along, hoping Vitia believed the horrible acting.

Mara quickly retreated and all but hid in the shadows.

Vitia stared at him with a virulent smile; he'd forgotten she had yet to inflict her punishment.

"I think I'll do this the hard way." She lashed out with a punch, catching him in his already tender ribs.

He gave an involuntary wheeze.

She paused. "What have you got in your pocket?"

He reacted quickly, pulling his legs up and planting his feet against her chest. She rolled backwards and he would've continued fighting had she not annihilated the feeling in his legs. He hung painfully, the rope cutting into his wrists.

Vitia dusted herself off casually. "It must be good!"

He cursed at her as she rifled through his pockets, producing Rosh's letter.

"What do we have here?" She didn't have time to read it as she followed Thahan's movements as he walked away.

Kade looked to see where the archer was going and saw Keegan standing across the clearing, dazed and disorientated.

‡‡‡

There was solid ground along her body, rocks digging into her, but the world felt like it was spinning, turning, and tumbling beneath her. There was a throbbing in her head; she reached up to touch it. A clump of dried blood crumbled between her fingers.

Groggily, Keegan opened her eyes and was assaulted by many brown colored shapes. As her vision became clearer, she distinguished individual trees. Jared was kneeling in the center of her vision and for reasons she couldn't understand, was shirtless.

He was mouthing something, and his eyes begged for her to understand—but the plea wasn't comprehended. She began to push herself up, body crying in pain, beseeching her to stay down.

Agonizingly, she made it to her feet while Jared continued mouthing frantically.

She mimicked him. R, r, ru, ru, ru, run. Run. *Run.* Finally, she understood, but it was too late; she'd failed to notice the man walking towards her.

He took her arm, setting her off balance.

She steadied herself and was surprised to be looking up at Thahan.

He shook her again, her body slamming into something solid. Another set of hands wrapped around her other arm and she turned to look at them. He too looked familiar.

They pulled her towards where Jared kneeled, a group from across the clearing meeting them there. As they approached, she saw Kade in the background, dark splotches on his face and blood trickling across his skin. He pulled at the branch that kept his hands raised, but the limb remained steadfast.

Though unsure of what had happened, what *was* happening, she still knew something was amiss. As she pulled against Thahan and the blond man, her heart stopped... there lay Cassidy. Her mind was suddenly clear. "Get away from me," she screamed, resisting in earnest.

As she continued to give screams of frustration, the Vosjnik froze.

"Get the ether," Vitia said, her tone conveying disbelief and fear.

A man pressed a rag against her face, and she broke into a fit of coughing, her throat burning as if the air had turned to acid. None too soon, the rag was removed, and she gasped for air, sagging between her captors.

"How did you manage that?" Vitia asked.

Her throat still reacting to the irritation, she gave Vitia a confused look.

"Show her."

They turned her around and the ground where they'd stood was raised in spikey waves, like fingers that had been reaching for them.

"Did I..."

"Yes, while still under the effects of ether. How did you come by your powers?"

"Hell if I know."

Vitia gave a laugh and pinched Keegan's cheek. "You're the only one I believe when they say that."

"Don't touch her," Jared yelled, awkwardly rising to his feet.

The men gave hearty laughs.

"Bring them over here," Vitia instructed. "Kade needs to be able to see."

293

While being pushed towards Kade, her foot caught on the hem of her dress and the fabric ripped.

"What's this?" Vitia questioned, returning her attention to Keegan. "Are you wearing trousers?"

She wanted to be witty, but knew it wasn't in her best interest.

The corners of Vitia's lips turned up. "No use having so many layers." She widened the tear, leaving only the bodice behind.

Keegan assumed it was a play to embarrass her. "What do you want with us?"

"They're here to take us to Caius," Kade said weakly.

A chill raced down her spine. "No. Please, no."

"Oh, that's not all we're going to do," Vitia said to Kade, running a finger along his jaw. "We're going to make you *suffer*."

"Opida," Kade spat.

Vitia lingered for a moment, giving him a pompous smile, then quickly turned on Keegan. "How do we get to the Lazado?"

"I don't know," she said. "I can't get anywhere in this world. But aren't they in Edreba?"

Vitia slapped her and she felt blood rushing to her cheek. "I wasn't asking you. I'm already aware that you and pretty boy over there," she pointed at Jared, "know nothing."

"Kade doesn't know either."

Vitia delivered a backhanded blow. "The only thing I want to hear from you is screams."

Keegan began to shake, not from fear but anger. Already, her mind was recalling the beatings she'd received from Caius, Kolt, and Braxton. "No," she snarled, driving her heel into Thahan's foot.

He released her and she clawed at Guthrie, her nails digging deep into the flesh of his face. He yelled but didn't let go. Before she could do any further damage, Thahan grabbed her arm and a fistful of hair, pulling hard, making her yelp.

"Evard, take Guthrie's place," Vitia commanded.

Evard made Keegan cringe, something about him making her feel threatened. Whether it was his disturbing smile or the fact that his grip was violently tight, she didn't know. Guthrie stepped away, blood running down his face.

"How dare you attack my men," Vitia hissed, coming within inches of her face.

Keegan's eyebrows furrowed into a deep scowl and she conveyed as much hate as she could. The look angered Vitia, causing Keegan's lips to turn up in the slightest show of arrogance.

Vitia stood for a moment before placing a foot on Keegan's left calf. "Wipe that look off your face." She applied pressure, and with a crack the leg broke under the stress.

For a moment Keegan felt no discomfort, then she looked at her leg; there was a clear bend. She felt an explosion of pain and gave a shrill cry, sucking in deep breaths as hot tears came forth.

Jared pulled against the men holding him, only yielding when struck in the stomach.

Vitia turned back to Kade, "How do we get to the Lazado?"

He stayed quiet.

"Fine." Vitia turned on Keegan and violently attacked her.

When done, Keegan could barely breathe, and a good portion of her face had gone numb.

The men holding Jared were beginning to struggle to restrain him as he twisted and screamed endless curses.

Several times Vitia asked Kade the same question and every time he remained silent. In retaliation, she struck Keegan, who was left slumping between Evard and Thahan.

In her half-conscious state, Keegan was barely aware of Jared repeatedly saying, "We don't know."

Slowly, she raised her head, knowing Vitia thought she was besting her. While it was true, she refused to give her the satisfaction. Placing her weight on her right leg, she rose to her full height—what little of it there was.

"Clearly, this isn't working," Vitia said, and pulled a knife from a sheath belted on her thigh.

"You wouldn't," Kade said, visibly agitated.

"Oh, I would." Vitia let the blade rest against Keegan's chest. "That is unless you tell me what I want to know."

Kade gulped. "I don't know."

"Wrong answer." Vitia drove the knife into Keegan's shoulder just below the clavicle.

She gave a shattering scream and hell broke loose.

CHAPTER 39

Aron crouched in the bushes, having a perfect view through the foliage. Evard and Thahan held Keegan while Vitia beat her. Slowly, he drew his bow, notching an arrow.

The man restrained by Dax and Brennian yelled profanities; it only made Vitia smile. Kade stared silently at her from his dangling position while Keegan sagged, barely keeping herself standing. She weakly raised her head and Aron saw a spark in her eyes as she lifted herself, putting all the weight on her right leg. He noticed the bend in her left calf, and grimaced.

Vitia unsheathed a knife and before he knew it, drove it deep into Keegan's shoulder.

Keegan released a wounded cry, which rang in his ears, and a force seemed to take control of his body. He sprang to his feet, shooting an arrow, which buried itself deep in Evard's jugular. The man dropped to the ground, pulling Keegan with him. Thahan, caught off guard, failed to release Keegan and tripped over her. She gave another cry as he scrambled back onto his feet and the rest of the Vosjnik looked for the source of the arrow.

Redrawing his bow, he pushed through the bushes. He let an arrow fly, aiming for Vitia.

She moved and it grazed her arm. "Who are you?" she spat, unable to recognize him with his hood drawn low, her hand covering her arm.

Calmly, he sent an arrow towards Kade; it sheared through the ropes around his wrists and he dropped to his knees. Aron notched three more, quickly aiming them at Vitia's chest and carefully stepped towards Kade, letting him take the sword belted around his waist.

Making his voice deeper than normal, he said, "Leave, I have twenty soldiers in the forest."

Vitia scoffed, "You lie."

"Are you sure?"

Vitia was about to say something when Mara interrupted, "He's lying."

Vitia laughed, "Fool. You thought—"

"He has forty men."

Aron was surprised, but happy to let Mara help. "Walk away now and my men will not pursue."

Vitia scowled but made a gesture and the Vosjnik began to slowly advance towards their horses.

Vitia was cruel to the extreme, but she knew how to lose gracefully. He would not call it caring for her comrades, more a way to make sure she lived to fight another day. "I said walk," he snarled.

Vitia gave him a glare before complying and the Vosjnik began to retreat.

As they reached the tree line, Aron stopped them. "Leave your weapons."

"No," Vitia said coldly.

He released an arrow and it found its mark in Brennian's hip, who fell to a knee, giving a strangled yelp. "Leave your weapons."

Vitia remained still. "You'll never be safe, not even in the Lazado."

Aron pulled the bowstring back further.

Vitia's men gave her worried looks, shifting uncomfortably. With a deep scowl, she unbuckled her belt and let its weight pull it to the ground. The others followed suit quickly, then backed into the forest.

Aron gave it several minutes before relaxing and rushing to Keegan, setting his bow down and throwing back his hood. She lay on her side and he gently pulled her over to face him. She gave a choked groan, dirt sticking to her face where tears wetted her skin.

"Aron?" she said in a whisper that only he heard.

Kade freed Jared and walked over to them. "What are you doing here?" he snapped, shoving him away from Keegan.

Aron wished he had held onto his bow. "Saving you."

"Jared, how's she doing?" Kade asked.

Jared gave Keegan a quick onceover. "Not well."

He pushed past Kade and returned to Keegan. Her eyes were closed, and he wished she were awake to speak on his behalf.

"Don't touch her," Kade snarled.

Jared gave him a quizzical glare. "What's the matter with you? He just saved us."

Kade tried to speak but found no words formed and cursed to himself.

For once, Aron was glad his father spelled all his men so none could speak of his sons' existence in the presence of those who did not know.

"He can't be trusted," Kade said finally.

"Why not?" Jared probed.

"I can't say; you just have to trust me."

"We need to leave," Aron suggested. "We are vulnerable here."

"What about the men with you, won't they protect us?" Jared asked.

"I was bluffing."

"Why would that girl lie for you?"

"Later," Kade stepped forward and scooped Keegan up. "Jared, can you carry Keegan?"

Jared mounted his large Clydesdale and held out his arms. Then turning to Aron, said, "Thank you for your help."

Aron nodded before cutting the Vosjnik's horses free and sending them trotting. Mounting his own, now named Osais, he announced. "I am coming with you."

"As you will. It'll be good to have another skilled fighter."

Kade gave him a deep scowl and stormed past him.

Aron figured he would refuse but seemed momentarily preoccupied by something else. With interest, he watched Kade cross the clearing to where someone lay, sadness overtaking him.

Gently, Kade lifted the body and carried it over to Arso, struggling to get it onto his back. Giving Jared a small nod, they left the clearing.

‡‡‡

Kade and the mysterious archer raced alongside him, and he swallowed his anger. He was furious; how could Kade have kept the fact that Nico was alive? But that was for later, presently, he had other things to worry about.

He looked down, Keegan's head lay on his shoulder and he held his arm up so it wouldn't loll. Just then, her eyes fluttered open and she gasped.

He reigned in Brewer.

"Why are you stopping?" Kade called.

"Keegan's awake."

"It's not safe to stop yet."

Jared looked at Keegan. "Can you make it a little further?"

Giving a dazed moan, she nodded.

There was no need to say anything else and he jabbed his heels into Brewer. With each footfall, Keegan gave a pained look. They covered a few more miles before he pulled Brewer to a stop again; enough was enough. She was in agony—as was he. He expected rebuke from Kade, which didn't come. Instead, he noticed him grimacing and wondered about the condition of his injuries.

The archer approached them and Kade gave him another angry scowl.

"What are you doing here?" Keegan questioned.

"Rescuing you," he answered softly.

"You know him?" Jared asked, sliding off his Clydesdale.

298

"Yeah," Keegan groaned uncomfortably. "He's the one who helped me escape from Caius."

Kade looked genuinely surprised. "We need to set a few things and bandage others."

"Unh," she groaned, shifting slightly, face crinkling in pain. "Jared, I have an extra shirt in my saddlebag."

He knelt beside her, "I can wait."

Kade turned to the archer, "Take a blanket and rip it into as many strips as you can. Then I need two sturdy sticks at least two feet long." He then asked Keegan, "What hurts most?"

"All of it."

Ever the austere one, Kade instructed, "Get her on her left side; I'll start with her shoulder."

Jared glanced at it, noticing the distortion, and wondered when that had happened, then imagined it must've occurred when Thahan tripped over her. He turned Keegan onto her side as gently as he could, but she still let out a stifled scream.

Kade took her right arm and raised it up as she sucked in shallow breaths. "Hold her still. On the count of three. One. Two." There was a loud pop as he pushed her shoulder back into the socket.

Keegan screamed but a look of relief also crossed her face. "What happened to three?"

Kade gave no answer, ripping her left sleeve off.

"What's your issue with Aron?" she asked.

Jared was surprised she could think past the pain.

"Can't say," Kade muttered.

"Bullshit."

Blood from the stab wound held the fabric to her skin and he had to pry it away. More began to flow as the wound was reopened. "I'd tell you if I could," he promised.

A yelp escaped her lips as he dabbed the wound with a wet cloth.

"I have to clean it," he chastised.

"I know, I know."

"Kade, is there anything you can do to heal her magically?" Aron called out.

"Ether's still affecting us," Kade answered, "and I'm an earth elemental. Keegan might be able to, but she's not particularly good at healing herself."

"She is an elemental?" Aron enquired.

"I'll explain later," Jared promised, knowing how convoluted the story was.

Once Kade finished flushing the wound, he wrapped Keegan's shoulder in one of the blanket strips and secured her right arm across her chest in a sling. "I'm going to set your leg now."

She grimaced, "Do it quickly." She half-watched as he carelessly went about it. After several minutes, with tears welling in her eyes, she asked, "Have you ever set a bone before?"

Kade glanced up at Jared to avoid her gaze. "Um... no. This was Vitia's domain."

"Archer," Jared said, "h—"

"It's Aron."

"Aron," Jared amended, "help Kade hold her still."

Aron gave an almost unnoticed raise of an eyebrow but did as asked, cradling Keegan's head in his lap.

Grabbing the knife from his boot, Jared carefully sliced through the fabric of her trousers, stopping at the knee to tear away the loose fabric.

Retaining her sarcastic nature, Keegan mumbled, "Kade must envy you."

Kade appeared to not hear and Aron looked mildly confused.

It was fortunate the bone hadn't pierced the skin, though, there was a large section of swelling. "I think it's a clean break," Jared said, taking two branches and tying them to the leg using the strips of blanket.

"Are we good to keep going?" Aron questioned. "Or do you need to attend to your own injuries?"

Keegan spoke before either could respond, "Don't be stubborn asses and carry on 'cause you need to look macho. Sort yourselves out."

Kade sighed, but every word she'd said was true. "Fine."

"There's an extra shirt in my saddlebag," Keegan mumbled again tiredly.

"Get some sleep," Kade told her.

She nodded, her eyelids already heavy.

"Thank you," Jared squeezed her hand. It didn't take him long to find the shirt and put it on and realize how chilled he'd been without it.

‡‡‡

Kade's ribs protested as he rose to his feet. Taking a damp cloth, he wiped his lower back where a griffin was now etched into the skin. Once clean, he wound a cloth around his abdomen. He would've liked to bind his ribs, but it would require help and he wanted none from Aron.

Injuries dealt with, he walked over to the horses. Seeing Cassidy's lifeless body lying across Arso's back, he felt a lump rise in his throat and fought to maintain his composure.

"Do you want help?" Aron asked.

Voice catching, he shook his head then headed into the forest to search for logs. The task didn't take long, at least he didn't think it did—time had little meaning right then.

After wrapping Cassidy in a blanket, he placed her on the pyre he'd fashioned, noticing that even in death she was beautiful. Seeing the larimar necklace, he gently removed it.

Aron placed a hand on his shoulder in condolence.

"Don't touch me," he said coldly, covering Cassidy's face, his body aching. His hands trembling as he endeavored to light a fire and he caught himself beginning to cry. He wiped his eyes—*I can't appear weak before Aron.* The pyre was slow to catch, but once it did, it raged wildly.

"We should pay our last respects," Jared said, standing beside him.

"No," Kade said harshly. As much as he wanted to, he knew he'd break. "Time to go."

"How do we get to the Lazado?"

"Don't worry about it."

"We're not going with you. Nico's alive."

Kade cursed. "Yes, he is. And the only way to help him is through the Lazado."

"I know. But we won't be arriving together."

"We are. I'll do the same thing to you I did to Keegan when she wanted to go back."

Jared drew his dagger. "I'm not Keegan."

"No, I thought you were more sensible. We need to leave; the Vosjnik won't be waylaid for long."

Jared turned to Aron, "I say we leave him. They'll be too preoccupied dealing with him to chase us."

Aron looked uncomfortable to be suddenly dragged into their quarrel. "I think he may have a use yet."

"Of course, I do," Kade said, "but you don't. You can leave."

"I set out to help Keegan."

"And you've done that," Kade snapped, picking Keegan up. Her head lolled and he felt a pit in his stomach. Being in the same squadron with Vitia for five years meant he knew all her evil tricks; this had the trademark of her poisoned blade.

"I intend to see her through until the end," Aron persisted.

"We don't need you. I'd tell you to go home, but no one there wants you either."

"I want him here," Jared said. "I need help protecting Keegan from *you.*"

"I don't recommend trying anything," Kade snarled. "We don't have time for this, so, either fight me and die, or be quiet and come with me."

Jared seemed conflicted, then stormed over to Brewer and swung into the saddle. "This isn't over."

"Of course not," Kade said sarcastically, handing Keegan up to him. "Leave," he told Aron.

Aron gritted his teeth. "You want me gone, make me."

Kade began to draw his sword.

"He comes," Jared blurted, "or I ride off with Keegan."

Glancing at him, he knew Jared would deliver on his threat. The entire thing had gone to vito, the secrets he'd kept to force them into compliance no longer holding sway; he had to bend and break now. He opened his mouth, about to protest again.

"Save it," Jared hissed.

But the bastard's the son of the king!

CHAPTER 40

Nico expected anyone but who walked into his cell that morning.

Braxton gave him a stare that had a mixture of sympathy, guilt, and—oddly enough—warmth. "Come with me."

"Where are we going?"

"See for yourself."

Nico hesitated before chasing after him.

The hallway outside was devoid of people and their footsteps reverberated off the walls, bringing faces to the bars of the cells they passed. Many had choice words for Braxton, who was unmoved by them, and soon they had left the dungeon behind.

"How old are you?" Braxton asked eventually.

Nico repeated his question, "How old are you?"

"Twenty-four."

"Fourteen." Nico looked around, wondering why there were no guards. He was tempted to run, but imagined it wasn't in his best interest. "Where are we going?"

"Almost there."

They made their way up another long, winding set of stairs and along a landing.

Braxton stopped at a door and pushed it open. Entering, he began, "This is my room. You will be sleeping on the cot over there."

"Wh—"

"I am your tutor. Until my father deems otherwise, at least. You will follow my orders without question, understood?"

"I didn't agree to this."

Braxton shut the door. "I know but trust me when I say this is for your benefit."

A chill ran down his spine. "What do—"

"My father is not a kind man. Neither is Kolt. This is the only way I can protect you. Please do not make this harder than necessary."

Nico scowled.

"Of course, you will not take my word for it. Not you, not my own brother, not even Keegan."

"You know Keegan?"

"I would have to use *know* loosely, but yes."

"Did she trust you?"

"I do not think so, but she must have realized I only did what I had to."

"Why should I trust you?"

"You should not." There was a pause. "I am just trying to minimize the pain you must endure."

Nico searched Braxton's face for any sign that he spoke false and found none. "What happens if I don't cooperate?"

"You have already experienced it. Worse is to come though, much worse."

The words were nothing but true and Nico knew he wouldn't be able to resist much longer. He recalled the flashes of kindness he'd seen from Braxton and began to think. "I'll make you a deal."

Braxton's eyebrows raised and the hint of a smile appeared on his lips. "I am listening."

"I'll let you tutor me if you promise nothing bad will happen to my family."

"I cannot promise that. There are many things outside of my control and my father does not have your family imprisoned."

Nico thought for a moment. "Then promise that if my family gets caught, nothing bad will happen to them."

"I cannot do that, but I will do what is within my power."

He understood nothing more could be truly asked—it was incomprehensible he was even able to propose the idea. "Then I'm your student."

✝✝✝

The sun shone through the branches of the trees ahead, blinding him every so often. Keegan was still in a blissful dream state. Jared supposed that was best, as she didn't have to endure the discomfort caused by her injuries—nor the lies Kade had told.

The sun was slow to set and cast them into twilight. By the time they stopped, the horses were grateful when their burdens dismounted.

He set Keegan near where they would build a fire and watched Aron and Kade work to set up camp, an icy silence between them. He studied her for a moment; her cheeks were heavily flushed, and she appeared to shiver. "Kade," he called.

"What?"

"I think something's wrong."

Without walking over, Kade answered, "I *know* something's wrong."

"What are you talking about?"

Aron paused to hear the exchange.

"She's been poisoned."

"And you didn't think it important to mention sooner?"

"How could you keep that to yourself?" Aron chimed in.

"There's nothing we can do about it," Kade said and to Aron, "And *you* won't be with us much longer anyway."

"Like nastor I will not," Aron said angrily.

Jared could see Kade wanted nothing more than to lash out but somehow restrained himself.

Kade placed a hand on the pommel of his sword. "You're not coming with us."

"I am."

Not interested in their quarrel, Jared interjected, "Enough; I already said he's coming. Now, we have more pressing matters. Tell us about the poison."

Kade snapped, "What's there to say, it's a poison."

"How was it introduced? What does it do?" Jared paused, "How long does she have?"

"When Vitia stabbed her in the shoulder. It's called Ramilla; it's made from the nectar of the dogwood flower and octopus' venom. It puts the victim into a deep sleep and slowly eats away at their muscle. As for time, with a grown man, three weeks, four if they're lucky. With her, maybe two."

"Is there an antidote?"

"Yes, but it's hard to come by." There was silence. "The Lazado might have some, but there's no telling for sure."

"How long will it take us to reach them?" Aron asked.

"It will take Jared and I—" Kade started.

"Us," Aron snarled.

"Why are you so desperate to come?"

"I promised someone I would look after her."

"Who?"

"No one you know and no longer living," Aron answered. "How long will it take us to reach the Lazado?"

"Three weeks. If we push, we can make it in two."

"We have to," Jared said. "There's no other choice."

"There is *one* other choice. But I'd only consider it if all else fails."

"What is it?" Jared asked, sensing he wasn't going to like the answer.

"We turn ourselves over to the Vosjnik. If it means Keegan lives, I'll do it without hesitation."

‡‡‡

305

"Remember the plan?" Carter whispered.

Lucas gave him a flat look. "Yes, I remember the royiken plan." He had no idea how Carter had managed it, but he'd talked him into going along with Elza's idea.

They hid in the darkness of an alleyway dressed in guards' uniforms, waiting for Elza to deal with the sentries at the door. There was a sudden shift in one of the men and he fell forward. The other, caught unawares, followed. In the dark, it was hard to see Elza waving them over.

Looking down the street to make sure no one was around, they snuck forward. As he neared the downed guards, Lucas could see the bloodstains creeping across their backs.

"Here," Elza murmured, thrusting a handful of keys into Carter's hand. "Dungeon's down those steps. The guards shouldn't be making rounds again for another hour."

"Got it," Carter said eagerly.

Lucas eyed Elza as he passed.

"Best of luck," Elza said with a scheming grin.

Lucas pulled a torch from its bracket and led the way. Soon, the steps leveled out, giving way to a long hallway lined with bars.

With excited anticipation, Carter began to fumble with the keys. The man in the cell seemed surprised and leaned against the back wall. There was a click of the lock and the door swung inwards. Carter gave a curt nod and moved to the next cell.

The man stared at Lucas.

"You're free to go," Lucas whispered.

"What's goin' on?" the man questioned.

"We're breaking everyone out."

"I don't know I'd do that now." The man stepped into the torch's light. He had a rough, scraggly beard that reached his collarbone run through by thick shocks of gray which also peppered his hair. Tired blue eyes gave him a questioning look.

"Why not?"

"Most of the men in here are murderers and thieves."

"Which one are you?" Lucas asked, placing a hand on the cell door.

"Both. But with good reason; I work with the Lazado."

"Can you prove that?"

"I can't."

"Hold on," Lucas told Carter, who was still fumbling with the second door.

"The name's Felix Isaacs," the man said. There was the sound of footsteps from the stairs. "I'd suggest runnin', lest the guards find us."

Lucas nodded and pushed Carter forward.

They were a good distance from the open cell when they heard a voice ask, "Where are they?"

"I swear I saw them come down here," Elza responded.

Lucas cursed; he knew the man couldn't be trusted.

"Check the rest of the cells," the voice ordered.

Ahead, they reached a set of stairs and quickly climbed them.

"You can hear them," Elza called.

"Go faster," Lucas urged.

"Sorry," Felix wheezed. "Sittin' in a cell's made me a tad unfit, lad."

"If you can talk, you can move faster."

They stumbled out into an empty corridor and followed Felix as he veered left. It wasn't long before a gang of guards appeared at the top of the stairs.

"Either ye lads got a weapon at all?" Felix asked, halting to a stop.

Carter glanced at Lucas then tossed his sword to Felix. Lucas drew his and turned to face the men racing towards them.

"Go ahead, lads," Felix said with a devilish grin, "I can handle this." When they hesitated, he turned to them. "Seriously, go."

Not in the mood or position to argue, Lucas pulled Carter down the hall. It wasn't long before the clanging of swords chased after them.

"You know where we're going?" Carter questioned.

"No," Lucas responded, taking a sharp left. They were rewarded with a locked door. When they turned back, they faced Elza.

"You son of a bwint," Carter growled.

Elza shrugged. "You morons played straight into my hand. Thanks to you two, I should be getting a promotion."

"We won't go down without a fight."

Elza laughed. "Only Lucas has a sword, so I don't expect this to be a very long one."

Lucas' heart pounded furiously as he gripped the sword tighter, instinct telling him to rush Elza and surprise him.

Elza was rightly caught off-guard and his sword dropped with a clang.

Unaccustomed to handling a weapon, Lucas' followed suit. His fist connected with flesh, sending the soldier into the wall. "Don't ever threaten my brother," he roared, his knuckles continuing to meet Elza, who began to slump, and he relented—a mistake. There was a sharp pain in his side, and he looked down to see the handle of a knife protruding from his abdomen.

Elza withdrew the blood-soaked blade. "I was prepared to let you live, but not anymore," he snarled, picking up his sword. "I'll make sure Carter suffers."

Lucas staggered and fell, clutching his side, then closed his eyes, waiting for pain to pierce him. Instead, he felt a warm liquid splash across his face. Opening his eyes, he saw Elza's gaping mouth and a sword protruding through his chest, which was removed, and he fell forward.

Felix replaced him. "Pig," was all he muttered, spitting on the body. "Help him up," he told Carter, taking the other discarded sword.

Carter wrapped an arm under the crook of Lucas' shoulder and heaved him to his feet. "We can't go that way. The door's locked."

Felix took in a deep breath and kicked it down. "That door?"

"Do you know where you're going?"

"I think so," Felix said, checking that the way was clear. "Do ye have somewhere we can go?"

"The house."

"No," Lucas wheezed, "Waylan's. Go to Waylan's."

"You know the way?" Felix questioned.

Carter nodded.

"Quickly now, before your friend bleeds out."

‡‡‡

Braxton found Nico's snoring atrociously loud. Finally realizing he was not going to sleep he rose and went to his desk. He lit a candle and checked over his shoulder to make sure the boy did not wake.

He looked down at the completed translation. 'While you have slaughtered — child of the dragon, she will rise again from the ashes by your own doing. Rule while you can, false lord, for it shall only be for the moment. A child will come who can defeat you. From the fire, from the earth, from adversity, from the path of exile this child will rise. But know it will be your own foolishness that will seal your fate, oh wicked king.'

He pulled out the page with the version he had been dreaming about and quickly read it; Jyken eya meki lunviyda zæ psodæ ri ayþ drackyn, æay woth viæn nuþ qalx ayþ æyscs fayo eyar oywn þen. Nackh jyken eya casne, fackyon ictotm, iruh du woth unla ryo iruh ayþ adæmno. Psodæ woth yarv rhæpn casne jappec eya. Qalx ayþ buna, qalx ayþ waysne, qalx okæpyio, qalx ayþ payn ri luxyen, zæ psodæ woth viæn. Astæm egreþer du woth ryo eyar oywn foylisha ghæ woth solcan eyar hayclen oh kævoka kunyi.

He compared it to the version he had found in the library; Jyken ey— —eki lunviyda — psod— ri ayþ drackyn, æa— woth viæn nuþ q— lx ayþ æyscs fayo eyar oywn þen. Nackh j—en eya casne, fackyon ictotm, —uh du woth unla ryo iruh ayþ adæmno. —od— woth yarv rhæpn casn— jappec eya. Qalx ayþ bu—a, qalx ayþ —aysne, qalx okæpyio, qa— ayþ payn ri luxyen, —æ ps—æ woth v—æn. Astæm egreþer —u woth ry— eyar oywn foylisha g—æ woth —olcan eyar haycl—n oh kævoka kunyi.

It was instantly clear where he had gone wrong. The addition of *zæ* in the original prophecy after *lunviyda* changed the meaning of *psodæ* in the first line from child to children. In the second part of the first line, he had assumed *æa*— was *æayu*, meaning her. Now, he realized it was *æay*, meaning they. Originally, in the fourth line he had used *dæ*, as for that word all he had to work with was —*æ*, instead of *zæ* which again, changed child to children.

He looked at the properly translated prophecy, 'While you have slaughtered these children of the dragon, they will rise again from the ashes by your own doing. Rule while you can, false lord, for it shall only be for the moment. Children will come who can defeat you. From the fire, from the earth, from adversity, from the path of exile, these children will rise. But know it will be your own foolishness that will seal your fate, oh wicked king.'

Until now he had thought the prophecy referred to one child. Alyck's words became clear, there was not *one* child of prophecy, but multiple—and he knew exactly who they were.

CHAPTER 41

The sun was just beginning to light the city streets. Lucas teetered beside Carter, his side sending painful flashes across his torso.

"Not much further, yeah?" Felix asked.

Lucas managed, "It's that shop there."

Felix followed his line of sight. "The blacksmith?"

"Yes."

Felix checked that the area was clear, then bolted across and began hammering on the door while Carter half-dragged Lucas over.

By the time they reached the shop, Waylan was opening the door. "The hell yo—" When he saw Lucas, he grew silent and ushered them in. "What the hell happened?"

"Later," Felix told the smith. "We need to stitch this up before he bleeds out. Get him on the table."

None too gently, Carter deposited Lucas on the tabletop after Waylan cleared it.

"Right," Felix started, "I need a needle, thread, a rag, water, a knife, and a lit candle."

Carter and Waylan started to move about collecting the items.

Felix turned his attention to Lucas. "How ya doing, lad?"

"Who knew getting stabbed hurt so noxþ much," Lucas groaned.

"I did. It's about to get worse now."

"What do you mean?"

Felix grimaced and placed a hand on his shoulder as Waylan and Carter approached, setting items on the table. Taking the knife, he ran it over the candle flame. "This is goin' to… burn. Try not to scream. Don't need to bring more attention to ourselves at all." He pressed the hot metal against the wound before Lucas could respond.

To Lucas, the sound of his sizzling skin was deafening. He clenched his teeth to keep from yelling and it felt like an eternity before the searing blade was removed. He sucked in deep breaths, blinking hard as darkness encroached on his vision.

"Impressive," Felix muttered. Taking the rag, he dabbed at the cauterized cut then took the needle and held it over the flame, watching the shiny metal turn red.

Lucas let his head fall back on the table, trying to mentally prepare himself. When the needle touched his skin, he flinched, when it pierced him, he bit down on the inside of his cheek. He tasted blood and for a moment forgot to breathe.

"Let go of your cheek, boy," Waylan snapped.

Lucas unclenched his jaw and took a gasping breath. Slowly, he counted each time the needle passed through his skin—nine in total.

Felix leaned back. "All better. For now."

"Take him upstairs," Waylan told Carter. "I need to have a talk with your *friend* here."

Carter was silent as he heaved Lucas to his feet. The trip wasn't a gentle one, Lucas banging into the wall with every step. They finally reached the landing and Carter deposited him into Waylan's bed. His eyes closed readily.

‡‡‡

Braxton lay staring at the canopy of his bed tiredly. Across the room, Nico snored to the point he questioned how such a small person could make so much noise. Light morning sunshine peaked through the window and he should at least be thankful for the few hours of sleep he had managed to get.

Rubbing his eyes, he threw back the covers and gave a small shiver as his feet touched the cool stone floor. Crossing the room, he shook Nico awake. As the boy pulled himself into reality, he slipped on a dark silk shirt. "Hungry?"

Nico said nothing.

"I am not going to hurt you." He gave what he hoped was a reassuring smile.

"Yes," Nico nodded. "Starving."

"Come on, breakfast is being served."

Nico slipped on his boots and followed timidly. As they walked through the halls, servants eyed Braxton scornfully and their looks turned to pity as their gazes shifted to Nico.

When they reached a section of hallway devoid of people, Braxton turned to him, "Do not let them dismay you; I have no intention of doing you harm."

"Caius may have other ideas," Nico pointed out.

"Yes, he may. So, let me amend my statement; I will not do you any more harm than I must."

Nico nodded in understanding.

As they neared the dining hall, Braxton felt a knot in his stomach. He prayed Kolt would behave.

Inside, his father sat at the head of the table, hands folded beneath his chin, a wide smile upon his face. Avoiding looking him in the eye, Braxton took a seat.

Food was brought out and placed before him. None was given to Nico. "Bring him a plate," he ordered.

"Yes, s—" the man started.

"A student only eats after his master has finished," Caius commented.

Braxton looked up at his father. "Bring him a plate."

Caius raised an eyebrow.

"He is my student; I shall treat him how I see fit."

Caius said nothing and not long after, a small plate was given to Nico.

The boy looked at him warily.

"Eat," Braxton commanded.

Nico needed no further coaxing and dug in, essentially inhaling the food.

"Bring him more," Braxton ordered.

"You do not want him getting fat," Kolt said.

Braxton had failed to notice his brother's entrance.

"Have you beaten him yet?" The dark bruises on his skin only seemed to enhance his brutal nature.

"No," Braxton told him casually.

"I will do it for you," a malicious grin ran across Kolt's countenance. "I do owe you something of that nature."

Caius spoke up, "His student, his way."

Kolt's grin faltered.

"I take it you remember where the training fields are," Caius went on.

"Yes, sir," Braxton answered.

"I expect to see results, mind you, or I will give him over to Evard."

"Evard is no longer the training master."

"Eamon then," Caius said irritated. As a second plate of food was set before Nico, he added slyly, "Get to it."

Braxton pushed his chair out, the feet scraping unpleasantly against the floor.

Nico quickly grabbed a handful of bacon and shoveled a few spoonsful of porridge into his mouth, then followed him out of the room.

‡‡‡

He landed on his back, the breath knocked out of him. Sweat dripped down the sides of his face and became coated in dust.

"On your feet," Braxton coaxed.

312

Nico gave a belligerent groan, pushing himself upright, "How much longer are we going to do this?"

"Until you get it right. Wait until the last moment before you raise a shield."

Nico muttered, "Or I could just attack first."

"No," Braxton sent an earthen projectile towards him.

He reacted too slow and was thrown into the dirt again.

"Sometimes, you cannot attack first. They say the best defense is a good offense, but sometimes you must take a hit first. Your brother is an earth elemental too, yes?"

He nodded.

"What did he teach you?"

"Attack fast, attack strong, don't give an inch."

Braxton chuckled. "And while you were attacking, what was he doing?"

Nico gave him a sour look and mumbled, "Defending."

"What was that? I could not hear you."

Louder, Nico repeated, "Defending."

"Did you ever get past him?"

"A few times."

"Learn to defend," Braxton said coolly, sending a projectile at him, "then you can attack."

✦✦✦

His body felt hot and sticky. Opening his eyes, Lucas found himself in a small room. Random smithy tools rested on shelves, a candle on the table illuminated the area, and a light-colored rug stained with many years' worth of dirt covered the wooden floor. He shifted slightly and pain raced up his side. He tried to sit up, but barely made it a few inches off the bed before falling back, giving a pained groan. Spots of fuzziness confused his vision as he heard footsteps approaching.

"Up already?" he heard Felix say. "Can't say I was expecting it."

"What—" he began, a displaced anxiety rising in his chest.

As if sensing his angst, Felix told him, "Relax, you've only been asleep. You suffered a trauma; your body needed time to rest and begin healing. Speaking of which, we should change your bandages."

Lucas gave him what must have been a baffled look.

"Do you remember what happened?"

"Yes," he croaked.

Felix took a glass that sat on the bedside table. "Here."

313

Gingerly, Lucas lifted his head and took a small sip. As the cool water raced down his throat, he realized just how thirsty he was. Bit by bit, he drained the glass.

"There's a good lad." Felix pulled a chair next to the bed. "Have you ever had an injury like this before?"

"No. But I've seen them. Caused them."

"It's not the same. To see that kind of damage on one's own body, makes it seem more... potent. I'd advise you not to look."

Lucas gave him a disregarding gaze as he pulled back the blanket.

"Good timin'," Felix muttered.

Going slightly cross-eyed, Lucas looked down at his chest. His torso was wrapped in white linen bandages, a small red spot beginning to peek through.

"Sit up," Felix instructed.

When he struggled to do so, Felix placed a hand in the crook of his shoulder blades and eased him up. He then started unwinding the wrappings.

Lucas winced as he neared the inner layers, blood clawing at the cloth, desperately trying to keep hold. When the last piece was pulled away, he looked down. He was never one to feel queasy at the sight of blood or open wounds, but regardless felt his face draining of color.

"I told you not to look," Felix chastised.

The words hurt his pride, and despite himself, he returned his attention to the wound. He could see clearly where the knife had penetrated; it was a clean, straight-edged cut, about three inches in length. The area around the wound was red and taking on a bluish tinge from inflammation. Black thread spiraled through, binding the rift's edges together.

Felix wetted a rag and gently dabbed the wound. Each time it touched him, Lucas gave an involuntary hiss. Felix placed sponging gauze atop the cut before winding clean bandages around him and pinning the end neatly in place.

Lucas' stomach gave a low growl.

Felix took the loaf of bread that sat on the table and brought it to him.

After a few bites, Lucas asked, "Where's Carter?"

"Downstairs."

"Can I speak with him?"

"I'd advise against it."

Lucas made to protest.

"It's the middle of the night. Let him rest, he'll still be here in the mornin'."

"I slept all day?"

"Sure did, and I expected you to not wake until tomorrow. Full of surprises you are." Felix gave a yawn. "Get some sleep." He didn't give him the chance to respond before blowing out the candle, casting them into darkness.

Lucas wasn't sure how he managed it, but Felix made his way through the room without a sound. The only way he knew he'd descended to the lower floor was the telltale creek of the stairs.

CHAPTER 42

Nico's body screamed as his back slammed into the ground. The day had barely begun and already he was spent.

"Better," Braxton said.

He lifted his head to give him a scowl. "It doesn't feel better. Everything hurts."

"Try creating a thicker shield. It will absorb more of the force."

"I have. It doesn't help."

"Give a bit of feedback," another instructor across the field called.

"Pardon?" Nico questioned.

"Give it some feedback." The man offered a hand to help him up. "Essentially, meet the attack with a counter."

Nico looked at him confused.

The man turned to Braxton, "Go on."

Braxton shot a projectile at him.

The man quickly raised a shield and when the projectile was close to making contact, gave a slight push forward. Instead of being thrown back, he remained standing, the projectile cracking and returning to the ground as stones. "Meet force with force," he said. Turning to Braxton, he added, "I can't believe you haven't explained this to him yet."

"I assumed it was common knowledge, Eamon," Braxton responded.

"Well, you know what I say about assuming.."

"Right you are. You can go back to your own students."

Eamon gave a mocking bow. "I'm always here should you require assistance."

"Who's that?" Nico questioned.

"Eamon Echols, the new training master. Not an awful guy to be honest."

"What did he mean?"

"When a force is applied, if there is no counterforce, you will be affected by it. However, when you meet it with a force of your own, you change the nature of influence, thereby giving you the ability to remain 'unaffected'. Understand?"

"Not really."

"Let me," Eamon said, approaching again. "Meet force with force." He reached over and pushed Nico.

Caught unawares, he stumbled.

Eamon went to push him again.

This time, he was ready and remained unmoved.

Pulling a rock from the ground, Eamon instructed, "React."

Nico quickly formed a shield and at the last moment, remembered to react. When the rock hit, it was sent back, and he stayed on his feet.

"There you go," Eamon said, placing a hand on Nico's shoulder. "Not so difficult."

Nico gave Eamon a small smile as he walked away.

"Well done," Braxton praised, sending another stone towards him without warning.

‡‡‡

Lucas awoke to daylight. Woozily looking around, he saw Carter crouched at the top of the stairs. "What's happening?"

"Shh."

"How many times do I need to repeat myself?" Waylan snapped. "I'm not go to the fucking Lazado."

"Waylan," Felix said, "be reasonable. It's where you and the lads will be safest."

"We're just as safe here. The guards don't know their faces; they're nothing more than a pair in thousands. Yours however, they know, and you will leave. The sooner the better."

"It'll be as soon as Lucas can travel. Like I said, the lads are coming with me. You, I can't make do anything, but I'd encourage you to follow now."

"Who are you to tell me what's going to happen in my own home?"

"A fellow Pexatose."

"Do you think I care?" Waylan snapped. "Pexatose, human, British, I don't listen to—"

"Irish," Felix snarled. "I'm Irish, you goddamn Yankee."

"I ain't no Yankee," Waylan barked, "Take it back, you fucking leprechaun."

They continued to argue, going in circles.

Bracing himself, Lucas pushed himself up, groaning.

Carter looked at him worried. "What are you doing?"

Lucas swung his legs over the edge of the bed, "Down there."

"What? Why?"

"They don't decide what we do."

Getting to his feet was harder than anticipated. He swayed slightly and Carter had to steady him. As he made his way downstairs, he leaned heavily against the railing.

The two men stood across the room, arguing passionately.

317

"Enough," Lucas said just loud enough to get their attention.

"What are you doing out of bed?" Waylan growled.

He ignored the question. "Neither of you gets to tell us what to do. We're grown men."

Both Felix and Waylan laughed.

"You may be grown, but ye're not men," Felix told him. "Nonetheless, ye do have a say. What would ye like to do now?"

"We'll go to the Lazado with you," Carter said.

"No, we won't," Lucas argued.

"Yes, we will. That's what Father said to do. Jared and Nico are probably already there. I conceded to staying when grief clouded me, but no longer. We should've gone with Virgil, and Felix is offering to take us, so we're going."

"Good lad," Felix said with a grin.

"What if I won't go?" Lucas asked.

"I'll make you," Carter said bluntly.

"The only thing left is to convince you to come, too," Felix said, returning his attention to the smith.

"No," Waylan growled. "I told you people I wanted nothing to do with you twenty years ago. My answer hasn't changed."

"We need you. The ability of a Pexatose, it… can win wars."

Waylan crossed his arms. "No."

"What's a Pexatose?" Lucas asked.

"A *very* special elemental," Felix answered. "A Pexatose is someone who shouldn't have powers, someone who shouldn't exist in this world, yet does."

Lucas and Carter gave him searching looks.

"Pexatoses come from another world. They're brought here by Nanagins and are granted great abilities. Waylan's an earth elemental."

Waylan shifted uncomfortably.

"But it's not earth he controls, it's metal."

"Where's your proof?"

"He bears a mark, just like any other elemental. Waylan, will you show them now?"

The smith gave Felix a look of fury, but nonetheless showed them the underside of his wrist. The mark was striking against his black skin, but only its outer border was white; the earthen symbol was a reflective silver.

"What about you?" Lucas asked Felix. "You said you're a Pexatose, too."

"Good ears, lad. I'll have to be mindful of that now." He showed them the underside of his wrist. The mark that scarred his skin was a simple black leaf. "I'm a life elemental, but I can't heal using magic."

"That makes no sense," Carter blurted.

"Let me finish," Felix said calmly. "When presented with an injury, I know exactly how to heal it with medicine, and I'm gifted with the ability to see in the dark."

A sudden overwhelming feeling overcame Lucas. Darkness covered his eyes and he had the sensation of falling. Light returned and he shook his head, surprised to find himself back in bed, his brother sitting beside him.

"Lucas," Carter said relieved.

"What happened?" he asked groggily.

"You weren't ready to be on your feet yet," Waylan said.

‡‡‡

Jared struggled to keep his eyes open and the setting sun was only making him feel drowsier. A few hours of rest had felt like the greatest reprieve and he yearned to return to that state. It was his watch though. Rubbing his eyes, he got to his feet and began to pace.

The sun inched closer to the horizon and as soon as the fiery ball touched the leaves, he roused Kade and Aron. Neither was happy, both giving displeased grumbles. Before leaving, they swallowed a few pieces of stale bread and jerky.

He scooped Keegan up in his arms and was heartened to find her skin cooler to the touch. He wanted to believe the poison was fading but knew better than to hope for that.

Kade clambered onto Arso, preparing to carry Keegan for the next leg.

Jared stared at him for a moment then made his way to Aron.

"What do you think you're doing?" Kade asked.

"Getting Keegan to the Lazado."

"W—"

"Enough!" he said, tired of the unexplained mistrust. While Aron had arrived in an unorthodox manner, it didn't mean he couldn't be trusted. Besides, they had all come together under strange circumstances. "He's given me no cause to doubt him. You have. He's only trying to help, and it's time you let him."

"You have no say here."

"You'll find I do."

319

Jared passed Keegan to Aron and didn't give Kade time to respond as he clambered onto Brewer and spurred him out of the clearing. He could hear the curses behind him, but that was good, it meant Kade was following.

‡‡‡

Nico headed straight to bed and promptly fell asleep, boots still on.

Braxton let him be, lit a candle, and opened the drawer to pull out the proper translation of the prophecy. His eyes glazed over as he stared at the page, having already memorized the words.

He knew he should tell his father, but something was stopping him. For days, he had tried to put his finger on the feeling, but it always slipped away. Maybe it was because the truth condemned Aron. He put the page away and readied himself for bed.

He was hard-pressed to find sleep that night. Since the griffins' release, he had not had one of his strange dreams. Each morning he awoke refreshed, but always went to bed with a feeling of unease. When his eyes did close, he was thankfully sent into serene darkness.

He remained in nothingness for a while then warm light filled the throne room. Forms materialized slowly until they became human. Six people, with heads bowed, knelt before him. He could hear sniffles from a few.

A seventh person took shape and asked the first one, "Woth eya sesuna eyar kunyi?"

"Naya," the man responded, spitting on the shoes of the one standing before him.

Braxton watched as a sword separated the man's head from his body.

The man moved on to the next person and again asked, "Woth eya sesunar eyar kunyi?"

The reply was, "Avu."

That answer was repeated four more times.

When it came to the last man, Braxton felt his heart catch. The grin on his face made the question redundant; it was asked anyway. "Woth eya sesuna eyar kunyi?"

"Naya," the man replied calmly, his demeanor not changing, even when the blade was poised above his neck. "Astæm az woth sesuna ayþ bindiar darvesen."

The people began to fade, the light going with them. Outside the window, Braxton could make out the night sky and watched his father

320

pacing across the room. A shadow moved in the corner and he saw it transform into a man, creeping towards Caius. Light was reflected off the knife he held.

He tried to warn his father, but no sound escaped his lips. He would have rushed forward, but his legs refused to move. Instead, he watched as the man drove the knife into the back of Caius's neck, instantly felling him.

Braxton jerked up, suddenly aware that he could move and make sound.

Nico stood beside him, a look of relief on his face.

"What is going on?" Braxton questioned, frantically throwing back the covers.

"You were screaming," Nico said, backing away. "A bad dream, I think."

"Yes, a bad dream," he said quietly. "Go back to bed."

Nico gave him a concerned look but did as told.

Braxton leaned back, his thoughts careening about his mind. He had just witnessed his father's death; he had to tell him about the prophecy now—it might mean Caius' life.

CHAPTER 43

Nico awoke to find Braxton sitting at his desk, so enraptured in what he was doing that he failed to notice him walk up behind him. The drawing was a rough sketch of a large pine tree.

"It's quite good," Nico said.

Braxton gave a slight start and tried to play it off. "Thank you. Not many people get to see me drawing."

"Is it a secret?"

"No," Braxton said, still focused on his task. "But it is something that does not oft follow me outside this room." He set the pencil down. "Come, time for breakfast."

As they walked, Nico noticed how tense his tutor was. The nightmare must've been traumatic. He also noticed dark circles under Braxton's eyes, signifying he hadn't followed his own counsel to go back to bed.

Kolt was not gracing them with his presence that morning and he was glad. Caius sat at the head of the table, giving them a knowing look that made him wary. Braxton seemed to be avoiding his father's gaze.

Breakfast was eaten quickly, and they headed to the training field. He could feel his muscles growing tense already; the day would be long if it was anything like the past few.

Eamon walked amongst several groups of men sparring. Most were working with magic, though a few fought with various weapons.

Braxton led him to an empty area, and they began.

He managed to remain standing after most of the attacks, but each one battered him, plaguing his muscles. A rock hit him in the back, sending him sprawling.

"Attacks will not always be where you can see them," Braxton reminded him.

"Obviously," Nico snapped. "Some warning would've been nice though."

"An enemy is not going to tell you his next move."

Nico got to his feet, readied himself, and although he didn't expect the strike to come from the front, the stone that hit his left leg produced an abundance of pins and needles.

At midday, Braxton passed him along to Eamon, saying he had other matters to attend to.

Eamon had one of his advanced students watch over the others as he worked with Nico. "What was Braxton working on with you?"

Nico considered lying but knew it wouldn't have a pleasant outcome. "Attacks from all directions."

"You mastered the shield already?" Eamon said with a raised brow.

"Braxton says so."

Eamon shot a rock at him and he quickly brought up a shield.

"Good. Close your eyes."

"How am I supposed to see anything coming?"

"You're not. You'll hear them, feel them. You can't always rely on your sight and you must learn to sense changes in your surroundings, to rely on your instincts"

Nico ground his teeth and closed his eyes. There was an instant before a rock hit his chest where he could hear it whistling through the air. Maybe Eamon was brighter than he thought.

✝✝✝

Braxton gulped as he neared his father's office. His heart raced and he almost turned away again. So far, he had spent the entire afternoon trying to work up the nerve to divulge what he knew—and subsequently explain why he had kept it secret. Each time, he got close to knocking on the door before skirting away.

He took a deep breath and approached the door again, fist raised. Before he could let himself think, he knocked. There was a moment of silence and he found himself praying his father was elsewhere.

"Enter."

He cursed and opened the door.

Caius sat at his desk, looking over a sheaf of papers. "What do you need?"

"The Child of Prophecy…" Braxton started.

Caius glanced up, curiosity and concern written across his face. "What can you tell me about it?"

"It—*she* is the only person more powerful than me. The Vosjnik found her twenty years ago—"

"But Rosh Broyker saved her, and she experienced a Nanagin."

"Correct. And we now know the girl Keegan is this child."

"Are you aware of Angela's last prophecy?"

"Of course."

"What did it say?"

"A careless pageboy dropped ink all over the sheet, making it difficult to read. But the essence of it is that a child will come to defeat me."

323

"So, it read something like this," Braxton stated, handing over one of the pages he had brought with him.

Caius took it and looked at it carefully. "Yes."

He handed another page over. "Here it is in its entirety."

"Where did you get this?"

"I would rather not say. But you can see the inkblots made it easy to mistranslate."

His father read it over and mumbled, "It was never one..."

"No, it is four."

"How did you come to learn this?"

Braxton gave a partial truth, "Alyck."

"Did he perhaps tell you who they are?" Caius pressed angrily.

"Yes." His heart pounded. "You were right about Keegan. The other three are Jared Sieme, Kade Tavin—"

Caius cursed at Kade's name and muttered, "Bastard was hiding under my nose the whole time."

"And..."

"Out with it!"

He gulped, "Aron Alagard."

Caius' face paled and he was silent for a long time.

Braxton was aware of the Death Deal that had been made; Aron was untouchable, as were he and Kolt.

"Train with the griffins," Caius said finally. "Ready them for battle."

"How are you going to get past the border?"

"Just do as I say!"

Braxton gave a bow and started to leave.

"Continue to train with the boy, I want him to trust you. He will be key in turning his brother."

"Why would Nico be what convinces Jared to submit?"

"You would be amazed at what people will do to protect their brothers."

Something in the words made Braxton believe he was speaking from experience.

‡‡‡

Walking upstairs, Lucas saw Waylan sitting on the edge of the bed, holding a small piece of parchment. "What's that?" he asked.

"A photo," Waylan responded.

He sat beside the smith. "What's a photo?"

"Think of it like a painting."

Lucas looked at the photo. The paper was worn and yellowed, but it still looked hyper-realistic, as if someone had stopped time and placed it on a page. There were three people: a man, a woman, and a child.

The man looked like a younger version of Waylan. The woman was a head shorter and held the child in her arms. Her hair was short and puffy. All three had dark skin and each bore the whites of their teeth in a smile.

"That's my wife, Ilene, and I," Waylan said, "and our foster child, Arthur."

"They look nice." He cursed himself for sounding so dumb.

"They were. Ilene used to always tell Arthur a bedtime story, before he died. She worked hard, did her best to help as many people as she could… She was the one who wanted to foster."

"What happened to the child?"

"He got hit by a car."

He was going to ask what a car was but seeing Waylan's melancholy, decided not to press.

Waylan tucked the photo away in a pocket.

Felix was suddenly at the top of the stairs. "Have you changed your mind?"

Waylan gave him an aggravated look. "Unfortunately."

"Excellent. We'll leave tomorrow."

"What changed your mind?" Lucas asked.

"You and my wife," the smithy answered.

"How so?"

"Ilene always said that if you take the time to help someone, you see that they get where they're goin'. I took you and Carter in; I need to make sure you get to where you need to be, which just so happens to be the Lazado."

"Virgil was right about you. You might be headstrong, but you've got a good heart. Thank you, Waylan, for everything."

CHAPTER 44

Lucas pulled the hood of his cloak low over his face. The pack felt heavy and he winced with every step. His wound was only just beginning to heal, it still oozed a white fluid onto the bandages. Felix had declared him fit to travel, but he didn't share the opinion. The sun was barely casting light across the street and was still well below the city walls.

They reached the gates as two guards watched the portcullis rise. A man was waiting outside the gate, a donkey in tow. He was allowed in without a word.

Lucas followed Felix as he approached the gate.

The guards stopped them. "Show your faces."

Lucas gritted his teeth and waited to see what Felix did. Even with the hood pulled low over his long face, he could see the whites of his companion's teeth as he smiled. There was no doubt Felix was a wanted man, but he had taken precautions to avoid being recognized by shaving his beard and trimming his shaggy hair. Now, he looked like any other graying, middle-aged man.

"Whatever for now?" Felix questioned.

"Because I said so," the guard snapped. He reached forward and threw Felix's hood back.

"Satisfied? You've exposed an agin' man to the mornin' mist."

"Remove your hoods," the guard instructed the rest of them.

Out of the corner of his eye, Lucas watched Carter and Waylan slowly lower theirs. He reached up and let the fabric fall onto his shoulders. The guard scrutinized him and lazily waved them through. Carter gave him a nervous glance and they were a good way down the road before anyone spoke.

"Do you intend for us to walk across the country?" Waylan questioned.

"Only a portion of it," Felix responded. "I hope to buy—or steal—some horses in the next town."

"Is that wise? You're already a wanted man—as are we all, I suppose."

"Caius has bigger problems than a renegade, a long-forgotten Pexatose, and two troublesome youths."

"What bigger problems?" Carter asked.

"There've been rumors of an immensely powerful elemental that's been running amok," Felix answered.

"Keegan," Lucas growled.

"Who?"

Scowling, Lucas told him, "An elemental my brother took in. She's the one who brought soldiers to our doorstep."

"Do you know where she is, lad?"

Lucas loathed admitting he was going to have to see Keegan again. "With any luck, the same place we're headed."

‡‡‡

Nico groaned as he opened his eyes; every part of his body ached. He sat up and his muscles complained.

Braxton was at his desk drawing again.

Some steps blinded him with a dull pain as he went to look over Braxton's shoulder, "Do you start every morning like this?"

"No, I have just had a bit of inspiration of late." Braxton moved his arm so Nico could see the picture—a portrait of him with an earthen shield half raised. He turned and gave a low whistle. "Eamon did a number on you. We will not train today."

"Why?"

Braxton raised an eyebrow, "I would have thought you would be glad for a reprieve, but, if you wish to train, we can."

"No," Nico said hastily.

"All right. Go see Ivo Pieper."

"Where can I find him?"

"Lower levels in the bathhouse."

Nico gave his shirt a sniff, "Do I smell?"

Braxton laughed. "No. Ivo should be able to take the sting out of those bruises. Get some breakfast before you go."

"What about Kolt?"

"Kolt has no power over you. Now go, before I change my mind."

Taking his cue, Nico headed towards the dining hall. Servants and pages bustled by, most paying him no heed; those who did notice, pointed and whispered. He hated that. Quickening his steps, he soon reached the dining hall. Caius and Kolt were already inside.

Kolt saw him and broke into a wide grin. "Learning your lessons, boy?"

"Yes," he said, averting his eyes.

A servant put a plate before him, piled high with eggs, a few links sausage, and strips of bacon.

"Yes, *sir*. Though, you may also call me Your Grace."

Coldly, Caius corrected, "You are no king, nor shall you ever be."

Nico couldn't help but smile.

327

Kolt saw it and reached for his mug.

"Put it down," Caius commanded.

Kolt did so reluctantly.

He shoveled in a few mouthfuls of food and taking several strips of bacon, made his exit. It was better to leave now while Caius made Kolt stay.

He struggled to find the bathhouse as it was well below the lowest windowed level. Several soldiers and guards were already soaking in the large pools. There were six, each a different color, with varying pungent smells.

A short, fat man approached him, his face red and covered in a thin film of sweat.

"Ivo Pieper?" Nico tested.

"That be me," the man said. "What can I help you with, sonny?"

"Braxton said you could take the sting from my bruises."

The man's face lit up. "Yes! Ivo Pieper knows how to fix many ailments with healing water."

"Really?"

"Oh, yes. Each bath contains a mixture of healing elements."

"Which one should I use?"

Ivo studied him for a moment. "Blue."

Nico pulled a towel off the rack near the door and headed towards the blue pool. Four men were already lounging in it, talking and laughing loudly. He stripped quickly and slipped into the water.

"This is the soldiers' bathhouse," a man snarled at him. "Servants are to bathe elsewhere."

"I was told to come here," Nico said, suddenly feeling small and vulnerable.

"By whom?"

Nico looked down at the water. "Braxton Alagard."

"Ah, you're the crown prince's bwint." The man leaned back, placing his arms along the wall of the pool. "It's a wonder you have any cock at all."

Nico clenched his fists, knowing this wasn't a fight he'd win.

"Tell me, how is it you became the prince's student? How many times did you have to lie with him?"

Let them say what they will. None of it is true.

The men laughed when he made no attempt to contradict them.

"Do you think if I had my way with the prince the king would make him *my* student?" another asked.

The others laughed malevolently.

"Now that's the best way for the crown prince to take your head," someone behind Nico announced.

He looked up to find Eamon and was suddenly aware his heart was beating furiously. Eamon slipped into the water beside him and his heart began to slow.

"We weren't talking to you," the man snapped.

"Ah, but you were conspiring against one of my charges, Luwis," Eamon said calmly.

"He's the prince's student."

"And when the prince is preoccupied, who do you think trains him?"

"You have no true hold over him."

"Tis true, but I do have hold over you."

Luwis and the others eyed him indignantly.

"I'm not an earth elemental," a third man said. "Your hold doesn't extend that far."

"Are you sure about that?" Eamon asked, the water rippling and sharp spikes pointed at the man's throat.

"Take your fighting elsewhere," Ivo yelled.

"'Pologies, Ivo," Eamon said, lowering the spikes. To the men he said, "I suggest you leave, and there'll be no more talk of harming the boy."

"Yes, sir," the men growled angrily, scowling as they pulled themselves from the water.

"You're not well-loved by many people in this castle," Eamon told Nico, "but you have friends in high places."

"What do they have against me?" Nico questioned.

"Most of these men were trained under Evard and other cruel tutors. None are strangers to brutality and pain. Yet, somehow, you were given to Braxton. He may put on a mean front, but behind closed doors, we all know he's gentle."

"I didn't ask for that."

"No one asks for the fate they must endure. Yet we always envy those whose path is kinder than ours."

‡‡‡

Jared was awoken just before the birth of day.

"A few hours," Kade instructed tiredly before falling into a heavy sleep.

While Jared was still exhausted, it was easier to stave off sleep than before. As the others slept, he tended to Keegan. He got her to drink a considerable amount of water and the red on her cheeks paled a little. Her injuries weren't healing and Kade had explained they wouldn't until the poison was neutralized. The only thing to do was to change the bandages and make sure the open cut on her shoulder hadn't become infected.

When the sun climbed halfway up the trees, he tended to the horses. They were just as appreciative of a night's reprieve. As the sun shone over the trees, he roused Kade and Aron; neither was happy to be up again.

"How far do you think we are?" Jared asked as they breakfasted quickly on jerky strips.

"About a third of the way," Kade answered.

"Is there anything we can do to hinder the poison?" Aron queried.

"If there was," Kade snapped, "don't you think I would've done it already?"

Jared took a deep breath. Even a night's sleep wasn't enough to kill the animosity. *Let them fight. Aron is just Kade's replacement for Keegan.* And it wasn't as if he were on good terms with Kade himself.

"We're wasting time," Kade told Aron.

They gave each other lingering scowls, then approached the horses.

"I'll take Keegan," Aron volunteered.

"No," Kade said, holding her protectively while waiting for Jared to mount.

"Share the load," Jared said, aggravated at Kade's continued misgivings. "He's not going to harm her."

"I trust him no further than I can throw him."

"Then trust me, trust Keegan. She trusts him; he can't be that awful."

"No."

Knowing this wasn't the day Kade gave way willingly, Jared clambered up onto Brewer and accepted Keegan. "You have to trust him at some point," he said in a hushed voice, "Just as Keegan came to trust you." Bitterly he added, "Just as I did."

"*Never.*"

‡‡‡

They had made exceedingly good time and now were just outside Agrielha castle. Thaddeus waited patiently to be pulled from the wagon and brought before the king, knowing today was going to end in at least one death.

As a group, they were herded in, the cool interior a welcome reprieve after being in the stuffy cart for several weeks, but he knew he was the only one who appreciated it. Reaching their destination meant death for anyone who refused to bow down, and servitude for the others. In his heart, he could feel his Calling humming happily; he was where he belonged.

The marching of their feet created a discord that resonated off the walls and they were taken to what Thaddeus assumed was the throne room. Ash sat between the stones and he smiled, knowing the mark of a Nanagin. They were made to line up and told to kneel. Only one man resisted but went down anyway when struck in the back of the knees.

They waited for quite some time—long enough for his knees to start aching. When the doors banged open behind him, he did not jump like the others. Four men came into view and he recognized the king and his kin instantly, Caius' unforgiving demeanor giving him away. The two younger men—one with hair black as a bruise and the other as yellow as dirty sunshine, stood beside Caius. He smiled; the curse was not as strict for the Alagards.

He turned his attention to the fourth man, who stood rigidly, his dark eyes staring at them with contempt, a hand resting on the pommel of his sword. It was he who faced the man who persisted on resisting, "Will you serve the king?"

He spat on the soldier's shoes. "No."

The soldier calmly drew his sword and brought it down across the man's neck. He then repeated the question to the others.

Thankfully, all answered, "Yes," even if tearfully.

Thaddeus smiled as the soldier came to stand before him.

"Will you serve your king?"

He looked up, "No, but I will serve the Blind Prophet."

A hush settled over the room.

"Leave," Caius growled.

The soldier gave the king a perplexed look.

"Leave! And take the others."

Slowly, the king's newest elementals filed from the room, stealing fervent glances at Thaddeus.

"How do you know about the Blind Prophet?" Caius asked tersely once the doors had shut.

"It is my job," Thaddeus answered.

The king gave him a questioning look.

"I am surprised you are unaware of Angela's second bloodline."

The muscles in Caius' jaw tightened. "Leave," he hissed at his sons.

They exchanged a glance before walking past Thaddeus.

"Who are you?" Caius asked in a voice that was meant to be cool.

"Thaddeus Broyker."

"I know that name."

"You should; you had the *honor* of murdering my son."

"I may give you the same honor."

"It will hurt you more than help you."

"How so?"

"I am one of the last Keepers of Prophecy. Do you know their history?"

"No, nor do I care to."

"And that will be your downfall; knowledge is power."

Caius' lips pulled back into an aggravated smile. "Then enlighten me."

"Angela Alga, as you know, was the first Blind Prophet. She had three children. Two were endowed with the magic that would allow either to become the Blind Prophet if necessary and became the Alagards. The third one was born without magic. This child stayed with Angela and as the visions made it harder for her to keep hold of reality, helped her to make sense of the world, thus becoming a translator of her visions. His name became Broyker."

"You might prove useful yet."

"I hope to be," Thaddeus said, bowing his head. Knowing Caius was about to dismiss him, he decided to use his only chance to save Reven. "Though, I should warn you about my family's curse."

Caius gave a disconcerted frown. "What curse?"

"The Broykers are only afforded one child per generation."

"You are the last then... since I killed your son."

"No, I have a grandson."

"Where is he?"

"Somewhere outside your grasp and he will never serve you. I just thought I should warn you to not kill him, unless you want to spend the rest of your life being harried by double meanings and twisted words."

"He will serve me. Everyone does, sooner or later."

"Only if you can find them."

‡‡‡

Thaddeus gave a slight bow as was expected of him and waited for a guard to take him to the Blind Prophet.

The walk was entertaining—at least for him. The accompanying soldiers treated him as if he were something of mystery and strength, rather than a wily old man.

His knees ached from kneeling so long, but it was for the good of many; telling Caius most of what he knew had ensured he got exactly what he needed: access to the Blind Prophet, the library, and Caius' secrets.

He was shocked to discover the Blind Prophet holed away in the depths of the castle like some plague. The door was unadorned, simple, inconspicuous; no one would guess one of the most important people in the world resided behind it.

The guards opened the door, allowed him to walk through, then shut it, the click of the lock audible. The torches along the wall were hardly enough to light the room—something he would fix.

A man emerged from a chamber, the entrance hidden in the gloom, "I was not expecting you today, brother."

"I am most definitely not your brother," Thaddeus informed him, "but we are distantly related."

"To whom do I have the pleasure of speaking with?"

"Thaddeus Broyker. I do find it curious that Prophets need a name to work with—whether they are told or hear it in one of their visions."

"More of a hassle for me. And, Thaddeus, it is a pleasure to meet you. I am sorry about your son, but he was the only one who could have done it."

"I understand," Thaddeus said, a pang in his heart. "And how should I address you? I assume *oh wise one* is too formal."

The Blind Prophet gave a hearty laugh, "I like you already. I am Alyck Alagard."

"A pleasure," Thaddeus answered, going forward to take his hand and shake it.

"Now, Thaddeus—Do you go by Thad? I am going to call you Thad—I have a few questions as to what you know."

"Which will be answered in due time," Thaddeus said. "I would like to rest now; it has been a grueling few weeks and a tiresome past few hours. I will answer all your questions later, just as I know you will answer mine."

‡‡‡

Kade kicked Aron's leg, and once sure he was awake, stalked away and gave himself up to sleep.

Aron rubbed his eyes, wishing he were still dreaming.

Time passed slowly and the only way he knew night had not come to a standstill was the movement of the moon. It sluggishly crept across the dark sky and his eyelids sagged, threatening to send him straight into dreamland. Shaking his head, he got to his feet and began to pace.

After so many days of hard riding, it felt good to stretch his muscles. Someone began coughing, but he paid it no heed. When the sound became raspy and pained, he turned his attention to Keegan. She struggled to catch a breath and her chest rose and fell heavily. Blood colored the spittle coming from her mouth. "Kade! Jared!" he yelled to wake the others.

They awoke groggily, fearing the worst. Kade stumbled to his feet, endeavoring to draw his sword. Jared tried to rise and pull a dagger from his boot, but it only caused him to ram his head into the tree he had been sleeping against.

Realizing there were no attackers, Kade snapped, "Why did you wake us?"

"Keegan," he answered, already kneeling beside her.

The sword in Kade's hand dropped to the ground as he rushed over. "No. We should have more time. No!"

"What does this mean?" Jared questioned, finally joining him, blood running down his face from a deep scrape along his forehead.

"We have less time than we thought," Kade answered darkly. "The poison's beginning to eat at her organs."

"What do we do?"

"Ride," Kade said, picking Keegan up, "and pray to Sola and Lunos we reach the Lazado in time." There was a pause, "Or, we turn around."

CHAPTER 45

His body rocked forward, and his eyes fluttered open as he had the sensation of falling. Jared grabbed onto the saddle, just in time to save himself from tumbling to the ground. Day had come and he realized he must have fallen asleep while riding. Looking around, he saw Aron doing something similar, while Kade held Keegan in his arms, riding stiffly.

"Do you want to switch?" he asked. He might still be angry, but with Keegan in such dire straits, their enmity was forgotten for the moment. After Keegan had begun coughing blood, they'd set out at once, and had yet to stop.

"No," Kade said in a low voice.

"You need to sleep," Jared argued.

"No."

Brewer shook his head and came to a stop. Jared jabbed the horse with his heels, but he only whinnied and pawed at the ground. "We need to stop. The horses are exhausted."

"No."

"It wasn't a question."

Arso's leg buckled enough to cause the horse to stumble.

"You'll kill the bovestun horses if you keep on."

Kade gave him a look of defeat. "Take her."

He dismounted and took Keegan, placing her against a tree. Although she was wrapped in a blanket, she still shivered.

Aron awoke dazed. "What is going on?"

"Stopping for a bit," Jared responded.

Aron nodded and stumbled over to a tree, slid down the trunk, and was fast asleep again.

"I'm not sure we're going to make it," Jared said quietly.

Kade dribbled some water into Keegan's mouth. "We have to."

"And what if we can't? The poison's progressing faster than you thought."

"We can make it."

"We could be nowhere near. Who's to say we've even been going in the right direction?"

"We are."

There was silence between them.

"You said it yourself, you'd do it if it meant saving her."

"I'm certain we can reach them."

Jared sighed. He'd never believed in Sola and Lunos, but if they were real, he prayed they would see them through.

‡‡‡

Caius paced across the throne room.

Braxton watched, noticing inconsistencies—the short stride, the wringing of hands, the fearful look in his eyes. Why did his father look so nervous? Caius never showed emotions—aside from anger or hubris.

A shadow moved across the room and began creeping forward. It formed into a man with hateful blue eyes and wild hair, then he raised a knife and plunged it into Caius' neck.

Light blinded his pupils and Braxton realized he was awake, still sitting at his desk, a half-finished drawing before him. He placed the sketch in a drawer and shook Nico awake. He knew—hoped—there was time before his vision came to pass. Maybe he could find a way to prevent it.

Together, they silently made their way to breakfast. He was aware of the whispers from the servants but ignored them. Kolt was not present, and he was thankful.

"Why was the boy not training yesterday?" Caius queried.

"I gave him leave to rest," Braxton answered. Dark bruises still covered Nico's arms and legs, though he no longer complained of soreness. "And I was looking into the business with the griffins."

Beside him, Nico choked on his food.

"Did you find the culprit?"

"No, sir. Whoever it was covered their tracks well."

"And Aron; any news on his whereabouts?"

"No." Braxton could not say he was genuinely concerned about his youngest brother right then, and considering all that had happened, had completely forgotten about him.

"He will come back sooner or later. The boy will never survive on his own."

Braxton had his doubts, Aron was more resourceful than anyone gave him credit for. He cleared his plate and left with Nico close behind, a strip of bacon in hand.

Once the doors to the dining hall closed, Nico asked excitedly, "You have griffins here?"

"Yes," he answered, for a moment remembering their purple blood splashed across his body.

"I though they only existed in lore."

If only. "No, they are as real as dragons and just as vicious."

Nico's eyes widened.

336

"Would you like to see them?" He regretted the words as soon as he said them; few were supposed to know of them and even fewer of their whereabouts.

"Can we?" Nico asked excitedly.

"Sure. But you cannot breathe a word of this to anyone."

"Deal!"

"Come on then." He looked around, making sure guards did not notice them slipping into the hidden passage. He knew the way well enough, but Nico struggled in the dark. They came out into the anterior room. Ahead of them, the way was murky, and he could hear the griffins stirring.

Pulling a torch from its sconce, he took Nico into the main chamber. Where the wall had once opened into nothingness, a heavy iron grate now barred the way. The five remaining griffins looked at him and gave snorts of anger.

The traitor returns, Niyth seethed.

He approached Myrish cautiously, the griffin's dark bronze feathers refracting the torch's light. *You know I tried to avoid bloodshed.*

The griffin snapped at him and he drew back. Slowly, he edged forward to just outside reach and stood his ground. Slowly, the Myrish relaxed.

We know, Crowlin admitted.

Braxton noticed Myrish held his wing awkwardly. "Your wing is broken, Myrish."

From when your chains grounded me.

"You named them?" Nico questioned, taking a step towards the wounded beast.

"Whoa," Braxton said, thrusting out an arm to stop him. "Griffins are particular about who they trust. Let him get a sense of you." *I will send someone to mend that later.*

Nico held still while the griffin eyed him.

Myrish strained against the iron links to sniff at the boy, then slowly pulled away. *I would sooner you not.*

"Now you can approach," Braxton told Nico, "and I did not name them; they named themselves."

"How?" Nico asked, "They're just beasts"

Myrish clicked his beak and gave a low hiss.

Beasts he calls us, Phynex raged. *Tell him we are no more beasts than the little beast before us.*

"They are no more beast than you or I," Braxton said, rubbing Myrish's head. "They are intelligent, as smart as any human."

"How could they tell you their names?"

"Telepathy. Myrish might talk to you if he is in a good mood."

"What are the others' names?" Nico asked.

"This is Myrish." He pointed out the others, "Crowlin, Niyth, Phynex, and Oxren."

Who is this boy? Myrish asked.

My student.

Myrish gave what Braxton had learned was their laugh. *You took a student? I can only wonder what possessed you.*

It was to save him.

I can see that. You have always had a good heart for a human. But I fear you will turn it to stone in the future.

You keep telling me that.

Nico's voice pulled Braxton away. "What do you use them for?"

"Nothing at the moment," Braxton said, then almost mentioned his father's plan to use them in battle.

Nico went back to marveling at the beasts.

This one is innocent, Niyth commented. *Such a shame.*

Braxton felt a twang of guilt. After a while, he said, "Time to go. You have to do some training today."

"Can we come see them again?" Nico asked as they headed towards the anterior room.

"Maybe." Braxton turned to look back at Myrish and a thought crossed his mind. *Do you know who released you?*

No, Myrish answered. *But he smelled like you—of anger, of sadness, of Seleena, of Alyck.*

‡‡‡

"We'll stop here for the night," Felix said.

No sooner had the words been spoken than Lucas dumped his pack on the ground. His shoulders sang as the weight was removed and his side gave a faint scream. He lowered himself onto the ground and took a long gulp from his water-skin.

The others began setting up camp while Felix attended to him, helping him remove his shirt. "Let's see." Once the bandages were off, he inspected the wound. "It's doing well, but it's going to scar."

"Better to be scarred and living than unscarred and dead," Waylan said, sending a spark jumping into a pile of tinder.

"Right you are, my obstinate friend," Felix noted.

338

Lucas looked down at the discarded bandages and noticed a clear fluid on them. "What's that?"

"White blood cells," Felix answered. "It means your body's doing its job."

"But blood's red," Carter argued.

"There's much about many things you don't know, lad," Felix said, "Don't presume what you know is the only truth."

"What do these white blood cells do?" Lucas asked.

"They protect against infections and viruses," Waylan answered nonchalantly.

Felix seemed surprised by the answer.

"I took high school biology."

"I often forget other Pexatoses know as much as me most of the time," Felix said with a grin.

Carter shot Lucas a look that said he had no idea what he meant; Lucas didn't either.

Felix wrapped fresh bandages on then set to making dinner. Tonight, it was a vegetable stew. Soon afterwards, they settled in for the night.

CHAPTER 46

Braxton walked the halls alone, having sent Nico to practice with Eamon. As they left the training field for a midday meal, he had realized something that could potentially help Nico—but really, it was more a precaution for himself. Nico was bound to learn about some sensitive topics, and he could not afford for others to hear of them.

He intended to have his father put a spell on the boy so he could not mention anything he should not, but telepaths could still get into his mind. Thus, Nico had to learn to shield his thoughts, and for that, he needed a tutor.

Telepaths were often found training deep inside the castle, as far from outside distractions as they could get. He found them one level above Alyck. Groups of men and women sat on chairs, eyes closed, stern looks on their faces.

"Doing your usual check?" a voice called out.

Ah, Rooth Oray, the telepath training master. "No," he said, searching for her.

She appeared from his left. "Then what is it you need?" Rooth was an older woman, her once golden hair turned silver. Her skin was wizened, but still held its former beauty.

"I need a tutor."

Her eyebrows rose. "For yourself?"

"No, for my student."

She began to walk away. "Train him yourself."

"I would if I could," he called after her.

A few of the telepaths flinched at the sound of his voice.

"You know I am no telepath. I came to ask nicely, please, don't make me demand it."

"What is your intention for the boy?" Rooth asked, turning back to scrutinize him.

He opened his mind to her.

Her face softened. "Fine. Azure."

A young man with the brightest blue eyes Braxton had ever seen came forward.

"I see why they call you Azure."

Thank you, the man said, bowing his head.

"I would appreciate it if you used verbal words," Braxton said.

Would if I could, but your father took my tongue while breaking me.

"A most unfortunate event I apologize for."

Wasn't your doing.

340

"Follow me," Braxton said leaving.

‡‡‡

"What do I do with him?" Nico asked, studying the blue-eyed man before him. He was tall and gangly with skin like the night. His dark hair was fashioned into thick cords that draped over his shoulders.

You learn.

Nico jumped and spun around trying to find the voice. "Who said that?"

Braxton snickered. "Azure. He is a telepath."

He was intrigued now. "Can he talk?"

Azure gave a strangled laugh. *You already heard me speak.*

"Actual words?"

"Um, no," Braxton told him. "Even so, learn from him." He gave it a moment before leaving.

The silence was straining.

"So w—" Nico started.

Quiet, Azure commanded. *Learn to speak with your mind rather than your mouth.*

"How am—"

Think. Let your thoughts drift outward from your conscious. It's easier than you imagine.

"How—"

Silence, please. Speak only with your thoughts. Open your mouth again and I have a right mind to take your tongue.

Nico quickly closed his mouth and set his jaw.

Calm, little one, it was only a jest.

He made to speak, but again Azure sensed he was going to.

Just think. I promise I'll hear you.

What am I supposed to do? Nico thought, fidgeting. He felt silly and hoped Azure didn't know that.

Azure's lips took a slight upturn. *It may seem ridiculous, but it's what you must do to be heard.*

‡‡‡

The trees were sparse now, barely more than twigs. Night had long since fallen and Jared was insisting, they stop. The horses breathed heavily and all of them were sleep deprived. If he could, he had no doubt he'd sleep for several days.

341

Jared shook his head to clear his mind and noticed Kade slumped forward on his horse, no doubt asleep. He spurred Brewer forward and grabbed Arso's reins.

Kade awoke with a jerk and snarled, "What are you doing?"

"You fell asleep," Jared explained. "We *need* to stop."

"We can't."

"We have to. None of us will do Keegan any good dead."

"You can stay," Kade said, taking the reins back, "but I'm continuing."

"Do not make me hurt you," Aron said.

Jared turned to see Aron had drawn his bow. "What do you think you're doing?"

"What I have to. Kade, we must stop. It will only be for a few hours."

Kade bore a look of fury as he spat, "Shoot me. It won't change anything."

An arrow whizzed past Jared. At first, he thought it hadn't struck, but when he looked at Kade, he saw a thin line of red across his cheek.

"That was a warning," Aron stated.

The muscles in Kade's jaw tightened and swung his leg over Arso. He slid to the ground, stumbling, and almost dropped Keegan.

"You could've hurt her," Jared seethed, also dismounting.

"Could have, but didn't," Kade answered irritably.

He reached out. "Let me take her."

"She's not yours to protect."

"Yes, she is. She's all of ours to protect."

"No, she isn't," Kade roared. "She's not your sister; she's not yours to protect!" He breathed heavily as he defensively held Keegan close.

"Did you just say *sister*?" Aron asked.

Kade took a breath. "Yes."

"How—" Jared started.

Kade headed him off, "It's a long story."

"Then you had better take a seat and tell us," Aron said.

"We don't have time for this."

"We're making time," Jared said, nodding at Aron as a signal that he should notch another arrow.

Kade glowered at him but did as instructed. "I didn't know any of this until a few weeks ago. Someone was sent to save her when she was born. Well... really, it could've been either of us, but he chose her. She was taken away and somehow ended up in her world. Twenty years later, she managed to come back."

The brief explanation left Jared angry and with only more questions.

Kade was slow to answer their queries at first, but the more he spoke, the easier they came.

When done, Jared was speechless. Now that he looked at them, he could see it. "We should get some sleep. There's still a good distance between us and safety." Besides, if Kade did any more talking, he was liable to have a go at him then and there. Some secrets were yours to keep; this wasn't one of them.

CHAPTER 47

Soft light spilled over the horizon when Kade stirred. Jared and Aron had already packed up camp.

"We thought we'd let you rest as long as possible," Jared told him when he asked why they hadn't woken him earlier.

Kade knew the real reason and brushing it aside, led the way with Keegan nestled in his arms. Jared tried to fight him, but his frustration burst forth telepathically and Jared let the matter go.

The trees around them grew sparser with every passing mile and by midday, disappeared entirely, opening into a desolate zone. He'd never seen the Borderlands before, and it was as bleak as the descriptions. The ground was gray, like a sick skin over the terrain. No living thing prospered here and the blight on the earth stretched for as far as he could see. He could feel pain and suffering radiating from the land.

"What happened here?" Jared asked quietly.

"War," Kade answered. "When Caius crowned himself king, the other races banded together to fight him. When they couldn't defeat him, they used spells to create a border that would stand for as long as he remains in this world. No one wishing harm to those on the other side may cross."

"Things should have regrown," Aron stated, jumping down from his horse. He took a handful of dirt and let the fine particles fall through his fingers.

"The land's cursed with the blood of the dead," Kade said.

"I do not like this."

Kade urged Arso forward, "No one does."

Arso gave a snort and pawed at the ground.

He dug his heels into the horse's side and reluctantly he started forward. The other animals were just as wary.

The sun was hot with nothing to shade them and sweat beaded on their foreheads to roll down their faces. It wasn't long before the sad excuses for trees were lost in the gray waste.

"How far across the Borderlands?" Jared asked stiffly.

Ahead, he could already espy the opaque blue wall denoting the border. It went up as high as he could see, well into the clouds and beyond. "Twenty miles," Kade answered grimly. "That is, *if* we can get across."

Soon, they were at its face.

"Why are we here?" he asked.

"To save Keegan," Aron answered.

"Keep that answer in mind."

Arso shook his head nervously, but tentatively stepped beyond the border when pressed.

As they passed through, a light feeling of electricity ran over Kade's body. "Almost there," he told Keegan. "Be strong."

‡‡‡

'He smelled like you—of anger, of sadness, of Seleena, of Alyck'. The words had been playing around his head for days, almost to the point of obsession. Braxton had been trying to decipher any hidden meanings but could think of nothing. Finally, he decided a visit to Alyck was due and Nico was left in Azure's capable hands for the afternoon.

The hallway near Alyck's door was desolate and he became wary when there was no telltale click of the lock being undone. Had Alyck finally taken leave of his duty? He pushed the door open and was disheartened to find the chair void. As he closed the door, a man emerged from one of the other chambers.

"Ah, you must be Braxton."

He stared and was about to ask what he was doing there when he recalled this was the man who had agreed to serve the Blind Prophet. "I never caught your name."

The man gave a polite smile. "Thaddeus Broyker."

Alyck emerged from another room. "Hello, Braxton, come to ask some questions?"

"Yes…" Braxton said, warily eyeing Thaddeus.

"No need to worry about Thad," Alyck said, "he will no more spill information than I."

Still uncertain, but knowing Alyck would be persistent, Braxton began, "I wanted to talk to you about something the griffins said. They said whoever released them smelled like me—of anger, of sadness, of Seleena, of you."

Alyck seemed taken aback by the last item. "Curious. Well, let us think, I am sure with a little thought you can solve this riddle. Firstly, what purpose would releasing the griffins serve?"

"To render them useless, cause us pain," Braxton said, growing frustrated that Alyck never made things simple. "To distract us…"

"See, all you had to do was put a little thought into it."

"How did he even know where the griffins were?" Braxton said, trying to convince himself the perpetrator was not whom he thought it was. "How could he have smelled like me?"

345

"Aron often made visits to me, much like you do."

Thaddeus began to pay attention at the mention of Aron.

"How?"

Alyck gave him a concerned looked, "I assumed that was fairly evident, with a key."

Braxton's head reeled with all the questions that arose. "I have to tell Father. You know that, right?"

"Of course," Alyck said, tilting his head forward in a nod, "but no one can touch him now."

Braxton turned to go, his head hurting. "I know Aron is a Child of Prophecy."

"As do I."

"You promised he would live a long life."

"And he will."

‡‡‡

Thaddeus was quiet as Alyck spoke to Braxton, knowing it was not his place as Keeper of Prophecy to interfere; his job was to record prophecies and help Alyck decipher them when necessary, which he never seemed to need. So many years without a Keeper had forced him to solve the riddles himself—and quickly. Now, he was curious and troubled at the mention of someone named Aron. From the way Braxton spoke of him, he deduced a familial connection.

After Braxton left, he approached Alyck, "Who is Aron?"

"The third Alagard boy."

His eyes filled with worry. "This is not good."

"Why?"

"The same curse that affects my bloodline affects yours, albeit in a slightly different manner."

Concern flooded Alyck's features. "Do you mean to tell me Caius and I can only have one child?"

"No, I said the curse similarly affects you. Whereas my family may only have one child per generation, the Alagards may have three. But only two will survive past their thirtieth year."

The blood drained from Alyck's face.

"Though, I am sure you can discern who will live with your abilities."

"No," Alyck said quietly. "I have never been able to see the path Braxton will take, only how he will affect the world around him. As for Aron, I can only see that he will survive the coming war—everything

346

after is darkness. I have never cared to foresee Kolt's future but now that I try, all I see is blood and death, though, I am not sure if it is his or others'."

"Time will reveal all," Thaddeus said, trying to reassure Alyck.

"By that time, it may be too late to save them."

"It is only too late if you say it is."

Alyck's eyes closed and his body stilled, "It is time for the leaves to fall."

‡‡‡

The Yarav forest had been visible on the horizon for hours now, slowly growing closer. As night settled, they reached the tree line.

We made it, Aron thought to himself, relief washing over him as they stepped into the forest. It was a moment before he realized it was deathly quiet.

"Something's not right," Jared muttered.

If Kade intended to respond, he was not given the chance; light exploded into existence.

Osais reared in fright and Aron fought to remain in the saddle. Once the palfrey landed, hands took hold of him and pulled him to the ground. He dropped onto the forest floor heavily, his wrist getting caught beneath his body and bending painfully.

He fumbled to draw a weapon and got tangled in his cloak. Hands grabbed his arms and he found Jared was similarly restrained.

Kade managed to stay on his horse, though an archer aimed an arrow at his chest.

Aron pulled against the men holding him until a dagger was placed under his chin.

"Who are you?" the archer asked.

"Kade... Digore, son of Kagen, ward of Thaddeus Broyker, subject of none," he answered calmly.

"Where do you come from?"

"A land of subjugation and hate."

"Why should we admit you?"

"War cannot be fought only in the minds of men. It must be fought on the field, with payment of blood, in the hopes that Sola and Lunos will see us through."

"And your companions, who are they?"

"Jared Sieme, son of the dead; Aron no name, son of a bastard; and Keegan Tavin, daughter of Korissa."

347

The archer lowered his bow and the men holding Aron and Jared withdrew. "I presume you seek refuge."

"Yes, and help. My friend's been poisoned with a dagger dipped in Ramilla."

The men around them gave a collective groan.

The archer went forward to take Keegan and placed a hand on her forehead, "How long ago?"

"About a week," Kade answered, dismounting.

"The poison's far advanced for having been introduced only a week ago. We may not be able to save her."

Kade paled.

"Edreba's another four days from here."

Aron's heart skipped a beat. All had been for naught.

"Jaako," the archer called.

A man materialized from the shadows.

"Take our fastest horse and get her to the city."

"Please, hurry," Kade said. "I can't lose her."

✝✝✝

They reached the town at nightfall. A torrential downpour had started a few hours past and had yet to let up. Lucas was soaked to the skin and quite unhappy, the deluge only serving to increase the aggravation of his wound.

Their feet sunk into the muck as they walked down the main street and they noticed a few brave souls dashing through the rain. Felix followed them slowly, being careful to not slip in the sludge.

Farther up, a door opened, spilling warm light into the night, the sound of chatter and laughter like a whisper through the deluge. As they neared, Lucas made out the sign above the doorway: a faded tankard.

Felix ushered them into the tavern crowded with tables and a large fire roaring in the hearth, making him long to sit beside it. "Room for four," he said to the barman.

"Gold coin," the man grunted.

Felix slid it to him and was given a key in exchange.

"First room on the third floor."

"Thanks."

The room was small and there was only one bed. Lucas dumped his pack on the floor and clutched at his side. Waylan helped him change the bandages and afterwards they slipped back downstairs.

348

They chose a table near the fire to let the heat warm and dry them. A wench soon brought them food and drink. Carter practically inhaled both, giving a burp when his plate was cleared.

In a low voice, Waylan said, "Those men in the corner have been eyeing us since we sat down."

Lucas glanced at them. Both were young, no older than twenty-five, but their faces were hard and weathered. They noticed him and gave a hard glare in return.

"They've been watching us since we got here," Felix said unconcernedly.

"I don't like the looks of them," Waylan said quietly.

Felix shrugged. "I'm sure they'd say the same about you."

The men shared a look before downing their ale, rising from their seats, and heading towards their table.

Waylan reached for the dagger at his waist.

"I don't think that'll be necessary," Felix told him.

One man stood at the head of the table while the other leaned between Felix and Carter, pressing a dirk into Carter's side. Lucas took hold of his tankard, preparing to leap across the table at the man who dared threaten his brother.

"I wouldn't do that, boy," the one at the head of the table sneered, grabbing the tankard from him and downing it. "Or Oslin sees how deep he can stick that blade."

Lucas clenched his fist and slowly rose to his feet.

Carter flinched as Oslin dug the steel into his side.

"Sit down."

"I suggest you do so, lad," Felix said, easily taking a sip of ale. "Can I help you, gents?"

"You're supposed to be rotting in a cell," the man said.

"With Nox and Indol. Yes, Caeyl, I should be."

"Where are they?"

"Decomposing—unless they were burned."

"Make no jests, Felix," Oslin snarled, "They were good men."

"That they were," Felix said with an air of sorrow. "But so are these men that you've seen fit to threaten, now."

"I see two boys and a nobody," Caeyl said.

"I see something quite different."

"And what's that?"

"Two stubborn young men who want revenge as much as you and a very well-trained blacksmith."

"Recruits?" Oslin questioned.

349

"If they so choose."

"Let's find out?" Oslin asked, digging the dirk further into Carter's side.

"Come now," Felix said, "you know decisions made under duress aren't one at all. And we fight for the same cause. Oslin, put your weapon away and share a drink."

"Not a very convincing argument," Oslin said, withdrawing, "but I do love a good pint."

Caeyl smiled and grabbing a chair from another table, sat down. "Tell us, old man, how did you escape?"

"These two here," Felix said, motioning to Lucas and Carter.

Caeyl and Oslin talked to Felix, asking him about his time in Tratoleck and in exchange filled him in on all that had happened since his incarceration.

Once it became clear Oslin and Caeyl were done with them, Lucas and Carter took their leave; Carter sported a spot of red where the dirk had pierced his skin. Lucas clenched his fists to keep himself from flying at Oslin and seeing how he liked a knife in the ribs.

‡‡‡

Alyck gave a pained sigh as he opened his eyes. "He is going to die."

"I cannot see how that is a bad thing," Thaddeus said. "The world has been baying for Caius' death for centuries."

"That is not the problem. Keegan is not the one to kill him."

"That contradicts all of your previous visions."

"I know. Nothing has changed surrounding the girl, but there is another player in my brother's demise now."

"As long as his death comes to pass, why does it matter who does the deed?"

"If it is by any hand other than Keegan's, I see my brother rising from the grave."

Thaddeus' heart caught. The dead rising was an impossible and frightening idea. "Can you see more about this figure who will kill Caius?"

"No," Alyck answered, rubbing his eyes. "He is too shrouded in shadow and hate for me to turn my attentions to him."

The door opened and Caius entered.

Call his name and he shall come.

"Are you going to tell me?" the king asked.

Alyck gave Caius a conniving smirk. "Yes."

350

Caius smiled arrogantly. "Where should I go to experience a Nanagin?"

Alyck thought for a moment, "To the place where it all began. To the place where you cast our stones. To the place you fear the most. To the place where we said goodbye."

The color drained from Caius' face. "You do not... you cannot... no. I cannot go there. Find another place!"

Alyck shrugged. "To get what you so desperately want, you must face your demons."

Thaddeus could see Caius was attempting—and failing—to hide his fear. "I cannot do that. You *know* why I cannot do that."

"Yet, you must. Face that which you cannot; it is the only way to get what you desire."

The king remained rooted in place for a heartbeat, before he all but fled.

"Where did you tell him to go?" Thaddeus asked.

"Home. He has to go home."

CHAPTER 48

"We will stop here for the night," Hickor said, swinging down from his horse.

Normally, Jared would've been glad for a reprieve, but not knowing Keegan's fate made him restless; he knew Kade and Aron felt the same. He was grateful to be in Lazado territory but felt naked without his weapons.

Once welcomed—if being attacked could be called that—they were fed and healed. With everything that'd transpired and worrying about Keegan, he'd almost forgotten that they too were injured. They'd spent a night at the forest's edge and in the morning, Hickor Gorell, an Alvor, and Halcyon Brygh, a Lazado soldier, started leading them to Edreba. This was now the end of their second day of travel.

Halcyon was thin, giving him a sly look that made Jared distrust him; his eyes were a hard black and there was a crook in his nose. Hickor seemed nice enough, but his form made Jared wary. He was tall, reaching just over six and a half feet, and more graceful than anyone his size should be. His hair was a medium brown but at times, he imagined seeing streaks of forest green. From the top of his head came two spiraling, black ram's horns and whenever he spoke, silver flashed in his mouth.

Halcyon easily started a fire while Hickor disappeared into the forest. The Alvor wasn't gone long, returning with several rabbits. Jared could only see a sword and dagger and wondered how he'd caught them. He abstained from asking, having a feeling he wouldn't like the answer.

"Have faith," Hickor said as bugs played dangerous games in the smoke, "your friend will live."

Jared eyed him suspiciously.

"You are a telepath," Aron said with an accusatory undertone.

"No," Hickor said docilely, "I am an Alvor."

Even Kade gave him a questioning look that barely masked his scorn.

"You'll have to explain further," Halcyon said, breaking the tension. "It seems these three aren't learned, just like most who show up on our doorstep."

"*My* doorstep," Hickor reprimanded. "This is only a temporary home for you humans." He turned his attention back to them. "Alvors are acutely aware of emotions."

Jared felt his muscles tense; telepaths or not, it'd be hard to hide much from them.

"Remember that if you try to betray my people," Hickor said in a light snarl.

Sensing the mounting tension, Halcyon intervened. "Hickor, easy, they're not Rowl."

"No, but they hold the same potential." Hickor got to his feet, went to the nearest tree, and scaled it easily.

"Who's Rowl?" Jared asked.

"An elemental we took in," Halcyon explained. "Hickor got close to the man and Rowl betrayed him."

"What did he do?" Aron pressed.

"Stole Hickor's child and gave her to Caius."

"What was the child's name?" Kade asked.

Jared was surprised that he cared at all.

"Vitia," Halcyon answered.

‡‡‡

"How are you feeling, Jakobe?" Lyerlly asked the boy lying in the bed.

"Better," he answered, pressing at his side. "I can hardly feel the tumor."

Lyerlly gave him a smile. "Get some rest and we should have it gone by tomorrow." She closed the curtains around his bed and headed towards the office.

The door to the hospital slammed open and she cringed at the sound of breaking glass. That was the third window this month.

"She needs help," a voice called.

"Put her on the bed," one of the nurses said.

Making her way over, Lyerlly was surprised to see Jaako; last she had heard, he was at the forest's edge until week's end.

"It's Ramilla," Jaako said.

"Get the antidote," Lyerlly commanded, taking over.

Elia rushed to the storeroom and the nurses who were not with patients hurried to help.

"Jaako," Lyerlly said, "go get my husband."

Lyerlly focused her attention on the girl. Her clothes were in ruins, torn and coated in dirt and blood. Her face was sallow and covered in a sheen of sweat. She was struggling to breathe and coughing blood.

"Henley, Ty, keep her heart and lungs going," she said, then yelled. "Elia, hurry with that antidote!"

The girl seized and gave a cough that splattered her cheeks in a mist of red.

353

"There's a block," Ty said, pulling away.

Lyerlly cursed to herself, placing a hand on the girl's stomach and lending her own power. Ty was right, something pushed back against her magic, making it difficult to assist. This was no simple case of Ramilla poisoning; it was in an altered state, creating resistance to healing. She pushed through the block and the beating of the girl's heart filled her ears. It was slow, giving a painful flutter every few seconds.

Elia returned breathless; a bottle filled with a pale pink liquid in her hands.

Lyerlly took it from her and pulled open the stopper, the sickly-sweet scent quickly filling the room. Carefully, she dripped the liquid into the girl's mouth.

Immediately, the coughing subsided, and her body eased.

Lyerlly stepped back, "Rebuild her organs. Once she can survive without your help, take a break."

"Yes, ma'am," Henley said.

Someone placed a hand on the small of her back and Lyerlly jumped. Turning, she gave a sigh; it was Bernot.

"Will she live?"

"Yes," Lyerlly sighed, "but only if she wants to. A few more hours and the poison would have taken her. But even at this point, she can still go to the void."

Bernot gave a small nod and studied the girl. Lyerlly saw his eyebrows knit together in concentration. He only got that look when he was planning something.

"Does Jaako know her name?"

"Keegan Tavin," Bernot said, "But I suspect it is an alias."

"Why would she do that?"

"Her companions gave it to her. Kade Digore, Jared Sieme, and Aron no name."

"Are those names supposed to mean something?"

"No. But Tavin… that is a name I have known for quite some time. One of the Vosjnik was named Tavin."

"Are you trying to tell me she is one of the Vosjnik?"

"No. More like someone gave her their name to shift suspicion from himself." Bernot reached forward and gently turned Keegan's wrist over to reveal five white marks. "Please keep me updated. And if Mahogen comes in here, give him something to do. The longer we can keep his father from finding out about her, the better." He smiled as he took his leave.

With him gone, Lyerlly examined the girl's wrist. Power exuded from the marks, signifying they were not imitations. She stared, uncomprehending.

Who are you and your companions?

‡‡‡

Fire surrounded her, roaring, eating at everything around her. The wood of the building crackled and groaned in pain and a hiccupped cry came from within the flames. Keegan looked around and saw a baby in the center of the blaze.

She desperately wanted to grab the infant and flee, but her body refused to listen. Helplessly, she watched as the flames began to singe the swaddling blanket, smoke curling around the child, but the fire never seeming to touch its skin.

She began to feel hot and saw the flames beginning to climb her legs. She told her feet to move, but they were rooted in place, no matter how hard she strained. Yellow and orange distorted her vision and was soon joined by gray. She knew this shouldn't've been happening but could barely see through tears of pain.

Come to me, a voice from the fire said.

"Who's there?" she called.

Come to me. Come to me.

She recognized the voice; it belonged to Caius.

"No!"

Come to me. Come to me. Come to me.

The baby began to scream, and a hole formed under it. A wind picked up and the flames started dancing and spinning about every corner, sucking the breath from her lungs, making her gag and gasp. Suddenly, the wind exploded outward, quenching the flames.

Come to me. Come to me.

She was thrown backwards, her head striking the wall and her body dropping heavily. Darkness quickly followed.

The voice began to laugh. *You will come back to me, child, and when you do, I will kill you. Come to me.*

CHAPTER 49

Caius walked to one side of the throne room then turned and headed back. He repeated this process, wringing his hands all the while.

The shadow shifted across the room, creeping along, and taking the form of a man with wild hair and sharp blue eyes. Nearing his father, the man jabbed a knife into Caius' neck. Caius gave a muted scream and crumpled to the floor.

It felt like he stood there forever, watching the killer hover over the body, blade still in hand. Braxton blinked and the world around him filled with a soft light. He sat up and realized he was in his chambers, Nico still snoring loudly across the room.

He dressed and prepared to wake Nico, then changed his mind. He wrote the boy a note, instructing him to eat and then report to Eamon.

When he entered Alyck's chambers, he found his uncle waiting expectantly.

"Do you know what I am going to ask, or are you simply hoping I will accidentally tell you?" Braxton said, remembering Alyck could see nothing of his future.

"Unfortunately, the latter," Alyck said, his customary grin faltering. "What is it you need to know?"

"Why am I having these dreams? Why can I see the future?" He spied Thaddeus hiding in the shadows, a knowing crease in the old man's eyebrows.

"I wish I knew," Alyck told him.

Frustration rose in his throat and there was a cracking sound that made them all jump.

Alyck slowly rose from the chair.

Braxton turned to see what his uncle was staring at. The stones above the doorway were cracked, a few pieces crumbling onto the floor. His heart began to race; it had been years since he had lost control of his magic and it had *never* been over something so trivial. Embarrassment began to rise in his chest while a blanket of worry settled over his shoulders.

Dust began to shake from the new cracks in the stones; he was losing control again. He rushed from the room, before he brought the ceiling down on them. Control over his magic was something he had learned and *mastered* as a child. Why was it happening?

He pushed the thought from his mind, refusing to believe he was regressing and made his way to the training field to work with Nico—to prove to himself he was still in control, that everything was as it should be.

‡‡‡

Thaddeus slipped into the main chamber to hear Alyck's exchange with Braxton. The questions he asked caused him to crease his brows.

How could Alyck, the man who put on a show of knowing everything—and oftentimes did—be unaware. He could see Braxton was becoming frustrated and watched as the stones above the doorway split, sending webbing cracks across their surface. After a moment, more dust spilling into the room, and Braxton fled.

Alyck turned to him, concern plastered on his face, "You seem to know the things I do not."

"Well..." he answered. "There are a few things I need to investigate first."

"Do it quickly."

Thaddeus bowed his head; the motion earning him a scowl from Alyck. "When did you start having visions of the future?"

"The day my brother cursed me to do so," Alyck said, anger dripping from his words.

"You were not meant to become the Blind Prophet?"

"No."

"Caius... he was supposed to become the Blind Prophet then?"

"Not as far as I know. He became overzealous and power-hungry after returning to this world and when he overthrew Seleena, he forgot someone needed to fill Angela's role. With him as king, I was the only choice."

Thaddeus nodded as he formulated his thoughts. Alyck was never meant to be the Blind Prophet, but neither was Caius—which went against all logic. "I have much more investigating than I thought," he muttered.

‡‡‡

Tiredly, Lyerlly stepped away. Night had long since fallen and she had dismissed the nurses hours ago, but she was not ready to give up. Thankfully, the Ramilla had been neutralized a day ago and there was marked improvement on the girl's condition—granted, they had fought tooth and nail. Keegan could survive without assistance now, but should she wake anytime soon, she would be hard pressed to even stand on her own.

While her friends had attended to her hurts in the field, none had healed because of the Ramilla. Lyerlly had left the little cuts and bruises to mend on their own and started with the major injuries. Hours passed and she had only just finished setting her broken leg. As it sat, any applied pressure would shatter the tibia. Gently, she pulled the covers over Keegan.

"How is she?" a voice said from the shadows.

Lyerlly jumped, heart suddenly pounding against her chest.

An Alvor emerged.

"Better," Lyerlly answered. "You know as well as I that you should not be here."

"I was curious to see the girl," he said. "My father has yet to learn of her, but it should not be long before he does."

"Even so, Prince—"

"Please, you have known me for far too many years."

"Even so, Mahogen, we are trying to keep her existence to a select few."

"Little good *that* has done. Half the city knows she is here, though most can only guess at who she really is."

Lyerlly sighed. "The trees really do whisper."

"Not as much as the people in their branches."

"I hoped this would not get out," Lyerlly said, crossing her arms. "No doubt Caius has a bounty on her head—one that might even tempt our best men."

Mahogen reached forward and turned Keegan's wrist over. "Then put a guard on her.".

"Would you care to volunteer?"

"I would," Mahogen said, taking the chair beside the bed. "There is great power in this one and I am curious to see how she will use it."

"Let us know when you tire."

He gave her a devilish smile, "By that time, you may no longer be running the hospital."

Lyerlly made her way to the office.

Elia was looking through a stack of papers. "Headed home?"

"Yes," Lyerlly responded, removing the white doctor's apron. "Try to rebuild some of her muscle mass every few hours. Use Mahogen if you grow weary."

"Would it not be better to finish mending the injuries first?"

"She will not be leaving that bed anytime soon, but she needs muscle if she is to make a well-timed recovery."

The night was pleasant and high up in the trees she could make out some of the lights of the city. The ladder was not far from the hospital, but in the dark, it could be challenging to find. When she had first started at the hospital, it had sometimes taken her an hour to locate it; now, she found it within seconds.

The way up was monotonous but calming and the higher she rose, the more she settled. She had been born in these trees and trusted them more than solid ground. In the treetops, bridges connected the canopy and houses nestled into the branches, a few even finding places inside the massive trunks. Only a few people strode along the walkways at this hour and she walked quickly, wanting to get home.

Their house was much larger than its neighbors' and peaked over the canopy. During the day, it offered a spectacular view of the rolling forest. Inside, she found Bernot sitting at the table, a book in hand.

At her entrance, he came to kiss her. "How is she?"

"Fine," Lyerlly said. "Hopefully she will wake soon. But it seems half the city knows of her."

Bernot sighed. "So, it does. We should put a guard on her to be safe."

"Mahogen has already volunteered."

Her husband was quiet for a moment.

"He has been your friend your entire life, do not distrust him because of who his father is. And, you wanted to keep him there anyway."

"You are right, of course we can trust Mahogen. I do not know why I worried."

"The blight of running a nation of rebels," Lyerlly said, kissing his brow.

CHAPTER 50

Kade could see no buildings, yet Hickor claimed they were in Edreba. Laughter floated in the breeze, but he couldn't find the source. They stopped beside a massive tree and Hickor and Halcyon dismounted.

"We want to see our friend," Aron demanded.

"After," Hickor said.

"After what?" Jared questioned.

"After you've seen our commander," Halcyon said.

"He can wait," Aron claimed, forgetting his ties to Caius no longer benefited him.

"We've been instructed to bring you to our commander as soon as you reached the city."

Knowing Jared was about to ask how they had received those orders, Kade told him, *Telepathy,* making him frown.

"There is nothing here," Aron stated.

"If you are going to live with us," Halcyon said, "you must learn to see past the bark on the tree."

Kade was just as confused as the others but knew it was best to watch and wait.

Hickor approached the tree and placed his hand on the trunk. Slowly, a doorknob protruded.

Inside, the tree was completely hollow, a spiraling staircase hugging the inner wall. In the center was a basket, which Kade assumed reached the top. The wood was worn smooth, yet the tree was still living.

"What is this?" Jared asked in wonder.

"The Gortlin Tree," Halcyon answered. "In every Alvor city, the tallest tree is dedicated to its citizens. They contain libraries and the offices of those who run the city."

"Where's your commander's office?" Kade dared to ask.

"Do not fatigue yourself," Hickor mocked, "you only have to climb to the first floor. Bernot is not important enough to the city itself to have a higher place."

Kade was unsure how to take that.

Halcyon initiated the ascent. The stairs weren't steep, yet, by the time they reached the first landing, even Kade was breathing hard. He glanced over the edge, to see they'd gone up nearly sixty feet.

They were then ushered through a door, leaving Halcyon and Hickor waiting outside.

The man sitting at the desk was much younger than Kade had presumed he'd be, probably no older than twenty-eight. His eyes were like obsidian and his black hair fell to just brush his jaw. His skin was swarthy and dark and when he rose, was looking down on all of them.

Kade didn't give him a chance to speak before he blurted, "I want to see my—"

"Sister," the man finished. "Yes, I bet you do."

His lips pulled into a snarl and he wanted to know how the man got past his wall.

"Calm, I have not intruded into your mind."

"Then how did you know?"

"I can see it in the shape of the face, the high forehead, the slight upturn in the nose, the hazel eyes, and rust hair. The truth is there if you are willing to see it."

Kade clenched his fist.

The man motioned towards three chairs, "Please."

Aron was the first to sit.

He and Jared followed suit warily after sharing a look that conveyed their disgruntlement.

"Let us start with names. I am Bernot Bællar. Who might you be?"

"I'm sure you've already been told," Kade growled.

"I have, but I would like to hear you name yourselves."

"I'm Kade Digore, this is Jared Sieme, and Aron no name."

Bernot leaned back in his chair. "Kade, I would appreciate it if you did not try to deceive me. I will give you one more chance to tell me who you are."

"I already did."

"You think me a lack-wit? You have plagued the nations for many years, Kade Tavin, and I must say, I never imagined you would end up here—willingly. You will have to create a better lie if you wish to fool me." Bernot came from behind the desk. "But you must really care for your sister to risk finding your death here."

"I may have slept with the enemy, but it was only so I could slit their throats."

"Your parents were good people," Bernot said, laying a hand on his shoulder. Before Kade could say anything else, he turned to Aron. "And, Aron Alagard, who would have thought the king's son would seek us out?"

"What?" Jared reacted in utter shock.

"That's why I don't trust him!" Kade bellowed.

"You knew?" Jared yelled.

Bernot held Jared back. "Even if he wanted to he could not tell you. The king places a spell on his men, which keeps them from talking about any aspect of his sons in the presence of the oblivious."

"A spell?" Jared questioned furiously.

"Yes, a spell. Spellcasters are rare, but they do exist. By saying a string of words in the Old Language, it is possible to do some amazing things. Much like what your own magical abilities permit."

"Too many lies," Jared snarled, lunging at Kade.

Bernot held him back. "Take a seat, Jared."

"And if I don't?"

"Take a seat."

Jared reached for the knife he kept in his boot, but realizing its absence, did as instructed. "Then how were you able to tell us?"

"Do I look like one of the king's men?" Bernot answered sarcastically.

"A better question would be, how did you find out?" Aron probed.

Bernot ignored him and turned his attention to Kade. "Tell me, Kade, is your sister truly the Child of Prophecy?"

"Yes," Kade answered, looking him straight in the eye. "As are Jared and I."

"There is only supposed to be one."

"Four," Jared corrected.

"How would you know this?" Bernot questioned.

"Thaddeus told us."

"Thaddeus Broyker?"

Jared nodded.

"I have found you board in a children's home," Bernot said, as Hickor opened the door.

"Take us to Keegan," Kade demanded.

"In due time. But first, eat, sleep, and try not to kill each other." As they left, Bernot added, "And next time, do not lie to me. It will make things so much smoother."

✝✝✝

Blood was what Jared wanted most—Kade's specifically. Too much had his 'friend' kept from him. Given access to a weapon, he would gladly dig some steel into him. He'd probably not aim to kill but definitely to maim and cause pain—actually, he might kill him if the fancy struck him. Fortunately for Kade, the Lazado had taken their weapons and Jared knew better than to attack him with fists.

362

When they emerged from the Gortlin Tree, they were dismayed to discover their horses had vanished.

"You will not need them where you are going," Hickor said.

Even Halcyon sensed the threatening undertones and made to ease their alarm. "Your belongings have been taken to the children's home already."

"And where would that be?" Kade snapped.

"In the city," Hickor said, walking away.

They followed him through the giant trees, twigs, and dead leaves crunching underfoot, creating a low rumble of sorts. Under different circumstances, Jared would've marveled at the forest. The trees were behemoths and by all rights, should've blocked all the sun's rays. Yet, the forest floor was bright, as if it was basking directly beneath the light. Woodland creatures hopped between the trunks, looking like miniatures of their true forms. Most creatures would have run at the sight of them, yet these beasts were at ease, completely ignoring them.

Hickor approached one of the trees and placed a hand on its side.

Jared expected another door to reveal itself; instead, a series of ladder rungs appeared.

"Climb," was the only instruction Hickor gave.

Halcyon followed the Alvor. "I recommend not looking down."

The climb was monotonous; one hand up, one foot up, other hand, other foot. Halfway up, Jared made the mistake of ignoring Halcyon's advice, and the world became a dizzyingly fog far below.

"Climb," Kade snapped when he froze in momentary fear.

At the top, wooden walkways linked the trees and houses rested in the high branches.

"A city in the trees," Aron said, taking in the view.

Neither Jared nor Kade were so enamored.

"How does no one fall from the walkways?" Aron asked.

"They have better sense than you ground-dwellers," Hickor responded sharply.

"And there are nets for those who don't," Halcyon added.

The walkways were bustling, and children darted between them, wooden swords clutched in their hands. Soon, they reached a tree whose leaves were a strange cream color. Halcyon pushed open the door and they were greeted with masterful commotion.

A few children saw Hickor and Halcyon and greeted them with smiles and hugs. Jared watched Hickor's tough exterior melt away and an easiness fill him.

363

"Hickor likes the children," Halcyon explained, pushing through the room, "He reasons they don't know how to be truly deceitful."

Jared was inclined to agree.

Halcyon took them into the kitchen where they found a plump, little woman scolding a boy. Seeing them, she sent the boy scampering with a playful kick to the backside.

"More charges for me, Halcyon?" she said turning to them, lips pursed.

"As usual. Though, I doubt these three will be as mischievous as the rest."

"But trouble they will cause nonetheless." She eyed them for a moment before dismissing Halcyon.

"Prepare room for a fourth."

"We require better accommodations," Kade said at once.

The woman put her hands on her hips. "Oh, is Behthany Rhyen's not good enough for ya? Do tell why?"

"We aren't children."

"How old are you?"

"Twenty."

She laughed. "A mere child."

"You're not much older than us."

Behthany gave another laugh and Jared saw a flash of silver in her mouth. "Your eyes deceive you, boy, I am well past my hundredth year."

"How?" Aron said incredulously.

Kade took a guess, "Half Alvor, half human?"

"Correct," Behthany answered.

"Would explain your longevity and the silver in your mouth, but the lack of horns."

"And why I am stuck with you lot. Anyway, your rooms are on the top floor. It is reserved for you *adults* who are still yet children. None of the youngins should bother you up there."

"I'd prefer to be housed away from *him*," Jared said, referring to Kade.

"And what makes you think I'd like to be forced to spend any more time with you or the bastard?" Kade argued.

It was hard to hear the words that came next as they all resorted to shouting.

"Enough," Behthany roared.

Jared found his voice stuck in his throat.

"You will act civil in this house, lest I need beat you with a belt."

They looked sourly at each other.

"You will act politely towards your companions, or so help me. There will be no bloodshed in this house. Am I understood?" When they declined to answer, she said louder, "Am I understood?"

"Yes, ma'am," they chorused.

"Good. Like I said, top floor. Dinner is at sunset. See that you are not late." She dismissed them with a wave. Under her breath, she muttered, "Bovestun well act like children but have the gall to call themselves men."

‡‡‡

True to his word, Mahogen watched Keegan through the night.

Lyerlly tried to dismiss him come morn, but he deflected her instructions.

He made no nuisance of himself, but she could feel his eager watchfulness as she healed Keegan throughout the day; she hated the feeling of being observed. "Mahogen," she eventually said sternly, "make yourself useful, or leave."

"Not used to being scrutinized?"

"Nor my authority being questioned."

Mahogen smiled. "How can I be of service?"

"Go help Ty clean the bedpans."

"I would sooner aid in healing the child."

"Bedpans."

Mahogen raised an eyebrow but did as instructed, saying, "Do not get too used to this."

"Never," Lyerlly said flippantly, returning her attention to Keegan.

All that was left of the broken leg was a hairline fracture, which should have taken no time to heal, but with the Ramilla's lingering block, took the rest of the day.

Mahogen wisely did not return until she was done.

Outside the hospital, twilight was setting on the forest floor.

She pulled the covers over Keegan as Bernot approached. He shared a few words with Mahogen and the Alvor slipped away into the office.

"How does she fare?" he asked.

"Better than before," Lyerlly responded.

"Is there anything we can do to wake her?"

"Not that I know of. Nor would I."

"I need her awake."

"Why?"

Bernot gave her a solemn look. "Because she has a part to play in the war."

"*What* war?"

"The one I intend to wage," he said, walking away.

War—the one thing her husband wanted yet could not have; the barrier saw to that. They were always welcoming refugees but had little use for them. The border had been raised to keep Caius and his militants out, but the spells also kept them from crossing.

"Bernot knows, as well as any, war cannot be waged," Mahogen said, retaking his seat beside the bed.

"Does not mean he is not going to try," Lyerlly told the prince, walking way. "Make sure you do not nod off."

"Never."

She left quietly, leaving the hospital in Henley's capable hands for the night. The journey home was not as enjoyable as usual, her mind elsewhere. On the walkways, wind pulled at her skirt, sending it whirling about.

Bernot sat at the kitchen table when she arrived home, maps and papers scattered across the tabletop.

"You know you cannot start a war," she reminded him.

"I am going to," he said stubbornly.

"How? No warring nation can get past the border."

"I will find a way. Otherwise, what use is having the most powerful elemental the world has ever seen?"

She took a seat across from him. "I am not sure."

Bernot reached across the table and took her hand.

"In time," she continued, "Sola and Lunos will reveal all."

"We don't have time. The world is dying under Caius' thumb. The border was meant to stand forever, but sooner or later everything falls. I mean for us to cause that."

"How?"

Bernot leaned back in the chair, "I am working on that. But Keegan is the key. That much I know."

‡‡‡

Thaddeus closed the book and set it back on the shelf. The guards behind him shifted, preparing to follow him as he continued searching the library. Caius had been easily swayed to give him freedom to roam the castle—and he was taking full advantage of it. He had spent the last two days in the library, searching for information on the Blind Prophets.

Thus far, his search had uncovered only two tomes. The larger one contained all of Angela's prophecies and a few of Alyck's. This book, he would be keeping in their chambers from now on and was going to endeavor to make Alyck recall previous predictions to record them, as well as enter any new ones.

The second was tiny in comparison and covered in dark moleskin. It gave the origins of the Blind Prophet but did not tell him much that he did not already know. There was also nothing on how the next Prophet was to be chosen, as Seleena had been the only queen to rule under Angela's guidance. There was however a spell engraved in the first few pages that appeared to be able to create a Blind Prophet and it told an interesting story. The handwriting told him it was Caius' work.

The tale the spell described was multifold. He could see where it extended and intertwined the Prophet's life with the ruling bloodline, where it took the Prophet's sight, and limited their powers to foresight. He re-examined that segment of the spell and suddenly understood—or at least had a theory. Thaddeus closed the books, took them back to their chambers, and immediately left again.

He struggled to make his way through the castle but surprised even himself when he reached his destination. He looked out the window next to the door and watched the sun near the horizon, casting magnificent hues across the sky.

He inserted a key in the lock and entered the room. He expected a lavish interior, fit for a king; it was anything but. The room was austere, with only the necessities and a single, small portrait hanging on the wall. The woman depicted was gorgeous, her lustrous black hair tumbling across the canvas in gentle waves. Her blue eyes held an air of despondency and the hint of a secret.

"Your wife I take it," Thaddeus said as Caius entered the room from an adjacent chamber.

"Yes, Seleena" Caius answered in a light growl. "What are you doing here? You are only supposed to come when Alyck makes a pertinent prophecy."

"It is something of that nature. Or at least it relates to the Blind Prophet."

Caius raised an eyebrow.

"You were supposed to become the next Blind Prophet."

Caius' features darkened.

"But you forced your brother to take your place. Why?"

"I did what I did for a reason, and it is none of your concern."

"I fear it is."

"Get out."

"As you wish, but I will continue to ask until you tell me what I need to know."

"You will lose your voice."

"But never my mind," Thaddeus refuted.

‡‡‡

The children's home was larger than Aron first presumed, as much of it was hidden by the branches it was constructed within and some of it was even built into the trunk. They had climbed sets of narrow stairs until they reached the upper floor.

The windows looked over the sprawling forest outside, the sun creating a fire of green as it touched the leaves. The layout of the floor followed the points of a compass; a pair of bedrooms and shared washroom were at three of the points and a kitchen at the fourth. In the center was a sitting area with a few couches and a dining table.

Jared and Kade scowled at each other and took rooms on opposite sides after snatching their bags from the table.

Having no desire to deal with either, Aron took a room in the third wing. It was smaller than his bedchambers in Agrielha, but still roomy, the bed able to sleep two people comfortably and covered in a pale, yellow comforter. The walls were a faded blue that had an airy feel.

Dumping his bag on the floor, he went to the window. Roosting birds dropped onto branches as twilight overcame the sky. Despite everything, he smiled; it just felt right. He was where he belonged.

He went to the washroom and was assaulted by his reflection in the mirror, looking strange compared to how he remembered himself. A scruffy beard covered his jaw and, combined with unkempt hair, made him look almost wild. His usually black-as-night hair had taken on subtle hues of a deep brown. The only thing that was unchanged were his indigo-colored eyes.

Not wanting to miss dinner, he promised himself he would shave afterwards. He doubted Jared and Kade would wait for him and made the trip downstairs alone. The table was crowded with rowdy children of various ages, from barely waddling behind older siblings, to looking at most a year or two younger than he.

Taking a seat, he glanced at Behthany, who seemed to be ignoring the fact that Jared and Kade were absent. There was enough food on the table to support a feast by all standards; dishes piled high with savory chicken breasts, bowls filled with mashed potatoes and peas, and loaves of bread were placed intermittently along the table.

Following the children's lead, he piled his plate high and dug in. The food might not have been prepared with a prince in mind, but it could have easily found a place on any king's table. As he ate, the only noise came from clattering forks and knives. As food diminished, voices began to join the clangor.

He felt a tug on his sleeve. "Where are your brothers?" a little girl asked.

"Uhh…" Aron faltered. "My brothers are far away in Agrielha."

"Not those brothers. Your other brothers."

"I have no brothers here."

"Yes, you do," a boy across the table added. "The ones you came in with earlier are your brothers."

Aron gripped his fork tightly. "They are *not* my brothers."

"Of course, they are," the boy continued. "We leave our families behind when we come here, but we gain new ones."

"Yeah," another child chimed in, "Hugie and I share no blood, but we're siblings. We have to look after each other."

It was hard to tell who was speaking next as all the children at once proclaimed who their siblings were.

"Enough," Behthany said from the head of the table.

They all quietened immediately.

"Aron, Kade, and Jared have just arrived, and it may take them some time to recognize themselves as brothers. No one is to pester them about it."

"Yes, ma'am," the children chorused.

"Good. Now finish your food and get to cleaning."

Dinner was completed in silence. After, the children took the dirty plates and cutlery into the kitchen, leaving him with Behthany. He hoped he could make a quiet exit.

"Tomorrow, you will help with clean up," Behthany informed him. "And make sure your brothers know not to miss meals. I cannot have you boys starving on me."

✜✜✜

The wall scraped open and Braxton stepped into the dimly lit stable. The griffins were already stirring, their chains clinking as they moved.

Where is your student? Crowlin questioned.

"Sleeping."

369

Should you not be doing the same? she asked as he faced her.

Her feathers were dark gray, bordering on black and reminded him of the night.

Probably, but I have been finding it hard to sleep. "Too much to think about."

"About what?" a voice asked from the shadows.

Braxton nearly jumped out of his skin and pulling his dagger, brandished it at the area where the voice came from.

"No need for that," the voice said, stepping into the dim torchlight.

"Thaddeus? What are you doing here?"

"Talking to you."

"How did you even know I would be here?"

"A mutual friend."

Sheathing his knife, Braxton gave him a sour look. "What do you need?"

"I want to talk about what happened earlier."

The muscles in his shoulders tightened. "There is nothing to talk about."

Clearly not, Crowlin said, nudging him towards Thaddeus. *Listen to this man; he bears the air of knowledge.*

"You can tell me. I promise I will keep it between us."

Braxton took a moment. "There is not much to tell. I... have been dreaming the future."

"That is not nothing, my dear boy. How long has this been occurring?"

He had to think, "A few months—since Keegan arrived."

"Ah, our ever-elusive Keegan. She seems to leave a wake of disturbance, does she not?"

"I suppose..."

"Describe your visions."

"Repetitive. I keep having the same dream until it actually happens. Or I figure out the meaning."

"What do you mean?"

"They are always in the Old Language."

"Are you fluent in the Old Language?"

Braxton shook his head.

Thaddeus muttered, "Interesting."

"We should both be going," Braxton said after a short silence.

"Of course, the paths set before us are arduous. But before we leave, I do have one more question. Why did you lose control?"

Braxton felt his stomach working itself into knots. "I did not lose control," he stammered. "It… must have been something else."

Braxton, Myrish said.

"What?" he snapped, turning to the griffin. As he did, the few loose pebbles that could be found in the stables clattered back to the ground.

"You are not aware when it happens, are you? How long has this been happening?"

"Today was the first time." The words were sticky in his throat. "Or at least the first time I noticed."

Thaddeus placed a hand on his shoulder. "Everything will be just fine. I will try to give you an answer; you have my word. Now, go back to bed."

Braxton nodded tiredly and opened the door to the secret passageway. He turned back to let Thaddeus through first and was shocked to find the old man had disappeared.

He left via the door, Phynex told him, giving a slight shuffling of his wings, which was as close to a shrug as he could give.

Goodnight, he told them, closing the wall.

Walking through the darkness was easy—dealing with his thoughts was not. He did his best to push them aside, to let himself believe that things were normal and fine.

Back in his chambers, he accidentally let the door slam shut, forgetting about Nico.

The boy popped up, groggily asking, "Wha'su goin' on?"

"Nothing," he told him, "Go back to sleep."

The child did not need to be told a second time before his snores filled the air.

He slipped into bed and stared at the ceiling. An oppressive sensation pressed against his chest and soon he realized he was afraid to go to sleep—afraid to see his father's death. Whatever was happening to him, he had to find a way to stop it. He could not live like this.

CHAPTER 51

A persistent knock pulled her from sleep. Lyerlly turned over and ran her fingers along Bernot's back to rouse him. "Want to get the door?"

"Not particularly," he mumbled.

"Please," she said sleepily, giving him a gentle push.

He grumbled but rose off the mattress. It was not long before she heard muted voices downstairs.

She expected Bernot to return shortly; when he didn't, she grew curious. Wrapping a shawl around her shoulders, she went to investigate, and found Bernot talking to a soldier; although minutes previously he had been fast asleep, he looked quite alert now.

"What is going on?" she asked, going to stand beside him.

"Keegan."

"Is she all right?"

"Yes, but we are both needed at the hospital, *immediately*," he told her, grabbing a jacket from the closet before heading into the night.

Dying candles lit the windows of a few houses and owls watched curiously as they made their way through the city. The climb down the ladder and walk across the forest floor seemed to take longer than she remembered.

Outside the hospital, the patients who could leave their beds were huddled in the night.

"What are they doing out here?" Lyerlly snapped at the soldiers standing around.

"We couldn't make them stay in there with the body," one stammered.

"Body...?" She pushed past the man.

The patients who had not been well enough to go outside had the curtains around their beds drawn. The floor was stained in a sickening crimson. Henley's body lay face up, her eyes glassy, staring blankly at the ceiling.

"Who did this?" she demanded.

"We're looking into it now," a soldier told her.

"Where is Mahogen?" Bernot questioned.

"With the girl."

Mahogen sat beside Keegan's bed, dabbing a cloth at her head where a gash spilled red blood over the side of her face.

"What happened?" Lyerlly asked furiously. "You were supposed to be watching her!"

"I was," Mahogen said calmly. "Henley thought she heard something outside, so I went to check. When I came back, Henley was dead and Keegan was on the floor across the hospital."

"Did you see who it was?"

"No."

"Did you sense who it was?"

"No."

She might have yelled at Mahogen had Bernot not joined them.

"Why would someone try to take the girl and then leave her behind?" her husband asked.

"My guess is they got scared," Mahogen replied.

"Lyerlly, I need to speak to you in the office," Bernot said, drawing her away. With the door shut, he told her, "I always knew we had spies, but I hoped none would be this bold. I am going to put a guard rotation on the hospital, and someone is to be with Keegan at all times."

"If you must."

"How much longer until she comes to?"

"If only I knew."

"She needs to be moved. Somewhere safer."

"We cannot move her until she wakes. If she were elsewhere and something happened, no one would be at hand to help."

"I want Mahogen guarding her at all times and I want him healing her as much as he can."

"Shall I tell him, or will you?"

Bernot did not answer.

She looked out into the hospital, the blood standing out like death in snow. She made her way back to Mahogen. "You wanted to help."

"I still do," he said dryly.

"Then it is your job to make sure *nothing* happens to her."

‡‡‡

The jolting motion of the horse sent pain up his side with every step, but he wasn't about to complain—not with Caeyl and Oslin present. Since meeting them at the inn, they'd joined their little band of outlaws. In different circumstances, Lucas might have liked them, but after they'd threatened Carter, he could hardly look at them without seeing red. The only good to come of them was the acquisition of horses.

Throughout the day, Caeyl and Oslin were rarely around. One was always scouting ahead and the other was behind, covering their tracks. He found the practice odd.

Carter asked why and Felix's response was, "Because you're valuable men."

Lucas doubted it—they probably only wanted something from them.

Since Felix had told the duo about Keegan, both had been incessantly asking about her. How had they found her? What did she look like? What element was she? How had she escaped from Caius? Had she really killed one of the Vosjnik? Was she really the Child of Prophecy? Any questions they couldn't answer, they had the tendency to repeat, as if hoping they'd remember later.

"How much further to the Lazado?" Lucas asked gruffly.

"Month or so," Felix answered. "Probably longer."

"You know the way?"

"Of course."

"Then why do we need *them*?"

"Let it go," Carter said. "And they're not that bad. Just 'cause they held a knife to my side doesn't mean you get to hate them forever."

"Oh, yes, it does," Lucas argued. "And what were they even doing that far from the Lazado anyway?"

"Finding us," Felix answered coyly.

Lucas would have pressed further had Waylan not stopped him. "He's never going to tell you, but they were most likely on a mission against the state. The less anyone knows, the better."

"Precisely," Felix said. "You know, under different conditions you and Caeyl might've been friends."

"I doubt that," Caeyl said, rejoining the group from scouting. "Nothing ahead, I'll check again in a bit."

"You lads are two sides of the same coin," Felix continued. "Both such stubborn and fierce protectors."

"And that's where our similarities end," Lucas snapped.

"I wouldn't be so sure about that. Give each other a chance and you might be surprised."

"Surprised at how well he can stick a knife in my back," Lucas muttered under his breath.

‡‡‡

Azure slammed himself against Nico's wall and it came tumbling down. Nico was frustrated, and sensing it, Azure made to placate him, *Very good.*

Not good enough.

374

They'd been working together for a week now and he'd mastered mental communication with a telepath. The next step was to fortify his mind against prying entities. It was difficult, but he was told he was learning quickly. The fact that he still succumbed to Azure's attacks proved otherwise.

This isn't something you master in a day, Azure said kindly.

"I should be doing better though."

Castles aren't built in a day.

But they fall in less.

Azure came forward and placed a hand in the center of his forehead. *Only if they are weak. I'd say you are anything but.*

Then why can't I keep up a wall against your invasions?

I've been making and breaking walls since before you were born. I didn't become this good in a week. It took years *of training. Ask Rooth.*

I believe you.

Then keep working. You'll get it eventually. But until then, excellent work, not many learn to create a wall this quickly—especially those who aren't telepaths.

Nico stood straighter at the praise.

Run along now, I'm sure Eamon's waiting for you.

"Bye," Nico called as he ran out of the room.

Stubborn child, Azure grumbled.

By Braxton's oversee, mornings were dedicated to working with Azure on telepathy and afternoons were given to Eamon for elemental training. He missed the brief time in which Braxton had worked with him. He wasn't sure what was keeping his tutor, but it had to be important.

Working with Eamon had also exposed him to some of the other elementals in the castle. Luwis and his group hadn't come to love him any more than before; if anything, they seemed to hate him harder. But Eamon kept them in line, so they were of no concern and thankfully, he'd made a few friends with some of the students his age.

"Nico," Auber called. She was a tiny little thing for a girl of thirteen, but that didn't stop her from besting men twice her size and thrice her age. "So good of you to finally join us."

"You know I work with Azure before lunch," he said, joining the group of boys around her.

"I don't see the point of telepathy training."

"You just want to spend more time with your love," Leander teased.

Auber punched him in the arm.

"More training, less talking," Eamon yelled.

Walking over to a free area, they began. Auber shot a rock at his head, which he easily blocked. The next attack came from two sides, one slightly delayed. He was beginning to anticipate attacks, but his brain still had trouble understanding the input, frequently earning him a bruise. He barely blocked one rock as the other struck him in the hip. Yelping, he shot her a glare.

She laughed.

He raised a stone from the earth and sent it towards her.

Effortlessly, she stopped it midair, turning it to sand, then crossed her arms and gave a haughty look.

He smiled in return, trying to hide his frustration. Mustering himself, he created an arsenal of projectiles and began continuously shooting them at her. Auber encased herself in an orb of earth. He let a few of the projectiles break against the shell then waited for her to lower the shield. She made no attempt to come forth and he wondered what she was doing when he felt someone grab the back of his shirt. As soon as he hit the ground, earth covered his body.

Auber stood over him, a smile on her face. "So much for getting better."

Nico let himself relax. "I'm still learning."

"I know," she let the earth recede. "You *are* getting better, though."

"I know," he said, making her sink into the ground.

She started laughing and he found himself joining in the merriment. After a moment, he realized this was the first time since everything had happened that he'd laughed.

✦✦✦

There was a soft rap on his door.

"What?" Kade groaned blearily.

It'd been easy to forget he was exhausted after their breakneck flight across the country. He'd meant to go to dinner, but once he'd sat on the bed, he'd fallen asleep and not moved until now.

"Bernot wishes to speak to you," Behthany said.

"Tell him he can go roy—"

"I *am not* a messenger and that *was not* a request."

Scowling, he threw back the covers and dressed. They had yet to be given back their weapons and he felt bare without his sword. He didn't know what Bernot wanted, but he had no intention of giving it to him.

Going out into the common space, he found Bernot sitting at the table with a woman. She sat elegantly, looking like a highborn lady. Her

376

skin was unmarred—smooth and pale. Chestnut colored hair hung freely about her shoulders and brown eyes gazed at him with a strange kind of knowing. Her figure was thin and Kade felt a warm power emanating from her.

"My lady," he said, remembering his manners.

"I am no lady by Arciolan standards," she responded coolly.

"This is my wife, Lyerlly," Bernot said, a coy smirk playing on his lips.

Kade felt like a small piece of him cried at the word wife, and another died as he remembered Cassidy. He hadn't had time to properly grieve and his emotions came to sit on a teetering precipice as memories returned. He reached into his pocket and ran a thumb over the larimar pendant.

Bernot motioned to an empty chair. "Take a seat."

He did so then realized Aron and Jared were also present. Jared scowled, which he reciprocated.

"I want to see Keegan," Jared demanded.

"In time," Bernot told him.

"What do we need to do to be able to see her?" Aron blurted.

"I see you have been trained in the art of diplomacy."

"Not really. What do we need to do?" Aron repeated.

"I want to know how all of you met Keegan."

"Why do you want to know that?" Kade snapped.

Aron decided to guess. "He wants to know if she really is the Child of Prophecy."

"You mean if *we*'re the Children of Prophecy," Kade corrected.

Aron gave him a bewildered look.

He remembered Aron hadn't been part of that conversation—and was more than happy to leave him in the dark.

"Correct," Bernot said. "Is she? Are you?"

"She is," Aron responded.

Jared added, "And we are. At least Kade and I are."

"How did she come to meet all of you?"

Aron took a moment to answer. "I freed her from my father's dungeon."

Bernot's brows twitched and raised slightly, but he remained quiet and turned to Jared.

"She found me," Jared told him.

"I saved her from the Vosjnik," Kade said.

Liar, Jared snarled.

"Kade, what have I told you about lying?"

Kade scowled at Bernot, presuming he had broken through his mental wall.

"No, I have not entered your mind. But I cannot ignore the emotions coming from your brother that tell me otherwise."

"We *are not* brothers," Jared bit.

"You came here together without family," Lyerlly said, her voice holding an air of assertiveness that Kade wasn't used to finding in women. "By all rights, the second you stepped over the border you became family."

"How did you come to know Keegan?" Bernot repeated.

"A long story, that you'd best hear from Keegan," Kade said, trying to redirect the question.

"I am not asking Keegan. But it does seem there is much all of you are not telling me. So, start at the beginning. Aron, I believe the first part belongs to you."

Kade glanced down the table, he didn't actually know much of her first days in Arciol, except how damaging her entrance had been.

Aron began with how she was found in the throne room, destruction all around her then spoke of his visits with Alyck and all he'd been told.

Bernot was highly interested in this and listened attentively.

Aron ended with Keegan riding off on Darkheart, now Bastille. "Kade has the next part."

"There's not much to tell," Kade said, keeping his face neutral. "The Vosjnik chased her west towards Lake Romann. When we caught up to her, there was a light, wind, and an explosion, and she disappeared. Jared."

Bernot held up a hand to stay Jared. "Describe the explosion."

Kade shifted uncomfortably in the chair. "It was like there were three suns and we were on the outskirts of a gale storm. The light and wind were pulling inwards, towards Keegan. Then, at its climax, exploded outward. None of us were harmed, but Keegan was gone."

"You know what that was," Bernot scrutinized him for a moment.

"Yes," Kade answered, "a Nanagin." He could see the wheels turning in Bernot's head, he just didn't know what conclusions he was coming to.

"Jared," Bernot invited, turning his attention to him.

"There was an explosion just before her horse brought her into my camp," Jared began. He told them how he had taken her home and how she had come down with some sickness, then how her magic suddenly manifested and the early days of their training, growing quieter as he neared the time his family was killed.

Something possessed Kade and he jumped in. He didn't look at Jared, but knew he was grateful; the subject still caused him heartache—as it should.

Bernot listened through the recounting of their flight to Suttan. Through the tale of Keegan's quick progression in telepathy and life magic, he sat back in his chair, a skeptical look on his face.

Jared took up the telling of their journey from Suttan, leaving most details about Cassidy out.

Kade knew he was settling his debt.

After their capture by the Vosjnik, Aron backtracked to tell of his own flight from Agrielha, and they were content to let him bring the story to a close.

By the end of it, both Bernot and Lyerlly bore looks of incredulity.

"A wild story from start to finish," she commented.

"This has been most informative. Is there anything else you *want* to tell us?" Bernot asked.

"No." Kade told him emphatically.

"All right," Bernot stood up.

Lyerlly stood with him.

"Hold on," Aron said, "we told you what you wanted to know. Now, let us see Keegan."

"Not just yet. There is still the matter of testing your skills."

"When can we do that?" Kade said, clenching his fists to keep himself from flying at Bernot.

"On the morrow. I will send someone to take you to the training grounds."

‡‡‡

Jared only had to look at Kade to see his frustration matched his own. However, he was in no mood to reconcile. Instead, he shot him a glare before storming downstairs to see if he could get some food from Behthany.

He found her on the first floor playing the maiden in distress. She saw him and picked her way across the room. A few of the younger children pulled away from their battles to chase after her, wrapping themselves in her skirts and giggling as she dragged them over.

"Wanting lunch, I presume," she said, hands on her hips.

"Yes," he answered.

"*Please.*"

"Yes, *please.*"

379

"There is bread and cheese in the kitchen. Help yourself and then come help me with these buggers," she instructed, reaching down and tickling a little girl.

He helped himself to a large slice of bread and a few blocks of cheese and washed it down with a cup of water. Peeking through the doorway, he saw the children's game had long since ended. They now sat around tables, reading or practicing arithmetic. He was about to go see what Behthany wanted help with but changed his mind and ducked out the back door.

He followed the path to the walkways out front, the sun high above, warm and pleasant. Without looking back, he shoved his hands into his pockets and walked for a time before coming to a junction between several trees.

A market was set up. Children ran through the crowd happily while adults haggled. He chose a random vendor and enquired where he could find the Gortlin Tree. The vendor obliged, and armed with a set of directions, he pushed across the market.

It was some time before he found the tree, its top even higher than the ones that held the city. A motley assortment of greens colored its leaves, causing it to seem as if it was an indecisive chameleon—they didn't have that creature in this world, but Keegan had explained it to him once. He set a hand against the tree like Hickor had done to open the door.

"It will not work for you," a voice said behind him.

Jared spun around.

"May I ask why you are here?" Bernot queried.

"There are a few more things I want to tell you."

Bernot kept a straight face and opened the door into the tree. "We will take the lift down."

The lift was little more than an expansive basket that lurched as they stepped into its confines and swung as they rode down.

"Why would the door not open for me?" Jared asked.

"You are neither an Alvor nor an agent of the Lazado yet."

They didn't talk the rest of the way and the lift creaked and groaned, making him wonder if it'd hold. Near the bottom, it jerked to a stop and they stepped onto the landing. He was glad to have solid footing again.

Bernot opened the door to his office, ushered him in, and took a seat behind his desk, "What is it you want to tell me?"

"Kade's a murderer and a liar."

"Nothing I am not aware of. If you want me to expel your brother, you will have to give me a better reason. His good outweighs the misdeeds."

"He's not my brother," Jared hissed. "Kade killed my family, then failed to mention he'd given my little brother to the king."

"Why would he not tell you this?"

"To make us come here," he said with disgust.

"Us?"

"Keegan and me. She would've gone back for Nico regardless of the danger to herself. And I would've followed."

"Then the lie was told in your best interest. Is that such a damning thing?"

"Yes, when in conjunction with the other lies."

"Such as?"

"He knew who Aron was and about Keegan."

"In regard to Aron, he could not tell you any more than he could control the changing of the seasons. Caius spells his men so they cannot mention his offspring in most contexts."

"You already told me this."

"I did, and the reasoning has not changed. I believe Kade, in his own way, tried to warn you."

Jared thought about how Kade had voiced his mistrust of Aron. Maybe he should've listened closer—and fought harder at the start. "Keegan," he continued, "doesn't know."

"Know what?"

"That she's Kade's twin."

"And you would have me tell her, so it does not look like you betrayed Kade?"

"No. I couldn't care less what he thinks of me. I'd rather she not be told."

"Why?"

"I know how people here will take to Kade. Let her deny any relation besides a forced one, so she won't be treated as a *monster,* like him."

‡‡‡

Lyerlly slowly climbed the ladder to the city, fireflies sputtering into existence around her like fleeting stars. On the walkways, children raced to catch the glowing insects, their laughter pure and innocent. At home, she found Bernot waiting for her.

"Any change?"

She shook her head.

"I cannot keep them away forever. What am I to do?"

"Let them see her," she told him. "Why did you have me come earlier?"

"Because, whereas I hear the person the words come from, you hear the words that come from the person. I know who they are, and that clouds how I judge what they say."

Lyerlly took a seat at the table. "What is it you heard them say?"

"Many things. The only commonality is how much they care for their sister."

"It would take a blind man to not see that. What else did you learn?"

"Several things. Some offered insight into Caius, and others explained some of the mysteries surrounding Keegan, while giving rise to yet more questions."

Lyerlly leaned forward on an elbow. "Do tell."

"Keegan is the Child of Prophecy."

"We already knew that."

"But so are her brothers."

She tilted her head. "I thought there was only one."

"No, that is what Angela wanted Caius to believe." He pulled a piece of parchment from his pocket and handed it to her. "Angela's last prophecy."

"Why did you pretend you were unaware of this?"

He shrugged, "I felt the deception might offer more insight."

Lyerlly turned her attention to the parchment and read: *Four children shall defeat the despot. To rouse, drive, intercede, and assuage his companions is one's self-given duty. A life of displacement another must lead. To right the wrong is the third's ambition. To sit upon the throne is one's right by ancient blood. Black and white yet compelled to stand in spite. To each their own misfortune; the lies of the mother shall condemn the first, the light before the thunder shall be the second's demise, the steel of the blade shall cast down the third, forbidden love shall be the ruin of the fourth. Twenty fingers from their birth we must count until the revolution begins, sparked by the one of all elements.*

"Four," she said, "and you think they are…"

"It all fits. Though, I do not believe Aron knows."

"Why would he not?"

"Because he was not with them in Suttan. The only person who knew about this prophecy, besides me, is the man who told me about it—Thaddeus Broyker."

"The man who fostered Kade."

382

"Keegan knows she is special—*knows* she is a Child of Prophecy. And I have no doubt she is also aware we are placing the fate of us all on her shoulders. But she does not know who she truly is in respect to this world and how she came to be as she is."

"Do you intend to tell her?"

"In time. The rest has only led to theories I need to investigate."

Lyerlly stood and cupped her husband's face in her hands, "You are going to rid us of Caius."

"No, they are. They will be the ones to swing the sword. Go to bed, my dear, we have a long path ahead of us. I have called a Council of the Nations and they should be here within the turn of the moon."

"Is that wise?"

"Necessary."

"They will tear the poor girl apart fighting over her."

"Something tells me it is not Keegan that will be torn apart. If she stands true to how her brothers describe her, it will be she who decides the terms of this war."

CHAPTER 52

Aron awoke to someone pounding on his door. Rising, he dressed quickly and went to the common area to find Kade and Jared waiting, the silence between them chilling. Both had gone to dinner the previous night and it had not been pleasant. They had refused to talk to each other, the children picked it up instantly, and not knowing how to break the tension, followed their example. Afterwards, they stole upstairs while he helped clean the table and dishes. When he went up, they had already locked themselves in their rooms.

Hickor escorted them to the forest floor, and somehow, the descent managed to be more racking than the climb.

They were led through the forest in silence and he let his mind wander. After a time, he realized it was the beginning of his twentieth year. Braxton and Kolt had thrown extravagant feasts and balls to mark the occasions. He doubted the same would have been done for him and was simply glad to be beyond his father's reach. In his wildest dreams, he could not have asked for a better gift on his birthday—even if it would go unmarked.

The training field was a fair distance from where they had descended, in a large, open field. The men there were segregated into a few classes, depending on weapon of choice. Most of the space was given to swordsmen and elementals while archers and those with maces and pikes were on the outskirts. Towards the back, a few men fought with fists.

Bernot was waiting for them. "What are your weapons of choice?"

"Sword and magic," Kade answered.

He was sent off with Halcyon.

"Magic," Jared answered.

Hickor went with him.

"What about you?"

"Bow and arrow," Aron answered.

Bernot led him to where the archers were practicing, rows of straw stuffed dummies acting as targets. Arrows stuck out of them like quills, yet despite that, they grinned devilishly.

He was handed a bow and a tube of arrows was set on the ground next to him.

"Start easy," Bernot instructed, "take a shot to the chest."

Aron notched and arrow and pulled the string back, feeling the muscles in his arms working to maintain the tension. As he breathed out, he let the arrow fly. It pierced the dummy's eye.

The archer next to him gave a disconcerted look and let his own arrow fly; it hit the target's shoulder.

"An impressive shot," Bernot commented, "but not what I asked for."

"No," Aron admitted. "This is what you asked for." He notched another arrow and let it go. It went through the target's heart. "When can I see Keegan?"

"As soon as we are done here." Bernot surveyed the training field behind him. "Do you see Kade?"

Aron turned and strained to find him in the flurry of motion. "Yes."

"I want you to shoot an arrow at him in such a way that it tears his clothing but leaves his skin unmarked."

Aron paused—what Bernot wanted was a test. He could either do as asked, showing he could follow directions, and that he was a good shot. *Or...*

Slowly, he pulled the bowstring back. As he was about to release it, he spun and loosed the arrow at the target. It sheared through its side, spilling a few golden rods onto the ground. "I am a good shot," he announced, "and as much as I dislike Kade, I will not do something that could potentially harm him."

"We might make use of you yet."

Aron did not like the implication, but kept his mouth shut. Bernot was a powerful man and he was unsure of where all the pieces fell.

"As soon as your brothers are done, we shall go see your sister."

✛✛✛

Come to me.

Nothing but blackness existed.

Come to me.

Unbelievably, the world was getting darker.

Come to me.

She was beginning to fade.

Be strong, came another voice, hardly more than a whisper. *Be strong.*

Come to me. There was a hint of worry in Caius' words now.

Be strong, be strong, be strong, each repetition louder than the last.

The darkness began to fade, and there was light in the distance.

The voice was practically yelling now, *Be strong!*

Light rushed at her like a bolt. Her eyes opened and strained at the overabundance of white. At first, it was all she could see, but slowly,

385

colors appeared. Her head felt like it was full of cotton and there was a dull ache in her muscles. Studying her surroundings, she saw the man in the chair beside the bed.

He looked human, save the golden horns protruding from his head that peeked above his bark-colored hair with deep gray undertones. He stared ahead, unblinkingly, like a statue.

She couldn't place where in time and space she was and after eyeing the man, quietly threw back the covers and swung her legs over the edge of the bed. Realizing she was in nothing but a long shirt, she eased herself off the bed, the tiled floor cool on her bare feet. She stood for no more than a few seconds before her legs buckled, sending her crashing to the floor.

"Keegan," the man said, and the chair scraped across the tiles.

"Where am I?" she began, pushing herself to her feet.

"There is no need to fight."

The words made her feel that something was wrong, and she tried to take a step. Her legs began to spasm and she fell, grabbing onto the curtain around the bed. The cloth was pulled from its hangings, revealing the hospital.

A few nurses looked at her curiously but made no attempt to help.

"Stay where you are," the man instructed.

"No!" Feeling defenseless, she tried scrambling to her feet, but only managed a few steps before collapsing onto her knees. She didn't know why her legs were so weak, but it only served to make her feel more unnerved.

"Stop."

Ignoring the man, she made a final attempt to stand, but crumpled onto the floor. Realizing she wouldn't get anywhere that way, she scuttled backwards. "Stay the fuck away from me."

"Keegan," the man said, taking a step forward.

"Stay away," she said, holding her hands out.

The tile cracked and rocks pulled themselves forth to float before her.

A woman in the background screamed and the world succumbed to pandemonium.

She could hear multiple voices yelling at her to yield and sensed someone trying to grab her from behind. She raised a column of earth and there was a loud "umph" as the person was hit in the stomach.

Soldiers rushed into the hospital, weapons drawn.

The man with the golden horns took a step towards her and she threw a projectile at him.

"Enough," he said as he used his forearms to shield his face from the attack.

There was something calming about his voice, but she was still on edge.

"Enough."

She began to feel fatigued and her eyelids drooped; slowly, the rocks began to lower. Now it was all she could do to keep herself sitting while people were still yelling all around her.

There was a flurry of motion and the horned man was sent stumbling. She couldn't see who'd attacked him, but others joined the fray.

Men and women in white aprons struggled to pull the attackers back while Keegan sat in the background, forgotten momentarily.

"STOP!" a woman yelled.

Everyone froze. Slowly, they disentangled themselves and a man and a woman walked into their midst.

"What on earth do you think you are doing?" the woman demanded.

‡‡‡

What I would give to have wings, Braxton said, leaning his head back against the cool stones.

Hmph, was Oxren's response. *They are freeing until someone clips them.*

You may find yourselves in the sky again sooner than you think, Braxton told him. *My father wants me to train you for battle.*

Myrish roared with laughter both mentally and audibly. *The only battle we will fight will to be to destroy Caius.*

"Of course, you cannot make life easy."

An easy life is not one worth living, Crowlin told him. *Have the Vosjnik captured the girl?*

Braxton shook his head, "I have not heard anything." *I am not sure if that is good or bad.*

No news is good news, Niyth said. *Do you actually intend to train us?*

Braxton felt guilt well up in his chest. *I'd rather not. But if I don't, my father will find a way to force you to.*

Ever the man with the seemingly noble intentions.

"But good intentions are worth *nothing*." He pushed himself to his feet, "I should be going."

They are worth more than you think, Crowlin said. *You are kinder than most humans we have met.*

"You have only met horrible examples of humanity." His foot struck a loose pebble, sending it skittering across the room. There was a loud thump and he followed the path the pebble had taken. It was now imbedded in the wall. He took a deep breath, forcing himself to maintain his composure.

There was a clicking of beaks as the griffins conversed.

You should talk to Alyck, Crowlin told him with concern. *Something is shifting with your magic.*

He would love to get answers, but it was painfully clear his uncle knew nothing on the matter. He would have to face whatever came without warning or advice.

‡‡‡

An ache was already forming in Lyerlly's head. Keegan sat on the floor, anxious and confused, deep gouges cracking the tile floor around her. Ty was hunched over on the ground holding his stomach. Keegan's brothers were all in a lather and poor Mahogen looked puzzled that someone had managed to land a punch on him.

"What on earth do you think you are doing?" Lyerlly demanded.

"Keegan—" Aron stammered.

"Quiet."

Bernot placed a hand on Lyerlly's shoulder. "Would one of you gentlemen help Keegan back into bed?"

The three brothers scrambled to help; Aron reached her first. Keegan gave him a curious look but consented to being scooped up into his arms, looking tiny, frail, and fragile.

The others followed him, and Mahogen wiped away a line of blood from his mouth.

Aron deposited Keegan on the bed, and she began spewing questions. "Where are we? What's going on? How'd I get here? Why does he have h—"

"Calm," Bernot said soothingly. "Lyerlly, is it possible to get a few more chairs?"

"Of course," she answered, sending Elia to bring some from the office.

"Where are we?" Keegan asked again.

"The Lazado," Aron answered, accepting a chair, and taking her hand as he sat down.

Absentmindedly, she ran her thumb over his palm. "But we were in Revod. And Vitia... and Cassidy..."

"Do you remember getting stabbed by Vitia?" Bernot said.

Keegan felt her shoulder.

"That blade was poisoned."

"How long?"

"Two weeks," Kade answered.

"And I'm gonna be fine?" she asked. "No lingering effects?"

"In time," Lyerlly told her. "The poison destroyed most of your muscle, so we have been doing our best to rebuild them, but the Ramilla was modified to inhibit that."

"What does that mean for me?"

"We will continue to artificially rebuild your muscles, but ultimately it will be better for you to do so on your own."

"We shall let you and your brothers talk," Bernot said rising.

Keegan knitted her brows together. "*Brothers?*"

Bernot smiled, "Those who come to the Lazado together become family."

The confused look did not fade from her face.

Office, he said to Lyerlly.

Lyerlly turned on her heels, "Mahogen, stay with Keegan and continue healing her."

Bernot leaned against the edge of the desk. "I never imagined she would be that powerful."

Giving a huff, Lyerlly responded, "None of us did. I have never seen anyone do so much damage while still recovering from Ramilla."

"She is the ace up our sleeve, but also the thorn in our side," noted Bernot. "We will need to be careful how we proceed with her."

Lyerlly crossed her arms. "And there is your problem, you are treating her like an object. You will never control her, but you may be able to guide her."

Bernot rose and went to hold her face in his hands. "How did I end up with such a beautiful and intelligent wife?"

✠✠✠

A good portion of the afternoon was spent watching Mahogen heal Keegan. Aron could find no reason he should distrust the Alvor, but something made him want to protect her. She looked a shadow of herself, but those who were fool enough to believe she was weak were in for a rude awakening. He had not expected her to be loud and outspoken but supposed he had not seen her true personality in Agrielha.

"Do you want to stay here tonight or come with us to the children's home?" Kade asked.

Bernot gave him a mild look of frustration while Mahogen looked away to conceal a smile, and Aron realized Kade had given them a chance to retake 'control'.

"Uh…" she began, looking towards Bernot, "I'll go with them. If that's okay."

"I cannot find a reason you should not," he said with a forced smile.

"Sweet." She swung her legs over the side of the bed, stood, and fell forward, tumbling into Jared.

"Easy," Lyerlly said, helping her up. "You are still weak."

Bernot led them outside the hospital and Aron was not thrilled when Mahogen joined them.

Keegan looked around confused. "Where's the city?"

Mahogen smiled. "Up in the trees."

There was a spark in Keegan's forest-colored eyes. "Like treehouses?"

"Exactly like treehouses."

Her excitement was obvious, but her face fell when she looked up at the canopy. "I don't think I'm strong enough to climb."

"There is an alternative," Bernot said.

Her smile returned and she readily let Jared help her along.

Aron realized they were being taken to the Gortlin Tree, where Mahogen opened the door with a touch of the hand. Keegan's jaw dropped when she saw inside, and even though he had seen it already, he could not help but marvel at it again either.

Bernot called upwards and a basket was lowered.

Aron questioned how sturdy it was, but Keegan had no misgivings.

"You will have to let Mahogen accompany her," Bernot told Jared.

"Why?" Kade snapped defensively.

"Do you know the way to the children's home from the Gortlin Tree?"

Scowling, Kade admitted. "No."

Jared seemed to want to contradict him but changed his mind.

"Then you need Mahogen to take her," Bernot said in a voice that was meant to be diplomatic. "I promise she is in good hands."

CHAPTER 53

The basket swung slightly as they rose. Keegan knew she looked like a star-struck child but couldn't care less. The Gortlin Tree was a spectacle; it was so high she wondered at first if it went on forever. A few people climbed the stairs spiraling the trunk, many calling greetings to Mahogen as they rose past.

"You seem popular," she commented.

"Princes tend to be," Mahogen returned.

"You're a prince?"

"Not in quite the same sense as Aron, but yes."

"*Aron?*" she said. "He's not a… is he?"

"Did you not know? Aron is Caius' son."

Keegan looked over the edge of the basket. "No, I didn't."

The basket stopped and Mahogen stepped onto the platform, offering a hand to help her.

She brushed it away.

Outside, the city was alive; large walkways were strung between the trees and houses nestled in the branches.

"Damn," she muttered. Even with the technology of her world, no one there would ever see the likes of this.

Mahogen offered an arm, "If you will, my lady."

My lady. For reasons she couldn't place, the words stung. She gave him a dogged smile and started forward without him; it wasn't long before she needed to lean upon him.

Through the city, Mahogen pointed out places of interest.

She feigned attentiveness, her mind preoccupied with Aron's ill-begotten secret, but soon they arrived at a tree with cream-colored leaves.

"The white leaves signify a children's home," Mahogen announced.

Inside was a large group of children—the youngest looking around three and the oldest seventeen or eighteen—sitting at a table, chattering over an evening meal.

"Behthany's in the kitchen," an older girl said, anticipating the question.

In the kitchen, Bernot and the boys were talking to a lovely looking woman, with a rounded face that made her look as if she were a cheerful person, but also looked far too young to be running a home.

As Behthany was about to speak, a little boy ran into the kitchen. "Bethsy, Bethsy," he cried, running into her arms.

She gave them an apologetic look before dealing with the child, shortly sending him on his way. "Apologies 'bout that. You must be Keegan," she said, smiling sweetly.

"Uh, yes, ma'am," Keegan responded. "And Bethsy, I presume."

"Behthany. Bethsy is an annoying pet name from a few of the children."

"It's cute though."

Bethsy raised an eyebrow. "Call me what you will, but none of these *men* have any right to use it."

"Yes, ma'am."

Bethsy lazily hit Bernot in the chest, "The manners on this one! Why can you not send me more like her?" She didn't give Bernot time to respond before walking away.

"She seems nice," Keegan commented.

"Just don't get on her bad side," Bernot warned. "The boys will show you to your accommodations. I will give you a few days to rest, but then I need to test your skills."

"Okey dokey."

Bernot gave her a perplexed look and a curt nod before walking away with Mahogen.

She was slow going up the stairs and as soon as the door to their floor closed, she turned to them, a look of betrayal on her face. "Why didn't you tell me?" she said, speaking to Aron specifically.

"Tell you what?" Aron asked, but she thought he knew what she was talking about.

"That you're Caius' son."

"I told you not to trust him," Kade blurted.

"You knew and didn't say anything?" Keegan thundered.

"Well— I— there, there's this—" Kade stammered.

Aron came to Kade's rescue. "He could not. My father spells his men so they cannot speak of me to those who do not already know of me and my brothers. Please do not hate me."

"I don't hate you," Keegan admitted. "It just would've been nice to know."

"Would you have trusted me?"

"When I first met you, no. But I wouldn't've trusted anyone then. I didn't."

"How can you trust him now?" Kade seethed.

Coolly, Keegan turned to him. "The sins of the father are not the sins of the son."

"What?"

"Just cause Caius has done some shitty things doesn't mean Aron should pay for it, nor does it mean he's the same as his father."

A vein appeared in Kade's temple.

"I don't like that he didn't tell me, but he's a good guy. And unless there's some other major secret he's not telling me, it is what it is," she shrugged.

Jared shot Kade a look, which Keegan noticed.

She put her hands on her hips. "Is there something *you* need to tell me, Kade?"

"No," he answered.

She gave him a skeptical look then noticing her saddlebag on the table, asked, "So, where's my room?"

"Over here," Kade and Jared responded, jumping at the chance to keep her close, but more importantly, away from the other.

Keegan scrutinized them. "Kade, you hate Aron, Aron, you hate Jared, and, Jared, you hate Kade. Do I have that right?"

"I don't hate either of them," Aron offered sheepishly.

"Brilliant. And let me guess, you each took a room in separate wings, so I have to choose between the three of you."

Silence.

Taking her bag, she walked away, choosing a random wing.

✢✢✢

"She is nothing like I expected," Mahogen declared as they walked.

"Cannot disagree," Bernot said. "The leaders are going to have a field day with her."

"You summoned them?"

"What choice do I have? We need their support if we are going to wage and win this war."

"You have not told my father yet... I guess that is why you encouraged Lyerlly to keep me in the hospital?"

"Nothing gets past you," Bernot sighed, giving his friend a wry grin. "Tell the old man tonight, just keep her location to yourself. I do not need him messing up my plans."

Mahogen gave a hearty laugh. "What do you think he's going to do?"

"Try to marry her to you!"

Mahogen shrugged.

"I did you a favor. I cannot save you again."

393

"The only person you helped was you. But I know you love her to bits, and I admit, you suit Lyerlly much better than I ever could."

It was Bernot's turn to laugh. "No woman has ever suited you. You much prefer the other type."

"You know me too well."

"Why is he pushing you to marry anyway?"

"He wants me to get him a powerful pawn. And he wants to see grandchildren before his third century."

"Regardless that you have not even reached your third decade?"

"That, and the other factor."

"Yes, well, tell him. And count on him not being happy we kept it so long. Any later and there will be some serious trouble."

Mahogen turned down a street, bidding him a fair evening.

Bernot headed back to his office and considered taking the basket down, instead, he took the stairs to prolong the inevitable. On his desk, he found four slips of paper. Essentially, they were all the same; the leaders of the other nations would be there within the fortnight.

‡‡‡

Lucas leaned back against the wall, glaring at the others across the room. Against his warnings, all of them decided to consume copious amounts of beer and were singing rowdily with many of the inn's other tenants. He brought his tankard to his lips, taking a small sip of the amber liquid.

A man he had failed to notice before took a seat opposite him.

"Go away."

"You should hear what I 'ave t' say first," the stranger said.

"You have nothing important to say."

"I know your brother."

The words made Lucas pause. "How do you know him?"

"He stayed with my grandfather an' I in Suttan. Came with a man named Kade and a girl named Keegan."

The mention of Keegan made Lucas pay attention. "Why should I care?"

The man shrugged, "I just thought you might like t' know he 's safe."

"Which brother?" Lucas questioned, noticing the singularity of the statement.

"Jared."

Nico was still unaccounted for—and possibly dead. Lucas felt his anger rising and stared down at his hands, noticing the four white scars on each palm. "Who are you?"

"Reven."

"You came over here for something other than to give me news of my brother."

"I also wanted t' offer you retribution."

"How?"

"With a single death."

"The king's?"

"Yes."

Lucas gave a loud laugh, earning a few curious looks from the people around them. "Are you mad?"

"Hear me out. The castle 's riddled with secret passageways, most o' which the king 's unaware of. It 'll be easy t' sneak into his chambers and put a knife in 'im."

Lucas wanted to tell him no, that this was a *horrible* idea but his mouth responded, "Yes."

"Can we count your other brother in?"

Lucas looked over at Carter; Oslin was helping him down another tankard. Carter would never understand, even if he was doing it for him, for Jared. If he could rid the world of Caius, they would be safe, would never have to run, never live in fear, never lose a friend again. He wanted to say goodbye, but someone would stop him, talk sense into him. He stood up. "No. We should leave now, while my companions will be none the wiser."

Reven led the way from the inn.

As he mounted his horse, laughter drifted from the inn. He forced himself to ignore it. He was out to make history, to make the world better.

‡‡‡

"I need something that will make your brother tell me what I need to know," Thaddeus said. "Something that suggests I already know or something enough to... shock him into giving up the information."

"There is only one thing that will accomplish that; you need to know about our parents' death."

Thaddeus took a seat across from Alyck.

"Before my brother experienced his Nanagin, we lived in the north. Our closest neighbors were miles away and we were self-reliant. Caius has always been a strong telepath with immense control over his powers.

But several months before his Nanagin, he began to lose that control and became moody and reserved. He never confided in me what was happening.

"The day of his Nanagin, a group of bandits fell upon our house. Our parents were passive people and gave them what they wanted. But they wanted more and while our parents complied, my brother began to grow angry, and at its peak, he lost control. The telepathic wave he released was painful..." Alyck gave an involuntary shudder. "Well, that wave killed the bandits, our parents, and it was only by some miracle I survived. Realizing what he had done, he relapsed and continued to lose more and more control. I do not remember most of what happened next, but I do recall a blinding light and a surge of wind. When I was finally able to focus, I was at our neighbor's house and had been babbling nonsense for a week straight. When I enquired about my brother, I was told his body had not been found. Caius was absent from our world for five months."

"What were your parents' names?" Thaddeus asked.

"Meloda and Braxten. Surprisingly, Caius is sentimental."

"What was he like after he returned?"

"Cold, calculating. And his control had returned."

"This has been most helpful; thank you," Thaddeus said softly. "I can understand how sore of a subject this must be."

CHAPTER 54

Keegan rolled onto her back, giving a sigh of contentment. Outside the window, birds tweeted gaily, and the sun shone warmly. She pulled the covers up to her chin and nestled into the mattress. It was some time before she cajoled herself into getting up.

No one was in the kitchen—as she expected. Last night she'd quickly discovered the boys *just about* tolerated each other. When no longer needed, they retreated to their rooms, all bidding her to go with them. She swiftly made it clear that if they wanted to talk, they could come to her or stop fighting and talk in the common room.

Kade and Jared decided to sulk.

Being stubborn herself, she left them to brood and headed downstairs. It felt odd to be wearing a dress again, but she had little choice as her clothes were filthy or shredded. She found Bethsy in the common room, endeavoring to instruct the younger children in their lessons.

Seeing her, she came over. "Do you need something?"

"Uh, yeah. Is there somewhere I can do laundry?"

"Put them in the hamper and I will get them later."

"Cool, thanks."

Bethsy made to return to her charges.

"Is there anything I can help you with?"

Bethsy raised an eyebrow. "Can you read?"

"Yeah."

"Can you write?"

"Yeah." Keegan scrunched up her nose. "I mean, my handwriting's shit, but—"

"Do you know arithmetic?"

"Yeah, as long as you don't ask me to do anything past algebra."

"Algebra?"

"Never mind. Yeah, I can math."

Bethsy chuckled, before sending her to help some of the children read.

‡‡‡

The door opened so quietly Lyerlly almost did not notice the man coming into the hospital. She grumbled to herself upon seeing who it was— Okleiy Ustor, king of the Alvor. Bernot had told her he had been informed about Keegan, but she would not have guessed he would come directly to her. Had she not known him so well, she might have assumed he was in a good mood.

"Lyerlly," Okleiy said, walking towards her with open arms.

It was awkward to be hugging her once prospective father-in-law.

"Where is the girl?" he asked quietly into her ear.

She pulled away and began making her rounds. "You will have to be more specific." She did not need to look at him to know he was irritated.

"Keegan Digore. Where is she?"

"At a children's home, I believe," she said after giving Ty instructions to see to a patient.

Okleiy grabbed her arm—not forcefully, but the threat was still clear. "I tire of these games, where is she?"

Lyerlly pulled away. "I don't know, so you will have to ask Bernot. And even then, I cannot let you see her yet; she is much too weak still."

"If that were so, she would still be here."

"Under normal circumstances, yes. Okleiy, I know you want to use this girl for your own gains, so I suggest you do not try to."

"Who are you to tell me what I can and cannot do in my own kingdom, *human*?"

"It was only a suggestion. Now, anything more you will need to take up with my husband." She did not give him a chance to refute her dismissal. *Bernot,* she tested.

Yes, darling, came his response.

Okleiy is coming.

‡‡‡

It was mid-morning before Aron rose. He considered knocking on Keegan's door to wake her but decided to let her rest. Kade was breakfasting in the kitchen and gave him a steely glare. So, he decided to take his chances downstairs with the motley residents.

He found Behthany in the kitchen, cleaning dishes.

"Wanting breakfast?"

"Yes, if possible."

"Help yourself. Just put things away."

"Do you mind if I take some up for Keegan?"

"She has already eaten; was down ages ago." A silent moment followed. "She is helpful that one." His look of surprise elicited a chuckle. "She has been helping me with the children's morning studies." She pointed with a soapy finger, "In there, if you are wanting her."

398

Children sat at the table quietly working on their own projects with a few young ones huddled around Keegan, a little girl on her lap.

"The pri, ince said, 'I only have ey, ees for you, fair ma, aiden'," the girl struggled.

"There you go," Keegan encouraged. She began reading and after a few paragraphs let the girl take over for a few lines again.

Aron leaned against the door frame and watched. Feeling a tug on his shirt, he looked down.

"Read," a chubby three-year-old demanded, holding up a book.

Keegan glanced up, smiled, and called the boy back. "Nieda, one more page and it's your turn."

Nieda gave Aron a lingering look before tottering back.

Aron went to stand behind her. "How are you so good with them?"

"I like kids," she moved the girl from her lap onto the seat next to her then struggled to lift Nieda.

Aron picked up the boy and deposited him on her knee.

"Why don't you read with a few of them," she suggested.

"I am not sure I would be any good."

"It's not that hard. Just encourage them and help them when they struggle." She turned to the children sitting on the floor around her, "Who wants to read with Aron?"

They looked up at her blankly.

"He's a prince," she enticed.

A few girls raised their hands squealing.

"Go on then," Keegan said with a tilt of the head.

Aron took the girls to an adjacent table, feeling he wasn't much use. He glanced at Keegan; the ease with which she interacted with the children creating a new allure. He felt a heavy tap on his shoulder.

"What's this word?" Luci asked with a pout.

"Uh... 'eventually'."

Luci crossed her arms. "Do you love her?"

"Pardon?"

"Your sister."

"I... she is my sister... so of course."

"No, like *love* her," Aura said. "Like want to marry her."

"I have not known her long and—"

Aura cut him off, "He *so* loves her."

"I do not," Aron argued. "I mean, I do. Not like that. I, well—"

"You're going to marry her," Luci proclaimed.

It was futile to argue. The feeling was definitely not love, but he supposed it could grow into that over time. He thought of Shiloh and could not see himself creating a life with anyone else. Perhaps he might come to love Keegan in a familial and platonic way, but anything else, he could not imagine.

‡‡‡

Bernot sat in his office, running figures for the upkeep of the Lazado. It was one of his least favorite tasks, but it had to be done. A rap came from the door, mercifully pulling him away from the work. "Enter."

Okleiy Ustor traipsed in.

Bernot groaned. The Alvor king was like a second father to him, but that did not stop him from trying to gain ground and power whenever he could. "I assume you are here about Miss Digore," he said candidly.

"You would be correct." Okleiy took a seat in one of the wooden chairs across from him. "Where is she?"

"I cannot disclose that currently."

"And why is that?"

"Because I am afraid you will try to sway her."

Okleiy began to speak.

"I know what you will say, but a heavy burden weighs on her. It will do no good if someone has more hold over her than the others."

"At least until after the summoning."

"At least until then."

"But you have access to her."

"Only to test her skills in a few days hence. After which, contact will cease until the summoning."

Okleiy looked at him skeptically before rising and leaving abruptly.

After the door closed, Bernot leaned back in his chair, running a hand through his thick hair. He might have staved him off for the moment, but the Alvor was tenacious. He would pry and search and bribe until he found her.

He rang the bell on his desk, prompting Olyver to come in. "Please tell Hernando Barnsed I need him." He returned to his figures until the captain arrived.

Hernando was an older gentleman, his salt-and-pepper hair faded well back on his head. He had once been a great warrior, but a peaceful life had let him gain a few pounds. The man might not be what he once was, but Hernando was still one of the best swordsmen in the Lazado— and a trusted friend and advisor.

"Been ah long time since ya' called on me," Hernando said jovially.

400

"Times of peace make little use of soldiers. I take it you have heard of the mysterious girl who came into our midst about a week past."

"I 'ave. 'Ave heard a fair few rumors, too. Some say she is the king's renegade daughter. Others, an assassin sent for you, who was fool 'nough to fall on 'er own poisoned blade. 'N those 're just the sensible ones."

"None are true, but she is *very* important. I need you to place a guard on her. She is at Behthany Rhyen's with her three brothers."

"An' if the girl decides to leave the house?"

"Go with her. You are there to watch over her, not place her under house arrest. Who are your best men?"

"That would be Halcyon Brygh, Rhyse Velaz, and Wexsley Grioux."

"Good, use them."

"May I ask why she is so important?"

"Yes, but I will decline to answer. Dismissed. Oh, ask Mahogen to help as well, I think he has taken a liking to the girl."

‡‡‡

"Why did you make Alyck become the Blind Prophet?" Thaddeus asked.

"You have been spending too much time with my brother," Caius commented. "Now, get out of my chambers."

"Tell me what I need to know. I would not be asking if it were not important."

"There is absolutely no reason for you to know."

"You might be surprised," Thaddeus said. "Just so you know, Meloda and Braxten's deaths were not your fault."

The blood drained from Caius' face. "How... how do you know that?" He paused. "Alyck."

"Yes, but I am sure you have more to add."

"It was not my fault. It was this stupid bloodline."

Thaddeus nodded with understanding; guilt had been eating at Caius. All he had to do now was listen.

"Do you know how terrifying it is to see the future? How terrifying it is to see your family's death? Your brother's death? The visions kept playing in my head until they came true. Except for one; the only one I was able to prevent. Do you think I wanted to become king? I was more than happy with my life before all of *this* happened. I was content with being on the Council of Elders, content with being *normal*." Caius took a breath.

401

"Naturally, this has caused pent-up emotions. Start from the beginning, so I may understand," Thaddeus encouraged, channeling his inner parent.

Caius looked like he wanted to be persistent in his unwillingness to talk, but the floodgates had already sprung a leak. He took the chair from his desk and turned it to face Thaddeus. "Clearly, you already know how my parents died, but... there is a part of that story only I know; the reason I lost control. Several months before... the incident, I began having visions of the future. At first, they were trivial, like a slaughtered cow or a small injury. But then I started having visions of Alyck's death. For weeks, I dreamt a bolt of lightning would cast him down, and each day, it never happened. My nerves began to fray and at times I found myself losing control over my powers.

"The day the bandits attacked, that control was completely gone for a moment, and in that moment, I lost most of what was dear to me. The only thing that saved Alyck was my Nanagin. But while in the other world, I was sure my brother was dead, and grief prevented me from using my powers.

"I survived and returned. It took some time, but I eventually learned Alyck was alive—and well—and my powers returned, along with the ability to cast spells. I was so strong I was given a place on the Council of Elders.

"Everything was fine for a few years, but then the visions returned. I *had* to find a way to save Alyck—and myself, as I was beginning to lose control again. And I did. By making Alyck become the Blind Prophet, he lived. That vision has never come to pass," Caius finished.

"Noble through and through," Thaddeus said kindly. "Now, I shall take my leave and let you rest."

"I expect you to keep this information to yourself."

Thaddeus bowed his head as he shut the door, "Of course."

CHAPTER 55

The past three days had been long and boring. Jared only emerged from his room at mealtimes, and even that was done begrudgingly. Keegan and Aron were the only ones who spent time outside of their rooms. Soldiers had been sent to guard them—or more specifically, Keegan. She seemed at ease around them and was becoming friends with them.

Jared came out for breakfast and found Bernot and Mahogen sitting at the table. "What do you want?" he asked, pouring a glass of water.

"I need to test Keegan's skills."

"Humph," was his response. "I won't be the one to wake her."

"No need, she already knows we are here, and is just changing."

"I'm coming, too."

"Excellent. We will make an outing of it; Kade and Aron are also coming."

"All good," Keegan said as she adjusted the bottom of her rolled up pants, then yelled, "Aron, Kade."

Downstairs, Wexsley, one of guards, was waiting for them. He was a snively-looking man with watery eyes and large ears and Jared doubted he could do much in the way of fighting but supposed he wouldn't be there if he couldn't.

Wexsley took Keegan to the Gortlin Tree to descend in the basket, leaving the rest of them to climb down.

As soon as they emerged from the trees, a quiet overtook the practicing men. They slowly moved to the outskirts of the field, pushing against each other to ensure all had a good view.

"How many skill tests do you think you can do today?" Bernot asked Keegan.

She shrugged, "I dunno. I'll let you know when I've had enough. And I don't know how to do air, fire, or water."

Bernot scanned the crowd. "Oskare Ber."

People pushed apart to let a man through.

"Yes, sir," Oskare answered, his back straight and head held high.

"Do your best," was all Bernot said before turning the field over.

Jared reached for his magic preemptively should Oskare go too far and had the feeling Kade did likewise.

Oskare started slow and Keegan lazily shot a rock at him, which he returned in kind. But rather than stopping his rock, she let it sail past, which wasn't her usual style; she was more likely to show her strength.

Jared crossed his arms, wondering what game she was getting at.

403

Keegan raised the earth around her and idly began to shoot sections at Oskare. He focused on blocking the projectiles and failed to notice he was sinking into the ground. By the time he did, he was entrapped up to his knees. Seeing he'd realized her ploy, she sunk him up to his shoulders instantly.

He seemed surprised she'd defeated him so easily.

Keegan smiled and offered a hand to help him up. He accepted warily and gave her an embarrassed glance before melting back into the mass of men. Snickers followed him and Jared felt a twinge of sympathy.

The subsequent opponent was an Alvor. Jared could tell she knew she was beat, but in her usual stubborn manner, attempted to fight regardless. The match didn't last long, ending with her kneeling, after the Alvor took her vision.

Bernot stepped forward for the telepathy skill test.

She appeared to be at her limit and Jared was about to call for Bernot to stop when he decided against it; she usually knew her limits and if he tried to save her, she would surely have choice words later. So, he watched.

Bernot's face was calm while Keegan had her eyes shut, looking as if she was struggling to keep him from her mind. She clenched her fists in determination and her eyes snapped open. Suddenly, Bernot was thrown across the field.

There was a hush as they all stared in shock then a few men rushed over to help him to his feet.

He brushed them off and went to talk quietly to Keegan, her eyes wide as she shook her head and shrugged often. He offered her an arm, which she accepted, and they walked from the field.

Jared started to follow them, but Wexsley stopped him. "I'm to walk you back home."

"But… Keegan," Aron argued.

"Bernot will take her back later, there are things he wants to discuss with her."

Jared looked back to the field and no longer could see her or Bernot. Aware that protesting was pointless, he followed Wexsley. He expected Kade to be fuming, and it was then he realized he wasn't with them either. "Where's Kade?" he hissed.

‡‡‡

As he watched Oskare test Keegan, he was pulled away from the match by someone asking, "Are you Kade Tavin?"

He turned to look at the man, an Alvor. He was tall and holding an air of grace, his brown hair was layered with leaf green streaks and large golden horns protruded from his head. "Who's asking?"

"The king of the Alvor."

His stomach dropped. It was never a good idea to insult an Alvor, even less if it was their king.

"Walk with me."

Kade stole a glance at Keegan.

"Do not worry, she is in good hands."

Feeling like he had no choice, Kade followed.

Once they were away from the crowd, the king introduced himself, "I am Okleiy Ustor. I believe you know my son, Mahogen."

In no mood for pleasantries, he forgot who he was dealing with. "What do you want?"

"I want you to be a bit more gracious," Okleiy scolded.

He swallowed his pride. "Sorry, my friends and I haven't been getting along of late."

"Yes, you and your brothers seem to be in discord over your sister. Though, you are the only one with the right to decide her fate as her *biological* brother."

Kade cursed to himself. "How do you know that?"

"It is hard to miss," Okleiy huffed. "You look so much alike."

"Keep that observation to yourself."

"Of course. Under one stipulation, you join me for dinner tonight."

There had to be something the king wanted, Alvor were notoriously tricky. "Sure. We'll join you tonight."

"No, no, no. Only you."

"Fine."

"Excellent, I will have Mahogen escort you."

Turning to head back to the training field he realized the tests had finished. He changed his path to take him to a ladder. Once reaching where one should've been, he realized he had no way to access it.

"Let me," Okleiy said, placing a hand on the tree, bringing forth the ladder.

He didn't bother thanking him and began to climb. Up in the city, he struggled to make his way back to the children's home. Upstairs, he found Jared and Aron sitting at the table anxiously.

"Where have you been?" Jared snapped.

"Places," he answered snidely. "Where's Keegan?"

"If you'd stayed, you would know," Jared fumed, storming to his room.

"Where is she?" he asked Aron.

"No idea; she went off with Bernot."

Kade glared at him, then went to his room, letting the door slam behind him.

‡‡‡

Bernot took Keegan to the Gortlin Tree and was surprised she had no qualms about leaving her brothers behind. His head was still pounding from the attack that had sent him across the field. Never had he seen, or experienced, something like that and was curious to know how she had done it.

They reached the tree and he was about to call down the basket when she stopped him, insisting she was strong enough to climb the stairs. She managed, even if going slow. Now, they sat in his office.

He inhaled before beginning. "I see you are well-versed in earth magic and have a good start on life magic. As for telepathy…"

"Yeah, sorry about that," she said, rubbing the back of her neck. "I'm not really sure how I did that."

She knows she is powerful but does not know just how much power she contains. "How did you come to this world?"

"Hell if I know. Magic probably."

"Do you trust Jared, Aron, and Kade?"

She raised an eyebrow. "What, you afraid they kidnapped me or something?"

He gave her an austere look.

"They might be childish and hard-headed, but they're good guys. Aron helped me escape from Caius, Jared took me in, and Kade, in his own twisted way, helped us avoid the Vosjnik."

"You still did not answer the question. Do you trust them?"

"I wouldn't've stuck with 'em if I didn't."

"You are free to roam the city after I give you your yewnes."

"Yewnes?"

"It is what will allow you to access the hidden ladders and doorways of the city."

"Ah."

"I do ask that you stay away from Okleiy Ustor until the summoning."

Keegan gave him a muddled look. "Couple of questions; who is Okleiy Ustor, and what's the summoning?"

406

"Okleiy is the king of the Alvor. And the summoning is where the leaders, or representatives from every nation convene. In this case, our reason is you."

"Cause we're the Children of Prophecy." She stifled a yawn. "If there isn't anything else, do you mind if I go? I'm beat."

"Beat?"

"Tired."

"Of course; let me walk you back." Bernot picked up the bag next to his desk and slung it over his shoulder.

"What's in the bag?" she questioned as he ushered her through the door.

"Your weapons."

"I bet the boys will be excited to get them back. Probably will use 'em to stick each other."

"I bet they will," Bernot chuckled, though he worried at the potential verity of her statement. He was glad to have spoken with her, even if his real reason was to keep her away from Okleiy, whom he had espied earlier.

As soon as she entered the children's home, young children flooded to her. Her face lit up and Bernot let her take her time, giving Behthany a passing acknowledgement.

Upstairs, Aron sat at the kitchen table reading a book. "There you are," he said with relief.

Bernot set the bag on the floor and extracted a bow and arrows, which Aron took excitedly.

"You can leave the rest," Keegan told him. "We'll distribute things."

"I still need to give you a yewne," Bernot reminded her and took her hand. He muttered a few words in the Old Language and when he pulled away, a small dot marked the side of her palm.

"What'd you do?" she asked, examining the mark. "That wasn't elemental magic."

"That was a spell," Bernot told her, repeating the process with Aron.

"But you would need to be a spellcaster..." Aron trailed off.

Bernot gave him a cunning smile then went into Kade and Jared's rooms.

On his way out, he stopped to talk to Behthany. "If you see Okleiy around here, let me know."

"Sweetie, if my father comes here, the whole city is going to bovestun well know about it," Behthany told him. "Do not worry, he will not be corresponding with your precious Child of Prophecy."

‡‡‡

For several days, Nico had noticed a strange scent on Braxton, and it'd taken him some time to place it. Once he'd realized Braxton smelled like the griffins, he decided to confront him about it. But to do so, he needed to catch him in the stables and had therefore spent the last few days looking for the secret passageway that led there.

So far, he'd found just about every other hidden corridor as he only roughly recalled where to find the entrance. Most of the passages led to empty rooms, though one led to the coffers. He was tempted to take as much gold as he could stuff into his pockets, then realized he had nothing to spend it on—and should he be caught, only bad things would come of it.

As always, he checked over his shoulder to make sure he was alone and began running his hands along the wall, eventually finding the divot. The wall scraped along the floor and taking a torch from its mounting, he made his way through the passage.

The trip was much easier with light and he wondered how Braxton navigated so well blind. When he came to the top of the stairs, he pulled a lever and the door opened smoothly. He peered around, and saw Braxton sitting on the floor, stroking Myrish's feathers.

Myrish turned to look at Nico, drawing Braxton's attention.

Braxton rest his head against the wall. "I knew your curiosity would hold you back only so long. Providing no one knows you know they exist, you are welcome to visit."

Not the response he expected. He closed the door and went to sit next to them. "I didn't come for the griffins."

Braxton raised an eyebrow. "Then why did you?"

"To see you."

"How did you figure I would be here of all places?"

"You smelled like them. It took me a bit to place, but then I recognized it: feathers and dust with a hint of iron and wind."

"What does wind smell like?" Braxton asked.

Freedom, a griffin with lackluster silver feathers answered.

"I'm sorry, but I don't remember your names," Nico said sheepishly.

The griffin laughed. *Our introductions were hasty, feel no shame. I am Niyth.*

The other griffins re-introduced themselves and Nico committed their names to heart. *I am glad to properly make your acquaintance,* he said, speaking to them telepathically for the first time.

We see your studies with Azure are going well, Oxren said. His feathers were black and mottled with white.

Nico was surprised they knew about it, yet somehow not. "Why have you been spending all your time here?"

Braxton gave him a sad smile, "Adult things. Now, run along, tomorrow's training is going to be trying."

Realizing he would get nothing from Braxton, he got to his feet. *Goodnight, Phynex,* he said to the griffin with a tint of red in its feathers then paused, trying to recall the name of the dark gray one. *Goodnight, Crowlin. Goodnight, Oxren. Goodnight, Niyth. Goodnight, Myrish.* He was going to have to use their names repeatedly to remember them. Then he turned back to Braxton, "By the way, whatever's bothering you, you can tell me about it; I'm good at keeping secrets."

CHAPTER 56

It felt right to have his sword belted around his waist again. It was even more comforting to have the hidden knife in his boot. Kade walked beside Mahogen through the city, dusk settling around them. He'd managed to slip from the house with only a few of the children noticing and Mahogen had been waiting for him a few houses down.

"Be courteous when talking to my father," Mahogen warned. "He can be a bit *touchy* with humans."

"He'll take what he gets from me," Kade said snidely. "I have no intention of playing games."

"Games may not be what you want, but games are what you will get. We Alvor live for play on words, so be careful when accepting a deal. It may not be exactly what you think."

"Why aren't you like that?"

"I choose not to be. It only sows mistrust and animosity."

They stopped outside a massive house nestled in the fork of a tree.

"And here is where I leave you," Mahogen said, motioning to the door.

"Aren't you joining us?" Kade questioned, suddenly realizing how helpful the prince might be.

"No, I was not invited."

He watched Mahogen retreat for a moment before turning to the house. Apprehensively, he stepped forward and knocked; it seemed an eternity before someone answered. He was greeted by a servant and shown to the dining room.

A massive chandelier hung from the ceiling, the crystals sending rainbows scattering across the walls. A long table was set for four, Okleiy sitting at the head with a woman on either side. One was older, whom Kade took to be Okleiy's wife. The other was young and stunning, her lips the color of a ruby. When she smiled, she revealed straight, pearly teeth. High cheekbones gave her an elegant look and long, honey-colored tresses were piled on her head with autumn red lowlights. The tips of two golden horns just protruded over the top of her head. She turned to look at him with rich blue eyes.

"Heh-hem," Okleiy said, bringing his attention back. "This is my wife Aster and my daughter Shyre."

"Pleasure to meet you," he said, more to Shyre than Aster.

"Take a seat."

Kade hurried to sit beside Shyre, a faint scent of pine emanating from her.

A plate of quail and vegetables was set before him, the smell making his mouth water. He almost began eating when he remembered his manners and waited for Okleiy to take the first bite. The quail tasted magnificent and after a few bites, he remembered to make small talk. "Shyre… you…" His brain chose that moment to stop working.

Shyre looked to her father disappointed, "I hoped this one would remember how to speak."

"—are beautiful," Kade blurted. As soon as the words left his mouth, he regretted them.

"How sweet of you," she said.

Her voice had a hypnotic quality that somehow calmed him. "I'm sure your husband tells you that every day."

"He would, if I had one."

Kade melted at the words.

"Make no rash promises," Aster said preemptively.

He looked at the plate in front of him guiltily.

"I think it would be a fine match," Okleiy said. "Of course, I will need something from you though."

There it was the real reason for this dinner. "And what would that be?"

"I have been trying for quite some time to find Mahogen a wife. It has been a hard task, but it seems he has taken a liking to your sister. I would propose a union between them."

Kade laughed, causing the Alvors to frown. "She'll never go for it."

"You can make her."

"Yes, just like I can make the sun rise," he said haughtily, making Aster purse her lips.

"I recommend you find a way."

"And if I don't?"

"There are numerous people who are calling for your head," Okleiy said calmly, "And I would feel bad if Caius was not reunited with his son. I know it is what I would want."

Kade wanted nothing more than to fly across the table. He couldn't care less about the threat to Aron, but those made to him weren't taken lightly.

"I protect my family fiercely," Okleiy continued.

"There's only so much I can do to convince her."

"You are her brother. As the head of your family, she must listen to you."

"But she—"

411

"Will listen to you. And, of course, this will stay between us until the vows are exchanged. I would have them said the day after the summoning. Now, let us talk of other matters. How are you liking the city?"

He was forced to make idle chatter, answering questions curtly and with little enthusiasm. Beauty had lost its charm, and he felt like a rat in a cage. None too soon he was saying goodnight.

Shyre walked him to the door and gave him a parting kiss on the cheek; it felt like a punch to the face. The sky was dark, a quarter moon adding its pale light to the lanterns along the street.

He walked away from the house quickly, pulling at the collar of his shirt, already feeling steel against his throat. He had no idea what he was going to do, but he was going to need a massive stroke of luck to pull it off.

‡‡‡

If he thought Tratoleck was a big city, he was mistaken; the city of Agrielha was monstrous. Lucas was amazed so many people could fit in one place. Reven seemed unperturbed and easily led them to an inn on the outskirts that possessed a certain criminal element.

Once they deposited their bags in a room, they picked a dark corner and settled in. Lucas hadn't asked much about Reven and his companion had done likewise.

Reven glanced around, making sure no one was paying them any attention and pulled a piece of parchment from his pocket, flattening it on the table. "Time t' come up with a plan."

"What's this?" Lucas probed, trying to decipher the squiggles across the page.

"A map o' the castle's secret passageways."

"Where did you get this?"

"I drew it. My grandfather made me memorize these tunnels as a child. I despised 'im for it at the time, but who knew it 'd become useful?"

"Explains why it looks like vite," Lucas muttered, wondering what kind of family Reven came from.

"There 're several outside entrances t' the castle, but only one that starts in the city." He pointed to a place on the map, "Here."

"You act like this means something to me. I can't make heads or tails of this royiken mess."

Reven gave him a frustrated look, "You do n't need t' be able to' read it. Now, the problem is, I do n't know where within this inn the entrance is."

"Wait, the entrance is *here*?"

"I just said that. For now, our problem 's finding the tunnel and doin' so without raising suspicion. Any ideas?"

Lucas' side began to throb as he was reminded of Elza's harebrained scheme. He got the feeling this mission might have a similar outcome. "I won't help you. This plan's going to get me killed."

"You can n't leave now."

"Why not?"

"You do n't know how t' get to the Lazado," Reven stated plainly, still looking over the map. "If you help me, I 'll take you there."

"I'm sure I can find a Kojote to take me."

Reven gave a snort of laughter, "Good luck. It 's hard enough t' find one in any other city; forget 'bout finding one here under Caius' ever-watchful eye."

Lucas pulled the knife from his boot and held it against Reven's side. "I won't help you." Dismay filled him when his hand, of its own accord, sheathed the knife.

Reven turned his wrist over, exposing his elemental mark, "Do n't threaten me. I will n't make you help me, but I would suggest it. You will n't be able to find a Kojote."

"Then you've played my hand for me," Lucas snarled.

"No, I 'ave simply presented you with the only option of getting to the Lazado—*and* back to your brothers."

"You'll pay for this."

"Not anytime soon."

‡‡‡

"Why does no one understand what causes a Blind Prophet to begin acquiring their powers?" Thaddeus fumed.

"Possibly because no one understands the magic surrounding it," Alyck suggested.

"That makes a deal of sense," Thaddeus agreed. "I might be able to parse it if I had the original spell."

"I can help with that."

"You know the original spell used to create the Blind Prophet?"

Alyck gave him a wry smile, "No."

"Out with it," Thaddeus said, not in the mood for games. It was often hard to remember that Alyck was centuries older than him—especially as he still acted the age he looked.

Alyck walked away but returned quickly, bearing a piece of parchment. "I think this what you need."

"Where did you get it?"

"From a very dear friend." There was sorrow in the words. "Now, I think I shall retire for the night."

Thaddeus gave him a nod of acknowledgement, his attention already on the spell. It was lengthy, taking up most of the page and well thought out; it took a few readings to fully understand all its facets.

He already knew that the Blind Prophet was linked to the ruling bloodline, but the interesting bit was that as long as someone of the lineage remained alive, the Prophet would continue to live. Thaddeus thought about the implications; Caius could be removed without Alyck suffering ramifications.

However, there was no mention of how the next Prophet was chosen, aside from the fact that they would come from Angela's bloodline, and there were no telling what factors caused them to obtain their powers. From Caius' story, it had taken years, and at one point, the process had ceased. He hoped the crown's successor was years away from taking the throne, otherwise Braxton was in for a rude awakening.

‡‡‡

There was a knock.

"Come in," Keegan called.

Aron poked his head through the doorway. "Want to go for a walk?"

She looked out the window to see sunset darkening the sky. "Why not?"

In the common room, Halcyon had to dislodge a few children off his lap to chase after them.

"Let's lose him," she said mischievously.

Aron raised an eyebrow but taking her hand, began to run and laugh.

When they finally stopped, she clutched at a stitch on her side, while fireflies danced around them like grounded stars. She pulled her hand from his and chased after the bugs; after catching one, she showed it to Aron. The firefly crawled across her finger before taking flight with a parting flash.

"I used to do this all the time as a kid," she said happily.

"It looks like fun," he commented.

"Wait, have you never caught fireflies before?"

"No…" Aron said, rubbing the back of his neck. "My father never allowed it."

"Oh, now you have to!"

"How do I do this?"

"See the bug and catch it. Just make sure you cup your hands, otherwise you're gonna have a squished bug."

Stepping back, she watched him attempt to catch one; he was close, though unprepared for the light to disappear. But once he got the hang of it, caught them as well as she.

They chased the fireflies until true stars replaced them and then started walking back; it wasn't long before they could see the children's home. Suddenly, Aron pulled her into a side alley, pushed her against the wall, and placed his hands beside her shoulders.

She gave him a questioning look, wondering about the gleam in his eyes. He answered by looking at her ardently and slowly moved forward. Too surprised to react, she felt his lips press against hers, begging for a retort. Caught in the moment, she responded in kind and he drew her closer, the heat of his body familiar and comforting.

Her senses were slow to return then she found her hands resting on his chest and pushed him away. Instantly hurt and confusion registered in Aron's eyes. Not knowing what to do, she ducked under his arm and ran back to the children's home, pausing in the doorway to see him staring after her. Leaving the door open, she hurried up the stairs, locked herself in her room, and sat against the door, running her hands through her hair as conflicting emotions raced through her.

‡‡‡

A sudden feeling of shame overtook Aron, and he silently berated himself for kissing her. How could she ever want someone like him? How could he let go of Shiloh so easily? Slowly, he returned to the children's home, taking a very round-about path.

Halcyon reappeared as he reached the doorway, angrily asking, "Why in tarnation did you two run off?"

He shrugged. Inside, a few of the older children lounged in the common room; none spared him a second glance. On their floor, all was quiet.

Walking to Keegan's door, he raised a hand to knock, then paused; forcing her to acknowledge what had just happened would only make things worse—for both of them. Turning on his heels, he went to his room and with nothing better to do, crawled into bed.

He intended to sleep, but his mind had other ideas, replaying his brash decision. The kiss had been euphoria, but now he resented it. He should have never done it. Why the royik had he?

The door opened and a figure slipped in. He wondered if it was Kade finally coming to stick a knife in his chest.

The figure tiptoed over. "You awake?" Keegan whispered.

He breathed a sigh of relief. "Yes."

She crawled into the bed and sat cross-legged beside him. "Can we talk?"

"Uh, sure."

"Look," she began, "I—"

"I need to apologize about… earlier. I really don't know what came over me…" It was hard to see the expression on her face, but he hoped it was soft.

"Who did you leave behind?"

"No one. She was murdered."

"I'm sorry," she said softly. "I understand. My family might not be dead, but they might as well be."

He was confused by the statement at first, then realized what she meant; she would never see her family again. "I never thought of you going through that."

She quickly turned the subject away from herself, "What was your girl's name?"

"Shiloh," Aron choked.

"Tell me about her."

"She was beautiful, and kind… and mine. Wonderfully mine."

They continued to talk well into the night, each word lifting a weight from his shoulders that he had not known was there. By the time they stopped, the moon was no longer visible in the sky.

He was not sure how it happened, but she fell asleep beside him. "Thank you for letting me talk. You will never know what it means to me," he whispered, draping an arm over her stomach and pulling her close.

In response, her fingers intertwined with his.

CHAPTER 57

Braxton looked away as his father was stabbed. When he opened his eyes again, he was in his room, morning light coming through the window, his father presumably alive. Throwing back the covers, he dressed, made his way to Caius' chambers, raised a hand, and knocked.

"Enter."

Braxton did so and paused; something was different.

Caius seemed nervous and gave an unsure smile. "What do you need... son?"

"I... never mind." He had come prepared to tell him about his dream, but this was not the man he knew.

"All right," Caius said, averting his gaze.

Out in the hall, Braxton lingered, brows knitted together. So much was not as it should be that he did not know where to begin. The wheels in his head turned, but nothing was coming of it. Giving up on trying to figure out what was going on with his father, he made his way to the griffins.

When Caius commanded him to begin training with the griffins, he had been too afraid to fly with them. Somehow, they cajoled him into taking them on their first flight no later than July twenty-second. He had put it off as long as he could, but the day had come to live up to his word.

He longed to go via the passageway but knew it would be suspicious if no one could account for where he spent the day. Inside the stable, the griffins were waiting excitedly, anticipation hanging in the air like electricity and poison.

"You promised to behave yourselves," Braxton said, approaching Myrish.

Believe me, I will, Myrish said.

Braxton took one of the saddles from the anterior room and situated it on Myrish's back.

The griffin stamped his feet impatiently.

Braxton did the buckles and pulled back the iron grate from the opening in the wall. "No funny business," he said, beginning to unlock the bond from around Myrish's neck.

Myrish did not answer, but the waves of joy were enough that Braxton knew he would do as promised. He took a breath and pulled himself into the saddle, feeling the beast's muscles tense. He quickly strapped his legs in before giving Myrish the go ahead.

The world froze for a moment before the griffin was running, his talons clacking against the stone floor. Myrish leapt through the opening, thrusting them into nothingness.

Braxton's stomach rose into his chest and pushed against his throat.

The ground below rushed towards them and Braxton closed his eyes, terrified that Myrish was too weak to stay aloft. There was a jerk as the griffin unfurled his wings and they soared on a wind current into the clouds.

You can let go now, Myrish told him.

Braxton slowly released his iron-clad grip on Myrish's feathers and looked down and, amazed by the beautiful scene below; the grass a magnificent green and spots of whites and yellow signified patches of wildflowers. His heart beat fast with excitement and the wind against his body was refreshing. *This is amazing.* There was something about flying that was exuberating, liberating. Here, the only prisons were the ones you created.

A humming sense of bliss came from Myrish.

A smile traced his lips and he let the griffin soar across the sky. When the castle became small behind them, he reluctantly told Myrish to turn back. All he had to do was let the griffin keep going and every bit of pain would melt away. But he could not leave the others behind—nor Nico.

Upon their return, the other griffins excitedly talked to Myrish in their wild language.

As he began to unsaddle Myrish, he noticed someone in the stable. "Nico?"

The boy came from one of the stalls.

"What are you doing here?"

"I wanted to see the griffins."

"You care for them?"

He shrugged. "I suppose."

"Good, I think I have a job for you."

"What?"

"Come back tomorrow and see. Now, I am sure Eamon has something for you to practice. And if I catch you here again during training hours, I will ban you."

The boy bit his cheek but left without another word.

What do you have planned for him? Crowlin asked.

‡‡‡

Two weeks passed quietly and Kade seldom saw the others. All interactions with Keegan were awkward, as he had yet to tell her she was going to marry Mahogen. There were times he tried, but the timing never felt right. When he was not hiding in his room, he was roaming the city or training. Swordplay was the best at helping him forget the predicament, but only so long as an opponent pressed him. The moment his weapon froze, all his worries came flooding back.

He emerged from his room, prepared to go to the training field but to his surprise, found Wexsley climbing the stairs to their floor.

"I'm here to take you to the summoning," Wexsley huffed. "Please dress in the clothes you were given."

His stomach dropped—he was out of time. "I'll get Keegan." He wiped his palms on his pants before knocking on her door. No response. He knocked again. "Keegan." Nothing. "Keegan!"

She pulled open the door.

It appeared she was wearing one of Aron's shirts—without any bottoms.

"What?" she said, rubbing the sleep from her eyes.

His mind blanked and he found anger rising.

She snapped her fingers, "Hellooo, earth to Kade."

He grabbed her arm and pulled her into the room, door slamming behind them. "What are you doing with him?"

"What?"

"You're wearing Aron's shirt; why?"

"Dude, it's my pajamas."

"Your what?"

"It's what I sleep in. What'd you need?"

"It's time for the summoning."

The color faded from her already pale features. She took a breath and pulled a pristine, white dress from the closet.

Knowing her, it wouldn't remain white for very long. "I need to talk to you."

"Can it wait?"

"Not really."

"Face the door."

He did so, heart beating wildly. "You know Mahogen?"

"Yeah...?"

"...You're going to marry him. Tomorrow."

She gave a nervous laugh.

"I'm not joking."

"What?" she exclaimed.

419

He turned back to face her and could see she was trying to keep calm. "You have to marry him."

"Like hell I do! Who the fu—"

He came as close to pleading as he would allow himself, "Keegan, please. You *have to* marry Mahogen."

"Why do I have to?" When he didn't respond, she snapped, "Kade!"

"Okleiy's going to hand Aron and I over to Caius if you don't."

Red flooded her face. "I'm gonna kill him. I swear to god, I'm gonna kill him." She eyed him. "How long have you known?"

"Couple of weeks."

She hit him in the arm. "A couple of weeks!"

"I'm sorry."

"Sorry ain't gonna cut it." She angrily pulled open the door. "Wexsley, I need to talk to Bernot. *Now.*"

"He's unavailable until after the summoning," Wexsley told her, taken aback by her anger. "Kade, get dressed, the leaders don't like to be kept waiting."

"It's important," Keegan persisted.

"My apologies, but it's not possible until after the summoning."

Keegan turned back to Kade. "Get ready, we'll deal with this later. Provided I don't frickin' strangle you first," she said menacingly. "And keep it between us. Lord knows Aron and Jared'll only make matters worse."

‡‡‡

The leaders and their adjutants sat around the concentric table. Bernot studied each carefully, wondering who would cause the most trouble. None knew why they were here—except for himself, Okleiy, and their adjutants. Okleiy had brought Mahogen, and he, Hernando. He had no doubt the other leaders would trample each other to get to Keegan once they learned of her.

We're here, Wexsley informed him.

May we begin? Tahrin said impatiently, speaking so that all present could hear.

"We may." Bernot went to a stand in the center of the congregation. "For centuries, we have hidden behind the border to evade Caius. He has made life for humans a Heill. We have all but given up on defeating him. Our only lasting hope was—"

"The Child of Prophecy," Garne Skaagg finished.

420

Bernot could tell the Torrpeki was already beginning to understand what was happening. "Precisely."

"Do you mean to tell us you found the Child of Prophecy?" Atlia Mahiako questioned, leaning forward.

The heir to the Merfolk throne was young and untried and Bernot was interested to see if she possessed her mother's intellect. Siene had not given a reason as to why her daughter was present in her stead, but it might be a blessing if Atlia was willing to join the cause.

"Not just one," Bernot told the crown princess, "all four."

The other leaders looked at him skeptically, most trying to figure out the game he was playing.

I see no children, Tahrin stated tetchily.

Bernot called for the doors to open and the first thing he saw was Keegan standing before the others, almost in a protective manner. She took a moment, before shyly joining him in the center of the room.

It was hard to believe these were the same people he had taken in just weeks past. The boys were clean-shaven and bathed—no longer frenzied-looking. Keegan appeared much stronger, with a determined air about herself—something that had not changed. He prayed *she* was not going to be the instigator today.

"May I present Keegan Digore, Kade Tavin, Jared Sieme, and Aron Alagard."

Kade and Aron received glares, their names being well-known.

Bernot took Keegan around the room and introduced her personally to the leaders. Tahrin and Rangi were the only ones to give her icy acknowledgments.

What makes you think these are the Children of Prophecy? Tahrin said, speaking to only the leaders.

Keegan stared at Tahrin with a look of astonishment.

Close your mouth, the dragon snarled at her.

"I- I- I'm s-sorry," she stammered. "I've just never seen a dragon before. You're really fucking cool."

Tahrin held her head a little higher. *Where is your proof?* Her tone was softer now; flattery went a long way with dragons.

"Keegan," Bernot held out a hand for her arm.

Sighing, she gave it to him, and he showed the leaders.

Only Hernando and the Alvor were not in an uproar.

The Buluo adjutant, Sabi, a youth with wily, wolfish features, vaulted over the table and snatched her arm. Thankfully, she refrained from clouting the boy, who began trying to remove the marks. When he could not, he snapped, "Prove it. Prove you can use all the elements."

421

She snatched her hand back, giving Sabi a nervous glare. Taking a deep breath, she caused a column of earth to rise and held it for a moment. She looked to the Buluo with a sly smile and a look of discomfort overtook the boy's face as he began scratching his armpits and hooting.

Garne chuckled unabashedly while Atlia was more tactful, only letting a grin flash across her features.

Once Keegan released him, Sabi slinked back to his seat beside Rangi, eyes diverted towards the floor.

"That was two," Rangi said.

"I can't do any of the others yet," Keegan admitted.

"Then what use are you?"

"She can learn," Bernot said, rounding the table to retake his seat.

"Which element?" Garne asked, already understanding.

"*That* is what we need to discuss," Bernot answered.

‡‡‡

They stood in the center of the room while the leaders talked. So far, it seemed like things were just getting started. Each leader was vying for control of Keegan, and seemed to have forgotten about him, Aron, and Kade. Once it was established they obeyed the laws of magic, they became of little interest.

"She should train under us," Garne, the Torrpeki representative, argued. "She is obviously most advanced in earth magic. We should focus on perfecting this element."

"No," Atlia argued. "If she is already versed there, teach her something new."

Jared shifted his feet. He was beginning to feel anger, but not his own. Pulling away from the discussion, he glanced at Keegan. Her fists and jaw were clenched. He nudged her. "Are you okay?"

"Shut up," she said through gritted teeth.

He gave her a questioning look but realized she hadn't heard him.

"Shut up," she repeated slightly louder, then in a normal voice, "Shut up."

Bernot grew quiet and patiently waited for her to continue.

"Shut up," she said loudly.

Tahrin heard and shifted her attention. *Excuse me?*

"Shut up!" Keegan yelled.

A wave of energy rolled over Jared and from the looks on the leaders' faces, they'd felt it too.

"What gives any of you the right to decide what *I* do?" she yelled.

Lower— the dragon started.

"Shut up!"

Jared opened his mouth and discovered he had no voice. Several of the leaders were coming to the same realization.

"None of you have any control over me," Keegan said, beginning a tirade. "I don't have to do jack-shit—let alone kill Caius. But it seems the goddamn universe has other ideas. So, here's what's gonna happen; y'all can't get across the border and until you can, I'm useless. I'm gonna spend six months training in each element. All y'all have do is decide which order it's in. I'd recommend going in a circle: earth, water, air, fire, life, or in reverse. Take your pick, I don't give a damn," she finished, storming off.

"Where do you think you are going?" Okleiy demanded.

"Away from you idiots. Oh, and I'm not marrying Mahogen. And Okleiy, if you *ever* threaten my friends again, I swear to god I'll rip your fucking head off."

"Do not threaten me," Okleiy snarled, rising to his feet.

"That wasn't a threat, that was a goddamned promise." She didn't give them time to stop her again.

Mahogen gave the tension a moment before chasing after her.

Jared started to go after her as well.

Who gave you permission to leave? Tahrin demanded.

"Kee—" he started.

Stay where you are.

He considered disobeying, but the look Tahrin gave him said it would be unwise.

‡‡‡

Although Nico knew where the griffin stable was, he would never have been able to find it if asked to go there via any way but the secret passage. He supposed this was done on purpose.

Inside, the griffins were waiting for them, along with two new additions, half the size of their compatriots and covered in dull brown feathers. In places, new fledging was beginning to show through with their true colors.

"Who are they?" Nico approached the newcomers and let them smell his hand before ruffling the feathers on their heads.

I am Ima, a feminine voice announced, coming from the griffin with the teal tint beginning to emerge on her feathers.

I am Harker, said the one with dark golden feathers mingling within the brown.

"Why haven't I seen them before?"

"Ima and Harker are hatchlings," Braxton explained. "They were kept in the nursery until yesterday."

Nico took a seat between Ima and Harker. "What was the job you had for me?"

"I am too big to fly with the hatchlings, so I want you to train with them."

"*Me?*" Never in his wildest dreams had he imagined flying. "Of course; I would be honored."

Braxton smiled. "Let us get them tacked up then."

Saddling the griffins was much like saddling Brewer, but much easier as Ima and Harker weren't nearly as large as the Clydesdale. He decided to fly with Harker first. The griffin tried to aid in his saddling, but often just made it more difficult. Rather than getting frustrated, Nico found himself laughing.

When he climbed onto Harker's back, anticipation, dread, and excitement mixed with his blood. The griffin carefully made his way towards the ledge, sticking his head into the sky.

Oxren, with Braxton on his back, barreled past, hurtling into the air, keeping his wings tight, and plummeted towards the ground. Just before crashing was imminent, he unfurled his wings, skimming over the top of the grass.

Nico leaned forward carefully. Processing how far up they were, he jerked back quickly. Gulping, he encouraged Harker to follow.

The hatchling gathered his courage and jumped. Opening his wings, he pumped them, and though they kept falling, it wasn't at an alarming rate. With each beat of the wings, Nico's heart bounced in his chest.

Oxren rushed past them, giving a caw. Nico could hear Braxton laughing and realized how exuberating it must be—well, when not on the wings of a fledgling. Harker did his best to keep up but was too inexperienced to do all the graceful maneuvers and it wasn't long before he was exhausted, and they had to turn back.

Braxton saw them returned safely before Oxren darted away again.

Nico unsaddled the griffin, then sat with the hatchlings. Harker fell asleep quickly and Ima was content to let him run his fingers through her downy feathers.

As he sat with the griffins, he realized he'd gained that which he thought he'd lost forever: family. He might not be of the same race as the griffins or the same blood as Braxton, but they were family.

CHAPTER 58

If it was possible to see the world in red, Keegan was close. Every time she thought she'd pushed her anger back into its bottle, it broke free again. She was beyond pissed.

"Keegan," Mahogen called.

"What?" she roared, turning on him.

"Walk with me," he invited.

She crossed her arms tightly across her chest. "To where?"

He offered an arm. "Find out."

To her own disbelief, she took it.

Her guards—Wexsley, Halcyon, and Rhyse—were just catching up.

"Where are you going?" Rhyse questioned breathlessly.

She pushed Mahogen as a cue to lead the way. "On a walk."

None of the guards argued and she was glad, as she was dangerously close to slapping the next person who told her no.

The trees began to decrease in size, soon dropping away entirely. They were in a small clearing, a pond in the center. Fragile waterlilies floated on the surface and birds flitted between branches, singing soft melodies.

"What is this place?" she asked, going to the water's edge.

"The Royal Koi Pond."

Large red, white, and orange fish swam serenely through the water. She turned to look at Mahogen, who had a satisfied smile pulling at his lips. "Whatcha grinnin' at?"

"I knew this would be just the thing for you."

"I'll give it to you."

He placed a hand on her head. "I am glad it makes you happy, but I need to get back to the summoning."

"Okay." She took a seat and returned her attention to the koi.

Mahogen didn't take his hand from her hair and after a moment sat beside her. "Realistically, they do not need me."

She smiled and together they watched the koi swim lazily. Keegan wasn't sure how long they sat, but a sudden tiredness overtook her. Finding she couldn't resist it, she lay down on the grass and fell into an easy sleep.

‡‡‡

It had been ages since Keegan had stormed out and the leaders were still deliberating. Aron was used to political proceedings, but even he was beginning to get frustrated.

"We should do as the child suggests," Atlia said.

That was no suggestion, Tahrin stated angrily.

"Suggestion, demand, order," the Mermaid shrugged, "what difference does it make?"

"Her plan is the best idea we have," Bernot added. "I call for a vote. Those in favor." He raised his hand.

Atlia and Garne joined him.

Aron hoped the Alvor would be on their side, but Keegan's threat had dashed that.

"You do not have the majority," Rangi said.

Aron raised his hand. "Yes, he does."

"You have no say," Sabi snarled, speaking for the first time since Keegan had humiliated him.

"I believe we do," Aron argued. "This is our fate as well and we still have the power to walk away; do not think we will not."

You would not, Tahrin tested.

"They would," Bernot said. "These three men would willingly give all they have and more to see that their sister is safe. Do not underestimate them."

"Then it appears we have reached a decision," Garne said with a smile that revealed his fangs.

Aron gave a mocking bow before turning to leave. At the doors, he found they would not open.

You are dismissed, Tahrin said in a needling tone.

Kade pushed him aside and began pulling at the door.

"It is not locked," Bernot said, joining them. "As you saw, your sister was able to leave."

Aron noticed a few symbols inscribed on the wall. "What are those?"

Bernot went to inspect them. "Spell runes. Someone has locked us in."

There was an ear-splitting scream that resonated through Aron's head and from the pained looks on everybody's faces, they had heard it too.

"What the royik was that?" Sabi asked, rubbing his temple.

"Keegan," Kade mumbled.

The floor shook, sending Aron to one knee.

Move, Tahrin demanded as they scrambled back. She bashed her muscular tail against the door for several minutes before it exploded violently outwards.

Aron rushed through, somehow expecting Keegan to be nearby. "Where is she?" he said frantically, when met with only splintered wood and dust.

"At the Royal Koi Pond," Okleiy said, pushing past him, fear and worry in his voice.

‡‡‡

Alyck stared blankly at the wall.

Any normal person would have feared the worst, but Thaddeus knew better. Alyck was having a vision—a long one—which left him in a mostly comatose state for the duration. The Blind Prophet twitched, and he moved closer. "What did you see?"

"Same thing I have been seeing for the past few weeks," Alyck answered.

Thaddeus knew he was referring to his brother's death.

"But something was different. There was a raven with the man who killed Caius."

"A raven?"

"Yes, a raven." Alyck rubbed his eyes. "Do you think it means anything?"

Thaddeus thought for a moment; ravens symbolized fate and deceit and were harbingers of change. "It could... maybe... I am not sure. Why would the vision suddenly change?"

Alyck shrugged. "Because Sola and Lunos would rather play with my mind than give me answers. This does not usually happen, but, when it does, the addition usually pertains to something vital."

"Describe the man to me," Thaddeus requested, fearing the raven might symbolize Reven, as he was crazy and determined enough to attempt it.

"Dark hair, blue eyes, average looking."

"Did he have a scar across his face?"

"No."

He sighed deeply, that seemed to rule out Reven. "Then I do not know what this change means."

"No one will until it comes to pass. I just wish it would happen soon."

427

Thaddeus considered advising against this, knowing it would lead to a new era—one without Alyck. Braxton was coming into his powers, meaning one of Caius' sons would not be ascending the throne.

They sat in silence.

Alyck broke it, "I know my time is coming, I just wish I understood the mystery of how two people can kill my brother." He gave a sly smile. "Sparing my feelings does me no good. Since Keegan's return, I have known my days were numbered."

"I cannot solve the conundrum of your brother's death, but I do know what is happening to Braxton."

"Do tell me."

"He is becoming a Blind Prophet."

The color drained from Alyck's face. "No... the fates cannot be so cruel."

‡‡‡

Feeling warm from lying in the sun, she rolled onto her back, yawned, and stretched her arms above her head. She should head back, the boys would be fretting by now, but all she wanted to do was stare at the sky and watch downy clouds float by.

There was a strangled gurgle and Keegan sat up. Looking around the clearing, she saw Mahogen lying face down on the grass several yards away. Wexsley stood by a tree, his back to her, a pair of boots sticking from between his legs. Getting to her feet slowly, her gut told her to do anything but stay there.

Wexsley stepped aside, revealing Rhyse, crimson spilling down his chest from a deep gash in his throat. Noticing her, Wexsley pointed the bloodied knife at her.

She turned to run and collided with Halcyon, who took hold of her wrists before she could pull away. She released a scream, which was quickly smothered as Wexsley placed an ether-soaked rag over her mouth. It seared her throat, her head felt fuzzy, and her knees buckled, refusing to hold her upright. After what seemed an aeon, Halcyon shoved her to the ground.

As she coughed, she managed, "Why?"

The men laughed and Halcyon pulled her head back. "Because you are worth a fortune." He turned to Wexsley, "Get the horses, I'll deal with these two."

Keegan glanced at Mahogen and realized he was still alive. Relief flooded her. She struggled to her feet, only to have Halcyon push her to

428

the ground again, making her feel like a ragdoll. "Don't do this," she pleaded, stubbornly struggling to her feet again.

"Quiet," Halcyon snapped, giving her a backhanded slap across the face.

The sting brought back memories. She knew she'd never be able to fight him, but was going to try anyway. She tried to run and when Halcyon grabbed her, clawed at his eyes. He struck her, sending blue and yellow spots floating across her vision. When the colors disappeared, she was on the ground again.

Halcyon wrenched her arms behind her back, placing strain on her shoulders.

"Please," she begged, the tears rolling down her cheeks.

Ignoring her, Halcyon wrapped rope around her wrists then pulled out a long rag, drenched it in ether. As soon as it was in place, she was coughing violently again.

"Have to take precautions," he said snidely. "I heard ether wears off quickly on you."

Wexsley returned with three horses.

"Take a last look," Halcyon snarled, placing a blindfold over her eyes.

✣✣✣

They sprinted into the clearing.

"Keegan," Kade yelled. No response. "Keegan!"

"She is not here," Bernot said.

"How do you know?"

"Because of that," Garne pointed.

Kade looked to where the Torrpeki pointed and saw Rhyse's body slumped against a tree, blood staining the front of his shirt.

"Who was with her?" Atlia asked.

"Rhyse, Wexsley, and Halcyon," Bernot answered.

Okleiy added, "And my son."

"Find the other two," Hernando ordered a soldier.

Okleiy stopped them. "They are not here."

"Did... whoever took Keegan, take them, too?" Aron questioned.

"I have a feeling Halcyon and Wexsley are the ones who did the taking."

Kade clenched his fists. If—no, when—he found those bastards, he was going to kill them.

"Where would they take her?" Jared pressed.

429

"Them," Garne corrected. "Mahogen is missing as well."

"Most likely, to the border." Bernot said, picking up a discarded rag from the ground. "Ether."

"Why would they do this?" Aron questioned.

"Money and titles, I assume," Bernot answered. "No doubt Caius will pay handsomely for Keegan. As for why they took Mahogen, I cannot pretend to understand. We must find them before they cross the border. Once they do, we cannot follow. Tahrin, fly ahead and see if you can spot them."

The dragon didn't look pleased to be given an order and showed it with a puff of smoke from her nostrils. Regardless, she spread her massive, red wings and took to the sky.

"The rest of us will follow on the ground," Bernot continued as a group of soldiers stormed into the clearing, extra horses in tow. He swung up onto a sable charger. "Hickor, can you track them?"

"Can I track them?" Hickor scoffed, spurring his horse into the forest.

Kade dug his heels into Arso, causing the dun to rear before racing forward.

The Alvor never slowed and he questioned how he could follow a trail so surely at this speed. After a time, they slowed and Hickor dismounted, a look of confusion muddling his features.

"Have you lost the trail?" Atlia asked.

"No," Hickor said. "There are two and no knowing which one leads to them."

"Then we split," Bernot announced calmly.

Kade was about to agree when he took a closer look at the hoof-prints. One set was perfectly stomped into the ground. "No, it's a ruse. We've done something similar before."

"Are you sure?" Garne questioned.

He looked at the trails again and his confidence wavered. "Not entirely."

"You are wasting time," Okleiy snarled, beginning to give directions.

"He is right," Hickor said, re-emerging from the underbrush.

Kade hadn't even noticed the Alvor slip away.

"They went this way."

"How could you possibly know that?" Okleiy snapped.

"Come see."

Jared gave Kade a perturbed look before following. The clearing they came to looked grotesque. Tree roots emerged from the ground like clawing arms and fear seemed to hang in the air.

"Who… what is this?" Okleiy muttered.

"This is Keegan," Kade answered quietly.

"But the ether…"

"Tends to wear off quickly on her," Jared said. "These fools learned that the hard way by the looks of it."

‡‡‡

He reached the crest of the hill and surveyed the land around him. Much had changed since he had last seen this place. The wild had overtaken what man had claimed and the house he had once known every nook and cranny of was barely more than a few piles of stone. The only true marker that this place had ever been significant were the gravestones.

Caius made his way over to the graves and lay a hand on the now weathered surfaces. Though time had taken its toll on these last tokens, the engraved names were still legible. He muttered a quick spell that returned the gravestones to their original standing, then another to prevent their destruction.

"The place where it all began," he muttered.

Though no one was around, he kept his tumultuous emotions beneath the surface. Too many times had he wished he could change the past, too many times had he placed all the blame on himself, too many times had he shed tears. He knew it was futile—they could never respond—but something made him start talking to his parents.

"Alyck is doing well. He is the Blind Prophet, and recently we found the Keeper of Prophecy. You also had a daughter-in-law. She was beautiful—the most beautiful woman to ever walk this earth; aside from you, Mother.

"Seleena was wonderful and it saddens me Aron never had the chance to know her. I guess I should also tell you that you have three grandsons: Braxton, Kolt, and Aron. All are doing well. Braxton has a long way to go before he will be able to handle being king, but has the potential."

Caius continued to talk as the sun made its way across the sky. He wanted to apologize for what had happened, for his lack of control, but every time he tried, the words stuck in his throat. Placing a hand on the stones, he said his goodbyes and stood up, realizing that his fear of was unfounded.

The sun was a breath above the horizon, casting stunning colors into the atmosphere. A light wind ruffled his hair and he smiled; the pleasant memories of childhood flooded back and were no longer clouded by shame and remorse.

He looked up as a rumbling nearby began to grow. The sky above him, clear at first, became warped and blackened. A hole opened in the center and he could see the other world through it, filled with bright lights, brighter than anything natural. The hole descended towards him and the wind grew into a storm. He grinned as the void swallowed him up.

The journey was painless, but as soon as his feet touched solid ground, it felt as if all energy was siphoned from him. He collapsed and could feel stones digging into his skin, but he was weak, too weak to even keep his eyes open.

‡‡‡

Lucas glared at Reven as he slipped into the cellar with one of the barmaids. They'd been in Agrielha about two weeks and the only thing Reven did was fool around. He claimed to have found the entrance to the tunnel, but a portion had apparently collapsed, and he was working on clearing it. Lucas doubted that was what he was doing.

He turned back to the customer he was serving and handed him his drink; the man tossed him a bronze coin and a smile before walking away. The morning after Reven all but forced him to help with his plan, they were offered jobs at the inn. Again, he wasn't entirely sure magic hadn't been used.

It was a slow night, giving Lucas time to ponder and his thoughts turned to his brothers. Somehow, he was confident Carter would make it to the Lazado. Jared might have made it there too, but with Keegan in tow, it was possible he was dead and buried. If that were so, Keegan wouldn't last much longer once he got hold of her.

He pushed his contemplations aside, finding he was becoming increasingly angry. The evening passed in boredom and Reven didn't return until well into the night. The inn's owner dismissed them and they headed to the small room they shared.

Once the door was shut, Lucas asked, "How much longer?"

"Not much, I just 'ave to clear a few more blocks and we can get through."

"Have you even thought about how we are going to find our way through the castle once we're there?"

"Magic."

Lucas blew out the candle and crawled into bed. He was trying to find flaws in Reven's plan, but he managed to refute them all. Presently, he'd resigned himself to the fact that he had to see it through.

CHAPTER 59

It had been two days and they had yet to catch up to Halcyon and Wexsley, even if there were obvious signs of the path they had taken. Tahrin had gone ahead but was unable to spot them from the sky.

They were able to get fresh horses at outposts along the way but were still pushing hard. Just ahead was the border outpost, where a new set of fresh horses awaited. They switched quickly and within minutes were in the bleak Borderlands.

Bernot could see out to the blue wall that divided them from Caius; not a living soul in sight. *Any sign of them?* he asked Tahrin.

The dragon was a red blur in the open sky. *No,* she responded, diving towards them, sending great shivers through the earth as she landed.

"They came this way," Hickor said, working to calm his balking horse.

I have not seen them, Tahrin growled.

"Then you must be blind," Kade snared impulsively.

Tahrin snapped at him, causing his horse to buck and give a frightened whinny.

"Easy, Tahrin," Bernot said. "I have a feeling they might have used an invisibility spell."

"What do we do then?" Aron questioned.

"Nothing," Rangi said angrily. "They have crossed the border; we cannot touch them."

"I'm bringing her back," Kade said defiantly.

"Even if you could cross the border, we will not allow it," Garne spoke. "You are a Child of Prophecy; we need to pro—."

"We saved her before, and we'll do it again," Jared cut him off.

A soldier from the back spoke up, "I might not make it across the border, but I'm willing to try."

Several others joined their cause.

"Why would you do this?" Bernot asked the first man to volunteer.

"Keegan helped my son with his sword fighting, giving pointers and offering to spar even when she could barely keep the blade up. I'd feel ashamed if I left her to Caius without at least trying," answered the man.

"Well said." Bernot spoke to the other leaders, "I, for one, am going. You may wait here or come." He knew all would come—attempt to at least—for fear of losing what little hold each thought they had over the girl.

434

The group rode across the borderlands, dust-clouds rising behind them. Kade plowed through the wall without hesitation, his brothers following. The rest of them stopped just short of the barrier.

Bernot's men took deep breaths before crossing, only a few getting stuck behind the line. He looked to the other leaders and began forward. Abruptly, he was midair and falling, hitting the ground with an "oof".

The other leaders gave him worried looks, but each tried to pass. None made it.

"Prepare for anything," Bernot instructed those who had crossed. "And bring her back."

‡‡‡

She was dropped onto the ground unceremoniously, her shoulder ramming into a tree root. The blindfold pushed up slightly and she could make out a few pairs of boots.

"As promised," Halcyon said, "Where's our money?"

"Here," a woman's voice said; the sound of clinking coins followed.

"That's barely a fraction of what you promised," Halcyon balked. Suddenly, he was gasping, choking on something.

Wexsley began pleading and soon fell silent too.

"Get her up," the woman instructed.

Keegan was yanked to her feet and the blindfold torn away. She blinked to bring her eyes into focus and recognized the Vosjnik. Guthrie held her, the gouges in his face from where she'd clawed him still healing. Frantically, she struggled against him.

He drew a knife and she managed an audible hiccup through the gag. Guthrie cut the ropes binding her hands and her first instinct was to strike out. He stopped her hand and she reflexively kicked him in the shin.

"Stop," Vitia said, using her magic.

Brennian reached for her other arm and removed the gag.

Vitia turned her attention to Mahogen, who had been pulled off the horse by Thahan. "Not what I asked for, but still a prize," she sneered, grabbing one of his golden horns.

Mahogen gave no reaction.

"Fancy seeing you here," Vitia said snidely, returning her attention to Keegan.

"Why can't you people just leave me alone?" she yelled.

"Nothing personal," Guthrie said, "but we have orders."

"Your brother won't be able to save you this time." Vitia jibed cruelly.

435

Keegan gave her an unwavering look. "Obviously, as they're a world away."

Vitia looked momentarily confused. "No, the brother you have in this world."

"Don't have any. Unless you mean by Alvor stand—"

"I mean your biological brother, Kade."

"What?" Keegan snorted. "He's not my brother."

Vitia produced a crumpled paper from her pocket and pushed it into her hands.

Keegan's haughty demeanor quickly melted away and by the end, she could scarcely keep herself from shaking. All she knew was wrong. "Where did you get this?"

"Your brother. Didn't he tell you?" Vitia said with a shrewd grin. "Let her go."

Keegan looked at her searchingly as Brennian and Guthrie obeyed. "Run."

She didn't need to be told a second time and, in her rush, stumbled over a root, earning a laugh. She glanced over, to see Vitia staring after her, Thahan beside her, bow strung and aimed.

There was a piercing pain in her shoulder, and she screamed, tumbling to the ground. She lay there, feeling defeated and realized this was what Vitia wanted. *Think again.* She pushed herself up, glancing back; the look of surprise on Vitia's face was worth the pain.

Keegan started running again and turned herself into an erratic target, using the trees as barriers. Branches snapped behind her and an arrow grazed her side, but she barely felt it with all the adrenaline coursing through her veins.

Suddenly, she fell, pain radiating from her left thigh; she looked back to find an arrow protruding from the muscle.

Thahan walked calmly towards her while Vitia smiled smugly.

She knew she couldn't outrun them, but she'd be damned if she was just going to wait for them. The pain in her leg and shoulder were searing as she struggled to her feet, nevertheless, she stumbled forward, placing a hand against a tree for support.

The scream she emitted when the arrow pierced her palm seemed to come from somewhere far off. She slid to her knees, face scraping against the rough bark, tears mixed with droplets of blood.

She took deep breaths, doing her best to give Vitia as little satisfaction as possible. There was a snap, and someone pulled her hand down the broken shaft of the arrow, the splinters at the end clawing at her flesh. She looked up, to find Aron, sword in hand.

436

"The cavalry is here," he said, dragging her into his arms.

She wrapped her arms tightly around his neck as he began to run.

‡‡‡

Aron knew the Vosjnik were occupied with the others, but he still needed to get Keegan somewhere safe. He had meant to get away on horseback, but the thing had spooked and run off. The sounds of battle fell away and he stopped, gently leaning Keegan against a tree. "I need to remove the arrows."

She gritted her teeth to keep from crying out. "Do it quickly."

He began with the one in her shoulder. Once the arrow was removed, he let her lean against the tree and moved to the one in her leg, which was deeply imbedded. He did not bother telling her what he was doing and quickly shoved it completely through her leg.

She yelped, beating her good hand against the tree. "You need to bind the wounds to stop the bleeding."

He tore away the bottom of her once white dress, ripped it into strips, winding several around her leg, while she tended to her hand. There was no easy way to bandage her shoulder, so he left it alone.

Kade, he said, remembering the others, *I have her, but lost my horse. Stay where you are.*

"Kade and the others are on their way."

At the mention of his name, she looked away. "Kade's... my brother."

"Who told you?"

Hurt shone in her hazel eyes. "You knew?"

He sighed. "I wanted to tell you, but Kade would not let me."

"Why?"

"You will have to ask him."

Her eyes became wide and fearful. "Aron."

He looked over his shoulder to find Thahan aiming a bow at his chest. He stood slowly, eyeing the archer.

"Step away," Thahan commanded. "I'd rather not do you harm."

Aron picked up his sword. "If you want her, you have to go through me."

"So be it." Thahan released the bowstring.

The arrow pierced his heart smoothly. Aron looked down at his chest calmly to watch blood color his shirt. A scream, not his own, filled his ears and the world lurched sideways.

‡‡‡

Kade rushed through the forest. The Vosjnik had fled, leaving Keegan and Mahogen behind. He wasn't sure why, but Vitia must have somehow achieved her goal. He pushed out with his mind to find Aron and Keegan; they weren't much farther.

He arrived to find Keegan leaned against a tree, red splotches staining her dress and Aron standing in front of her protectively as Thahan aimed an arrow at his chest, which he released, and hit true on the intended mark.

As Kade revealed himself, Thahan reached for another arrow, but was too slow. In one clean motion, his head was rolling from his shoulders.

He was aware Keegan had screamed, but now, the world was deathly quiet. He looked at her, finding her unconscious, the arrow that had been in Aron's chest clenched in her fist. Where there should have been a hole in Aron's breast was seamless flesh.

Aron jerked up, gasping. "What happened?"

"Nastor if I know," Kade answered. *Jared, you need to bring the horses. Keegan's done... something and needs immediate attention.*

On our way.

"You would have died for her," he said to Aron.

"Of course."

"Why?"

"Same reason you would, which is what I have been trying to show you this entire time. I may be Caius' blood, but I will never be him."

"What happened?" Jared asked, arriving with the others.

"Not sure," Aron said, "I have a feeling I should be dead though."

Mahogen examined Keegan. "She is still breathing. We need to get her back to the Lazado."

"You're a life elemental," Kade stated.

"Ether," Mahogen said plainly.

"Hickor could heal her," Aron suggested.

"My strengths lie elsewhere," Hickor told them. "We need Lyerlly."

"Edreba's days away," Jared argued.

"By horseback," Mahogen said slyly.

‡‡‡

A gale buffeted the hospital, rattling the windows in their holdings.

Lyerlly rushed outside to find Aron sliding down from Tahrin's back, Keegan dirtied and bloodied in his arms. "Where are the others?" she asked, after yelling into the hospital for assistance.

"Riding back from the border," Aron answered, allowing Ty to take Keegan from him.

"What happened?" Lyerlly questioned, undoing Keegan's field dressings.

"Thahan shot her several times before we got away. He found us again and shot me in the heart." He paused and Lyerlly noticed the hole in his shirt. "When I came to, she was like this."

Lyerlly pointed to his chest. "I assume that is why they sent you back with her."

"Yes," he answered almost ashamedly.

She returned her attention to Keegan and could sense no poison— the only injuries were the evident ones. Yet, somehow, she was barely hanging onto life, as if someone had syphoned the energy from her. She slowly began to transfer her own to see if there was a response. Keegan's heart began beating faster and her body drew away from the brink.

"Aron," Lyerlly instructed, "I need to transfer energy to Keegan. Find some soldiers and bring them here."

"Use me."

"You do not have near enough."

"Start with me."

She really did not have time to argue. "Fine." She placed a hand on his arm and began to pull energy and was amazed at how much he had— enough for two people. She drew enough to leave Keegan in a deep sleep, then left Elia and Ty to attend to her injuries.

She took Aron to another bed and drew the curtains. "Remove your shirt."

Aron's chest was muscled and unscarred with no sign an arrow had pierced him. She placed a hand on his chest to assess the internal damage. There was nothing wrong. "It is like you were never injured."

Aron pulled his shirt back on. "How?"

"I am not sure, but it *was* Keegan's doing. What truly concerns me is that she did it in an instant while still under the effects of ether. That should be impossible."

CHAPTER 60

The sounds were of a busy area; people chatted, but she couldn't make out any words clearly. Shoes clicked on a tiled floor. There was the scrape of a chair. A curtain slid against a rod.

Her eyes opened slowly. Looking around, Keegan realized she was back in the hospital. Kade and Jared sat beside the bed, talking quietly.

Jared noticed she was awake. "Hey, how are you feeling?"

"Confused," she answered truthfully, pushing herself upright. Wexsley and Halcyon's betrayal resurfaced. Kade was her brother. Vitia had let Thahan use her as target practice. Aron had rescued her... "Oh my god, Aron."

Kade and Jared looked at each other dumbfounded, neither doing anything to console her.

"What did you do?" Aron asked. "I walked away for a minute."

"Aron," she exclaimed, pulling him into an embrace. Tears still falling, but now they were of relief. "But..." she remembered the arrow piercing his chest. She scrabbled to lift his shirt. "The arrow..." His chest was smooth, unbroken, whole. "How?"

"You," Aron answered, taking her hand.

"*How?*"

"We are not sure; we were hoping you knew."

Lyerlly pulled the curtain open. "Shoo," she said, sending the boys away. "How are you feeling?"

"Fine."

"Do you remember anything after you escaped with Aron?"

"I remember Thahan shooting him."

"Do you know how you healed him?"

Keegan shook her head.

"You can go back to the children's home today if you wish. But before you do, the leaders want to speak with you."

"Oh, *joy*. Let's get this over with."

Mahogen slipped in behind Lyerlly. "How are you feeling?"

"Jesus! Is everyone going to ask me that?" she asked sarcastically. "I've been worse. I'm glad you're okay, too."

"So am I."

"Why'd they take you as well?"

The Alvor shrugged.

Lyerlly returned with the leaders and Mahogen slipped away. Tahrin was too big to fit into the hospital and settled with observing through a window.

"I don't know how I did it," Keegan said, heading them off.

So you say, Tahrin responded.

Keegan shot her a glare. "Is that all y'all're here to talk about?"

"No," Bernot said calmly. "We thought you might like to know the path you will take."

"Ooh, do share," Keegan said, glad their games were over.

"You will start with the Torrpeki, then go to the Merfolk, Buluo, Dragons, and then back to us," Okleiy informed her.

"Good deal. Now," she said, swinging her legs over the edge of the bed. "I'm going home."

No one stopped her.

Lyerlly stood behind the group, arms folded across her chest. The order on the doctor's face was painfully clear

"Yes ma'am," Keegan sighed, crawling back into bed.

Lyerlly's expression softened. "I believe that is what you all came here for. That being completed, I need to do a few more things before Miss Digore may leave. Should you need her for anything more, you may talk with her at the children's home. *Tomorrow.*"

‡‡‡

Nico gave a yell of excitement as Ima dove towards the ground. The wind pulled his hair back, making it look like his head was on fire.

Crowlin followed them at a breakneck speed, the air cool against Braxton's skin. The griffin pulled out of the dive and returned to the clouds, leaving Ima struggling to follow.

You are doing much better, Braxton told Ima.

The hatchling gave a crow and dove towards the ground.

Braxton urged Crowlin to follow.

The griffin tucked in her wings and began plummeting towards the earth.

Suddenly, the world fell away and darkness was all around. He felt his stomach drop and found himself in the throne room. A wild man snuck up from the shadows, knife poised and ready, then jabbed the weapon into the back of Caius' neck. His father gave a silent scream and fell to his knees.

The attacker's face transformed and became Kolt's, a sneer plastered on his lips. Braxton looked back at his father and saw it was now himself being stabbed. A scream filled his ears and the world burst into light.

The first thing he realized was that he was falling, the air ripping from his lungs. The next, was that Crowlin was chasing after him. She wrapped her claws around his biceps, stopping his free-fall, the jerk he felt as momentum stopped making it feel like his shoulders were pulled apart. His feet touched the ground and Crowlin released him. As he rolled across the grass, his body somehow found every rock. When he came to a stop, he just lay there, his body throbbing.

Out of the corner of his eye he saw Ima land and Nico jump off her back.

The boy raced over to him. "Braxton! Braxton, are you all right?"

The griffins followed behind him, worry emitting from them both.

He pushed himself upright. "Yes. What happened?"

Nico crouched beside him. "I'm not sure. You were fine one moment, then you fell... Did you faint?"

"No..." A shooting pain presented itself behind his eyes and he gasped in pain.

Braxton, Crowlin said worriedly.

"I am fine," he managed. "But let us stop for the day." Not in the mood to deal with everyone's obvious concern, he swung up onto Crowlin's back. It took all his strength to not curl up into a ball and he let her guide herself home. Through the pain, he could see one thing clearly, Kolt stabbing him in the back.

‡‡‡

Once Lyerlly approved Keegan's departure, she was anxious to return to the children's home. There was something eating at her and Kade might've asked but had a feeling it would blow up in his face. Behthany greeted them warmly and Keegan was overtaken by a few of the younger children. It took Behthany shooing them away before they could make it upstairs.

Once on their floor, Keegan turned to face them, a pained look on her face. "Can I talk to Kade, alone please?"

Aron and Jared shared a worried look before going to their rooms.

"Wha—" he started.

"How could you keep that from me?" Anger and pain rode on her words.

"Keep what from you?" he asked, genuinely confused.

"We're siblings." Her voice wavered, "Were you ever gonna tell me?"

"Maybe."

"*Maybe*? You shoulda told me so I didn't have to find out from *Vitia*."

"You were never supposed to know."

A look of complete betrayal overtook her features. "That's not something you get to keep from me. Do you know how many years I spent looking for a family?"

"I was just trying to protect you."

"From *what*?"

"From how people would treat you. From people using that relationship against us."

She gave him a disappointed look. "Like how you treated Aron? And sibling or not, I would've been treated like that for simply being your friend."

Somehow, he knew she wouldn't hold this against him forever.

"Is there anything else you wanna own up to?"

He looked at the floor. "Nico's alive."

The color drained from her face. "What?"

"Nico's—"

"I heard you the first time! Nico's alive, and we could've saved him. What about the rest of Jared's family?"

"Alessandra is dead. I let it happen."

"What about Lucas, Carter, and Jude?"

"Who?"

Keegan took a step back, shaking her head. "I can't tell you how much I wanted to simply... be a family with you," she started, "But I don't think I want to associate with a liar and murderer."

He knew she wanted to say much more but was too angry to find the right words.

She stared at him, her eyes speaking what her mouth couldn't and eventually stormed to her room, the door slamming behind her.

✢✢✢

Bernot took his seat and looked at the men across from him. The older gentleman was dark-skinned, with his coarse, wiry hair beginning to lose its color. He was a large man, and Bernot did not doubt he was accustomed to strenuous labor. The other could hardly be considered more than a child, probably not past his sixteenth year. There was something familiar about him that he could not yet place.

"Why did you bring them here? Any of the Initiators could have dealt with them," Bernot said, not pleased that Felix was placing more work on his already overladen plate.

"You told us to bring Pexatoses straight to you," Felix said, motioning to the older gentleman.

Bernot looked towards the boy, "And what about…"

"Carter," the boy provided.

"Yes, what about Carter?"

"Carter has no magic," Felix explained, "but knows Keegan."

Of course, he knew to whom Felix referred but had to erase any doubt; and he hoped Carter was not one of Jared's brothers. "There are numerous people named Keegan, you will have to be specific."

"Keegan Digore," Carter snapped. "The one who leaves a wake of destruction in her royiken path."

"You must be a Sieme then."

"How do you know that? Are my brothers here?"

"Jared is."

"What about Nico? Lucas?" Carter pressed, his hands gripping the chair's arm.

"I have heard nothing of Lucas; I do believe Jared thought he was traveling with you."

Carter looked at the floor. "He was until a few weeks ago."

"The boy's headstrong and I have a feelin' he went to do something stupid now," Felix spoke up. "Would you be willin' to let me take a few men to go look for the whanker?"

"No," Bernot said.

Carter gave him a furious scowl.

"There have been some unfortunate events that require me to keep as many men as I can at hand. Also, there would be no way to find Lucas; he will have to come to us. And Felix, do not think you have gotten out of telling me what happened to you."

"Expected nothin' less, sir," Felix said, leaning back against the wall.

"What about Nico?" Carter pressed.

Bernot paused before answering, "Caius has him."

The color drained from Carter's face. "Are… you… what's being done to save him?"

"Nothing. As I said before, there have been some important things happening here." Before Carter could lash out in anger and pain, he added, "But I have no doubt Caius is keeping him alive. Have no worries." He cursed to himself; that was never the correct thing to say.

"How can you tell me not to worry? My brother, my *little* brother's captive to the king, having Sola and Lunos knows what happen to him."

"We will rescue him. However, things like this take time. I cannot say he will be saved today, or tomorrow, or even a week from now, but it will happen. You have my word." He knew Carter wanted to argue, but the boy had the foresight to realize doing so would get him nowhere. He turned his attention to the Pexatose. "I apologize, but I seem to have not received your name."

"Waylan Piscol," the Pexatose answered, his large arms folded across his chest.

"Ah, I wondered when you would decide to join us. You are the metal elemental, if I remember correctly."

"It was done begrudgingly. And yes, I'm the metal elemental."

"Do you use your powers in your line of work, which is...?"

Waylan answered, "I'm a blacksmith, and no."

Whatever Waylan's reasons were for not using his powers, they were his own. "Excellent. You will be given work in a forge and you can work towards having your own."

"When Lucas arrives, I'll require him as an assistant."

"That can be arranged," Bernot said, pulling some papers from his desk. "Will you be wanting Carter as an assistant as well?"

Carter spoke up, "I worked with a shoemaker."

"I may have a job for you," Bernot said, recalling the increased demand in carpenters of late. "It is a carpentry position though."

Carter gave a nod of acceptance.

Bernot scanned the sheets of paper in his hands until he found what he was looking for. "Carter, there is room for you at Zaire's children's home. Waylan, there should be room above the forge if that will suffice."

"That's fine," Waylan said gruffly.

"I take it Jared and Keegan are at Zaire's," Carter commented.

"No," Bernot said. "I cannot allow you to see your brother yet... it would create complications."

"What kind of complications?"

"Jared is set to leave in a few days and I have no doubt your arrival would keep him here. That, and I am sure you would convince him to go search for Lucas and make a fool-hearted attempt to rescue Nico."

"What if I swore not to?"

"Even then I would say no. Jared cannot afford to be distracted— the world cannot afford for him to be distracted. Once he has left, I will inform him of your safe arrival."

"You can't keep me from him," Carter argued, his desperation evident.

"Unfortunately, I can, and I must."

Carter made to continue arguing.

Felix placed a hand on his shoulder, stopping him. "I know it's not what you want to hear, lad, but trust me, Bernot's doin' what he thinks is best now."

"Thank you," Bernot said. "Now, Felix will take you where you need to go and I promise, you will see all three of your brothers again. But you must be patient."

CHAPTER 61

There was a wailing in the distance, and he forced himself to open his eyes. The world around him was ablaze and it was a wonder *he* was not on fire. Caius pushed himself to his feet, trying to gauge where he was, but there was too much smoke and flame to make out much.

Heat began to register, and he pushed through the flames. Nothing impeded him and when he cleared the smoke, he stopped to take in his surroundings. He was in a grassy field with several clumps of trees. There were a few patches of grass with strange white markings, as if the lines created a border, and a structure across the field was made of brightly colored material with a spiraling tube coming from the topmost point.

The wailing became painfully loud and was accompanied by flashing lights. He knew he could not be seen there; if people of this world found him, there would undoubtedly be torture involved. The buildings surrounding the field were behemoths, their spires reaching as high as the castle of Agrielha, and higher. This was not the world he remembered, and a bolt of fear shot through him. Steeling his nerves, he pushed into the maze of edifices.

Metal contraptions raced by on the road and he hugged the buildings, fearing he would be hit. There were a few people about, who gave him curious looks. Exhaustion plagued him and he felt himself succumbing to it.

Ahead, he noticed an alleyway and stumbled into it. Hisses in the dark told him he had scared a few cats. Something smelled pungent, but he could not locate its source, and honestly, that was the least of his worries. He got far enough into the alley to where the lantern on the street was dim, and keeled over.

✚✚✚

His nerves were on edge, then again, they had been that way for the past few weeks. *July 27th, the day history changes,* he thought as he followed Reven into the inn's cellar.

Reven moved a crate to reveal a small hole in the wall.

"That'd better not be how we're getting into the castle," Lucas snapped.

Reven ignored him, dropped onto his stomach, and crawled through the opening.

447

Lucas looked at the crate and considered moving it over the entrance and simply walking away.

"Do n't even try it."

Taking a deep breath, he edged inside, where it was dusty and dark. "Let's get this over with."

There was a spark, a light burst into existence, and Reven started forward.

Lucas was more than happy to let him lead; it meant he wasn't the one walking through never-ending spider webs. He glanced back and was disheartened to find he couldn't see the opening; he was truly committed now. Touching the knife at his waist, he realized there was more than one way out of this. He drew it and raised it but after a moment, lowered it again. "Why do you want to kill the king?"

"Now is n't the time for this."

"You seem to know my motivations, but I hardly know anything about you. Why is it you want to kill the king?"

"'Cause of what he did to my family."

"What did he do to yours that he hasn't done to everyone else's?"

"Killed them."

"His soldiers do that every day."

"No, he actually wielded the blade. My father died savin' a Child of Prophecy—Keegan. And you 'ave no idea what that did t' my family. My mother was never told my father 'd been murdered and thought he 'd left 'er. She turned to drink, and it killed her. My grandfather was an amazing spell-caster but when my father died, grief overpowered everything. Now, he 's dead, because o' a supposed friend's betrayal."

"Did you see your grandfather die?"

"No."

"Then he could still be alive."

"No one survives long in the Suttan dungeon."

The walk through the shaft was excruciatingly long, and with no sunlight to gauge time, it felt forever. But eventually there was an end.

Reven suggested. "We 'ill wait until dark."

"How do you know it's not night already?"

"I have my ways."

"Then why did we come so royiken early?"

"T' make people think we 'd left the inn." Their constant butting heads was beginning to wear down Reven's usually placid nature. "Sleep if you like, there 's not much else t' do."

‡‡‡

448

The room was blissfully dark and from his open window, Aron could hear owls hooting in the night. After Keegan and Kade's fight, she had disappeared from the house. He had gone to check on her and found an empty room with an open window. He debated telling the others, but she probably needed time alone. Sooner or later, she would come back—at least he hoped.

The air between Kade and Jared grew worse with the discovery that most of his family had survived the Vosjnik. Jared had immediately gone to Bernot to ask for leave to look for them. From the slamming of his door when he returned, Aron assumed he was refused.

He heard a rustling outside his window and a shadow climbed lithely through. He was wondering why an Alvor would climb through his window when he realized it was Keegan.

"You up?" she whispered.

"Yes," he responded, sitting up.

She climbed into the bed and sat quietly.

From the small streams of moonlight that made it through the leaves, he could see something glistening on her face. "What is wrong?" he asked, reaching for her hand.

"It's all too much," she answered. "I... I don't want to be part of this world. None of it makes sense."

"What does not make sense?"

"Everything," she hiccuped. "How can people keep so much from me? Why do I have to save everyone?"

"I cannot answer the latter," Aron said, wiping away the trail of tears. "But they—we—keep things from you because we are trying to protect you, because we care about you."

She pushed his hand away angrily, "It doesn't protect me!" Quietly, she said, "I should've never come here." She shifted, about to get up to leave.

He took her hand again, "Do not fault us because we are doing what we think is right."

"How do you know it's the right thing to do?"

"We do not." He pulled her into an embrace. "But we try, and that is what matters."

Her sobbing made it impossible to respond.

Aron stroked her hair in an effort to comfort her and slowly the tears subsided as exhaustion overtook her. Gently, he laid her down and covered her with the blanket. Knowing she needed space, he was about to head into the common room to sleep on the couch.

She grabbed his hand. "Stay. Please."

He hesitated, then climbed back into the bed.

She nestled against his body. "Thank you."

He waited until she was asleep and gently kissed her forehead.

‡‡‡

Someone was shaking him.

Reven pulled away just in time to avoid Lucas' flailing limbs as he jerked back to reality. "Time t' go," he said, picking up the torch with one hand and feeling the wall with the other.

Lucas wondered what he was looking for until the wall sprang open. He crept past Reven and peered into the corridor.

"See anyone?"

"No," Lucas answered, hand on his knife.

Reven pushed past him.

"You know where you're going, right?" He was sure the "map" wasn't as accurate as he believed.

"Through the halls, no, through the secret passages, yes."

Lucas gritted his teeth, feeling exposed, and tiptoed after him.

Reven felt along the wall again and his hand pressed against a stone, opening another hidden door.

Lucas let him lead again and when they came across pitfalls, was glad he found them first. It wasn't long before they came to another dead-end. This time, Reven pulled a lever to open the door. The room they stepped into was nothing extravagant, quite plain, but comfortable, and on the wall hung a painting of a woman with sad eyes.

As they explored, Lucas felt the painting's eyes following him. He crept towards the bed, expecting the king to be fast asleep. The covers were tangled and empty. "Where is he?" he hissed.

"How should I royiken know?" Reven snapped back.

"This is your noxþ plan, find him."

Reven stormed to the door and threw it open, stomping out. When he returned, he dragged a guard in.

The man's eyes were wide with fear but he did'nt resist, clearly, under Reven's control.

"Where 's the king?" Reven asked, throwing the guard to the floor.

"I don't know," the man answered, fighting against Reven's control. "Where is he?"

The guard gave a scream through gritted teeth. "He didn't tell me."

Reven drew his knife. "Where is he?"

The man eyed the blade before saying, "You'll kill me even if I tell; do your worst."

Reven crouched in front of him. "Oh, I was never going to kill you. But I 'll make it so that you wish I had."

The guard gave him a cold stare.

Reven returned the look.

Pain began to wash over the guard's features.

"This can end well if you tell me what I need t' know."

The guard only managed to stay steadfast for a few more moments. "In the throne room. He always goes there when he can't sleep."

"Thank you." Reven raised the knife and smashed the butt into his head.

✝✝✝

Caius pried his eyes open through lids akin to sandpaper. His body felt like stone and his muscles were tight, as if they had not been used in years. He took in his surroundings; he was still in the alleyway.

The buildings on either side of him were made of brick and immaculate gray mortar. The ground beneath him was un-cobbled, though, not dirt, and littered with garbage. Across the alley was a large, green, metal box with a black lid, where black bags of a material he was unfamiliar with, overflowed from the top. An odd humming came from somewhere nearby.

He got to his feet and approached the box, the smell emanating from it potent. He felt one of the bags and was shocked to find that it was smooth and malleable. Glancing around the rest of the container, he noticed similar bags in white.

"What's wrong, hermano?" a voice called, "Ain't you seen a basurero 'fore?"

Caius looked towards the voice. A group of young men stood at the entrance of the alleyway, all wearing blue-colored pants that sagged around their hips, revealing brightly colored bits of cloth underneath. They wore thin white shirts that for some reason were devoid of sleeves.

"You perdido, man?" one of the men asked.

Caius gave them a bewildered look and walked towards them. "Where am I?"

"El Paso," someone answered.

"You ain't from 'round here, are you, hermano?" the first man said. "Mi nombre is Carlos."

451

"Where is this... El Paso?" Caius asked, an unsettling feeling in his gut. He noticed metal handles resting in the waistbands of several of the men's trousers.

"Texas, hermano," Carlos answered.

A man behind Carlos snarled, "El jefe introduced himself, what kind of rude hijo de puta are you, chico?"

"Calma, Juan," Carlos snapped. "Hermano ain't from around aquí."

"Cabron es grosero," Juan muttered.

Caius did not understand the uncivilized language they spoke, but knew an insult when he heard one. He lashed out at Juan, sending him sprawling. Juan quickly got to his feet, spewing curses in his beastly tongue. The men around him held Juan back while Carlos talked to him quietly. Several of the men came towards Caius and he backed into the alley.

"You shouldn't've done that, hermano," Carlos said. "I was trying to be simpatico, but you don't get to hit mi familia. I'm gonna let Juan te patee tu culo."

The men holding Juan let go of him and he pulled the metal handle from his belt. The object was misshapen, bending at an angle, which Juan held at arm's length, almost as if he were afraid of it.

Caius laughed and drew his sword. "I shall be nice and spare your life for the little kindness Carlos has shown."

"You loco, bastardo," Juan said. "Only hijo de puta dyin' hoy es you."

He was too far away to strike and began closing the distance. There was a loud bang, taking him by surprise. Caius paused to look for the source when his attention fell on Juan's hand. "Your weapon is sound?"

Juan looked confused, "What are tu talkin' about, cabron?"

"Sound will do nothing for you," Caius said, rushing at him again.

Juan's eyes opened wide and there was another deafening bang.

For a moment, he felt nothing, then there was excruciating pain in his chest. Straight away it became hard to breathe and he collapsed onto the ground. Blood washed over his throat and he began to choke.

Juan stood over him, his mysterious weapon of sound aimed at his head, Carlos beside him.

A loud, screeching, wailing sound filled the air.

"Hoy, es your lucky day, hermano," Carlos said. "Don't let mi find you around here de nuevo."

Carlos and Juan took off with the rest of the group, leaving Caius struggling to breathe past the blood in his throat. The wailing was so close now it sounded like it was on top of him. There was yelling and two men entered his field of vision. Both wore dark blue suits and had an assortment of weaponry belted around their waists.

"We need an ambulance," one man said, speaking to his shoulder. "Victim's been shot in the chest—lung puncture possible."

The second man approached him. "Hang in there, help is on the way." He then placed a hand on his chest and applied pressure.

He could feel himself fading and darkness closed in around him.

‡‡‡

"Are you sure this is the right one?" Lucas asked aggravated.

So far, Reven had taken them everywhere but the throne room. Apparently, his map of the castle's secret passages wasn't as solid as he thought.

"It should be the right one," Reven answered, uncertainty in his voice as he opened the door.

They were finally rewarded. The door spit them out into the shadows of the throne. The back of the throne was plain, with a few words scrawled on it: The future is mine to make, break, and bend.

He drew his knife and made his way to the shadows lining the walls. Immediately, he spotted Caius; thankfully, the king didn't notice him.

The man was nothing like he imagined, beginning to show the wear of age and a sense of anxiety surrounded him as he paced across the room, eyes never leaving the floor.

Lucas waited until the king had his back turned before creeping forward. His heart pounded, pumping adrenaline through his veins as his nerves sat on edge. He was within feet now. He took a deep breath, before driving the knife into the back of Caius' neck.

The king gave a loud cry and collapsed to his knees.

Lucas removed the knife and Caius fell forward, blood seeping from the wound.

There was banging on the door. "Sir, is everything all right?"

"Lucas," Reven called, frantically motioning for him to return to the secret passageway.

He stole a last glance at the king before sprinting across and was instantly swallowed by the shadows as the doors burst open, spilling in guards.

Reven quickly shut the door and started running; he didn't need to be told to follow.

They only stopped when they reached a dead-end that required them to move from one tunnel to another. Their dash through the open hallway was quick and soon they were safe once more. They continued for a while longer and when Reven finally stopped, bearing a large smile. "Congratulations, you just killed the king."

✣✣✣

"This poses a problem," Rangi stated. "Caius will undoubtedly use the boy to turn his brother."

"I know," Bernot said calmly. "I propose we send parties to extract the boy."

"That would be suicide for your men," Atlia stated. "Caius will understand the value of Nico Sieme and have him heavily guarded."

"Our men," Okleiy corrected the princess.

"No," Atlia said. "I have agreed to train the Child of Prophecy, but I promised no help in the war you want to wage. I am not yet queen and cannot grant you forces."

Bernot had a sinking feeling. He had assumed that when the leaders agreed to train Keegan, they would support him in the war as well. "How many of you will stand with me in the war to come?"

Only Okleiy answered his call.

Bernot felt a weight fall on his shoulders; there was no way the Lazado could defeat Caius alone. "I need your assistance if I am to overthrow Caius."

Caius is not wreaking havoc in our lands, Tahrin told him. *We have our own concerns. The dragons will gladly train Keegan, but we cannot offer anything more.*

There were similar answers from Rangi and Garne.

Bernot looked to Okleiy, hoping he might put his conniving skills towards a greater good for once, and was rewarded. "Will you consent to give us use of your Pexatoses?"

"Pexatoses are allowed to make their own decisions as free people of Arciol," Rangi told them. "We will ask them to help, whether or not they do is up to them."

The door burst open and a flustered soldier rushed in.

Tahrin bared her fangs. *What do you think you are doing interrupting this meeting?* The man spared her a glance, "I need to talk to Bernot; it's urgent."

"Pardon the interruption." Sighing, Bernot followed the man outside. "What is so important?"

"The border... the border's gone," the man answered frantically.

"What do you mean *gone*?"

"Gone! It no longer exists. How is this possible?"

He ignored the man's question. "Tell Hernando Barnsed to increase the number of men at the border and make sure you tell no one else of this."

The man gulped, clearly wanting to argue. "Yes, sir."

He steadied himself before re-entering the room. "My apologizes. You must all forgive me but there are some unforeseen events that require my immediate attention. May we finish this discussion on the morrow?"

Tahrin showed her irritation with a puff of smoke. *Courtesy aside, we have no choice.*

Bernot bowed his head. "Thank you."

The others stood and began making their way from the room.

He called out to the Alvor, "Okleiy, we need to talk."

Okleiy had the sense to wait until the doors closed before asking, "What has happened?"

"The border has fallen. Caius is dead."

"I have already agreed to join your cause."

Bernot knew to be wary of a gift from the Alvor, especially Okleiy. "But at what price?"

"I want the same thing I did before."

"And what would that be?" Bernot asked though he already knew.

"I want Mahogen to be matched to the Child of Prophecy."

Bernot took a deep breath to give himself time to think. For once, it was hard to keep the smile that pulled at the corners of his lips. "Fine, Mahogen will be matched with a Child of Prophecy."

Okleiy grinned, thinking he had won. "My men are yours. Use them wisely."

Bernot gave Okleiy a nod before walking away. Thankfully, he had left himself some leeway. He never promised when a union would take place, but that would stave off Okleiy only so long. The true ace was that while he had promised Mahogen would be matched with a Child of Prophecy, he had never promised which one. Now, all he had to do was find the one of the same mindset as Mahogen.

CHAPTER 62

The castle was in pandemonium.

Braxton was called upon, which meant Nico was roused too and whatever the soldier had said to his tutor was enough to drain the color from his face. They dressed quickly and all but ran to the throne room.

There were so many guards standing outside the door that Nico wondered if someone had died. None of the men would look at Braxton.

Inside, they found the cause of the commotion: Caius' body. Nico recalled his mother's death and instantly knew what Braxton was going through. He also knew he should feel sadness, but his heart was singing; he might finally be free.

If Braxton had been pale before, blood had stopped circulating in his face now. He went to stand above his father, face devoid of emotion.

Nico followed but gave him the space to not feel intruded upon. He noticed the wound on Caius' neck and something struck a chord, as the cut was directly in the center of his neck. He knew it wasn't easy to stab someone through their spine and most people would have felled the king anywhere else. But there was one person he knew who insisted upon using a knife between the vertebrae to deliver death: Lucas.

His brother had always done this to kill whatever small farm animals they needed, saying it was painless and less bloody than slitting the animal's throat. He tried to convince himself there was no possible way Lucas could've done this—been in Agrielha—but the precision was too telltale.

The doors slammed open and Kolt stormed in. He was almost as pale as Braxton and when he saw Caius, began screaming as if someone was trying to kill him.

Braxton didn't seem to even notice.

Nico looked between the brothers, trying to figure out how they could have such differing reactions.

Braxton turned on his heels and began to walk from the room. As he passed the guards, he ordered, "Take my brother to his room. Drain his energy if he will not go quietly."

The guards gave each other concerned looks, before doing as told.

Kolt wasn't happy and threw a punch. Other soldiers quickly came to hold him back and someone sapped his energy.

Nico ran to catch up to Braxton. "Where are you going?"

"Back to bed."

"But—"

"But nothing."

✦✦✦

It was hard to believe, but it had happened. He had been having the same vision for weeks and it had finally come to pass; his father was dead. Braxton stood over the body, Kolt beside him. A sheet covered Caius' body, but his face remained visible. Braxton knew he should feel sad, but all he felt was apprehension; he would be crowned in a few days.

What he understood from the guards was that his father had been in the throne room—alone. There was no way someone could have snuck past them to murder the king, so his death had come at the hands of the Sola and Lunos.

He knew better—man had dealt this death.

Kolt was surprisingly silent and sullen.

This was the only time Braxton could recall him showing an emotion other than hate, arrogance, or contempt. He almost wanted to console him, wanted to forget the animosity and cruelty between them.

"The funeral should take place no later than tomorrow," a prioress said.

Braxton had not noticed her enter the room. Prioresses were uncommon in Arciol, with each city only having a few, but they played a major role in the burial of the dead, as most still upheld belief in the old gods.

"And what about the coronation?" Braxton asked, suddenly realizing he had no one to guide him.

"Whenever you think would be best," she answered. "My duties only concern the dead."

"The funeral will be tomorrow," Kolt spoke up.

Braxton had no reason to argue and for once, was content to let him decide.

"As you wish," the prioress said apathetically, covering Caius' face.

Braxton gave her a small nod of thanks and started walking away.

Kolt lingered. "And the coronation the day after that? Would you like me to take care of the preparations?"

Braxton stopped to scrutinize his brother and could see no signs of trickery—something he had learned to discern like a smile. "That would be *incredibly* helpful." And as much as he wanted to question Kolt's sudden kindness, he also did not want to snap him out of his stupor.

There was so much he wanted to do—needed to do—but he could not muster the energy. He dazedly made his way back to his chambers and sat on the bed, staring blankly. Eventually, he sank into the mattress.

457

He was suddenly in the throne room, a mass of people standing around him, all facing the throne. Braxton turned his attention there and was disappointed when the person sitting in the gilded chair was unrecognizable.

A priest lowered an ornate crown onto his head, saying, "Ell poyla ayþ kunyi."

The scene darkened and two men stood alone. He thought he was reliving his father's death until he realized the two were, he and Kolt. Braxton watched helplessly as Kolt drove a knife into his back.

‡‡‡

There was a persistent knocking and Kade groggily opened his eyes. "What?"

"You're needed, immediately," a person returned.

The voice was unfamiliar, and he was about to question it when he remembered what had happened to the old guards. He wasn't surprised Bernot had found replacements so quickly, but he wasn't going to allow anyone near Keegan. He dressed quickly and went into the common space.

Bernot was waiting for him along with several men.

"What's so urgent?" Kade asked.

"We should wait for the others," Bernot said, taking a seat at the table.

He knew Bernot to be calm and collected but today he was clearly anxious.

"What happened?" he pushed.

"Many things. Many things."

He apprehensively took a seat. Jared was the next to show his face, and it wasn't a pleasant one for him. The revelation that most of his family was alive had not worked to amend their feelings.

Kade felt anger course through his veins when Keegan emerged from Aron's room and clenched his fists to keep from flying at him. The prince had proven his intentions to be honorable, but he still wasn't entirely willing to trust him. *What are you doing with him?* he snarled.

Whatever the hell I want, Keegan snapped back.

They took a seat, Keegan pulling her knees up to her chest and pressing her shins against the table. "What's up?"

Bernot gave her a confused look before answering, "The ceiling…"

She chuckled, "No, I mean what happened?"

"Oh." He paused before continuing, "Caius is dead."

458

She dropped her feet onto the floor so she could lean over the table. "What! How do you know he's dead?"

"Last night, the border fell. And the only way that could happen was if he were… dead"

"How are the two correlated?"

"In their last stand, the Council of Elders wove an enchantment that would protect the rest of the world from Caius' tyranny. As long as he was in this world, it would stand."

"So, what does that mean for us?" Jared asked. "We're no longer needed if the king's dead."

"I believe Caius has left safeguards so that his sons will ascend the throne," Bernot told them. "I fear we will need you to aid in deposing them."

Aron spoke for the first time. "Braxton will not need to be deposed; he is nothing like our father."

"The chance of him being like Caius is too great a risk," Bernot insisted.

"You want to get rid of him before he can even disprove your worst fear? I would be willing to wager that before you met me you assumed, I was like my father."

"You would be right."

"Give Braxton a chance."

"It is a risk the world cannot take."

"He's not like Caius," Keegan said quietly.

Bernot sighed, "What is it you propose I do then?"

Aron thought for a moment. "Put your forces in place, but do not attack."

Bernot grinned.

"You were already planning on doing that."

"I was. But I needed to confirm that it was the right course. By both yourself and Keegan's words, it would be against better judgment to not give Braxton a chance. But Keegan, I do want to ask why you vouch for him?"

She was pensive for a moment. "Because he didn't want to do the things he was forced to do. So, where does that leave *me*?"

"I still want you to train in all the elements, but clearly, you cannot go to each nation to do so. They will have to come to you. Kade, Aron, and Jared, your roles have not changed, and you must train to become warriors."

"Gladly," Kade said. "When can we begin?"

"Now, if you like," Bernot answered. "But Jared, I think there is someone you will want to see first."

Jared creased his brows together. "Who?"

"Carter."

Jared jumped out of his seat. "Carter's here?"

"He is."

"And Lucas?"

"I think you should hear that story from Carter. Now, let us go, I am sure he will be just as excited to see you."

‡‡‡

Following Bernot was pure torture; his pace was slow and Jared wanted nothing more than to scream at him to run. His thoughts tumbled around themselves as he struggled to create an explanation as to why Lucas hadn't made it to the Lazado.

Bernot stopped outside another children's home and casually entered. In the kitchen they found Carter sitting at the table.

Shock and joy morphed Carter's features. "Jared."

He rushed forward and pulled his brother into an embrace. There were so many things he wanted to ask, so many he wanted to say, but his voice was stuck in his throat. Carter returned the embrace and he realized they were both crying. "I was sure I'd never see you again," he choked. "I thought you were dead."

Carter managed to laugh. "I'm glad I'm not."

Jared pulled away and studied him. Carter's childlike features had melted into the features of a man. There was wear on his face and there was no doubt he'd been tried and tested like the rest of them. "Where's Lucas?" he questioned, turning to the topic that was eating at him.

Carter gave an aggravated sigh. "Wish I knew so I could slap him upside the head."

"Do you have any idea where he might've gone?"

Carter shook his head and gulped before asking, "What happened to Nico?"

Jared turned away, emotions roiling within. "I don't know, but the Vosjnik have him. Or did. Braxton must have him now. I should've never let him stay home."

Carter placed a comforting hand on his shoulder. "You couldn't have known what would happen. What matters now is what we do to save him."

460

"I would do anything to do just that, but right now there are things outside of my control."

"What things?"

"The world needs me… here. I'm a Child of Prophecy."

"There's only one and that *one* is Keegan."

"A lie. There are four of us. Keegan and I are two. You can meet the others if you'd like."

"Then you can all help me rescue Nico?"

Jared's heart was splitting in two. He knew what he wanted to do, what he should do. "No. We'll never be allowed to."

"He's your brother," Carter yelled. "Our baby brother."

"You think I don't know that? I want nothing more than get Keegan and go rescue him, but we can't. We'll find a way to save him, but we have to entrust the mission to someone else."

"You would leave him to be tortured by the king?"

"The king's dead."

Carter's face became neutral before turning to shock. "That doesn't change anything."

"It might. The man to ascend the throne is supposedly a good person. We may not have to do much to get him back."

"You can't know that for sure."

"No, but I have faith that Nico will return to us. Whether by force or otherwise, we'll get him back."

CHAPTER 63

Bernot waited patiently while the leaders trickled in. He had decided to inform the Children of Prophecy of Caius' demise first and was now wondering if that had been the right decision. Except for Okleiy, the leaders all looked annoyed. Atlia gave him a small smile in passing and he hoped he already had the Merprincess on his side. There was also something else in Atlia's look, something akin to sadness.

The leaders took their seats slowly.

Tahrin did not bother to hide her distain for being dismissed. *Where did we leave off?*

"You promised to ask your Pexatoses if they would provide aid in the coming war," Bernot said. "I am going to ask for your help once more."

"We already gave you an answer," Rangi said.

"You did," Bernot admitted, "But the circumstances have changed."

Rangi huffed.

"We will not be waging war against Caius Alagard; we will be waging it against Braxton Alagard."

The leaders gave him baffled looks.

"Last night the border fell, which can mean only one thing; Caius is dead."

"How?" Garne asked. "And by whose hand?"

"I am not sure," Bernot admitted. "The only thing I know is that Caius is gone from this world."

"Do you have any operatives in Agrielha?" Rangi questioned.

"Not since Rosh Broyker," Bernot answered. "I ask now that you join forces with me. I intend to wait, to see what kind of king Braxton will be, but should he prove to be like his father…"

"I will stand with you," Okleiy declared.

There was silence from the rest of the leaders as they shifted uncomfortably.

Only Tahrin had the nerve to look him in the eye. *No. This is still not our war.*

The others made similar statements.

Atlia had been holding her tongue but finally spoke. "I will join your crusade."

"You are but a representative for your mother," Rangi reminded her.

Atlia was mute for a moment, as if composing herself. "Unfortunately, as of this morning, that is not so. My mother has passed."

Bernot understood the look he had noticed before. "My deepest condolences." He truly meant the words.

Atlia gave a slight dip of the head. "I remember a world in which we did not feel threatened by Caius. My people are far beyond the reach of anyone but Sola and Lunos, so I cannot imagine what those under his rule feel. I have no reason besides compassion to give my support, but sometimes compassion is the best reason to do anything." When none of the others made a motion to add theirs, she concluded, "You are fools for believing our trials are over."

What would you *know of waging war or ruling a nation?* Tahrin seethed.

"Nothing," Atlia admitted. "But having watched my mother and learned from her mistakes, I *know* this is the right course of action."

"I cannot justify going to war," Garne said, "Not now at least."

"So be it," Atlia said. "I just pray to Sola and Lunos that you come to your senses before it is too late."

She stood and Bernot thought she was going to storm from the room; he was pleasantly surprised when she did not.

"As per my people's custom, I have gifts for all the leaders here today. With what is to come, it is imperative that we are able to contact each other quickly. Thus, I offer each of you a small Looking Glass."

They were indeed small—she pulled them from a hidden pocket in her dress and began handing them out. "To use them, speak the name of the race you wish to contact in the Old Language." Once she was done passing them around, she turned to them, "Now, I do believe there is a Child of Prophecy who needs training." She smiled, baring her small pointed incisors, and left.

Bernot wanted to chase after her to thank her, for she had taken a bigger risk than he would have ever dared. Instead, he held his place, and watched as resentment crossed the faces of the other leaders. Atlia's actions had simultaneously angered and shamed them. He just hoped her words and actions would push them into action—sooner, rather than later.

‡‡‡

Keegan paced across the common room while the boys lounged in the chairs watching her anxiously. For the longest time after Bernot had left, no one said a word—as if they were afraid that if they spoke of Caius he would rise from the dead.

"Is he really dead?" she finally managed, her thoughts beginning to cohesively come together. "Like... nothing's ever *that* easy for us."

"Why would Bernot lie?" Aron countered.

"Idk," she said, beginning to talk with her hands. "Just... there's no way he's dead. Good things don't happen to me—to *us*."

"Good things do happen to us," Aron argued. "Maybe just not in the most straightforward way."

Keegan addressed Kade and Jared, "What'd y'all think?"

"If the border's down, Caius is dead," Kade said plainly. "There's no way to cheat the spell."

There was a knock at the door.

"It's open," Keegan called, expecting one of the children in the house and unprepared for the woman who entered.

She was an ethereal creature, who possessed more grace than Keegan could ever hope to. The woman's skin was a pale blue with hints of silver scales scattered across her body. From below the collar of her dress, she could make out the head of a shark tattoo swimming beneath the collarbone.

Caught off guard, she struggled to remember the Mermaid's name, "Uhh... Atlia... right?"

"It is," she responded, gently closing the door. "Atlia Mahiako."

An awkward silence followed, and Keegan rocked on her heels, "Is there something we can help you with?"

"I was hoping to help you," Atlia said. "With Caius dead, Bernot wants to wage war and you are woefully unprepared. I am willing to train you in water magic."

Keegan shrugged, "When'd you wanna start?"

"Now."

"Eh, what the hell; ain't got nothing better to do."

Kade started to protest and she shot him a glare. He still wasn't forgiven for his omissions.

"Do you want us to come with you?" Jared asked.

"No," Keegan answered quickly, "I don't think Atlia's gonna try to kidnap me."

"That's what we thought about Wexsley and Halcyon," Kade said audibly under his breath.

Ignoring Kade, she followed Atlia. She expected to go to some watery training field, instead, the Mermaid took her to the kitchen downstairs, where she simply filled a glass with water and took a seat at the table.

"Do you know where the water paika is?" Atlia asked, leaning back in the chair.

"Reven told me once," Keegan said, racking her brain, "but I don't remember."

"In the right eye."

"Why's it there? It seems so irrelevant."

The Mermaid laughed, "So it does and I have no answer."

"I assume water magic should be similar to earth and life magic."

"I would agree, but I am only a water elemental so I cannot confirm it."

"Right."

Keegan closed her eyes. It felt awkward to be searching in her eye for a paika, but she found it easily enough. As per everything in Arciol, nothing made sense. The paika was bright orange, as if it were on fire. She took a breath and tried to smash it like she would the earth paika. Her hand passed through the gem and she switched her approach to resemble how she would gain access to the life paika, gently endeavoring to pick it up. Again, her hand passed through it. She opened her eyes, "Why can't I get hold of it?"

Atlia smiled, "What element are we working with?"

"Water," Keegan answered, unsure of what she was getting at.

"Then treat the paika like water."

She creased her brows, having an idea of what Atlia wanted her to do, but not sure of its validity. She decided to try it, rather than look a fool and ask for explicit instructions. Re-entering her mind, she found the paika again. Taking a deep breath, she reached towards the gem and simply let her hand rest inside.

A rush of power surged through her, though, it was different from the way it felt to use earth and life magic. The power flooded over her and felt like a wave lapping at her seams. Ripples of magic shifted and coursed through her body like blood through her veins.

She sent the magic towards the water in the glass before her and imagined it rising. When she opened her eyes, the water had done exactly as she wanted. She smiled to herself and decided to try something harder. With a quick furrowing of her eyes, she willed the water to freeze. The effect was almost instantaneous. Pleased with herself, she melted the ice and returned the water to the glass. She glanced at Atlia and was concerned with the stare she was getting. "What?"

"You have never used water magic before?" Atlia said quietly. "Are you sure?"

"Positive. Why?"

"What you just did is not something most water elementals—even Merfolk—do within the first few minutes of practice."

Keegan shrugged. "I've been getting a lot of that since I got here."

"Something special you are. Well, I suppose this is a good start. We will continue tomorrow."

"Sounds good," she said, taking a sip from the glass. She watched Atlia leave, then slipped out the back door.

‡‡‡

"Good morning," Alyck said as Thaddeus entered the bedroom.

"Good morning. Any interesting news?"

"I am not sure. The world is amuck today."

"What do you mean?"

"Nothing is clear," Alyck said, sitting up. "Clouds cover everything."

"I wish I knew how to help you."

"Me too. I see something about the coronation. Something... I am just not sure what though."

Thaddeus came to squat beside the bed. "Do you want me to do something?"

"I am not sure." There was a pause. "Look after Braxton."

"I can do that," Thaddeus said, patting Alyck's knee then standing and walking from the chambers allotted to them.

He made his way through the castle, doing his best to blend in with the servants scurrying around. A few guards recognized him, but all knew he had free reign—at least he had during Caius' rule and assumed the courtesy would extend into Braxton's.

He first looked for Braxton in his chambers and ran into Nico. The child was alarmed to see him and Thaddeus slipped away before he could do much questioning. The next place he checked was the dining hall, where he met Kolt. He was unsure if the boy knew who he was and his place within the castle but was not about to ask, knowing his volatile reputation.

After that, he went to the griffin stables. The beasts eyed him eagerly but there was nothing he could do to save these magnificent creatures from their fate; that was something only Sola and Lunos could do. He did however offer some small comfort. "Caius has left this world," he said before disappearing back into the secret tunnels that he preferred to use.

Clicks from the griffins called after him, begging for more than those simple words.

He was about to head back to Alyck's chambers when he realized where Braxton was. He would have done the same if the opportunity had been allowed him.

The way to the Chapel of the Prioress was unfamiliar. The doors were ornate, and even more terrifying than those that guarded the throne room. One was a deep black with a pearl white dragon soaring across its inkiness. The other, white as the sun, had an onyx dragon faced its opposing counterpart. The expression shared between the two beasts was not one of hatred, but of love.

Thaddeus pushed open the white door and entered. If the doors were beautiful, he had no words to describe the Chapel itself. Colored windows scattered rainbows across the room, suggesting the opposite of death and shadows. Elegantly crafted statues of women crying out for lost loved ones circled the room. In the center was a stone altar, upon which a body lay; Braxton stood at its head.

He carefully made his way over, noticing how no tears fell down Braxton's face, in spite of his look of utter shock. "There was nothing you could have done," he said softly.

Braxton was slow to pull his eyes from his father's body. "What if there was?"

"How could you have known?" Thaddeus asked, placing a hand on his shoulder. Considering how things were moving, he could have been aware.

Braxton looked to him. "I did know. I have been... having visions."

"What did you see?"

Braxton looked back at his father.

"You can tell me," Thaddeus encouraged. "I will not tell another soul."

"I saw the future."

Thaddeus feigned surprise.

"It is hard to discern what the visions are at times. And I never know when they will come to pass."

"It is all right," Thaddeus said, forcing Braxton to look away from the body by pulling him into an embrace. It was then he felt tears soaking the fabric of his shirt.

"Sometimes I wished him dead. Sometimes I wanted to kill him."

We all did. "But *you* were not the one who killed him."

‡‡‡
‡‡‡

He hated the feeling of nothing existing in the world, nothing but his mind. The air was stale and hot and there was the distinct tang of iron. He loathed that smell, but there was no way to be rid of it, not until he could wash his hands and find a change of clothes.

"Stop," Reven called.

Lucas jerked to a halt, the silence suffocating him once again. There was the sound of something scraping against the floor and a breeze flooded through the tunnel, washing away the smell of blood. Light flooded his eyes and he shied away.

"Quickly," Reven whispered, "'fore anyone realizes we 're still down here."

Lucas crawled from the tunnel and Reven re-covered the entrance. He looked down at his hands, amazed to find so little blood on his person; only the tips of his fingers were red, and he could only find a few droplets on his clothes. He wondered how such a small amount could create such a strong smell.

Reven tossed him a rag. "Wipe your hands."

Lucas wrung them in the cloth, but almost none of the blood came away. Taking his water-skin, he wetted the rag, and tried again. This time, the blood transferred readily. He stared down at it, captivated by its power.

"Quit gawkin' and walk!"

Lucas watched as Reven crept up the stairs from the cellar, freezing for a moment before continuing. When he followed, he saw why Reven had paused; a man stood at the bar, his back to them. He wondered why the man didn't turn, then realized Reven was controlling him. Bile rose in his throat. No one should have their body used against them. "Let him go."

"I 'ill when we get out o' here. I do 't like doing it any more than you."

Knowing there was no other choice, Lucas crept through the inn after Reven, stealing a glance at the man as he exited and saw Reven had kept his word.

In the stables, the horses weren't saddled, but their bags were packed and all they needed to do was get the bovestun things on the animals. They quickly set to work, making sure they left nothing behind, and were ready in what felt like seconds.

"Now, we go to the Lazado," Lucas said, swinging up into the saddle.

"Yes."

‡‡‡
‡‡‡

Aron paced across the common room. Jared and Kade had long since eaten and retired, regardless of their concern for Keegan. That morning, she had begun training with Atlia. The Merprincess had since left, but Keegan was nowhere to be found.

Bernot had been notified and soldiers were searching for her. Aron prayed she had just wandered off and this was not a repeat of before.

The door opened and there she stood. His insides became butterflies as his stomach filled with relief.

She looked at him with pursed lips and entered the room, two men and Bernot coming in behind her.

Aron rushed forward and pulled her into a hug. "Where have you been? I—*we* have been worried sick."

She rolled her eyes. "Calm down, mom. I just went for a walk."

Bernot gave her a stern look.

"A really long walk."

"Do not get yourself into any more trouble," Bernot said, opening the door to leave. "Ezekhial and Zavier will be staying to make sure you do just that."

Aron wanted to protest but Keegan grabbed his arm and pulled him into his room. He started to talk, but all it earned him was Keegan shushing him.

"Where were you?" he blurted.

"I actually did just go for a walk. Didn't mean to scare y'all. Just kinda forgot how *important* I am. Bernot found me hours ago."

"Why didn't he bring you back immediately?" he questioned. She was beautiful and... he pushed the thought aside; Bernot was an honorable man.

"He wanted help picking my new guards."

"The two men outside?"

"They do have names," she teased. "Ezekhial and Zavier. As well as two others."

"Why did he want your help picking them?"

"Telepathy. Plus, I pretty much said I'd keep sneaking off if he assigned guys I didn't like."

Aron shook his head, sighing, "You are the only person who could ever demand something from a man like that and get it."

"Perks of being me."

"Why did you go for a 'really long' walk?"

"To think."

He took a seat on the bed. "Do you want to talk?"

"For once in my life that'd actually be helpful," she said, sitting beside him. "Since I got here, I've felt like I've been in a vise. When we were told Caius was dead, that vise tightened more. At least before, I knew what I was supposed to be doing, and there wasn't much anyone could do to make me do anything. With Caius dead, all bets are off."

Aron furrowed his eyebrows. "I am not sure what you are afraid of."

"Not really anything." She bit the inside of her lip thinking. "I just don't know how I fit into this world anymore, I guess. Not that I fit in before."

"No one is going to force you to do anything."

She laughed. "Oh, I know that. But I just got demoted from king to pawn."

"What?"

"Do y'all really not have chess here? Anyway, what I mean is that I went from being the person who has the power to the person who's getting controlled."

"We are all in that position."

"I know. But I don't like it."

"None of us do."

CHAPTER 64

Nico sat with his legs dangling over the precipice, Ima on his left and Harker to his right.

Are we going to fly today? Harker asked, looking up at Nico with his glossy black eyes that exuded innocence.

"No, Braxton's burying Caius. Not much of anything is going to be happening besides falsely shed tears."

Was Caius a bad person? Ima asked.

Nico was about to scoff at her question then remembered how young she was—barely a year old. "Yes, he was a very bad person."

What about Braxton? Harker said, laying his head in Nico's lap.

He had to think. Braxton was one of the few people who'd shown him kindness since his ordeal began but he'd also heard the rumors. "I'm not sure I can answer that."

They were silent for a time and watched the sun make its path across the morning sky. He'd considered going to the funeral but knew it would bring up too many painful memories. Already thoughts of his mother were resurfacing, and he had to push them away before his emotions broke forth. He wiped his eyes to cover the evidence.

When can we fly again? Harker asked.

Nico smiled, thankful for the griffin's young age and resulting short attention span. "After Braxton's coronation." For as antsy as they were to return to the skies—to temporary freedom—he felt their sentiments.

When is that? Ima said.

"Tomorrow."

Then what happens?

"I'm not sure. I hope things will return to the way they were before."

Including the Vosjnik using us as sky horses? Myrish said behind them.

Nico whipped around to look at the bronze-tinted griffin. The adults didn't usually have anything to say to him.

"I don't know Braxton's plans," Nico admitted. He wanted to say more, assure Myrish those monsters would never get to experience what it was like to fly.

Instead, he focused his attention on the horizon as his thoughts turned to the future. With Braxton as king, there was a chance he'd be given back his freedom. There was a chance he could walk away from all of this.

‡‡‡

The Chapel of the Prioress was filled to capacity and he could feel the hundreds of eyes that pretended to cry staring at him; he hated the feeling of being watched. The chapel filled with incense and he knew the funeral was about to begin in proper.

The sounds of a hymn drifted through the air, sweet and melodic, carrying feelings of sorrow. The words were in the Old Language and he could pick out a few. He knew he should be shedding tears of grief, but his eyes remained dry. He stole a glance at his brother and saw tears beginning to gather.

He refocused on the body before him. His father was wrapped in white linen with a red sash tied around the torso. The sash was meant to represent the blood that flowed through all men and the sin that came forth after death. He huffed, knowing so much more sin should be showing.

A line of prioresses reached the body, all garbed in dresses made of pale pink silk accented with blue, while white chiffon veils covered their faces and draped over their arms. They were beautiful, like seraphs sent by Sola and Lunos.

The singing stopped and turned into a droning hum. The cloud of incense grew thicker and the smell clogged his nostrils. The room became quiet as if death himself had descended.

A single voice filled the atmosphere. It was ethereal and at first seemed to have no origin. Then Braxton realized it was the prioress he had spoken to the yesterday. Her face was unveiled, and painted ichor-colored tears streamed down her face. The air in the room seemed to instantly clear of the smell and smoke.

He then noticed his father's body—or, the place it had lain, for incredulously, it had disappeared. Panic rose in his chest.

"Today, we have sent a king to an eternal life with Sola and Lunos," the prioress spoke. "His worldly body has been laid to rest within the soil of this earth. The elements that created him shall reclaim him. Blood and bones will turn to dust and water and replenish the earth. Death creates life."

The prioresses began to sing again, and Braxton felt something slide down his face. He reached up: tears. He willed them to cease, but they only fell quicker.

There was a hand on his shoulder, and he turned to find Kolt, tears also spilling from his eyes. They shared a look and for the first time, Braxton realized Kolt did care, did have a heart. He pulled his brother into an embrace and they shared their sorrow.

472

‡‡‡

Aron had been awake since before sunrise. He and Keegan had talked until eventually falling asleep. In the middle of the night, he had awoken in a cold sweat and even now his father's face floated across his vision. Knowing he would never fall back asleep he had crawled out the window and sat on the roof—Keegan had showed him this hideaway; his father's death had finally sunk in.

It was barely midday, but the sun was hot and the few sparse leaves at the crown of the tree offered little relief. He felt a pang in the pit of his stomach and recognized it as the same feeling he had felt after Shiloh died. Why? How could he feel anything but joy at Caius' departure?

"Hey," a voice called.

His attention snapped to Keegan.

She climbed onto the roof and sat beside him. "What's wrong?"

"I… I am not sure," he admitted.

She pulled him into a hug. "It's okay to be sad; he was your father."

He was unable to do or say anything for what seemed an eternity. Then slowly, and of their own accord, his arms wrapped around her as tears began to fall down his face. "Why am I upset?" he managed.

"Because, regardless of how shitty a person was, he was family and he loved you. I kind of understand. It's why Kade did what he did—or at least in part, anyway."

"My father never loved me."

Keegan rubbed his back, "In his own twisted way, he did. Why else would he've kept your identity secret? Why else would he've let you live the life you did?"

"Because he had to." He wiped his eyes and took a deep breath. "My father made a Death Deal with my mother when I was born, he could not kill or grievously hurt me."

"Seems a bit extreme."

He shrugged and returned his attention to the rolling forest covering the horizon, knowing Keegan wanted to do something, or say something to comfort him. He put a hand on her knee, giving it a gentle squeeze.

"If there's anything I can do, let me know."

When he did not respond, she clambered down from the roof.

He felt a lump in his throat and drew his knees up to his chest. He did not care about his father, not after everything he had done and let happen. Yet, he did care, and there was nothing he could do about it.

473

CHAPTER 65

Jared brought the mug to his lips and let the steam waft through his nostrils before taking a sip. The people of Edreba had a peculiar morning custom of drinking this strange tea made from ground beans. Keegan called it coffee and refused to drink it. He quite liked it. Across the table, Carter scarfed down a plate of food.

"Slow down," he chuckled, "it's not going anywhere."

"It's been ages since I was allowed to eat as much as I wanted," Carter said through a mouthful.

Jared let him return to his breakfast. Since reuniting, he hadn't been able to stop smiling and not even Kade's presence could make it fade. In what was becoming a habit with Keegan, she'd disappeared the previous night and hadn't return until well past sunset. Thus, she had no idea Carter was now living with them.

There was a knock on the door before a man entered. "Is Keegan awake yet?"

"Who are you?" Jared questioned.

"Ezekhial Dorehiem, one of Keegan's new guards."

"I don't think so. After Halcyon and Wexsley, I don't trust anyone around Keegan. No offense."

"None taken, but since Keegan chose me herself, I don't think you have much of a say."

"When did she do this?"

"Yesterday. There are four of us who will be in rotation."

"We'll see about that."

Carter rolled his eyes. "Calm down. He seems like a good man."

"So did Halcyon and Wexsley," Jared countered.

Carter leaned back in his chair. "I keep hearing those names. What did they do?"

"They were Keegan's guards. They killed another guard, kidnapped Keegan and Mahogen, and handed them over to the Vosjnik, who caused a whole other set of problems to arise."

"Like?"

"Like us learning you and Lucas were alive," Jared said angrily, his hatred of Kade rising. "Like Keegan learning she's Kade's twin."

Carter, who was taking a sip of coffee, just managed to stop himself from spitting it out. "What? You're kidding, right?"

"I wish." The door opened and closed and when he glanced up, he saw Keegan.

When she saw Carter, her face lit up and she rushed over to hug him. "When did you get here?"

"Last night," Carter responded, cautiously returning her hug. After a moment, he hugged her in earnest.

"What's with the new guards?" Jared tried to keep his tone even.

She gave an aggravated groan, "Bernot's idea." When he tried to protest, she held up a finger to quell him. "I said I'd be fine with y'all looking after me and he essentially said either we agree or we don't, but I'd still be getting guards. So, I caved a bit, and he let me choose them."

"Did you choose them randomly? I can't say I trust Ezekhial."

"No. Used a bit of telepathy."

"I still don't like them."

Keegan rolled her eyes. "Figures."

"What are your plans for today?" Carter asked.

"Probably some training," Keegan answered, making herself a plate of food. "Maybe some running away."

Jared gave her a harsh look.

She rolled her eyes again. "Kidding."

There was a knock before the door opened and Jared was surprised to see Atlia. He knew the Mermaid was training Keegan but had expected her to hand her over to some tutor.

"Hey, Atlia," Keegan said, greeting her as if they were life-long friends.

"Are you ready?" the Mermaid asked.

"Yeah," Keegan said, shoving food into her mouth, "let me eat right quick."

Though Atlia was one of the leaders, Jared still felt a hint of distrust.

"Quit worrying," Keegan grumbled, picking up on his feelings and pushed back from the table. "I'll see y'all later."

✝✝✝

It felt good to be fighting with a sword—even if it was only against a straw-stuffed dummy. Kade let his muscles lead his hands and feet. His body acted without much instruction and he fell into a rhythm: cut, slash, hack.

"That dummy must've done something to donp you off," a voice behind him said.

Kade whipped around, his mind instinctively telling him to keep his weapon raised and poised to attack. There was a clang as two swords met.

"Watch it there, I don't pop back up like that dummy."

He quickly took in the man, who was shorter than himself by a few inches. He had brown eyes with a laugh about them, crinkles about the corners, and was missing half of his left eyebrow, presumably from a fight.

"Who are you?" Kade asked, stepping back.

"Elhyas Wealsh," the man dropped his sword, so its point went into the ground.

His usual desire to be left alone presented itself in his tone. "Can I help you?"

"You can drop the attitude to start with. I was just wondering if you wanted a proper sparring partner."

Kade felt bad for his gruffness. "Yes, I would appreciate a partner— a living one."

"Care to switch to sparring weapons, Kade? Or do you think you can best old Elhyas?"

Kade heard warning bells. "How do you know my name?"

Elhyas laughed. "Son, everyone here knows your name. And the name of that pretty sister of yours and two brothers to boot. You four are the celebrities of the town."

"Why do you want to spar?" He was suddenly concerned the man might be seeking retribution.

"I want to see if you're as good as everyone claims. People boast of the great Kade Tavin and his skill with a sword and magic. I think it's just chalked up bulla vite."

Kade lunged forward, "Let's put it to the test."

Elhyas easily blocked his attack and quickly parried. Back and forth they went, their swords clanking together as if they were in true battle. Kade could feel sweat on his skin and pushed Elhyas harder, realizing this man was his equal. His muscles pleaded for him to give ground and give up, but his mind pushed, knowing there was much more left.

For a moment, he was distracted and that was all Elhyas needed. Elhyas struck the flat of his blade near the guard and the weapon slipped from his grip. Before he could even comprehend what was happening, Elhyas had the sword at his throat.

Elhyas smiled and pulled away. "Not bad, sonny."

"Not bad?" Kade exclaimed, "I am—was one of the king's best swordsmen."

"I can see that." Elhyas took a long drink from a water-skin. "But you're used to fighting coerced men and peasants. Still, you're better than most of the men on this field." He offered him the water-skin.

Kade looked at it skeptically before accepting. "You say I'm good, but I'd wager you'd say I could become better."

"You'd be right." Elhyas flashed him a smile. "Would you care to do exactly that?"

"Of course," Kade said, crossing his arms. "But who's going to train me—you? You barely bested me."

"'Tis true, but only just besting you with my non-dominant hand."

Kade stared dubiously at him then glancing at his hands noticed his palm and fingers were clearly more calloused on his right hand, but recalled he'd been using his left. "Then train me, oh master," he said sarcastically, giving a bow to enhance the statement.

"You got a mouth on you, sonny. We'll start tomorrow."

"Why not today?"

"I have things to do," Elhyas said, picking up his sword and walking away. "Keep going at that dummy though; I'm sure he's done something to deserve it."

✝✝✝

The muted sunshine filtering through the leaves dangling off the giant branches above made the atmosphere feel cozy as Keegan followed Atlia. She knew they would train today but had wrongly assumed they would do so at the children's home again. Ezekhial trod along behind them, doing his best to go unnoticed. She made sure that while her guards were treated like friends, they still make themselves ghosts when she wanted privacy.

So far, Atlia hadn't said a word and she was more than happy with the silence, taking in the beauty of the treetop city and surrounding forest as they walked. She'd spent far too little time on the forest floor to recognize where they were, but the path felt familiar and haunting. It wasn't long before the trees began to diminish and fell away altogether.

Atlia led her into a clearing, the sun's full force greeting them warmly. It took Keegan a moment before she knew where they were. Nature had long since washed away the blood, but the memories remained.

Her heart pounded against her chest. "Why'd you bring me here?"

"Because you must learn to face that which you fear," Atlia commented, making her way over to the pond.

Keegan paused, a lump in her throat. She could so clearly see Halcyon and Wexsley's faces that it felt as if they were back from the dead. Her eyes snapped open, dispelling the vision and slowly took a seat beside Atlia. "I don't fear them."

"No," the Mermaid said, letting her fingertips brush across the water's surface, "you fear the betrayal and memories." She sat back and a ball of water rose from the pond, one of the koi trapped within. The fish swam along the rim of the bubble like nothing was amiss, its webbed fins fanned out elegantly. "This fish is you," she began, "and your world is the water in the pond. That comfort was taken away, but you keep swimming."

There was a caw and Keegan looked up to see a hawk circling.

"You can see your enemies but cannot stop them. Then there are your friends and family. Your enemies threaten them, and you forget about the threat to yourself."

The hawk began plummeting and Keegan flinched, knowing it was going to scoop up the koi in its talons. There was another caw and she reopened her eyes. The koi was still swimming serenely in its floating bubble. She looked towards the hawk and saw a squirrel struggling to free itself.

Atlia continued, "Sometimes, the enemy you perceive has their sights set elsewhere. Today, you are safe, but there will come a time when you are under attack. Now, I pose a question, will you sit and watch calmly, like this koi, as danger catches you in its snare—or will you look that danger in the eye and keep it at bay?"

"I want to fight," Keegan said, her heart inexplicably calm.

"Then forget the hurts of enemies past." Atlia lowered the koi back into the pond. "That danger has gone. Learn from it, but let it haunt you no more."

"Easier said than done. You've got your mother standing behind you. I've got the entire world fighting over me, and danger likes making a joke of my life."

Atlia turned and gave her a sad smile. "No, I am alone in my duty to guide a nation. Fear clouds my eyes and I fight every minute to clear it. The danger we come to meet head-on is no longer a danger to us, as we become a danger to it. You are so much stronger than you think, Keegan. Do not let your fear stop you from becoming a force no one can reckon with."

A silence settled between them.

Keegan willed her heart to slow, but it fought against her, pleading to flee. The world cooled and she felt her body beginning to shiver as she battled fear. Memories of Caius surfaced, and her muscles tensed. Recollections of Vitia came forth and she felt her body begin to shiver.

Halcyon and Wexsley pushed forward and she felt an icy stab in her heart. The cold became overwhelming and she opened her eyes.

The pond in front of her was frozen over in inches-thick ice.

"What'd you do?" Keegan said quietly.

"This was not me," Atlia said. "Magic is born from fear and is controlled by it. To control magic, we must control our fears, or our fears control our magic and us."

"How can anyone get rid of their fear?"

"That is an impossible quest. Remember, I said you must learn to control your fear, never banish it. Fear is what keeps us alive, but it can also kill us if we lose control of it. And to control it, we must face it."

✝✝✝

It was hard to believe the bright cheerful halls Thaddeus now walked had been covered in black hangings only a few hours past. There had been a quick transition from funeral decorations to gay ones for the coronation. Bright banners bearing the Alagard emblem hung from the walls, dispelling any traces of mourning. He was not surprised the world would rather rejoice.

The air was alit with laughter and there was a plethora of people bustling about. The higher within the castle he went, the fewer people there were. When he reached the level where the crown prince, soon to be king resided, there was only gloom.

He gently knocked on Braxton's door and entered when given permission.

"What do you want?" Braxton asked quietly.

"I just wanted to see if you were all right."

Braxton turned to face him. His eyes red and puffy and there were wet splotches on his shirt. "What do you think?"

"I know what it is like to lose someone." He came to stand beside the prince. "I know how much it hurts."

"You lost your son."

"And my daughter-in-law, and potentially my grandson."

"How have you not drowned in tears by now?"

"Because it will not bring them back. I did my share of mourning, but there comes a time when you move on. Wear the loss like a badge and do something great with it. Make the lives of those around you better."

"How would you suggest I do that?"

479

"That is something you will have to figure out. But I do know taking the crown tomorrow and being a fair ruler will put you on the right path."

"What if I do not want to be king?"

"That is your choice."

"What if I want to be king but it is not my fate?"

"Then there is nothing you or I can do except help he who does take the throne." A pause followed and Thaddeus felt there was cause behind the prompted questions. "Is there something you saw?"

"Yes. I saw myself—I think it was me—sitting on the throne. Then, Kolt was stabbing me in the back."

"Kolt stabbed you in the back?" He instantly knew there were two possible meanings.

"Yes," Braxton looked at him with fear in his eyes. "I know Kolt has always wanted the throne, but do you suppose it is possible he would be willing to kill for it?"

"I do not think so," Thaddeus lied; he had no doubt that without Caius keeping him in check, Kolt would do whatever he pleased. "The visions are not always what you think. Sometimes, they offer clues and symbols about the future, rather than the future itself."

Braxton looked like he wanted to argue. "I am sure you are correct. After all, you would know more about this than I."

"Do not worry about tomorrow or even the day after. I know in my heart of hearts you will be one of the greatest kings this world has ever seen."

"Thank you."

Thaddeus could tell the prince was tired and he headed to the door. Braxton called him back. "Could you do me a favor?"

"Of course."

"Will you present me to the gods tomorrow at the ceremony?"

"It would be an honor."

Braxton gave him a grateful nod that dismissed him.

Thaddeus was slow to return to Alyck's quarters, Braxton's vision weighing heavily on his mind. There were too many ways, both literal and metaphorical, for Kolt to stab Braxton in the back for him to even begin trying to thwart the prince.

CHAPTER 66

The world around him was soft and comfortable, though, the sheets were coarse against his bare skin. There was a smell in the air that he could not place, for, in reality, it was like he was smelling water. Aron arched his back and stretched.

His arm brushed against something warm in the bed beside him. Warily, he opened his eyes and was assaulted with a riot of rust-colored hair splayed around someone's head like a halo. Guilt overwhelmed him as he racked his brain. *Who is this?*

She gave a sleepy groan, rolled over, and his eyes widened as he stared at Keegan. She pulled herself close to him and nestled into the crook of his shoulder. He lay there, his mouth agape as he struggled to recall the events of the previous night.

He had hidden on the roof for most of the morning until the sun had heated the shingles to an unbearable temperature. At that point, he relocated to his room and spent the day sulking, not emerging once. Just before dinner, Keegan came to check on him. He had not managed to get a single word out before she ran out. Feeling worse than before, he skipped dinner.

Well past dusk, she returned, a flask clutched in her hand like it was gold and a mischievous grin that told him she was up to no good.

"What is that?" he asked.

She simply opened the stopper and let him take a whiff, the pungent smell immediately giving the answer: alcohol. She took a gulp before handing it to him.

There were misgivings, but after seeing the gleam in her eyes, he took a sip. The alcohol burned as it traced down his throat, leaving a warm feeling behind. He coughed through the after-burn, "Where did you get this?"

"Let's just say I owe Behthany a favor. You ever had vodka before?"

He took another sip. "What is vodka?"

"Right," she took the flask back, "y'all wouldn't call it vodka. It's what you're drinking now."

"No, I have never had it."

"This is gonna be fun."

After that, everything became a blur, his head feeling heavy. Most of what he remembered was bringing the flask to his lips several more times and the warm burning sensation that followed.

He watched as Keegan inched closer to him. Then, before he could pull himself away, their lips were melded together. Her breath was warm and carried passion. His hands found themselves on her shoulders, intending to push her away, but instead pulled her closer.

Her clothes felt soft under his fingertips, but all he wanted was to feel her skin. He scrabbled to pull her shirt off. She pushed him back, staring at him breathlessly as guilt washed over him. It took only a moment for the entire mood to change.

She started to pull at him desperately. Her hands pushing his shirt up and he pulled it off, throwing it to the side and returning to her. Her shirt was gone and his hands roamed the smooth contours of her back. She pulled him towards the bed and together they fell onto it.

His mind refused to think of anything other than what was happening, anything other than Keegan. Their bodies came together, like forgotten lovers, a lock and key, puzzle pieces… Nothing else in the world except them and then existed. The act was soon over but the air still coursed with electricity. Their breaths came heavily, his heart begging for more.

Keegan nestled against him and it wasn't long before she was asleep.

"I love you," he had whispered, kissing her head before he too fell asleep.

Aron ran a hand through his hair; how could he have let this happen? He glanced over at her and Keegan gave an incomprehensible groggy mumble. Gently, he lifted himself from the bed, doing his best to not wake her. He quickly dressed and then all but fled the room.

How could he have done this with Keegan? How could he have done this *to* Keegan?

‡‡‡

"What is our first move?" Okleiy asked.

"Uh…" Bernot mumbled, for the first time in a while struggling to come up with a plan. "That is what we are here to figure out."

"The Children have asked you to wait," Atlia said calmly. "And did you not agree to do so?"

"I did," Bernot admitted. "But sometimes waiting is not an option."

"So, you lied to them?" Atlia accused.

Okleiy leaned back in his chair, clearly enjoying seeing Bernot flustered. "What do you want us to do?"

"Something…" Bernot answered.

"The Children were right," Atlia said, "Waiting is our best course of action."

"Why?"

"Because jumping into water without knowing what lies at the bottom ensures injury."

"We cannot appear weak," Okleiy argued. "We have to show that we will not stand for another tyrant king."

"The Children told you what we need to do. Listen to them," Atlia said, anger tingeing her voice.

"What exactly did they suggest?" Okleiy asked, anger in his voice, too.

"That we wait," Bernot told him, "but place soldiers at the border so we would be prepared should Braxton prove to be like his father."

"Which is an excellent plan," Atlia exclaimed. "It lets us show that we will attack need be, but that we do not want to."

"Yes, but it also might cause Braxton to retaliate."

"How? We would have done nothing to warrant retaliation."

"Sometimes, the threat of attack is as good as an actual attack."

"We cannot sit and do nothing," Okleiy yelled. "That is how you got into this mess in the first place!"

"This is not Caius," Atlia snapped. "This is his son. Someone who is not *exactly* like his father."

Bernot rubbed his temples as the Alvor and Merqueen continued to yell at each other. "Stop!" he roared, slamming a hand on the desk. "Bickering gets us nowhere."

"Then decide," Atlia snarled.

He was silent as he drowned out Okleiy and Atlia.

"Bernot," Okleiy snapped.

He took a breath before starting. "We wait."

Atlia's lips transformed into a smirk and Okleiy began to protest.

"But we also attack."

"You cannot do both," Atlia said.

"We can. We barely have enough soldiers to do any damage without the Merfolk, so until they arrive, we wait. But we attack with diplomacy. We send word to Braxton asking to make peace."

Okleiy huffed, "You think that will work?"

"It is worth try," Atlia agreed. "If it works, lives will be spared. If not, we are already prepared to face that possibility."

"And how do we convince the other nations to join us?"

"If this works, we will not have to," Bernot answered.

‡‡‡

"Rise an' shine, arse face" Reven said, prodding Lucas with his boot.

"Shut the royik up," Lucas grumbled, turning onto his back. As he rolled, he felt his vertebrae cracking. The sun had yet to rise over the treetops and thus was not blinding. He sat up and rubbed the sleep from his eyes.

Reven tossed him some jerky. "Hurry up. We 're burning daylight."

Lucas quickly packed his bedroll and they left the clearing at an amiable trot.

"Wonder what the funeral was like," Reven said.

"What?" Lucas questioned.

"Caius' funeral—I wonder what it was like."

"What difference does it make?"

Reven shrugged. "Was just wondering if people cried or celebrated."

Lucas rolled his eyes and was glad when Reven said no more; he found it straining to not throttle him when he talked. But he did find himself considering the question.

He supposed Caius had people who cared about him—though, he couldn't fathom who. As far as he knew, Caius had never been married, and never had children, so his parents might be the only people who grieved for him—assuming they were still alive. But that was impossible as the king had been over two centuries old.

His heart began to feel heavy as it continued down this train of thought. If he were to drop dead today, who would miss him? He wasn't even entirely sure Nico and Jared were alive. Carter might assume he was dead after his disappearing stunt. Reven... He would probably be the only person who would mark his passing. He shuddered at the thought. "How long until we reach the Lazado?" he blurted.

"Few weeks," Reven said, "Maybe less if we push."

"Let's push."

Reven laughed, "Got a girl to see?"

"No, family. Family to make sure that's still alive."

"Then let 's get going. Would n't want to keep 'em waiting."

‡‡‡

Thaddeus reached over and straightened the sash that crossed Braxton's chest. "There. Perfect."

Braxton gave him a weak smile. "Thank you."

"Are you nervous?"

"My stomach is in knots."

484

"Good, remember that feeling and use it to help you make good decisions."

"Is that not what I have you and Alyck for?" Braxton said, giving a genuine smile.

Thaddeus returned the smile as trumpets sounded from inside the throne room. "Are you ready?"

"No."

"That is all right." Thaddeus took a deep breath and pushed open the doors, the griffins carved into them eyeing them scornfully.

He turned his attention to the people in the room. Bright colors covered the bodies of everyone; women wore elegant up-dos and priceless gems, and men wore dashing coats, embroidered in silver, gold, and bronze. Hundreds of faces turned to smile at them and get a glimpse of the prince to be turned king. Flowers accented the room and banners bearing the Alagard coat-of-arms hung from the walls.

Together, they walked towards the throne. At the bottom of the steps, Thaddeus stopped. Braxton looked back, gave him a reassuring nod, and slowly ascended the steps.

Thaddeus knelt, "Long live the king." Seeing the smile playing on Braxton's lips, he knew he would be fine. He then walked back down the aisle and exited the throne room. Walking down the hall, he frowned; the corridors were completely empty—of guards, servants, everyone. Probably nothing, everyone was at the coronation.

Worries aside, he put a spring in his step, knowing Braxton would make a great and just ruler. Reaching Alyck's chambers, he inhaled deeply, knowing as soon as he crossed the threshold he re-entered a prison of sorts. "Alyck, I am back. You should see the throne room." When there was no response on how that was impossible, he called again, "Alyck?" Concern rising, he made his way to the sleeping quarters.

Alyck sat on the bed, staring emptily at his hands, looking nothing like he had when Thaddeus had left him. As the Blind Prophet, he was exempt from the ravages of time so long as Caius and those of his blood remained on the throne. Now, he looked like he had aged thirty years. Gray hair covered his head, sunspots dappled his skin, and wrinkles pulled at his body.

Thaddeus rushed to him. "What is happening?"

"Change," Alyck answered.

"How do we stop it?"

Alyck smiled. "You do not."

Thaddeus watched as the transformation continued before his eyes. The now gray hair began to fall from his scalp, lying across the bed like macabre snowfall. Alyck's breaths started to come in raspy wheezes.

"There has to be a way to stop this."

"Oh, there is," Alyck said, letting himself fall back onto the bed. "But I do not want to." He took a shuddering breath and stilled.

"No!"

Then, in a moment, Alyck returned to his former self. His face became youthful, the wrinkles ironed themselves out, and his black hair regrew in an instant. He bolted upright, eyes wide and afraid. "No. NO! This was not supposed to happen. The bastard!"

"What are you talking about?" Thaddeus questioned, simultaneously relieved he was alive and worried about this new threat.

"Go see our new king for your answers. Then tell him I will never serve him."

✝✝✝

The air seemed to catch in his throat as he watched Thaddeus leave. Somehow, the Keeper of Prophecy had come to be a source of stability and comfort. Braxton pushed the thought away and focused on the priest standing before him.

"Are you ready?" the priest whispered.

He nodded, his stomach like a great snake trying to tie itself into a knot.

"Citizens of Agrielha," the priest began, speaking to the observers.

Braxton droned out the words, his mind taking in everything around him, from the decorations to the people—to the lack of Kolt. Try as he might, he could not locate his brother. At first, he was disappointed, then an uneasy feeling settled in; he had no time to dwell on it as the priest returned his attention to him.

"Do you swear to uphold the laws of this nation?" the priest continued, "Do you swear to uphold justice for those who misstep? Do you swear to uphold faith in your people? Do you swear to lead this nation in peace and war? Do you swear to rule with wisdom and kindness?"

Braxton gulped, understanding the weight about to be put on his shoulders. "I do. I swear to uphold the law strictly, but to show mercy to those who might be led from the path of violence. I swear to ride into battle with my soldiers should the time come but pray for peace and prosperity instead. I swear to rule with the wisdom of those before me and with the guidance of those who wish to give it. I swear to all of this so this nation and its people may prosper."

The priest picked up a bowl of ash and smeared it along Braxton's jaw, "Rule with the strength and fierceness of your father." Ash was smeared in a line that traced the bottom of his eyes and ran over the bridge of his nose. "Rule with the kindness and understanding of Seleena." Ash went on his eyebrows, "Rule with the courage and wisdom of The Dragon King." The priest turned to pick up the crown.

This one was different from the one that had graced Caius' head; each ruler had their own. The one Braxton would wear was made of red gold with a single ruby imbedded above the space between the brows. Kolt had designed it and he felt pride knowing his brother had done well.

His thoughts returned to the fact that Kolt was absent. He forced himself to focus on the priest and the crown. Just as it was about to rest upon his head, the doors burst open and soldiers flooded the room.

The priest withdrew, as shocked as everyone else.

Braxton slowly got to his feet, spotting Kolt amidst the soldiers. "What is the meaning of this?"

"An excellent question, brother," Kolt said, slowly approaching, the soldiers falling in behind him. "Did you think I would miss my own coronation?"

"This is not your coronation."

One of his signature sneers was plastered across Kolt's face. "Are you sure?"

Before Braxton could get another word out, hands latched onto his arms. His first instinct was to reach for his magic, but he had barely reached the paika when he felt cold metal around his wrists. He lost the connection to his magic and try as he might, could not regain access. "What is this?" he demanded as soldiers pulled him off the throne and down to where his brother stood.

"Call it an overthrow," Kolt said, taking a seat upon the throne.

"You cannot do this."

"Just did. Take him away."

In vain, Braxton struggled against the men who pulled him down the aisle and towards the doors. "You will pay for this!"

"Stop."

The soldiers froze, while Braxton continued fighting.

"I want him to witness history." Kolt turned to the priest, "Do it or die where you stand."

Braxton could see how petrified the priest was as he picked up the bowl of ash and prepared to repeat the words he had said earlier.

"Skip the bulla vite," Kolt snarled.

Carefully, the priest put the bowl down and picked up the crown.

All too slowly, the crown descended. All too soon it was resting on Kolt's head.

The priest stepped back, "Long live the king."

"Long live the king," the people in the room echoed in warbled, fearful tones.

In a daze, Braxton no longer fought the soldiers as they dragged him away. The castle around him disappeared and he was thrown into his own mind. How could he be so stupid to believe Kolt would do anything good? He should have known. He should have known, and now everyone was going to suffer. He had known, and now he was going to suffer.

‡‡‡

His heart was in his throat. None of this should be happening. Braxton should be on the throne, not Kolt. Nico desperately wanted to do something, but fear kept him rooted in place as he watched in horror as Kolt was crowned and everyone's lives were thrust into uncertainty.

As soon as he found the ability to move, Nico slipped from the throne room. He journeyed through the halls briskly at first but was now practically running and almost flew past the secret passage, having to skid to a stop.

He pressed the stone and quickly began making his way through the walls. A few of the steps tripped him up; his shins would bear the marks in the morning. When he reached the stable, the griffins were all sitting peacefully.

All could tell he was frantic and their black eyes oozed concern.

What is wrong? Niyth asked.

Nico spoke between sharp breaths, "Kolt… Kolt is king."

The adults quickly got to their feet and agitatedly began pulling at their tethers.

This is not good, Crowlin said, hissing in anger.

The griffins began conversing in their tongue.

Having nothing else to do, he paced.

You came here for a reason, Myrish said. *What is it?*

"I… was going to release you and…"

Run away with us? Harker said excitedly.

Quickly, boy, Oxren said, *who knows how long before Kolt thinks to pay us a visit.*

"I don't have the key to your chains," Nico stammered, realizing how useless he was.

The griffins' heads lowered.

Then we are doomed to suffer under Kolt as we did under his father, Myrish said.

"I wish there was something I could do," Nico said, feeling feathers under his hand. Looking down, he found Ima staring up at him. "You're not chained."

Save them, Phynex begged. *Please.*

Nico nodded, pushing himself into action. He headed to the wall to grab one of the juvenile's saddles. As he lifted it up in his arms, the door to the stable slammed open.

Kolt entered, several soldiers at his back. "Where do you think you are going?"

Nico's heart pounded in his ears. How had Kolt known to come here so soon?

"Did you really think I did not know of this place?" Kolt laughed coldly. "Did you think I would not notice you all but running from my coronation?"

He noticed the crown on the prince's—the *king's* head.

"What I want to know is how you got here without any of my men seeing you?"

Nico set his jaw. He would remain silent for as long as he possibly could, though he was certain Kolt would break him before long.

"I presume you 'will never tell me'." Kolt gave another cold laugh. "We shall see about that." He snapped his fingers and the men behind him took a hold of Nico and dragged him from the stable.

He knew he should have fought, or at least tried, but it would earn him nothing but pain a bit sooner. Nico let his mind enter a blank bliss as he was marched down the hallways. This would need to be something he got good at if he was going to last long.

He was shoved into a room and the door closed heavily behind him. He barely heard the click of the lock as he took in his surroundings. He was in Braxton's chambers, or rather, theirs, since he'd become his student. What game was Kolt getting at?

CHAPTER 67

"What is this?" Okleiy queried, holding up a package.

"We know as much as you," Atlia snapped. "Bernot and I have not opened ours yet."

The three parcels for the leaders had arrived that morning, ostensibly from Agrielha. He had sent word to Braxton about creating a treaty only yesterday, so these had to have been sent some time before, which made him wonder if they were from Caius. They had each found a package outside their bedroom door that morning; likely, they had arrived by magic.

Slowly, Bernot undid the twine around the package. Inside was something wrapped in tissue paper and a note. He turned his attention to the note first.

7/31

Dear Bernot Bœllar,

I assume you have sent me a message requesting a peace treaty. Your want is unfounded; you will find one is unnecessary after I destroy you. However, there is a way for this to end peacefully. Surrender yourself, Keegan Digore, Kade Tavin, and Aron Alagard and I might pardon your people for fleeing from the crown. Deny me and I will annihilate you.

I will give you and the other races time to pledge your loyalty. I expect a response within a week. Bow down or die.

Kolt Alagard
King of this world

"Vite," he cursed.

"This is not good," Atlia said. "We have to go to war."

Bernot turned his attention to the package that had come with the note. Folding back the thin paper, he revealed two golden bracelets. It took several moments of scrutiny before he realized what they were and quickly dropped them onto the desk.

Atlia glanced up, worry etched on her face. "What are they?"

"Slajor manacles."

"Impossible. We destroyed them all when Caius became king."

"Apparently not," Okleiy said. "That, or they figured out how to make more."

"That spell was lost centuries ago," Atlia argued.

"Bernot," a voice called.

He looked around, trying to find the source.

Okleiy gave him a baffled look while Atlia struggled to hold back laughter, which earned her a menacing glare from the Alvor for daring to laugh during such a serious situation.

"Where is it coming from?" Bernot asked, realizing Atlia knew the voice's source.

"The Looking Glass," she said, nodding towards his desk drawer.

Bernot yanked open the drawer, almost pulling it from the desk, and rummaged around until he found it. The piece had the faces of Tahrin, Rangi, and Garne squashed onto its surface.

"Did you get a package?" Rangi asked, distress in his voice.

"I did," Bernot answered. "Did you all get slajor manacles, too?"

"Yes," they responded.

Bernot paid attention to the voice that answered for Tahrin; it was not hers and belonged to a man. "Who is speaking for Tahrin?"

"I," the voice said, the Looking Glass shifting to show a face.

"Ah. What do you intend to do about this?" Bernot asked, hoping he would finally get what he wanted.

"War," the man answered.

Rangi and Garne were slow to answer but said the same.

"We cannot allow Kolt to threaten us like this," Rangi said. "I will have his head. How dare he believe he could ever hold us in subjugation? Has he forgotten who created humans?"

"I am human, too," Bernot reminded him, "say no ill of us or you may find yourself with more than one enemy."

"Is that a threat?"

"You may have created humans, but we are your equals, so do not think less of us."

"He is right," Atlia said loud enough to be heard by the other leaders, "but let us turn the conversation to the present dilemma."

"War is our answer now," Garne provided. "Have you begun preparing?"

"Partially," Bernot answered. "We were waiting for Atlia's men before marching past the border. Now, we will wait for all of you. And we must be quick before Kolt decides to launch an attack of his own, which I am sure is not far off."

"We will move with haste," Tahrin's speaker said. "We dragons can be at the border within three weeks or so."

"We will need more time," Rangi said. "We are still nomads and it will take a while for us to reach out to all the tribe leaders. I hope we can reach you in less than a month but realistically it will be longer—much longer."

"Expect a month or so for the Torrpeki to reach you," Garne told him.

Bernot gave him a nod. "Until then. Meanwhile, we will stop Kolt from getting further than the border."

"We shall be seeing you soon," Tahrin's speaker said, disappearing, and was quickly followed by the others.

"We have much to prepare for, I will tell my generals to hurry here," Atlia rose from the chair.

"I will prepare mine," Okleiy followed Atlia.

To war we go. To death we march.

Bernot walked with them to the landing and watched as they began the descent down the Gortlin Tree. A flash of red caught his eye at the bottom of the staircase, and he peered over the landing.

Keegan paused to looked up and even from that height he could see the terror in her eyes.

He cursed and wondered if any of his men could intercept her. The chances were slim as she always seemed to have a way of avoiding people when she wanted. He decided to let her go. The other Children of Prophecy knowing the situation would not cause a problem—at least he hoped.

‡‡‡

Jared sat on the couch, trying to read a book on earth elemental techniques, though his anger was making it difficult. Carter had gone to his job at the carpenter's, something he intended to put an end to; if the rest of them didn't have to work, why should he? Aron was sitting at the table, apathetically refletching his arrows.

The door to the common room creeped open to reveal a white-faced Keegan. Both he and Aron stopped what they were doing.

She took a wavering breath and slowly closed the door.

"What the royik, Keegan?" Kade said, emerging from his room. "I've been able to sense your emotions since you left the forest floor." When he noticed her face, he muttered, "Vitt."

"Take a seat," Jared said, pulling out a chair.

There was pure terror in her eyes. "Kolt is king."

A dead silence enveloped them.

"Who told you that?" Kade asked quietly. There was something in his voice, not quite fear, but close to it.

"I overheard Bernot, Okleiy, and Atlia talking," she responded then began shaking her head and struggled to make her mouth form words.

Aron gulped, "Did you hear anything about Braxton?"

Her eyebrows knitted together in sympathy, "No, I'm sorry."

Kade rubbed his jaw. "You were slated to kill Caius. Kolt will be child's work."

Keegan shook her head again. "He made something called slajor manacles."

Kade cursed. "You're still stronger than him."

"But I'm not. None of us are. Kolt has no problem throwing away his humanity."

Jared hated himself, but now wasn't the time for grudges against misguided good intentions. "Then we work together. The prophecy spoke about it taking four children to defeat Caius." He glanced at Kade. "I can never forgive what you did to my family."

"I don't expect you to," Kade said.

"But if working with you means my brothers live, I'll do it. And maybe in time I'll see you as a friend again."

"I won't hold my breath." Kade turned to Aron. "I appreciate what you've done for Keegan lately, but I still don't like you. But I respect you enough to fight alongside you."

Aron didn't respond, it wasn't as if Kade truly cared that much anyway.

Jared returned his attention to Keegan, who still looked petrified but had at least regained some color. Dropping to his knees, he took her hands. "When we work together, nothing is impossible."

TO BE CONTINUED

Nanagin Pronunciations and Translations (Glossary)
Old Language

Æay [ay]- they
Æysc [ay-sc]- ash
Adæmno [ad-aim-no]- moment
Astæm [as-tame]- but
Avu [av-oo]- yes
Ayþ [ay-th]- the
Az [as]- I
Bindiar [bin-dee-ar]- blind
Bovestun [bove-est-un]- bloody
Bulla vite [bull-ah vie-t]- bullshit
Buna [boo-nuh]- fire
Bwint [b-win-t]- bitch
Casne [cas-nay]- can
Caxone [cax-own]- barrier
Darvesen [dar-ves-en]- prophet
Drackyn [drack-in]- dragon
Du [do]- it
Egreþer [eg-reth-er]- know
Eya [ey-ah]- you
Eyar [ey-ar]- your
Fackyon [fack-ee-on]- false
Fayo [fay-oh]- by
Foylisha [foy-lish-ah]- foolishness
Ghæ [gay]- that
Hamoomph [ham-oom-f]- heal
Haxnug [hax-nug]- stop
Hayclen [hay-clen]- fate
Hiell [hi-ell]- hell (phrase, though more akin to a place)
Hynak [hi-knack]- whore
Ictotm [ict-ot-m]- lord
Iruh [ih-roo]- for
Jappec [jap-pec]- defeat
Jyken [jai-ken]- while
Kævoka [kay-voke-ah]- wicked
Kunyi [coon-yih]- king
Lunviyda [loon-vee-da]- slaughter
Luxyen [lux-yen]- exile
Marmarda [marm-ard-ah]- murderer

Meki [mek-e]- have
Nackh [nack-h]- rule
Nastor [nas-tore]- hell (phrase)
Naya [nay-ah]- no
Noxþ [knockx-th]- damn
Nuþ [nuth]- again
Okæpyio [oak-ap-ee-oh]- adversity
Opida [oh-pee-dah]- bitch +7
Oywn [oywn]- own
Payn [pain]- path
Plazde [plaz-day]- please
Proytyct [proy-t-i-ct]- protect
Psodæ [ps-ode-ay]- child/children
Qalx [o-a-lx]- from
Rhæpn [rap-n]- who
Ri [re]- of
Rimbor [rim-bore]- remember
Royik [roy-ick]- fuck
Ryla [rye-la]- am
Ryo [rye-oh]- be
Sarig [sar-ig]- sorry
Sesuna [ses-oo-na]- serve
Solcan [soul-can]- seal
Soucer [sou-ker]- hero
Unla [oon-la]- only
Viæn [vee-an]- rise
Vite [vie-t]- shit [as in "piece of trash"]/excriment
Vito [vee-toe]- shit (as in "jack shit"/"oh shit")
Vitot [vee-tot]- piece of shit
Waysne [way-sn-ay]- earth
Woth [woth]- will
Wye [why]- now
Yarv [yar-v]- come
Zæ [zay]- these
Þe [the]- do

Place Pronunciations
Agrielha [ag-re-el-uh]
Arciol [are-see-ole]
Averit Volcanoes [av-er-it vol-cane-oh-s]

Aylentowne [aye-len-town]
Bouyne [boone]
Drath [drath]
Edreba [eh-dreb-uh]
Glensung Plains [glen-sung plains]
Gortlin Tree [gore-t-lin tree]
Gydrick's Inn and Tavern [guide-ricks in and tav-ern]
Illeria Mountains [i-leer-e-ah mount-ains]
Lake Romann [lay-ke roh-man]
Magnenpie [mag-nen-pie]
Móverth [mauve-earth]
Ohvenail [oh-ven-ail]
Revod [rev-odd]
Suilenroc [sull-en-rock]
Suttan [sut-tan]
Tatat River [tat-at riv-er]
Tratoleck [trat-o-leck]
Whendell [when-dell]
Yarav Forest [yar-av for-est]

Other Pronunciations

Alvor [al-vore]- (life elementals)
Arciolan [are-see-ole-an]- someone from Arciol
Buluo [boo-loo-oh]- (air elementals)
Claymore- sword with a cross hilt that slopes up, Scottish variant of the two-handed sword
Dragons- (fire elementals)
Estoc- sword with a cruciform hilt
Ether- agent used to temporarily inhibit magic use
Kojote [koh-joe-te]- a person who secrets elementals across the country to safety
Larimar [lar-ih-mar]- pale blue stone
Lazado [laz-ah-do]- Revolutionaries
Merfolk [mer-folk]- mermaid-like people (water elementals)
Nanagin [nuh-nah-gin]- magical portal between worlds, specific in time in place to each person
Northron accent [north-ron ack-cent]- accent indicative to someone from the far north of the human region
Paika [pie-kuh]- source of elemental magic in the body

Pexatose [pex-ah-toe-s] = alien humans to Arciol- someone from the other world (may possess any element)

Ramilla [ram-ill-uh]- a poison made from octopi venom and the nectar of the dogwood flower

Rimor [rim-or]- earth immobilization technique

Torrpeki [tore-pec-ee]- (earth elementals)

Vosjnik [voz-nick]- a group of the best warriors in each of their fields

Yewne [yew-nay]- marker that grants access to the hidden Alvor cities

Zoutsi [zout-see]- earth immobilization technique

About The Author

Growing up, you were just as likely to find Haley playing outside as you were to find her with her nose in a book. She particularly enjoys stories focusing on worlds of magic and adventure. Often joking that she is part mermaid, Haley pursued a marine biology degree from the University of North Carolina, Wilmington, graduating in 2017. She then proceeded to attend the University of Miami in the pursuit of a Masters of Professional Science for marine conservation; she aims to graduate in December 2018.

With an English father and an Italian-American mother, Haley had a colorful upbringing in Charlotte, North Carolina, which she has accentuated by traveling as much as she can.

She says her biggest inspiration for writing is that she simply needs her characters to be quiet, so she can think. Currently, she divides her time between scuba diving and living in Miami.

Conquest

Chapter 1

Braxton watched a soldier pull a man past his cell. It had been nine days since Kolt had upended everything. From where he was, it had not seemed like much had changed, but he knew everyone must be on edge trying to gauge the alterations that would inevitably be coming—if they had not already come. The guards never said a word as they passed him—no matter how much he screamed and cursed.

All in all, he was not entirely upset with the situation. He had no worries or responsibilities. The cell was not terribly cold. While the cot was nothing compared to the feather bed he was accustomed to, it could be worse. He was given three meals a day that were brought from the king's own table. Kolt's upheaval might actually be a blessing.

There was a squeak from a rat, hidden in the impermeable darkness that shrouded most of the cell, and the momentary lapse in judgment fell away. His hatred for the cell, the situation, and for Kolt returned and magnified. He dove into his mind and found the earth paika. For all his anger and determination though, he was still unable to break the blood-red gem.

Kolt had done something to him at the coronation that had robbed him of his magic. He knew the golden bracelets he now bore were the source of the block but could not understand the magic they possessed to inhibit his magic so completely and unfailingly. They had also stopped his visions of the future. For as long as he had wanted the revelations to stop, he had come to rely on them and hated not knowing what was coming. He loathed admitting that to himself.

"Hello, brother," a voice from the hallway said.

Braxton scrambled to his feet and rushed to the bars. He knew that voice better than anyone and would give *anything* to stop it from ever speaking again. His hands gripped the iron bars so tightly his knuckles turned white in a matter of seconds.

Kolt was shrewd enough to stand just outside of reach.

"What do you want?" Braxton snarled.

"Many things, dear brother."

"Why did you do this?"

"Because you are weak," Kolt answered. "You would have allowed peace between us and the nations that once enslaved us. You would allow humans to become lesser beings again. Right now, we are feared—we are strong."

There was too much of their father in Kolt. "No." Caius might have been brazen, but he knew where to draw a line. Kolt was going to obliterate it along with who else knew what. "We are weak right now, splintered and afraid. You are going to take us into a war that will ensure we never stand as a nation again."

Kolt examined his nails, "I doubt that. I have taken some precautions to guarantee we are left victorious."

"What are you talking about?"

"I never knew you were so thick," Kolt chuckled. "Do you not wonder why you have become ordinary or why I was father's favorite?"

He spat at Kolt's feet. "You were father's favorite because you are cruel like him."

"No, I was father's favorite because I am a spellcaster just like him."

Braxton balked at the thought. "Impossible. You are as ungifted as they come. If not more so."

Kolt's face soured. "That is what I would have people think. It is true that I was ungifted until I was eight. Then my powers came. I find it so unfortunate that spellcasters must wait to get their powers, unlike elementals who cannot remember life without them."

"You give no proof."

"Buna," Kolt said in a clear voice.

Fire engulfed Kolt's hand and he pushed back from the bars, afraid to be burnt, knowing full well he would be denied medical treatment. "Why would you want to hide something like that?"

"When you are normal, no one suspects you of doing great things." There was hurt in the words.

Had it been anyone else he might have been sympathetic. "You cannot suppress my magic forever."

Kolt laughed, "I already have with those slajor manacles."

"The last set was destroyed at the beginning of father's reign." For the first time, true fear raced through his heart. Slajor manacles meant Kolt could effectively make every elemental he caught useless. There were only two ways to remove them: the person who made them detached them or the person wearing them died.

"I made more," Kolt said, "and tested them on you. They seem to be doing the job."

Braxton fought to suppress his fear and anger. "Why visit me now? Why wait so long?"

"Let us just say that I have been reaping all the benefits of being king. Now, I have a proposition for you."

"I would rather die."

"See, I knew you would say that. Which is why I am not going to touch a hair on your fat head. But I cannot say the same will be true for the griffins and the boy. Serve me or I will *personally* make them suffer."

Braxton wanted nothing more than to enter a frenzy and rip Kolt limb from body, but he kept his face as neutral as he could. How could he ever let his brother hurt the griffins, those innocent beings born of the wind, or Nico, the child forced to look Lunos in the eyes?

"I see I have hit the right point. Do not worry, I will give you time to think things over. Just know that when you do bow to me, you will become the new archer for the Vosjnik." Kolt walked away, giving an antagonistic wave.

Braxton let himself back away from the bars slowly. There was no way to defy his brother and protect the few beings he had come to care for. It was either sacrifice them or sacrifice himself.

CPSIA information can be obtained
at www.ICGtesting.com
Printed in the USA
FSHW021728291120
76286FS

9 781945 286353